Fabio Goran is a flight attendant. When he doesn't travel the world, he teaches music and gives piano concerts. He lives in Montreal with his partner.

Nella Robertsen works for a courier company. She is a painter, regular gym goer, and Yoga enthusiast living in Montreal.

Dedication

We dedicate this book to all the mothers in the world. Thank you for the life you gave us and for your sleepless nights. With deep respect for those we have not met and eternal love for moms: Violetta, Kankica, Hélène, and Vera.

Fabio Goran and Nella Robertsen

YUGOOPERA

AUSTIN MACAULEY PUBLISHERS
London · Cambridge · New York · Sharjah

Copyright © Fabio Goran and Nella Robertsen (2018)

All rights reserved. No part of this publication may be reproduced, distributed, or transmitted in any form or by any means, including photocopying, recording, or other electronic or mechanical methods, without the prior written permission of the publisher, except in the case of brief quotations embodied in critical reviews and certain other noncommercial uses permitted by copyright law. For permission requests, write to the publisher

Any person who commits any unauthorized act in relation to this publication may be liable to criminal prosecution and civil claims for damages.

Ordering Information:
Quantity sales: special discounts are available on quantity purchases by corporations, associations, and others. For details, contact the publisher at the address below.

Publisher's Cataloging-in-Publication data
Goran Fabio and Robertsen Nella.
Yugoopera

ISBN 9781641820028 (Paperback)
ISBN 9781641820004 (Hardback)
ISBN 9781641820011 (E-Book)

The main category of the book —Fiction / General

www.austinmacauley.com

First Published (2018)
Austin Macauley Publishers LLC.
40 Wall Street, 28th Floor
New York, NY 10005

USA
mail-usa@austinmacauley.com
+1 (646) 5125767

Acknowledgments

Our heartful thanks go to Jelica for her continuous support and to Alexia, Jennifer, Elizabeth, and James, who proofread the manuscript, gave us precious feedback and a thumbs up. Also to our cats, Poppers and Archie, who supervised the editing by purring from the top shelves of our computer desks. A very special appreciation for my partner, Georges.

Table of Contents

Act I	19
Somewhere in the South	19
Act II	39
The Call of the Big City	39
Act III	103
Transformations	103
Act IV	147
Who Turned off the Light?	147
Act V	179
Adagio	179
Act VI	231
The Sound of Freedom	231
Act VII	317
Enchanted by the Song Without Words	317
Act VIII	441
God Has More than One Name	441

Welcome

To the first night of the Opera!

It is called Yugoopera.

We wish you a comfortable and pleasant journey into the accords and harmonies of words; the course of events will take you far-away, to a world of imagination and beauty. Tonight's première is full of surprises and unusual moments, for that's the way of an opera, isn't it?

This is neither opera buffa nor a tragic one, so we will simply call it the opera of reality, for it is sincere and authentic.

Everybody is ready for you: the actors, singers, and musicians. They wish you a delightful night.

Through the enchanting music transformed into sentences, paragraphs and stories, this opera will take you to a long voyage into my heart and from it, with the power of emotions and torrents of some other words, into Nora's.

You may wonder at the two hearts beating in the same rhythm of the newly composed magical opera.

We know you will like it, because it is pure.

Genuine.

Innocent.

Warm.

This piece is a work of four hands and two pairs of eyes.

It contains both sides of the coin – his and hers.

Woven on the spinning wheel by Nora's and Nikola's spindles, creating the tapestry of light of a night and darkness of a day.

Depicting the noise of silence and a silent echo in the midst of noise.

Enjoy.

Cloakroom

All opera houses in the world have a nice cloakroom where you can leave your coats or fur coats to reveal a stunning dress and glittering jewelry, or a new suit and a silk tie.

Cloakroom is a safe place where all coats sleep, guarding their secrets. Some of them are designer, very elegant and hand-stitched, while others have holes in the pockets and are frayed at cuffs and collars. Some fur coats are sad because they were made from dead animals, but are worth more than a condominium in downtown; others are made of artificial fur, more or less reflecting the original.

Cloakroom is the only place in an opera house where the distinction between the rich and the poor doesn't exist. The extravagant Siberian fox of that lady with huge rubies in her ears and the worn-out denim jacket of this young guy hang side by side.

Each person is wonderful in their own way, in bodies sculptured from birth and endowed by brains that can think, learn, and create but also forget, hate, and destroy. When you are angry, it's just a coat, the old shabby one, for deep down in your heart, you are certainly a good person. Cloakroom is for all of you who enter this temple of music unhappy, tired, disappointed, hurt, distressed, or irritated. There is plenty of room in the cloakroom for all your ailments. We hired, especially for this occasion, lots of gorgeous young men and women to be at your service and help you shed those coats of suffering, so that you can shine in your beautiful clothes of hope and happiness.

We would like to ask you not to be cross with us for the sporadic use of words that might not be appropriate for such an exquisite night. They spilled directly out of our fingertips, carried away by an avalanche of emotions from our souls.

You are kindly invited to come into the main hall.

The program is here:

Tuning

Before performing any piece of music, the instrumentalists have to make sure they are perfectly tuned. It all starts when the oboist plays the tone La or A1, which has the same pitch all over the world. Oboe is always tuned to 440 Hz. This beautiful tone is then taken over by the first violin, followed by string and brass wind instruments.

Let's tune into this book: Southeastern Europe, Balkans.

I was born in Yugoslavia – now Serbia; centuries ago, Turkey, and once part of the Roman Empire.

The town I was born in is located at 202 meters altitude, latitude 43°19' north and longitude 21°54' east. If we add up the last two numbers, we get 6473 which, translated into musical language, gives us:

La – Fa – Si – Mi

Or, we can rearrange them as:

Naissus was the Latin name for my hometown in which Constantine the Great (Flavius Valerius Aurelius Constantinus Augustus) was also born. He was a famous Roman emperor, founded Constantinople (now Istanbul) that later became the capital of the Byzantine Empire, established Christianity in 313 AD, and proclaimed religious tolerance throughout the Empire.

If you try to look me up on the Internet, you'll find next to nothing, for I'm neither a ruler nor a well-known person. Still, in the next few hundred pages, I will take you to a leisurely walk through my life and to Nora's side of the moon that's neither darker nor clearer than mine. You will have the chance to meet lots of interesting characters, friends, and those who are not.

This story begins in a town that's beautiful to everybody's eyes except mine.

Sometimes it gets on my nerves.

But that's the way it is.

The present name of my hometown is Niš.

Ouverture

The street that cradles my earliest memories is lined by chestnut trees; they freely spread their branches from both sides of it. On a scorching July mid-afternoon, when even the birds are too hot to fly, hiding from the scalding sun's rays, it feels like an oasis in a desert. Heavy fronds on the left side demurely caress the ones on the right, creating a tunnel of love, shadowy and deep. An accidentally-lost driver, driven by the summer heat and the over-brightness of the day, finds himself suddenly in the cool of the green passage where the microclimate reigns for about half a kilometer. The street is at its best in the spring, when the wide-open white chestnut blossoms proudly sprawl all around. After a quick rain, they stick to the soles of your shoes, as if wishing to travel with you somewhere far-away.

A friend of mine in my teens said that chestnut blossoms smelled of sperm, so it should be called Sperm-Scented Street. The condensed scent of millions of them is certainly unusual, thick and a bit sugary, but I didn't agree with my friend.

On 12 Chestnut Street, hidden behind the leafy branches of apricot and pear trees, a house could be discerned: not too small, not too big, with a plain white façade, windows facing north and west, a 16-step staircase and a well in the garden. This is the house I was born or reincarnated in. From the very beginning, I felt at odds with destiny choosing this particular place for my present incarnation, without my consent to the decision of the powers of the Universe.

I was born in the body I still hold, and spent a good deal of my childhood exploring the surroundings and people; attempting to figure out, grasp, comprehend, and accept their role in my life, at the same time endeavoring to find my place under the sun.

The actual birth happened in a hospital (as is usual) and I have no recollection of that. My mom was in a serious crisis after giving life to me, but with the help of God, managed to survive and stay in this world. Her love for me has always been too strong and almost suffocating.

My early memories of my father are foggy. His constant complaining, grumbling, and doing everything possible to make our lives miserable forced me to put sort of a veil, like a defense mechanism, between him and myself. Mom says he loved me dearly when I was a baby; he used to hold me in his arms, and I always laughed in his lap. I have no recollection of that, either.

My psychotherapist says: "What he needed to leave, he left to you. What he didn't give you, you'll carry as dissatisfaction and sorrow forever." Just why on earth do I pay this woman $80 per appointment?

My father wasn't famous. His name never made it to the newspapers, his contribution to this world didn't consist of big things, sculptures, poetry or anything valuable and important – other than the fact that he gave me life: the sparkle of birth and the chance to open my eyes, breathe the air, walk, and talk.

His role was fulfilled by my birth, although never accomplished. According to my psychotherapist, as she looks at me through the glasses on the tip of her nose: "You need him, but since you didn't have him, he comes to your dreams, to be with you, to give you advice and scold you if needed."

At any rate, I've been feeling emptiness in that respect ever since my early years. That side of the coin has always been washed out. I've been lacking a man in my life; my childhood days were void of a gentle man's hand and a soft man's voice.

My childhood revolved around tons of children I was constantly with, only to be left alone in the end. My days were full of laughter and my nights filled with sadness or loneliness. My 'illness' was incurable; I could not stand being alone. I was afraid of it, so I packed my garden with some kids I didn't even know, let alone like. I generously shared my toys, just to keep them with me a bit longer. Night would fall irrevocably and the kids would leave me alone with the toys.

Books lit a new light in my life. I was in their company 20 hours out of 24, absorbing words and thoughts. Children became less and less a part of my days. They gave way to heroes from wonderful books: to Knight Legardeur from a marvelous book by Paul Féval, and to Aureliano Buendía from One Hundred Years of Solitude, one of the best books I have ever read. Kids' laughter was replaced by funny characters from children's books. I also read some serious stuff, cried inconsolably over the death of Camilla in The Lady of the Camellias by Dumas, and was deeply touched by the love of brother and sister in The Mill on the Floss by George Eliot. The scene from The Paul Street Boys by Ferenc Molnár, in which the poor little Nemeczek dies, brought me to the edge of despair and worried the whole circle of people around me.

Books became a part of me and I became a part of them. All of a sudden, everyday situations became different, nicer, and more interesting, filtered through colors of my reading adventures.

In those remote days of the early 1960s, TV was a big thing and was black and white. It didn't impress me much; books were more powerful. It was interesting only when it came to cartoons: Donald Duck, Flintstones, and especially Maya the Bee on Sunday mornings at 10:30. I would glue myself to the screen, following adventures of the lovely Maya and her sleepy friend, Willy, into the wonderful world of flowers and secrets of fields and forests. Even today, far away from childhood, I sometimes watch Maya and Willy and think how much healthier for children they are than this new Japanese animation, where characters cut each other's body parts and turn into some beasts and monsters.

My ritual of watching cartoons was accompanied by a few buns, a mandatory Nutella, and Diana orange juice that marked the first eight years of my life. Every time I go back to those days, I can feel the taste of the sweet chocolate cream spread over hot buns.

Books created whatever they wanted in my head. New worlds and galaxies were opening up before me, more and more each day. Soon, they became an obsession as much as love. I lost the ability to communicate 'normally' with the world around me.

My friends, kids like me, couldn't understand me. Our plays turned into playing school (where I was the teacher, of course), educational games, and quizzes.

The moment came when I was left completely alone; it was too late to change myself and call them back. So I just decided to turn to people older than me, hoping that my brain would find shelter in their harbors of knowledge and skills. My views were too large for such a small-town. I was a black sheep and an ugly duckling, a needle in the eye of every idiot – Achilles' tendon to all mediocrities and Rubik's cube to morons.

My presence bothered both, the younger and the older than myself. Most of all, it bothered those my own age.

Then it all happened overnight: the childhood was gone and I started going to school, proudly wearing a blue sweater hand-knitted by my sweet aunt Kankica.

Act I
Somewhere in the South

- Ball
- Nora's Impressions
- Rendez-Vous with the Piano or Re-birth
- Life in Six Boobs

Ball

The drama of Ana Karenina, more dramatic than the original one, would begin every day with the school bell announcing recess and end with its shrill sound calling to come back to the classroom. I hated recesses. I despised the herds of children rushing outside, shrieking with joy in anticipation of playing with Ball.

Ball – my lethal enemy.

Ball – synthesis of deadly sins and deep-rooted hatred.

Ball – disgusting, round mix of plastic and shit.

Ball and its family: foot-ball, basket-ball, volley-ball, or just an ordinary ball for every day.

We met during the first recess. Shakespeare's tragedies couldn't describe the enormity of my suffering at the meeting. Ball and I didn't have a chance to get to know each other, since my early childhood was somehow incubated when my whole family (my mom, her sisters and friends, that is) took care of my health (which was very frail according to them); organizing crowds of kids to come, eat, and entertain me, in order to tempt me to taste all the imaginable foodstuff prepared in our house. My food was to watch the kids swallow delicacies that my mom and aunts cooked, sautéed, and baked for me, which I didn't touch.

My preschool years were filled by volumes of books. Ball simply didn't have a place there and nobody had ever introduced us.

Our first and last experience was dreadful.

Recess is the time for running, screaming, ball-playing (in all its versions), or chatting. Being born as a male with a name in the masculine gender, I was automatically put into the group that played a game called foot-ball. Figuring out the micro-elements of Titanic or the subconscious states of Patagonian white owls would have been easier. Besides, the Ball and I didn't have the slightest wish to get acquainted.

The code of conduct in the South of Serbia says: "Boys play foot-ball from the beginning of their lives."

I am a boy.

No, I don't play foot-ball.

I have no idea what it's all about!

Good news travels fast and bad news travels even faster. You should have seen the speed with which the news about me spread through the school corridors and classrooms. After that fatal recess, it struck like a thunderbolt; here was someone who didn't know how to play foot-ball, didn't even want to learn the game that had symbolized all male generations since times immemorial (like the warriors and kings throughout history couldn't do without it).

Impossible, nothing like that had ever happened. It the worst thing on earth to befall upon anyone in this town!

"He'll never get married," said the cleaning ladies, leaning against brooms full of dead flies.

"Poor his mother," said teachers, watching me attentively as I approached girls during the recesses. "Poor woman."

"All those stupid things he picked up from books should be kicked out of his head," said a neighbor.

"Whoever saw any good come from books," another one commented, lighting up a cigarette.

From my point of view, there was nothing wrong with me and I couldn't sense the disaster in the making that would turn my school days into War and Peace (more war than peace). The school awaited me at the same place as always; painted in tasteless yellow, with poplars on the north side of the schoolyard. My casual attitude only intensified the reactions of my schoolmates.

"Who does he think he is? He can't even play foot-ball!" They whispered behind my back in the corridors.

My top grades suddenly lost their luster. It went without saying that I had to be an excellent student since I couldn't play foot-ball.

That experience made me realize how somebody who is in any way different from the others must feel. I was 'a fat girl, a stammering child, a simpleton, from a very poor family, limping, blind'; a kid with all the 'anomalies' who didn't fit anywhere. I was all of those in one single moment.

In my school days, I was sheltered by girls, for they found in me someone similar to themselves; someone they could open up their infant hearts to and talk about their loves and wishes. They protected me during recesses, with their bodies, skirts, and dolls. In return, I was telling them white lies: about how amazingly pretty they were, how they would marry great guys who would adore them, kiss them all the time, and cover them in diamonds and silk. At the age of nine, I was mature enough to know that the majority of them would fall in love with the first idiot, spread out their legs, give birth to a child or two, and spend all their time washing his filthy clothes, raising children, cooking, cleaning, and living a totally loveless life; the one of ordinary housewives, so unappreciated in the Yugoslav society of the early 1970s.

I couldn't tell them how silly they were. I needed them and liked them. I couldn't tell them there was no way for a man they would marry one day to be nice and gentle, capable of giving love and respect. I couldn't find it in my heart to tell them they were doomed, and soon, in a few short years.

The rule of our provincial town and of all the provincial towns in our country stated that:

A girl has value only if she is a virgin until marriage.

A guy has more value the more girls he shags, especially virgins.

The usual scenario:

He meets her and promises her all the riches of the world. She's young and inexperienced, he's young and a bit more experienced.

They get together behind the school or in a park.

He wants to fuck her as soon as possible.

She feels so very important, all those four minutes.

He impregnates her.

They have to get married.

They live unhappily ever after.

She tells her daughter, "Don't you dare make the same mistake I did and then suffer for the rest of your life! School is more important."

She tells her son, "If I see a girl with a bastard on my doorstep, I'll kill her, and you as well!"

The husband is silent. He's drinking fizzy wine and watching TV. Sports. Foot-ball.

The husband has been silent for the last fifteen years.

"There are worse men than me," he often thinks. "At least I don't beat her." He takes a drag on his cigarette as he looks at the female singer on TV. "This one needs to be screwed," he sighs.

The wife has forgotten she's a woman. She's been wearing the same stained dress for months.

"A woman is cursed," she keeps telling her daughter before going to sleep. "A woman is like a donkey, just that she can cook," her voice trembles.

She goes into the solitude of the bedroom. The bed is cold and empty, just like her womb.

The husband has been sleeping on the living room sofa for years, a cigarette butt in his cramped fingers, the lights on, and the hum of the TV long after the program has finished.

"I hate him," she whispers sleepily.

"C'mon, get up, I'm hungry!" His voice booms through the closed door. "Just lying there like a cow, aren't you!" he yells.

She gets up and opens the window. Fresh spring breeze brings in the scent of linden blossoms that fills the room. The sun warms the little birds on the branches, impatiently waiting for their parents to fly back with fresh worms.

She makes scrambled eggs, wishing to spice them with poison. She looks at his back bent over the morning edition of sports newspapers. The smoke from his cigarette twirls from his fingers to his face and hair. She puts coffee on the table and sits across from him.

He slurps his coffee.

He doesn't notice her.

He eats his scrambled eggs and bread and then stands up.

He opens the door and stops for a moment, blinded by the early April sun.

The morning is preparing the day with its vibrant scents and colors.

He closes the door.

She hears him swearing.

She opens the kitchen cabinet and pours herself a small glass of brandy. Maybe two today. Maybe two.

My school routine got disturbed one day when we were passed on from our dearest, sweetest teacher, to many unknown teachers. As many school subjects – as many new faces.

My happiness was endless when I saw a gorgeous blond woman who was our Arts teacher; I was happy since I always loved to draw, paint, and spill colors all over the place. Luck was also on my side with the appearance of such a pretty and gentle Music teacher.

"Bingo!" I thought. "They're all women and they are all beautiful!"

My love for women was more powerful than the solar energy. My attachment to them was even stronger than to myself. I enjoyed watching them, talking to them, feeling, and looking like them. In that empire of women, I was surrounded with my mother, her friends, my aunts, and teachers; all had a significant influence on my everyday being, on the development on my brain cells, and on my personality in general.

Many years later, when *The Woman* materialized in my life: the most beautiful one in the world, with long black hair and deep dark eyes, who cuddled in the warmth of a white fur coat to protect her from the strong Belgrade winds, I realized the true secret about women. We, men, can't understand them, try as passionately as we might.

The woman who became my reality was the best. She was the loveliest, gentlest, and kindest one on earth, but alas, she wished to please me. Her inner and outer beauty was enormous, but submitted to me. I neither wanted, liked, nor understood that.

I loved her for herself.

A woman is made of molecules dissimilar from a man's, and we'll never understand each other completely, no matter how hard we try.

If you ask me, all loves should stay at the stage of getting together, pleasant evenings, long walks, holding each other's hands and enjoyable trips. The moment electricity bills, snoring, mutual friends, and the whole sack of other banalities get involved, all is lost.

The communist-infused days of my elementary school were dragging on, progressing at a snail's pace through socio-realistic movies featuring World War II and national heroes. Everything was sort of made up, yet so comforting.

I was growing up and developing in all the spheres of my being. I was getting smarter, I cried less if somebody hurt my feelings, I read even more, and then I discovered music as the most wondrous thing on earth.

Ball remained my state enemy # 1, and foot-ball, a nightmare.

Nora's Impressions

No, I don't want to get out of my mom's womb; it's so warm, cozy, and safe in here! Eventually, I have to make an appearance to save my mom from the long labor, since the doctors and midwives are giving up. So I pop up, stick out my tongue to everybody concerned, and take a look at the world I don't want to encounter but seems like I have to.

"This is a baby all in eyes!" the midwife says.

I'm tiny, but healthy. I don't want to leave the hospital yet on the pretext that I develop baby jaundice. I scared my mom, but I am biding my time. When I finally decide to face the outside, happens to be the day J.F. Kennedy gets assassinated, back in November 1963.

My father is God-knows-where, so my grandpa comes to take Mom and my little-self home. He brings a cloudy white pillow and a throw, crocheted by my grandma and so, cuddled, I take off.

They say that when a powerful person dies in the reign of a Scorpio, another Scorpio is being born, like a phoenix kind of thing, rising from the ashes.

Without attempting to make any analogies between J.F. Kennedy and the baby me, I can say only one thing for a fact: I was born with a white hair in my left eyebrow, and that's apparently a sign of a wise person.

Whatever; on my bumpy journey in this life, I happen to meet the most extraordinary person whose story I'm a part of.

Through good and not-so-good times, we have been best friends for almost thirty years. And it will stay this way, I think, till the end of our time on this earth.

I met him on a crazy bus ride to a village on the outskirts of Belgrade, Serbia, where I involuntarily got a position of the English teacher in an elementary school. He was practicing for his exam in Conducting; spreading his arms all over the place, packed with chicken and stinky old cheese mixed with human body odor.

There was such pure beauty in his movements and his facial expressions that made the filthy bus look sparkling clean. I realized then and there that I really wanted to get closer to this person.

And so I did.

Sharing his story and mine now.

The centerpiece in the white mansion, the baby me is brought to, is a baby grand-rosewood piano from one of the palaces in Vienna, Austria, where my great-grandaunt was a governess around a hundred years ago. The noble family gave it to her as a token of appreciation when she retired. It's an heirloom, my grandma inherited it from her, then my mom (all three, talented musicians). So it goes without saying, it should pass on to me.

I am expected to carry on the tradition established by my dear njanja (my grandma that is), born in the Austro-Hungarian Empire. As I grew up, I preferred playing in the huge garden, climbing the cherry tree, smelling hydrangeas, digging my fingers deep into the soil, eating slugs, making sand castles, and practicing some boring études glued to the chair.

Like, I have music running in my veins, but as an accompaniment to movement, dance, rhythm, the energy of my soles and tiptoes; the gipsy part of my Hungarian blood, I guess.

My mom is clearly disappointed. All her eager efforts to get me musically educated are repaid to her, however, only years later, when Nikola appears. With fluidity in his fingers that barely touch the keys of the baby grand-rosewood piano, he makes the whole house reverberate with pure elation of sonatas, symphonies, and concertos! It looks so easy, just that I have never figured out how to do it myself.

Anyway, the two of them (Nikola and my mom, that is) click so totally perfectly on the first accord, making me the odd–one-out.

Never mind, I fly across the skies, beyond times and places, and observe.

The thing about me that puzzles even myself is this: like physically I'm experiencing the here and now while spiritually watching everything from above.

Whatever.

Rendez-Vous with the Piano or Rebirth

The piano and I met in October 1980. It was upright, shining in its high-polished brown wood on the fourth floor of the biggest department store in town.

It was love at first glance.

We couldn't afford it. There was no chance my love could move into our house. Still, with the help of a family friend and a loan, a miracle happened and the beautiful piano settled in my room.

The affection was mutual. Music was swimming throughout my body. I played before washing my face in the mornings until the last atom of my strength at nights.

I was already fifteen and had no previous education in piano studies, but had a wish more powerful than anything; without a slightest chance of backing off.

I practiced Bach, Chopin, and Mozart. Played endless boring scales, passages, and études.

Caressed Beethoven's early sonatas and the quiet, lonely Debussy.

I saved some time for my friends, then rushed back home to my love that waited for me to touch its black and white keys.

Piano was my ticket to freedom.

Piano was my white light after death, leading to eternal Paradise.

In more rational terms, piano would make possible my entrance into the capital city, far away from this provincial town. Farewell to the south of Serbia!

My high school of Music was a kind of a zoo with rare animals: fantastic, strange, and peculiar. There were just a few of us there, somehow apart from the whole external world.

Days were unrolling in never-ending classes (usually eight a day) and in-choir singing every evening, led by the alcohol-induced, unstable hands of the Conducting teacher.

My deadly enemy was the Physical Education teacher. I was sort of doomed to go from one school to another without a positive turn in that respect. The fact that I had all the highest marks in the most difficult music subjects and got awards for my piano playing and singing meant nothing to this woman, who would take us outside to the nearby park and give us boys a ball (oh, the horror!) while sitting on a bench with the girls and gossiping about other teachers and older guys in higher grades.

She made a point of making my life miserable since I offended her a few times with my remarks about her absence of makeup, smelling of sweat, and by saying that no man on earth would fuck her. I wouldn't have been so rude if she hadn't attacked me with nicknames such as 'Mom's pussy' and 'Pissy' because I didn't play foot-ball.

The war between us was in full swing; nobody could stop it. Not my teachers, not my mom, not even the principal.

She was really ugly and stank of the unwashed. Her hair was greasy and her track suit was dirty. She didn't talk properly and constantly picked her nose. She tried in every possible way to humiliate me, but I always pissed her off.

One day, we happened to be alone.

She swore she would make me fail the year, even though I was by far the best student in the school (she had to admit that). Why? Because she could just kill all men who were not strong, masculine, and muscular males. In the next class, she gathered us all together and announced:

"Girls and boys play foot-ball from now on. If you don't play, you fail the year."

Everybody started running to the playground. She looked at me victoriously.

"What are you waiting for, stupid horse?"

"For a stinky mare to ask me what I'm waiting for." I gave her an envelope.

"What's this?"

"Doctor's certified note stating I can't do Physical Education because of a heart condition."

The cat ate her tongue as she slowly walked towards the playground.

A couple of months later, she resigned.

"One to null, sister!" I chuckled to myself.

Life in Six Boobs

Let me introduce you, proudly and lovingly, to the family of my dearest high school teacher.

She walked into the classroom in a flowing, colorful dress, with brightly-painted lips and a cloud of smoke hovering above her. She must have just put out a cigarette in front of the door.

"I shall be your lead teacher in the next four years," she said simply.

We were listening to her.

"We will have to discuss some mandatory issues in due course, but I will not allow a single minute to be wasted from the Literature classes."

She taught World Literature, loved her subject with all her heart, and remained true to her word. During her classes, there was no mention of school trips, petty fights, or problems with some other teachers. Those forty-five minutes were reserved for Literature.

My teacher lived with her mother: a real lady born before World War I, a mighty person with a strong character who, in her 90s, would sit on a high chair in the kitchen, supervising the cooking of her daughter and advising (nagging, my teacher would say), "Less salt, a bit more pepper, some herbs…"

Her ears sported two huge diamonds, a gift from her deceased husband, a long time ago. Her hands were well-maintained and soft, hands of a woman who had never lifted anything heavier than a silver spoon.

Before presenting the youngest member of the family, sweet Yvette, let me invite you to their apartment.

When you walk into that upscale six-bedroom space, you are at first confused. You cannot see a thing from the cigarette smoke. The grandmother and mother smoked 80 cigarettes a day each. That's 160 cigarettes.

The wallpaper was deep beige, with lovely motifs of some exotic flowers. I guessed its original color used to be light apricot or lemon, but the smoke had its say.

The living room was gorgeously furnished in baroque style, with rare and valuable objects, brocade drapes, and leather armchairs. The centerpiece was a massive mahogany table, surrounded by elegant, high-backed burgundy chairs. On the table, there were playing cards in a silver case encrusted in mother of pearl, crystal bowls with sweets, and ashtrays: small, medium, large, made of Venetian glass, Royal Delft porcelain, and Rosenthal china… a sea of ashtrays. Fascinating old oil paintings in elaborate wood frames hung on the walls. I loved them all; I couldn't decide which one was my favorite.

The floor-to-ceiling windows spread all along one of the walls, potentially providing a panoramic view of high-rise buildings and traditional low brick houses outside, were it not for the double café au lait curtains and amber drapes that made sure the microclimate within remained undisturbed.

Dark-orange armchairs were equipped with velvet cushions and soft blankets. I imagined the three women relaxing, each in her respective armchair at the end of lavish dinner parties they often threw, after the last guest had gone home.

The first thing I would do, still standing at the doorway, before settling into the warmth of their place, was to light up. That seemed to be an appropriate greeting.

Theirs was a home to all of us who respected and loved them. It was a home of culture, interesting stories, ease, and music. If incidentally (very seldom, though), a topic of conversation got exhausted and silence lasted for longer than a minute, somebody would sit at the piano and we would all start singing. Dinners at their home stayed grooved into the record of my reality in those years of 1979–1983, as a symbol of beauty, friendship, and love.

My teacher and her mother nourished my soul with wise words and adventures from their trips and my body with elaborate dishes and sandwiches with most exquisite combinations. We used to talk for hours.

We spent many an evening like that, sitting at the landmark table, three women: 'Six Boobs' and I. There was nothing insulting about the phrase. In those days, we laughed our hearts out when I said I'd write a 'Six Boobs' story one day.

My teacher liked to talk about her ex-students, following up to their adulthood. She had only the best words for everyone, never judging, always loving. She spoke four languages fluently, beautifully; the way, she herself was.

The Six Boobs toured Europe in summertime and winters were invariably spent in a luxurious romantic hotel on the far north side of the Adriatic Sea, where everybody knew, respected, and loved them. They had their usual three-bedroom penthouse suite filled with vases of fresh flowers, enjoyed the sea view while eating breakfasts prepared specially for them on the marble terrace, and took short trips to Italy. Three weeks later, they would come back full of impressions and with ten suitcases full of dresses for the youngest pair of boobs, Yvette.

Yvette was very young when I first met her, a child that came late to a lovely mother and an old father whom her mother divorced when she was a toddler. She was brought into that baroque castle as the last of the Mohicans.

She was a sweet, darling girl with already-imprinted characteristics of an old lady. She was fourteen at the time, but her dress code and manners belonged to someone who was at least sixty-five. Squished into lacy blouses and dresses, pink, white and red, with ribbons and bows, matching bonnets, coats and gloves, she often appeared as if fallen from another planet. Yet, she was still charming in her own way, and nobody could imagine her otherwise.

She played the piano for hours, sang opera arias for hours. She spoke four languages fluently and perfectly, just like her mother.

She lived in that apartment by the routine established by the older of four boobs, trying to catch up with them. During those wonderful evenings with endless stories, she also wanted to get noticed, since all attention was focused on my teacher.

Yvette would often interrupt her mother halfway through an account, "Mom, now say what (this or that person) said! Mom, now tell us that story! Come on, Mom…"

Mom was strict with her, and Grandma with me.

There was always tons of food. Their home was simmering with cooking, sautéing, frying, and baking. Coffee was consumed in gallons from dainty porcelain cups originating from an Austro-Hungarian palace.

I could hardly wait for them to come back from their vacation from the North Adriatic.

Stories waited to be told and suitcases to be unpacked.

And then – the magic door opened wide and my teacher would start describing innumerable courtiers to young Yvette. I was listening to her, imagining a chubby and slightly confused Yvette, who refused or accepted the courtiers, danced with them or watched them through the net veil on her hat during an official dinner. I was picturing those courtiers as well, sons of rich fathers, who didn't go to discos or to the beach, where they could smoke and drink a bit, kiss, and touch the girls. Similar to our Yvette, they probably lived the lives of Three Cocks.

Ballroom dance evenings at the hotel were the Six Boobs' style. There were fifteen to twenty such evenings in the season, so they would take a taxi to Trieste, Italy, on the first day, in order to buy cocktail dresses and garden party ones and evening gowns for the young Yvette.

That's another world, I thought, looking at suitcase after suitcase of dresses spilling out into the living room, in all the imaginable colors, shades, patterns, and decorations. Under the antique chandelier, light mixed with thick cigarette smoke; they became alive and danced in front of me: joyful, frilly, flowing, pleated, silk, velvet, and the finest cotton dresses, one after another.

Walking slowly home, late at night, I wondered what they could possibly do with all those dresses. There were no such parties in Southern Serbia, where in another world, Yvette could be flirting, gently swaying her hips, in such extravagant attire.

In the later years of my youth, Yvette had grown into a young woman. She started to belong to the present times, but not always precisely. At least she stayed in the same century and more or less in the same decade.

When I left my hometown for the University of Belgrade, I also left those long evenings filled with talking, eating, and coffee drinking with the Six Boobs. Coming back home a few times a year, I never failed to pay them a visit. Later, there were Four Boobs, because Yvette went to study somewhere far away. And then, only Two Boobs remained, my old and tired, but still beautiful, teacher, all alone in the six bedroom apartment. My teacher stopped smoking.

When she disappeared from this world, a deep piercing pain shot through my heart.

I missed her a lot. I longed for more of her stories and jokes; I wanted to prolong those get-togethers that became just a reminiscence.

Yvette is rich and famous now, and lives in a big city on the other side of the Atlantic (from Serbia, that is). I might find her if I wanted to, but maybe it's better the way it is. It would not be the same any more.

Life in Six Boobs permeated my high school and my adolescent years with its spectrum of tales, laughter, beauty, and above all, with somehow an unreal space where we were sitting, drinking coffee, and talking; wrapped up in the scent of freshly-baked cookies and enveloped by the dense fog of cigarette smoke.

Act II
The Call of the Big City

- **Snow in More Than One Way**
- **The Scent of Wild Flowers**
- **A Fairy Tale of a Young Teacher**
- **One Glass and Vivaldi**
- **Mira and the Small Children**
- **Nora**
- **Nora's Impressions**
- **Flooding**
- **Nora's Impressions**
- **University Vs. School, Teacher Vs. Professor**
- **Nora's Impressions**
- **Zora**
- **Nora's Impressions**
- **Is It a Pie or Is It Not a Pie?**

Snow in More Than One Way

I have always loved snow. One of my greatest joys has always been to feel the snowflakes on my face.

Now, many winters later, there are moments of silence in me, when the memories of my first Belgrade winter start warming.

My first student days in Belgrade were painted by dark colors of poverty and injustice.

The hues that an imaginary painter's brush would use to depict my thoughts, feelings and life at the time, would be all the shades of gray, of deep brown, and all the possible nuances of black, along with some light-blue sparks. Light-blue was the color of the Belgrade sky, radiant in its glorious luster, right above me. I couldn't blame the sky for whatever was happening on the earth.

There were just about a dozen of us at the Faculty of Music Piano and Ethnomusicology department. My colleagues had money for the books and for going out; and after the lectures or nights out, they had warm homes to come back to. I had none of that. Still, my heart filled with happiness that I managed to leave the South of Serbia. There was no place for jealousy.

As a child, I read a story, one of the folk fairy tales carried over from generation to generation.

The narrative describes God as an ordinary man, just like we all are, living on bread and water only and sleeping on hay one day and enjoying wine, delicious food and a soft mattress with silk covers the next. Days varied in degrees of poverty or richness. At the end of each day, God would say aloud to those who were born on that day:

"As it is for me now, may it be for you forever."

Maybe this story was really true. Maybe I was simply born on a 'poor man's day'.

On the other hand, my absolutely favorite singer of all times, Josipa Lisac, sang:

Who knows, maybe a new world's waiting for me,
Who knows, from dark a lovely flower may grow,
Maybe the lucky one,
One in a million
Will be me.
Who knows?

I lived in a tiny basement room that contained my piano, a narrow bed, and a chair doubling as the dining table. There was a small stove, just big enough for a coffee pot. On the walls, mildew created modern paintings and emanated the smell of poverty.

The only way to enliven my little room was to put a few nice posters of the setting sun, of mountains and clear lakes, blue and deep. I also had silk thread curtains that my auntie Kankica, from the South, lovingly crocheted for me. They framed the two windows, each one the length of about twenty centimeters. That minuscule room had to mark the beginning of my life in the big city. It had to be my home. No matter what, it was mine and I was going to be happy in it, and in the big city!

The landlady was nicknamed 'Vida, the Gossipmonger' because of her insatiable hunger for gossips. She lived by herself in the house and rented several rooms. In the room next to mine lived a couple who constantly fought. Then, exhausted by fighting, they would fuck like crazy. In the room next to that one there were two guys from Lebanon, students, who left soon.

Vida had a husband who was almost always away, leaving her to her plots. In the mornings, she would walk into my room and glide her old gnarled hands over the blanket, exploring my body. I didn't let her do it, which made her mad. That toothless woman became my nemesis. First, she turned off the heating, so that the water in the sink froze, and then complained loudly about my piano playing.

There was nowhere else to go; it was wintertime and I could barely afford even those meagre lodgings. I had to clench my teeth.

Many a morning found me with frost on my eyelashes and frozen ears. I would get up and run outside to get some snow, put it in a small pot, and melt it on the stove to make some warm coffee. That was my breakfast and dinner. I would leave for my lectures at the university, carried by buses, study all day, and come back to my room to study some more and practice the piano in the evenings.

Practicing the piano was the hardest part. No matter at what time, which was always decent, I would start playing. Thumpings would be heard from the floor above, coming from the landlady, a mentally-deranged woman; and from the room next to mine, occupied by a drug addict couple who slept all day, fought at night, took some more drugs, and fucked themselves senseless. Even though my piano had a pedal to make the sound almost inaudible, which I always kept pressed on, it irritated them. My music was bad for their taste.

I used to buy bread from a bakery owned by an elderly man who sold two or three-day-old bread at half price. My gourmet cuisine consisted of 'snow fried' stale bread in the heated pot for a couple of minutes, until the snow melted and made the bread softer. In rare moments of 'richness', having some extra cash in my wallet, I would spread cream cheese or pâté on it.

Out of all the ways life can make us sad, nothing, nothing can be compared to hunger.

Hunger is stronger than depression, pain, lovesickness, or any kind of suffering. Hunger is quiet and doesn't hurt in the belly but in the brain. It creeps deep into your dreams and doesn't leave you alone.

Still, my joy of being in the capital city and at the university was so great that hunger didn't have a chance to break me down, not one bit. I accepted it as a roommate in my little home.

The beauty of that big city, fascination with its boulevards and parks, its steep winding streets almost impossible to walk on when covered with ice, those gorgeous old façades of landmark buildings and tastefully decorated shop windows; all was a part of an expanding fairy tale. I had dreamt that fairy tale for eighteen years and not even hunger could separate me from it, not in the least. My place was in that city, among its people, on its sidewalks!

When my mom came to visit me for the first time in my new home, she burst into tears. A born actress and an expert in hiding her emotions, she cried inconsolably nevertheless. Everything she saw pained her. I tried to cheer her up, explaining that in spite of the current circumstances, I was happy being where I was, but it didn't bring her much comfort. She returned to my hometown resolved to work as hard as possible to help me out, for she couldn't stand the misery I lived in.

At the time, poverty was present in lots of homes. Since the death of our President Tito, so many things changed, affecting our standard of life in the early 1980s. People were slowly sinking, abandoned by comfortable socialism and unprepared for a change.

Days, weeks, months, and years in my mom's life were measured by my phone calls and letters. In those poverty laden days, she used to knit up to nineteen hours a day. A neighbor who lived next window to Mom's, once said to me that she used to go to bed at midnight and fall asleep by the sounds of Mom's knitting machine. When she went to the bathroom around four in the morning, she would see my mom still awake, knitting.

The knitting machine was a basic metal one, with some mechanical stuff incomprehensible to me. Mom used it only for big chunks and then would take her crocheting needles and start creating fantastic details she invented herself, out of her artistic soul, for sweaters, tops, dresses and leggings, and for her friends who got her new clients every day. Mom became the most popular knitter in the South Serbian world!

Everybody loves Mom; she has always been held in high esteem by neighbors and friends.

Only my paternal relatives couldn't stand her. It was a conflict of mentalities, for my mom's background is honest, hardworking, and school oriented, while the family on my father's side was made up of quite different people.

Never, for as long as I live, will I be able to understand why an educated woman with her looks, her imposing posture, and inspiring presence, chose to marry a man like my father. In distant, sleepless nights of my early teenage years, listening to the echo of his voice yelling at Mom because this or that wasn't 'done properly', I was thinking intently, trying to find the reason and unlock the secret of my birth.

Why do women let these things happen?

Why do they let men beat or torture them psychologically? My mom stoically stood all of my father's rages, angry outbursts, swearing, and maltreating. All that under the banner:

"For your own good, Son."

My love for my mom cannot be measured; such a measuring tape hasn't been invented yet. Still, all these years, especially since I left that part of the world, it drives me nuts when I remember the phrase:

"For your own good, Son."

She wasn't right. I have to utter it, even though it hurts when I do so, for I have only the most beautiful thoughts and words for her. She was wrong there. She convinced herself into something and tried to convince me as well. Of course it worked when I was younger, but as I grew up, my brain evolved, so I realized it was a lame excuse.

She could have:

a) Left forever.

Her answer: "Yeah, so he stays the proud owner of the house I paid 80% for. I carried the bricks and stirred the plaster myself!"

b) Divorced him.

Her reply: "He would kill us both."

c) Called the police.

Her response: "Right, and when they leave, he cuts me into pieces."

So she lived her life with him, me being an accidental passer-by for the first eighteen years of my life.

My mom knitted for working women, housewives, teachers, and doctors. She didn't charge much and made the most beautiful knitwear in the world. Even though I was poor, I was super dressed and had the most unique sweaters at the university. Mom was imaginative and created extraordinary pieces. She knitted day and night. That tempo of work brought my mom many a gray hair and sadness in the eyes, but she made it possible for me to buy books for my studies and to pay for that little room in Belgrade.

A year later, when I got a job, changed the apartment, and had lots of private students, I asked her to slow down with her knitting. She listened to me, but didn't stop. That may have been her contract with herself. Anyway, Mom continued knitting even when a few years later I got a job at the university. She was doing it for her friends and their children.

Suddenly, as if by magic, she stopped, put the knitting machine away, and decided to rest.

All her sleepless nights were mine as well. All my exams were also hers. As my life was assuming clearer shades of the palette, as I was getting better off, she could experience the effects: from new dresses to a new fridge. I sent her to hairdressers, to spas, bought nice bags and shoes for her. Her hardworking, suffering past was simply – the past.

At the time of this story, however, during the bitter winter of 1984, Mom was in deep poverty and misery, just like me.

Snow was freezing the windows of her house, distorting the outline of her face bent over the knitting machine; while at my place, it obscured what little light I had in that small room in the basement.

God is just and good to everybody. I grew up at times when God was banned in my country, but thanks to my mom's stories, I realized that even though we weren't allowed to talk about Him, He existed and protected us all. I asked Him, in those unbearably cold nights, tucked in old blankets insufficient to provide me with warmth, when times would get better for me; when the sun would illuminate my days.

God answered by sending me two Angels: Lela and Marko.

Lela

I met Lela at the house party of my girlfriend at the time who I wanted to break up with but was waiting for an appropriate moment. Lela and I were going home together in the small hours, walking briskly under the chilling wind. She opened her heart to me, gave it to me on the palm of her hand and I accepted it and gave her mine.

Lela lived in a dilapidated house on the outskirts of the city. Her mother was an alcoholic and she took care of her and her father, an unspeakable tyrant; Lela always getting the worst of him. Still, she laughed with all her heart and was full of joie de vivre. We took to each other instantly, tenderly, like brother and sister.

Our friendship started on telepathic notes. Lela got rid of the mildew on the walls of my little room and scared the landlady to death threatening to get the sanitary inspection to her doorstep if she didn't provide me with heating. From all her warmth, my faucet defrosted and I didn't have to wash myself with melted snow any more.

Her eyes were teary when she saw my daily 'menu': wet bread on the small stove.

"I'll be back in two hours," she said. "Practice Bach, you know you have an exam soon."

She came back bringing a bigger stove, a proper pot, a frying pan, and a bag full of flour, oil, eggs, ham, salt, pepper, and what not! My little room was infused with the scent of scrambled eggs with ham. She also had a piece of chocolate for me.

Lela was compassionate and caring. Her love shifted from motherly to sisterly, we never crossed the line that would take us to some other spheres of love.

She would take my laundry and secretly mix it with her family's. She would put aside some of her breakfast or dinner so she could share it with me. The winter was getting warmer.

She admired my piano playing. She was a good listener. She knew how to share happiness.

Lela was a princess without a castle, I was a knight without a white horse.

She was studying Pedagogy and I was helping her with music subjects. I can still see her in a worn-out yellow-ish coat, the wrong cut for her body frame. I see her all smiley and cheerful. She and I didn't know the meaning of 'sadness', unless we heard a song. We would cry our hearts out to a melody or lyrics.

Evenings with Lela were full of doing things, singing, and playing Yamb. She enjoyed when I revealed secrets of this or that composer while I studied for the Music History exam. Lela's and my path never crossed the physical plane of love; our friendship glowed with a more powerful flame.

Sometime after Christmas, she introduced me to Marko, her next door friend she had grown up with.

Marko

A curly-haired Marko, in a short brown jacket entered my life and just like Lela, did his best to help me and make my life better and more beautiful. He found some old shelves and painted them, so I got a cupboard. He brought me a lamp for the piano so I could see clearly the small print notes during my late evening practice. He also brought his guitar that he never parted from.

I was teaching him music that he loved so much. He absorbed all my words about harmonies and their functions. He virtually lived with me, went to school in the morning, and came back every afternoon to his music lessons, bringing me some home-made food, cookies, or anything else he thought I might need.

In our spare time, the three of us used to go to the huge park of Košutnjak, more like a wood, and walk for miles. Marko would make fun of my southern accent, only to be reprimanded by Lela.

I was studying hard for the exams. I knew only one thing – I had to pass them for the existential reason: I'll never go back to the South, so I've got to make it here!

The Scent of Wild Flowers

My former high school of Music in the south organized a trip to Poland for one week, which included tickets for The Chopin Festival. In spite of my dire financial situation, my heart was glowing with a wish to be there, at the greatest of all Chopin competitions.

The team leader of the organizers was my wonderful teacher (the middle pair of Boobs), who wanted very much to get Yvette to listen to the top pianists. She contacted me and convinced me with few words to go with them. They were leaving from the South and I was to join them at a certain spot in Belgrade. She understood my lack of money and found a way for me to pay in ten installments, so I sighed with relief. She had always been such a darling – so compassionate.

The bus I boarded a few mornings later was full of my high school teachers, their children, and students. Almost all of us knew one another. The seat next to Yvette, who had been looking forward to our meeting, was waiting for me. She changed a bit, grew up, but was still a cheerful lady-like self, dressed in an impossible tangle of bows, ribbons, lace, and frills. The same old Yvette.

My teacher took the front seat, next to the driver, because she had to smoke. She carried with her a metal, travel size ashtray which she regularly emptied after every fifth cigarette (that is, every ten minutes).

Her mother reclined on the window seat, also smoking.

The bus drove through Budapest in the middle of the night, which was a pity, since I wanted to see its luxurious streets and opulent façades.

We crossed the border of Czechoslovakia (as it was called then), followed by the fierce blowing of the mountain winds.

Poland was waiting for us, unable to provide a warm welcome. At that time, with the exception of the red and white flag, Poland was gray, dark, unsatisfied, and sad. Our faces glued to the bus windows were greeted by long lines in front of the stores, empty shop windows, and sullen people miserably dressed. We were looking, not knowing then that it would become the mirror image of our country only a few years later, and that our grayness would be colored in much deeper and darker shades than the Polish one.

Warsaw conquered my heart with its wide streets, cathedrals, and palaces, but also with its socio-realistic buildings. Warsaw defied poverty and remained beautiful. On a rainy September morning, love was born between Warsaw and I; between Poland and I. That love will expand, become a marriage, and then an eternal unbreakable platonic relationship.

As I was taking the room key from the hotel reception that morning, I was asked several times if I needed to exchange some money. Foreign currency trade was a source of income for the unemployed Poles then (the exact same thing would happen in my country some short years after).

I exchanged $20 and got a lot of Polish banknotes in return.

My teacher and her daughter decided to go shopping and I joined them.

"It's good that we speak Russian, all three of us," my teacher said lightly. "It will help us, since none of us speak Polish."

It turned out not to be a bright idea. At the sound of the Russian language, Poles became very unfriendly and frowned at us. We soon realized it was easier to use body language.

Poles didn't like Russians at all. Who would, when they imposed such a regime and misery upon them!

The Festival started and concerts were performed three times a day. Out of about sixty candidates, fewer and fewer remained in the competition as the hours passed. There were so many of us sitting on the floor, tightly pressed against each other. The concert halls were overbooked (a typical Eastern European logic: sell a lot more tickets than there are seats, make more money), so the audience had to use every available surface to sit down.

Between the concerts, I walked the city streets and went into empty stores. Chopin's music could be heard at every step. Ill-disposed shop assistants drank tea from water glasses, looking at us foreigners pass by. Chopin's music was ever present, adding up to an already too melancholic autumnal reality of Warsaw.

And then I started to listen more attentively to the language, unpleasant to the ear at first, but so beautiful as it went on. I started to listen to it and to love it.

The melancholy of Warsaw, Chopin's music, and the sound of the Polish language, made me fall in love with the city and the country. I loved my Warsaw and Poland. I had some quick and passionate sexual affairs in my hotel room on the eleventh floor, late at night, instead of getting together with my teacher and her daughter; always ready for yet another waltz on the dance podium of the Polonia Hotel.

In the Philharmonic Hall, the competition was tight, there were only six pianists left. I wanted Krzysztof Jabłoński to win; he looked so much like young Chopin, was wonderful, and played angelically. My second choice was Marc Laforet from France or Bernata Blocha from Canada. Still, the winner was Stanislav Bunin from Russia. There was no end to general disappointment. Honestly, he was excellent. His reward was well-earned for, even though it didn't fulfill Yvette's and my expectations.

We took a tour to Chopin's birth place and walked in the Old Town of Warsaw, by the Vistula River. Wrapped up in my thoughts, I wasn't listening to what Yvette was mumbling about, a big red scarf covering her head and mouth. My thoughts were directed towards this city. How do I get back here again? How do I *live* here? I didn't know what magic potion Warsaw gave me to drink, but I was intoxicated.

At one of the concerts, I met Alfred: a well-off gentleman in his early fifties, whose heart was touched by my love for Warsaw. He promised to make it possible for me to come here often and was true to his word in the following four years.

I sent postcards to my mom, my aunts, and to my dear elementary school teacher. The postcards were not of the best quality, wrinkled and with colors washed out.

Every night, another body slept in my bed. Every night, Chopin's music filled my hotel room from a small radio on the bedside table. There were too many prostitutes in restaurants and bars. Poland was in a really bad shape in 1985. Once a great nation, strong and proud, now diminished under Russian domination.

We felt rich there; even me. For only a couple of US dollars, you could get the most delicious dinner in a high class restaurant. We could have bought everything, but there was nothing to buy. Scary shelves of nothing gaped at us, eager to be filled.

My souvenirs were my sexual Polish nights and the concerts, one after another. Those two passions flowed through my body.

The bus was driving the same way back. Budapest in the middle of the night again. This time, I didn't mind. I dreamt of Warsaw; resplendent, freed of grayness.

One of the most memorable days during my first year in Belgrade was when, exhausted after tons of lectures and classes, my head buzzing with musicians, notes and harmonies, I went to the university café and lit a cigarette over a strong black coffee.

"Fuck them all, I'm resigning!"

Sladja was an attractive blonde with less attractive manners and least attractive language.

Red in the face, she slumped on the chair next to me.

"I am fed up with peasants and primitives!" she burst out and lit up.

"What are you talking about?" I asked.

"Shit, I've been working in that bloody village school for eight months now. I can't take it a day longer," she kicked the leg of the table. "It's too far. I hate the children, and the teachers there even more!"

"You have a job?" I said, astonished. "But you're only a freshman, just like me."

"C'mon, don't be daft. They'd fuck themselves in their dirty asses to get someone with a high school diploma," she laughed. "Nobody wants to go there."

I couldn't believe my ears. A job. A job for me. Maybe God granted my long prayers to relieve the hunger and suffering in my tiny basement room. Maybe the Almighty decided to give me that job, so I could finally buy fresh bread instead of the stale and mildewed.

"Do you think I could get the position?" I asked, transfixed.

"Of course," she said matter-of-factly. "Just call them, here's the number."

I rushed out of the café and into the phone booth. I dialed with my left hand and prayed.

Sladja had a question mark in her eyes when I got back. "So, how did it go?"

I could find no words, my heart wanted to jump out of my chest of happiness.

"I'm going for the interview right now," I said.

"Good luck."

"Thank you!"

As I exited the main door of the Faculty of Music, the sun made its way through the heavy three-day old clouds, as if wanting to give me a sign that everything would be fine.

And it was. It was more than fine. It was like a fairy tale.
A beautiful, village fairy tale.

A Fairy Tale of a Young Teacher

The village that the commuter bus was approaching looked unusual: spread out over hills, gorges, and valleys. Some houses were built so high up, I wondered how people could get there. After yesterday's interview with the principal, today would be my first day of work. Ecstatically, I awaited the last stop.

I felt a twinge of guilty consciousness having missed the Music History class that I enjoyed, but this was more existential than the history of early music of the 12th century.

The bus stopped at some kind of a plateau, after an hour and ten-minute ride. I got off and looked around. The road led uphill and there were a post office and a bank, both very small. About two hundred meters away, a school could be discerned and an outline of the church steeple behind it. Just like in every village: school and church close to each other. On the small square, there was a newspapers kiosk and a variety store. That was the main crossroad in the village from where five roads forked; intersected by distant paths leading to who-knows-where.

The sun was shining on the freshly cut grass in front of the post office and the bank. I started walking uphill towards the school.

The school looked nice and inviting, hugged by pine and birch trees. Tito's picture hung proudly on the central wall of the teachers' room. In the middle of nowhere, that school emanated a certain beauty that immediately endeared it to me.

In the course of two months, I managed to be respected and liked by all the colleagues and most of the children. It was impossible to be liked by all kids because I was strict from the very beginning and didn't allow inappropriate behavior during classes.

On the last day in May of that far wonderful 1985, I got my first salary of 1920 dinars. I felt like flying, only if I had wings! It was a modest part-time teacher's salary, but for a poor student from a province with the minimal earnings imaginable, it was like winning the lottery.

From that first salary, I bought my mom a handbag – since the one she had was falling apart, a lipstick, and an eye shadow. I treated all my friends to coffee and cakes from the best pâtisserie in the city, and myself to a box of Bajadera chocolates: my symbol of taste.

On the last day of school, at the end of June, before the summer vacations, the children asked me after each class:

"Teacher, will you please teach us again in September?"

"I hope so, my little ones," I said. "I sincerely hope so."

Oh, if the little ones only knew how much I needed that job and what it meant to me! Over the following few days, there were teachers meetings and sessions which I had to attend. Regardless of the fact that I was a part-time employee, there were lots of things to be discussed and tons of paperwork to be done.

Out of the blue, a law came in vigor, demanding only Cyrillic alphabet to be used in school registers. A few of us teachers exchanged glances. I never wrote in Cyrillic. Of course I knew it, I was taught it in elementary school; but all the time it had been Latin alphabet from the street signs, adds, books, to the subtitles on TV. I decided then to start looking into the matter more attentively and to make sure I could write properly.

It was the beginning of summer. The sunshine was plentiful, but the teachers' room was in a shade of huge trees outside, protecting us from the heat. For the first time in my life, I was in teachers meetings, fully participating.

I was happy and proud. If it could, my heart would have jumped out of my chest. We talked about the school children and their potential, about those who were very good or not so good. As always, most of the time was spent on 'problematic' kids who were undisciplined or destroyed school possessions.

I used to sit next to Mira, the Physical Education teacher, who already became my friend. The two of us often gossiped, whispering into each other's ears. Teachers were a very specific kind of people. The principal was trying to shush and calm down the louder ones, but his efforts were in vain; for once the two Serbian Literature teachers started a debate it grew into a heated discussion, resulting in a verbal war. Coffee would be brought in, thus tempering the tempest. We all smoked and the teachers' room was submerged into bluish fumes.

July and August went by fast in preparations for the next academic year at the university, in practicing Bach, and trips to the South, to visit my family. Everybody was proud of me, for I had completed the first year of my studies.

And then September came, and my heart started to freeze with fear in case somebody else applied to work in the village school. I was scared someone would snatch away from me the job I needed so much.

Luckily, it remained mine. I worked three days a week, in different shifts. I knew it would be extremely hard to coordinate classes at the university and the school, especially the commuting that took at least two hours in each direction, but I was ready for it.

And so, timidly, love was born between me and the profession, love for teaching, and for the children.

On the days when I worked the morning shift, I would wake up at 4:30 a.m. and from a suburb of Belgrade where I lived, take a night bus to another part of the city where I waited for the commuter bus. I would get on at 6:05, for the next one left at 6:20 which was too late, leaving me without a chance to have the early morning coffee at the school canteen in the basement. The bus was full of locals going back home from night shifts or wild parties, sprinkled with us 'outlanders' who traveled to the village to teach young locals.

There was an understated demarcation line between native teachers and the commuting ones, considered sort of vagabonds. The kids figured it out and treated us respectively.

Mornings would start with us 'vagabonds' rushing to the basement, where the cooks baked pastries for the kids to snack on. The usual conversation involved previous night's TV shows, scandals in the newspapers, and running gossips in the style 'who, when and with whom…'.

It might have been due to my young age or to my kind words; at any rate, the two cooks liked me a lot and were all beaming when I went downstairs for my first coffee of the day and a chat. They were telling me about all the marriageable girls in the village, recommending some of them. There was a Biology teacher, good looking and very a tall girl. The cooks said we were made for each other. I laughed at that. She wasn't my type at all.

So a few of us early risers would enjoy coffee, talking about this and that, what happened the day before, what a politician said and what movies were playing. It was a good start of a good day. Each day was good to me in that school.

Then we would go to the second floor and get ready for the classes.

The bell would ring at 7:45 a.m. and I would emerge from the smoke-soaked teachers' room, heading for the classroom where my heart opened music vistas to the curious village kids.

The warm September sun shone on my smiley face.

I won!
I'll never be hungry again!

One Glass and Vivaldi

If Antonio Vivaldi had known how his Concerto No.4 in F minor, Op.8, L'inverno would deeply touch children's hearts, I believe he would have been contented with my transmission of the message. Winter conquered the village, offering us views from the school windows to white hills; dreamy snow covered roofs and chimneys, smoke whirling out of them carried away by the never-ending dance of snowflakes.

I decided to share with my little students Vivaldi's Winter. The record player was old and the record I brought cracked, but it was all negligible when violins, violas, and cellos started to blend into that morning. Kids were looking at their village, paths to their homes and the rooftops, inspired by the melody of L'inverno. When it ended, silence descended upon us like an encompassing music hug.

"Did you like it?" I asked.

"Yeees!" they said in unison.

I played the record again, more quietly now, for I wanted them to listen attentively to exuberant thrillers and sequences in the movements.

1. Allegro. The children experienced it as a snowstorm, winds blowing on windows at night. Cries of trees exhausted from the battle with the wind.
2. Largo. They felt it as a moment of silence, the show falling softly and fire crackling in stoves in their homes. Some said it reminded them of the smells of winter, of smoked meat, pickles, and apple sorbets.
3. Allegro. A constant fight between the sun and the snow. Who is going to win?

I enjoyed listening to them, I loved their warm, smiley faces. In certain moments, I had a stone in my heart knowing that most of them wouldn't continue schooling. They were bound to stay there to work on the fields. Girls would marry early and bear children, and boys would get old before their time, drinking beer in the local bar. Education wasn't exactly the guiding principle in those parts, for the fields had to be ploughed and gardens to be planted. The cycle of life irreversibly gives and takes. I often felt like sort of a muse of music and arts, offering those wide-open eyes for at least a few years a bit of beauty that might a little, a tiniest little bit, engrave some artistic sense in their brains and souls.

One evening, I found myself in the classroom in front of about thirty women. Their heads covered with scarves and tight expressions on their faces. That was my first meeting with the parents. Only mothers came to teacher-parent meetings, it wasn't a 'male thing'.

I greeted them politely and introduced myself:

"I am only a nineteen-year-old teacher, but please be assured that I will take a good care of your children, teach them to the best of my abilities, and definitely not let the older students bully or beat them."

The women turned around and looked at each other. One of them, after coughing out a bit, stood up and said:

"Hey, teacher, you should beat them; we'll bring you some nice branches for whipping."

Her words were approved by other women. They scanted loudly:

"There's no learning without beatings!"

"A whip makes the school go round!"

"Just be strict with them!"

There were some other requests, totally illogical to me.

After each class, teachers would gather in the teachers' room to have some coffee, smoke a couple of cigarettes, and eat pastries always waiting for us.

There was a jug of water on the table and a glass. Only one.

I didn't notice anything wrong about it in May when I first came to the school; nor in January when the severe winter enveloped the village in white transparency, causing the buses to run late and us commuters to wait forever, frozen, on the clearing in the center of the village, whipped by cold mountain winds. I noticed it only the last week, on one of my last days there, before I left the magical village school.

So, there was only one glass. Teachers would come in, one by one, pour the water from the jug into the glass and drink, one after one, and I with them. It had never occurred to any of us that it wasn't healthy or hygienic, with all those germs spreading and us possibly catching a contagious disease. Nobody would have cared anyway; if you are thirsty you drink water, if there's only one glass, so be it. As simple as that.

Coffee would arrive, one of the cooks would bring a platter full of small cups that emanated a seductive smell.

There were about twenty of us teachers and we didn't all work always on the same days, so we never ran out of subjects for conversation, discussion, jokes, or gossips, to catch up.

Our greatest fun was to witness frequent arguments between two colleagues: Stoja and Mira.

Stoja was a Math teacher, a wonderful woman with a strong ethic sense. She was a mother to two sons who were well-behaved and good students. After teaching Pythagoras theorem and arithmetic, she would go to a nearby village, pull up her sleeves, and roll the dough. She would bake the most delicious pies and cakes, cook, fry and sauté; filling, with mouth-watering aromas, her warm home, peaceful and full of love.

Stoja always came to the school in nice hand-knitted blouses and skirts (made by herself) in soft pastel colors, as was appropriate for a woman her age. On her hands, she had engagement and wedding rings and a gold watch, a gift from her husband for their 25th anniversary.

Mira was very fit and youthful looking. She wore tight jeans and t-shirts or turtlenecks, with tons of bracelets, chains, earrings, and other accessories. After a gymnastics, core strength or sports class, she would sprint into the teachers room where we were all quietly talking about a book or a movie, and start shouting from the top of her lungs:

"Sitting there like grandmas!"

"Is there anything to eat?"

"Shit, you've eaten everything!"

"Who's taking the 7 o'clock bus tonight?"

"I've got to book the ski resort soon, the prices are going up!"

"Girls can't have periods three times a month, it's just an excuse not to play basket-ball!"

"Are we getting a raise? What's the government doing about it?"

A torrent of questions, an overflooded river of words flowing through the inexplicably strong voice of such a small woman would shake us up, Stoja most of all. Stoja calmly resisted Mira's innumerable comments, but if Mira kept on being unstoppable and unbearingly loud, Stoja would stand up and say firmly:

"Calm down Mira, you adolescent girl!" And she would give her a piece of her mind.

It eventually turned out that Mira was a few years older than Stoja, but due to all those physical activities, she stayed young in an unspecified age.

We all enjoyed watching the cross exchange between the two of them.

In addition to the teacher's job, my classes at the university were multiplying, with exams following one another. Since the job took a lot of my time, I would take with me all the material, books, scores, and note paper, so I could study while commuting. A day before an exam, on the bus, Mira would take my music books and ask me random questions to make sure I was well prepared. She often yelled with her sonorous voice at the people there to keep their hens quiet, since I couldn't concentrate on conducting because of the noise. Hens were frequent passengers on those trips.

At the end of each semester, there was a long session after the classes, with all the teachers, the pedagogue, the psychologist, the librarian, and the principal. It was boring to death, but comical at the same time. While eagerly expecting what Mira would say to provoke Stoja to lose her balance, we were amused by an elderly Literature teacher who sounded more authoritative than the principal, with his refined language, ways of expression, and accent; which annoyed the latter big time.

The principal invariably started with:

"Good evening, comrades, and especially good evening to our colleagues from caves, to our cave people."

When I first heard it, I turned around in alarm, horrified by the mental image of some surviving cave people miraculously transported into our teachers' room, expecting wild hairy creatures with sharp long nails. I was sort of disappointed when I saw two sweet old ladies.

It was actually Caves, a small village a few kilometers away, where those two women taught children: grades one to four, before delivering them into our hands.

There were some other local teachers. The principal always took the side of the locals and didn't like us commuters at all. He wanted the school staff to be eventually composed only of 'our people', as he used to say.

Mira and the Small Children

Our friendship was born on the commuter bus. Mira was back to work after maternity leave. She encountered some changes in the school, me being one of them.

We clicked on first sight and got attached to each other, more than a brother and sister would. She invited me to her home. I met her two little daughters. We established our pizzeria evenings in downtown Belgrade once a month, sharing the details of our lives that couldn't be told on the bus, over piping hot pizzas and cold beer.

Mira is an extraordinarily strong woman, rational, quick-witted, and fast talking. She talks loudly, extremely loudly and laughs her heart out. She has always been projected into positive thoughts and deeds, and has no idea what sadness means.

When her husband left her, there was no place in her for tears or defeat. Mira managed her household even better, all the while teaching in a far-away school surrounded by hills. She wished for a job in the city so she could be closer to her daughters, and it was granted to her a couple of years later.

She supported me in my studies and exams. I supported her in bringing up the little girls. We have remained inseparable friends over decades, with a mutual memory of the village suspended in the air.

Mira has always had a way to make ends meet, finding the smartest methods of paying with post-dated checks or by buying, selling, and reselling. Her energy is the most vital ever seen in this world, her strength draws from the pure survival instinct.

Mira's life is sport. Incredibly well-built, all lean muscle. Not a tiny trace of fat on her. Her thighs and butt are cellulite free. Mira walks through life with fast and steady steps. She dyes her hair blond which suits her perfectly. The good food of Vojvodina, in the North of Serbia, its mild climate, and early life in a village where she grew up may have contributed to one of the most beautiful skin textures on the planet, which she possesses.

She is older than most people around her, the oldest one at the school sessions she has to attend, with the looks of a girl in her late twenties! She has that magical power to look gorgeous without a bit of concealer and with just a touch of mascara. She is slim and totally fit, just the way she should be.

Friendship with her has always been easy going and enjoyable. For over a quarter of a century, never once have we quarreled or disagreed with each other in any way. Of course, I've been irritated with her hundreds of times, as she's probably been with me, but these little things only add spice to a friendship and make it stronger.

Whenever I send her an email or a postcard from my trips now, I always start with: 'Dear Mira and the small children'; for when I first met them, her kids were really very small: two sweet angels, two beautiful girls, one dark-haired with deep brown eyes; the other, blond with a soft, gentle gaze. They used to jump and clap their hands when I brought them chocolates.

Now they are all happy when I bring them makeup and perfumes.

Time goes by and everything changes.

Heraclitus, a Greek philosopher, said that the only constant thing in life is change.

That's why each change is a reason for celebration.

Nora

Caught up in a waltz she didn't want to dance, carried by the wind that was too strong for her, Nora entered my life unexpectedly one morning, when I started classes at the school later than usual.

She was sitting in the teachers room, smoking.

Actually, the first thing I saw was her hair: long, thick black hair. It cascaded in waterfalls down her body, stopping just short of her hips. She was sitting quietly, reading. Out of that sea of hair, I could discern only the tip of the cigarette and the contour of her nose.

I introduced myself and went to teach the class.

At the break, she was still there, silent, smoking, and reading, unbothered by Mira's and Stoja's verbal fights, paying no attention to the Literature teacher's political comments or to the principal's remarks. She was cocooned in her world of nymphs and like them, didn't give a word out of herself. Still, her aura was almost palpable. I could feel the vibrations of her heart.

The day was surrendering to the reign of the night. We finished our classes and waited for the bus. Colors, yellow and red, were competing in tree fronds that fall. Which one was going to win? The autumnal winds were swirling her hair, but she was far away from that reality.

On the bus, I sat down beside her. We talked.

Her voice was quiet and the words carefully measured, precise, and perfect. Our friendship and love were born there, on the four wheels of the old rickety bus somewhere at the Three Lamp Posts stop.

And then suddenly, days started to be filled with her presence. I managed to fit her into a tight time-frame, barely available from all the classes at the university, the school, and lots of private lessons I was giving. That frame was small, but was worth more than all the others.

She entered my heart.

The school children were talking about her and asked me if I had met her.

"I've met her," I said.

"Have you seen how beautiful she is?"

"I have."

The children loved her and were running to her as if drawn by a magnet. Once, I walked into the classroom where she was teaching, intrigued by the noise coming out of it. This is what I saw: half of the kids jumping on the desks, imitating Tarzan cries, while the other half, mostly girls, were all around her, snuggled in her lap, and playing with her hair. Nora was like a fairy, totally undisturbed by the unusual class setting, whispering some English poems into their ears. When the moment of astonishment passed and I managed to close, still in wonder, the wide-open door, I shouted:

"Go back to your seats before I count to three – one, two..." They were already sitting down properly.

No matter how hard I tried to explain to the children the importance of the English language and the impact it may have on their future, and the basis of being attentive in the classes so they could learn more, it was all smart talk, only to disappear in the strands of Nora's hair. They loved her a lot, enjoyed being close to her and sharing jokes with her. There were no bad words or nasty behavior in her classes, just childish, funny chaos.

Nora wasn't into small talk or chatting. Everything she said sounded condensed, squeezed out of sentences, as if she was always filtering long paragraphs, managing to reduce them to a few words.

She wore quite unusual clothes and I liked that. Some of her tops were definitely not appropriate for the school, but luck was on her side, for her long thick hair served her as a cloak and a shawl.

The colleagues didn't understand her.

They didn't gossip about her, not a lot anyway.

In the beginning, nobody knew we were getting together, but shortly the news spread, of course.

"She's very good-looking, you have to give her that," the colleagues said.

"Such a pretty lass, what's she doing in our village? It's not for her," the cooks commented when I went for my early morning coffee in the basement.

She was extraordinarily beautiful.

Nora entered my life quietly and stayed in it intensively. I have never met a person who has been changing so much as her. The constant flux is her essence, her perpetuum mobile.

Nora would change with the cold winds of November, with the first buds of lily of the valley in shady gardens of the early spring. She would transform dramatically, impulsively, guided by her Scorpio instincts. No treasures in the world could ever tempt her to stop changing.

Her love for me was growing and getting stronger day by day, but it often took on different shapes, making it sometimes hard for me to comprehend and accept it. She was a dreamer and very rational at the same time. Her feet were firmly rooted into the ground (in spite of the high stilettos she used to wear), but her head was in another hemisphere.

On the days of her powerful spiritual currents, she would offer me too much love, affection, and attention, while on some other days she would long for a long discussion, using the tiniest of excuses to start an argument, to express her love.

She was like a poem made up from pieces of Picasso's canvases, from verses of melancholy Jacques Prévert, flamboyant Laza Kostić, and gentle and sentimental Desanka Maksimović (the latter two were eminent Serbian poets). Then this canvas should be hung on a wall of glass, so it's always lit – by the radiant sun by day, and by the silent moon by night.

Nora's Impressions

A carefree sparrow, cheerfully chirping and chuckling, fluffing its feathers, hopping from branch to branch, chatting happily with its little friends. That's me, in case you haven't guessed.

And that's because I'm simply, genuinely, and irrevocably in love, for real! Like, you read about those colossal loves that consume the whole being, about whirlwinds of passion that sweep everything else from the lives of characters, but nothing can be compared to the most basic yet mighty feel of the body chemistry working its way, hormones going wild, carried away by whatever process is taking place.

Feeling weightless, with veiled gaze and fluttering heart, levitating rather than walking, I run to Mom to tell her everything, even though nothing has happened yet. Mom is sort of pleasantly surprised seeing the normally composed me in such an ecstatic state, and gives me her full support.

So, enamored and fortified, I go on.

"Is he going to fall in love with me, no, to love me forever and ever and happily ever after, till the end of time? Oh my God, what shall I do? How do I approach him? How do I attract his attention? Maybe change my eye shadow – and what about the lipstick, the nails? He's a musician, you know, so he might prefer short nails on a girl. My mom's obsessed with filing them because she plays the piano, too. Do I trade my leggings for elegant dresses? What do I say to him to sound like easy going to get him interested in me? Aargh. What do I do? Tell me, tell me, please!" I risk suffocating to death my best friend Lina with my endless pleadings for reassurance.

"Hey, slow down, take it easy, just don't scare the hell out of the guy, let him be," she says, exasperated.

The two of us diligently work on perfecting my makeup and I get a facial followed by a complete body treatment, all with full waxing, manicure, pedicure, and massage; Lina being an esthetician. The procedure is enjoyably accompanied by gallons of coffee, cigarettes overflowing the ashtrays, and an occasional glass of vodka, just to calm my tingling nerves, which has a reverse effect, making me even more garrulous.

In the end, to put a stop to my incessant bugging, Lina retreats to the last resort and starts reading my destiny from an overturned coffee cup (we're talking Turkish coffee here. It leaves a thick layer of drags on the bottom of the cup, which form all sorts of various shapes when you turn the cup upside down) and in Tarot cards, just to confirm the favorable prognosis. I have a slight suspicion she's making it all up or embellishing it at least, but I let myself get softly lulled into the predictions.

"Ascendant in Gemini, Sun, Mercury, and Neptune form a stellium in your Sixth House. Moon in Virgo, Venus in conjunction with Mars in the Seventh House, hmm... that's the House of Libra, it rules the relationships... It's in Sagittarius, you're quite adventurous! Right, I have it. His Ascendant is in Sagittarius!" Iva, another friend of mine, creator of psychedelic etchings and amateur astrologer, is reading my birth chart.

"He needs your water to drench his hard soil." (Even I can figure this one out: I'm a Scorpio – water and Nikola is a Taurus – earth, so stands to reason, but I let Iva continue.) "Your spirit of creativity, your internal fire... You will be his inspiration!"

I let this one pass. Like, it's too much. I have a deep respect for real psychics, but my dear Iva is just attempting – although honestly – to be one.

Whatever, everything she says is actually nice and I can't wait to go teach the village kids some English, and Nikola some rumba (when you dance your body has to be close to your partner's, so here's my chance!).

I'm getting accustomed to the fact I'm earning for a living, even though I don't have to. My existence is not being threatened by anything and my living conditions well over average. So, I basically use my salary as pocket money to get even larger quantities of cosmetics and books than usual. Shopping sprees for some new clothes are conducted by Mom, since she has a more refined sense of style than I do. Like, I'm happy in jeans and all kinds of pants, fitting t-shirts, and tops, as long as the colors are coordinated; while Mom is into more romantic stuff: flowing dresses, full skirts and frilly blouses, all soft and pastel. I let her guide me, it may lead to conquering the love of my life.

Once, I left the wallet containing my monthly earnings in a bookstore (head in the clouds kind of thing), which Mom promptly substituted with: money and a new wallet on top of it! God bless her soul, is all I can say!

Now, I'm not a spoiled brat, even though I have grown up in a huge house, sporting mahogany and marble furniture, silver, ivory, and amber decorations, German porcelain, Polish crystal, and Venetian glass; and where lavish parties are the order of every second or third day of the week. Nor is it my 'fault' that I got to see Michelangelo's Pietà in the Vatican when I was barely thirteen, and visited Paris twice by the age of fifteen.

The day finally comes when I'm invited for coffee to Nikola's place and I am so totally impressed by its originality! The apartment is an open concept, with tastefully furnished kitchen, dining room, living room, salon, bedroom, and bathroom; the whole space being about the size of a large walk-in closet! Just how is it possible that his dressing table is bigger than mine?

Has anyone ever made love to your hair? Lightly touching it, burying their nose into its depths, breathing in its scent to the top of their lungs, kissing it with full lips, lingering above it… Gentleness incorporated, so soft and pure, and ethereal and eternally engraved in my body. Never has every cell of it pulsated in such orgasmic shocks! A moment encapsulated.

Never in my life have I seen such a multitude of books, records, and paintings in so tiny a place. This is like my dream kingdom! The reign of Literature, Music, and Art! All you need is to inhale the beauty of them, nothing else. Except, you have to eat sometimes.

Now, I've never been much into food and my eating habits are quite erratic. Eating is such a waste of time, in my opinion, for there are so many more fulfilling things to do in life!

Just think about it: first you have to make money to buy food, then go to a supermarket, drag the heavy bags home and unpack. Next comes washing, peeling, cutting, slicing, shredding, grating, chopping... all of which create a lot of garbage in the process. And then you boil, stew, fry, sauté, bake...what not. Then put everything together. Set the table, all with matching tablecloth, plates, cutlery, and napkins. Eat (too time consuming to chew). Clean up, wash the dishes. And the next day, everything goes into the toilet, like a literal waste. I have often wondered why, in spite of the incredible development of modern science and technology, nobody has ever invented a pill containing your daily intake of the perfect carb-protein-fat-vitamin ratio appropriate to your body type, that you take in the morning and are done with the food thing for the day.

All this said, I really enjoy savoring delicacies in Nikola's Castle of Arts. He introduces me to the most sophisticated concoctions from pea soups to spicy and baked delicacies; just to the point chicken liver and wings (in my non-vegetarian days); to prženija, a yummy South Serbian dish of fried onions, peppers and tomatoes, and to a home-made pizza! Pizza has always been my feast food, reserved for pizzerias in Trieste, Verona, Florence, and Rome, but now I learn you can actually make it at home, every day if you want!

OK, Nikola's looks and personality conquer my heart, but his pizzas win my belly!

Oh, Nikola's looks! Tall and slim, long-limbed and with movements of a ballet dancer (which he used to be), Slavic face, high cheek-bones, sensual lips, melancholy-honest eyes (if you look deeply into a dog's eyes, you'll get the picture), head crowned by an unruly bush of curly hair. His coloring is dark, hair and eye wise. His skin is porcelain white. He is very fast, able to do, like, thousands of different things a day, running from one end of the city to another. He also tells the funniest and most incredible stories in the world! There's immense goodness emanating from him and a powerful charisma; like a strong magnetic field drawing people into his circle where they feel protected and privileged.

Nikola's apartment is actually a converted garage, but luckily, the window stretches all the length of the wall. There are translucent-white curtains and light-green drapes, tied up with white ribbons on the sides of it. Morning glory is blossoming in the window boxes.

Every inch of the space is used to its maximum, creating a little microclimate oasis. There are shelves everywhere, above the dining room table (doubling as a study), on the floor, on the top of the wardrobe. Also knickknacks, trinkets, and souvenirs all over the place.

"What's this?" Little Ana, Mira's younger daughter, grabs a small pewter jewelry box and spills its contents on the floor. I notice that the carpet could do with a bit of cleaning.

Ana is a lively kid, in her phase of asking questions and excessive moving. She jumps on the chair and nearly knocks down the bust of Chopin from the piano. Then, she rummages through the extensive collection of Alan Ford comic books, kicks a vase with dried flowers and a bowl filled with water lilies, starts systematically pulling out Nikola's underwear from the drawers and makes for the bathroom where she performs an alchemical act by mixing variously scented shower gels, bath oils, and body lotions and pouring them all into the bathtub.

She is a ballerina now, dancing at the National Theater in Belgrade and touring the world. Her first inquiring steps were made at Nikola's place.

Flooding

There are and always will be certain things in life we'll never be able to completely understand, or comprehend because they can't be fully explained.

Why don't some people eat meat, while others don't drink milk? Why is it somebody can't stand summer, somebody else, winter? One person may like wearing shirts, another one, sweaters. The same goes for taste in women: blondes or brunettes, tall or short, plump or thin...

One of the things I most strongly dislike is thunderstorms.

In my early childhood, I used to hide under the dining room table when it thundered, and tightly close my eyes before the splitting rays of lightning. The skies of Southern Serbia, where I grew up, became threatening, dark gray, and leaden. Not even my mother's soothing presence could release my fear. I would make us both run to the neighbor next door, where we stayed until the thunderstorm subsided, because the clouds looked less frightening to my child's eyes from her window.

My student days beaded into enameled necklace made of rare pearls from exotic seas. In a year and a half in Belgrade, I acquired new friends, lots of colleagues, top grades at the university, a job, and tons of private students.

I could afford to live in an apartment.

Actually, in a garage converted into one.

From the street, an incline path led to the entrance where the garage doors had been replaced by a slim white door and large windows, spreading along the wall. My windows had snow-white curtains and soft-green drapes, tied with white bows.

The apartment was small but equipped with all the essentials, and felt warm. It became an empire of beauty for my friends and acquaintances who often came over for a relaxed chat, some food, drinks, and music. In addition to a decent size room that I divided in two with a wardrobe and bookshelves to create casual and working areas, there was a cozy alcove for the bed, a kitchenette, and a bathroom with a proper bathtub.

I loved that place from the day I came to an open house visit and found the landlord talking to prospective tenants. He asked lots of questions. I said I was a musician and had a piano, but would be careful regarding the times of day when I played, so as not to disturb anybody. He wanted to make sure I had sufficient means to pay the rent.

"Of course, I have a job," I said, proudly.

And he rented it to me!

That was my third living place in the big city. After the initial minuscule basement room, I moved into a bigger one but got an even worse landlady.

The most glorious day was when I left that pigsty where the nasty old hag tortured me every single day with her petty thefts, by locking the washroom and doing all kinds of disgusting mischiefs only she was capable of.

The hag had a son, a fat drunkard who she raised by herself, spoiled, and eventually came to hate. He drank and yelled at her all the time. She haunted – like a witch ghost – the numerous rooms she rented, inhaling our smells; scents of students she stole everything she could from.

I walked out of that hell of a house.

My mom sighed a sigh of relief when she saw me living in an apartment, instead of in a tiny room in the basement with pigeonhole windows. Her face was telling me she was more relaxed and eager to help with organizing and interior decoration. Yes, it was a garage; which could be easily transformed into an upscale restaurant serving delicious food to all of my friends, or into a concert hall when I entertained by giving piano recitals, or into a romantic séparé, lit by candles, made for love.

There were few tenants in the building: a family on the top floor and an elderly gentleman in the apartment above mine. When the landlord gave me the keys, he warned me:

"That one above is grumpy. If he doesn't like you or if you play late at night, or have noisy company, he immediately dials my phone number and complains."

"Please be assured there won't be a single phone call." I said.

There were neither calls nor complaints in the full four years I spent in that lovely garage; the most beautiful living space on earth. Days unrolled pleasantly and peacefully, without drama.

Mom would come every three months and plant flowers in my window boxes, paint the bathroom, or sew the curtains. With each visit, in addition to mouthwatering dishes she made, she would also fix this and that, always leaving her artistic trail behind her.

Winter came, spreading the big whiteness in front of my windows. I have always loved winter. The north-wind blowing into my face on an early morning at the bus stop never bothered me, nor did the snowflakes densely settling on my eyelashes late, very late at night, on my way back home from lectures and private students.

Spring pushed the winter out with blossoming tree branches on Ada Ciganlija Island on the river Sava which I saw from the bus on my way to the university. Days started getting longer, as well as my practicing the piano, for the piano exams were coming closer. The other ones had to wait for a place to sit down on the bus to be studied.

All in all, in spite of all the duties and responsibilities I had to fulfill, there was always time for coffee with Nora, pizza and beer with Mira, and wonderful moments with my dear friends Lela and Marko.

Every now and then, I would go for a walk on the wide streets of the capital, enjoying the smell of asphalt and the noise of cars and passers-by. I have always been a big city kid.

Some people were born to love meadows, woods, grass, and endless spaces of nature. I love high-rise buildings, stores, cafés, trams, and buses.

From the very start of it, the summer was hot and humidity infused. The clouds, round and white, with heavy rain pouring over my city every afternoon. While playing the piano, I would often gaze up to the street that was above me, because of the steep concrete path, looking at torrents of dirty water flowing into a narrow grid just below my windows and the entrance door. As if I had sensed what was going to happen, I made a mental note to check the drainage hole and make sure it was clear, in case of a big thunderstorm, but I would soon forget about it; carried away by my music.

I was going back home one evening, after a busy day. The thunderstorm had apparently been raging over Belgrade but I couldn't see it coming from the south side, from the village school I worked in. Stepping out of the bus, I realized that nothing looked right; trees were bent, flowers pulled out of their roots, streets turned into canals. The sky, the color of lead, released and emptied out, gazed hollowly at the devastation.

I was approaching the apartment in the garage with fast steps and growing apprehension in my heart.

Then I saw it.

Water invaded my apartment. The drainage hole in front of my door was too small or clogged, and all that heavy rain rushed into my living space. Gruesome, almost half a meter high water, black and muddled, gaped at me.

My heart sank. In my mind's eye, I could see the landlord evicting me for not keeping the apartment in good condition. I could see myself leaving this place I loved so much.

Tears were rolling down my cheeks.

Somebody knocked on the door. In that moment, I thought I would die. The landlord, I thought.

No, it was naughty Sale with his mother, a woman who brought her restless little boy to piano lessons that he hated, only because she loved to be in my company. My friends said she was in love with me, but I paid no attention to that.

As if nothing had happened, she stepped into the water, walked in, sat on the bed, and lit a cigarette.

"So is there going to be a class?"

I looked at her speechless.

"No, unfortunately not, since I have to get rid of this water."

"But why, I don't mind it," she was persistent.

"Believe me, I do. The piano is halfway under the water and can be badly damaged."

Disappointed, she put out the cigarette and walked out. Her son was very happy to skip a piano lesson.

They left.

I called Nora.

The rest of my friends were unavailable at the moment.

Nora came.

Nora took a bucket and started to throw the water away.

I was so scared of the landlord hearing about the incident that I didn't want any of the neighbors to know about the flooding in my apartment.

I pretended I was washing the carpet.

While Nora was emptying bucketfuls of water into the toilet and the bathtub, I took the big soaked and muddy carpet outside and spread it out on the concrete, on the steep slope in front of the entrance. It was already dark, so nobody could see how wet and dirty it really was.

I scrubbed it and cleaned it with detergents, then went back to the apartment. Nora was picking up the last drops of water with cloths and sponges. I got an idea.

"Nora, I'll turn the heating on to the highest, so the heat will dry out the damp from the corners and surfaces."

She thought that was smart.

I opened the windows a bit, just enough to let the air flow, but pulled on the curtains so that nothing could be seen inside and went to sleep at Nora's place that night.

After two days of heating to the maximum, everything was back in place: dry and clean. Even the carpet looked almost like new, having been freshly washed.

Only my brain was in panic. What if it happened again?

I asked the drainage specialists to check that hole and tell me if it was alright and they said it was.

I was still scared.

For luck, I bought a little bird and called it Olja. She was a cute, tiny finch with a red beak and a shrilly voice, waking me up with her chirping every morning at sunrise. I would put a cover of black fabric over her cage at night, so she couldn't realize when it was dawn. That way, I could sleep a little bit longer.

Olja had been living at my place for about a month when Nora and I decided to spend a day in Pula, on the Adriatic Coast, just to walk in the Arena dating back from the Roman times, have lunch at the square facing the house where James Joyce used to live at one point, sip a drink by the seashore, and return to Belgrade on an evening flight.

The day was filled with loveliness and joy, our stories, walks in the Old Town, brilliant under the sun of that gorgeous summer day.

Going back to my apartment with my mind still in Pula, I opened the door and immediately went towards the cage to see how my sweet Olja was doing. To my dismay, the cage was wide-open and the feathers were scattered all over the floor.

I started crying and then froze with horror.

What if it was a rat or a wild cat, what if it was still in here? I started making noise and hitting the furniture, but nothing moved. The windows had been open all day, a cat must have heard my Olja's song, walked in, overturned the cage from the piano, and attacked.

Nora came as soon as I called her.

She was sorry for Olja.

That evening, water invaded my apartment again, but not as much as the first time, which meant that the drainage had been fixed, but it had apparently rained too heavily for the small hole to absorb all that amount of water.

I was now getting seriously worried about tomorrow and the day after tomorrow. If it went on like that, I would have to get rid of water every day, dry and clean ad infinitum.

It couldn't go on like that!

As it happened, my cousin Neško, an engineer, was doing the last three months of his military service in Belgrade at the time and often dropped by for a good talk, music, and some dinner. He came the day after the flooding, smiley, like always. I told him about my problem, listing all the details. We went outside. He thoroughly checked the whole hydraulic system, the pipes that took the water away, and the hole into which it went, digging his hands into the fittings, valves, and tubes, and observing the functioning of the whole thing. Then he pronounced the diagnosis:

"See, the opening is too small for the sudden influx of water that a rainfall brings. It can't hold it, so that's why it overflows."

It didn't help my increasing headache. At that very moment, a rainstorm was about to hit Belgrade.

"Hey, don't be so scared," Neško said. "You're white as a sheet."

I didn't look at myself in the mirror, but I guessed I looked like a ghost. Fear overtook me. I had already gone through two floodings, I didn't want to experience the third one now!

The downpour was spilling its wrath over the beautiful part of Belgrade in which I lived. Fat raindrops became fast speed showers. The rain was turning into the gray curtain of my despair. The drainage hole was overflowing. Flooding threatened, second by second.

"How about closing tight the entrance door?" Neško suggested.

"The water will get in from underneath, the door can't close hermetically. That's how it got in both times." I was desperate.

We closed the door. Water was gushing from the hole, making its way towards the apartment and to us.

"Give me some cloths, towels, socks, whatever!" Neško shouted.

He was trying to fill up all the empty spaces between the door, windows, and the floor.

When the rain subsided, we made a plan of action. We cemented those few centimeters underneath the door, so that water couldn't enter any more.

I slept easier that night.

And the next.

And all the following nights in that apartment.

I made a promise to myself, in the course of those events, that one day, when I had enough money to afford better living conditions, who knows where, I would live on high floors of high-rise buildings.

The touch of destiny, which is sometimes truly in sync with our wishes, granted it to me. My next apartments were on the twelfth, then sixteenth, twenty-second and currently on the twenty-seventh floor; from where I am writing this.

Still, my childhood fear of thunderstorms mingled with those floodings.

And many years later, living far away from that garage, whenever thunder roars and lightning splits the sky in two and torrential rains start pouring, I catch myself thinking: "Is the garage alright? Is it flooded?"

Nora's Impressions

"Nora, come quickly, something terrible happened!" Nikola's alarmed voice doesn't elaborate, and I sprint into the night to catch the first available cab.

As I enter his apartment, I find myself almost knee deep in water. A really bad case of flooding has happened here, caused by thunderstorms and heavy rain. The whole place has been turned into a watery muddy mess!

Nikola's valuables having been safely stored along unaffected surfaces, forming a kind of Noah's Ark, we proceed with emptying the apartment of the water, bucket by bucket, sponge by sponge. A major cleaning of the place happens in the process, unplanned, and even the carpet is properly washed, so everything's fine!

The biggest job, however, is saving his most precious possessions, his gramophone records, that is. There are tons of them and they are soaked through. We pack them into a cab which takes all of us to my place, release them from their sleeves, and spread them all over my apartment to dry.

Honestly, it's been real hard work, but thoroughly cleansing. The place has been in dire need of a major exfoliation for quite some time, so it's done. Like, you remove the dead cells from your skin so that the new ones can grow. You get rid of the stuff you don't need any more to make place for the fresh energy to circulate. Cleaning your living space equals to cleaning yourself, like inside out; muscle work included. You want to make it welcoming to yourself and to your friends, right! It's like breathing: you exhale to push out the stale air, so you can fully inhale to fill your body with life force.

An image is coming to me now. I know about Nikola's fear of thunderstorms, originating from his childhood and still present. Not going into psychoanalysis or maybe past lives' underlying causes, I'm seeing this picture clearly in my mind's eye. It takes place at the same time but at different places.

We are both just little kids, not knowing about each other's existence. He is hiding under the table and running with his mom to the neighbor's house. My mom is shutting all the windows and doors in our house, rushing me inside. I'm running outside, to the terrace and the garden, enjoying the spectacle of sound and light in the sky, indulging in the wind and the rain, happily performing, barefoot, some Aboriginal or African dances.

Just goes to show how different yet how compatible we all are, like a Yin and Yang kind of thing. Isn't that amazing?

University vs. School, Teacher vs. Professor

As much as I loved my studies, colleagues, and lectures, I also enjoyed the opportunity to work and earn money necessary for living, books, and rent. As it had often been happening in my life, until the present day, I was in between the two fires. Both of them were glowing with beautiful flames.

This is something that will follow me throughout my life, till my last breath, this needs to be spread out into various doings and different places simultaneously, without any time left for myself, to simply sit down and rest, let alone take a nap in the afternoon. That's been my 'curse' or my 'companion' all along. I have always been torn apart all over the place, but always able to manage everything.

In those days, I used to wake up at the crack of dawn in order to arrive, two buses and two and a half hours later, to the school on the hill outside of the city. Then, after the classes, by some other buses, I journeyed to the university, to attend the afternoon lectures. After or in-between of which I would give some private lessons. Attendance to some of the lectures wasn't mandatory, so I studied those subjects on the buses, if I was lucky enough to find a place to sit down and open a book.

My university professors often reproached me for not coming to their classes regularly or for being late. One of them, a glorious queen, breathed down my neck more often than the others. In her thick accent, she would 'attack' me in front of all the students.

"Sir, just where have you been? You know that we start at 3 p.m. sharp!"

She knew she was intimidating me, that it was not very professional on her part, but she enjoyed it.

"I know, madam. I was at work."

"Oh, sir, then you don't need the university diploma, you are already earning a lot of money. You don't need the Faculty of Music." she used to say.

Says who? I thought. You are rolling in money, my dear, you don't give a damn for me or anyone of us!

I believe that deep down, she was a good person, but I didn't feel her goodness at the time. It certainly didn't manifest during the rehearsals of Mozart's Requiem for a major concert performance. It happened that just then I was overloaded with work at the school and couldn't come to every single rehearsal. I knew that her wrath would spill over me at the last one, when she was making sure we were all perfectly impeccably ready to perform, but I was well prepared. I knew the baritone and tenor melody lines by heart, I didn't even need to look at the score. The professor was checking us out in quartets, each one of us singing one of the four voices.

It was an early Friday morning. I was in the first quartet.

Requiem aeternam
Dona eis Domine...

Everything went flawlessly. The professor was playing the orchestra part on the piano while we sang. Requiem is a complex music genre and it took us about forty minutes to finish it. She made some comments on the other student's singing but was generally satisfied and let them go. I was ordered to stay.

Dies irae
Dies illa
Solvet saetium, in favila...

Then, she called three more students and it started all over again. Then three more. Around two o'clock in the afternoon, when I thought I would pass out for I hadn't eaten anything nor had a sip of water since eight in the morning, it was my closest colleague Veronica's turn to sing. After having done her part masterfully, she turned to the professor:

"Madam, don't you think you have gone a bit too far with Nikola? He has sung at least six times both the baritone and the tenor, what more do you want?" She was angry.

The professor spread her lips into a tight smile.

"Next group," she said.

Confutatis maledictis
Flammis acrimus addictis...

So, I sang the whole score all over again.

"Thank you, sir. You have passed," the professor finally said.

"Thank you, Professor," I replied.

Veronica was waiting for me outside, visibly shaken up.

"Here, I've bought some puff pastry, you've got to eat something," she said, sympathetically.

I ate, rather swallowed, the warm pastry melting in my mouth.

"What a cow!" Veronica said.

"She's made me pay for those days when I missed the rehearsals. That was her point."

"I know, but that's not fair."

"Life's not fair, Veronica."

She sighed.

We walked to the bus stop. The 37 bus took us to my apartment where we continued preparing for the upcoming exams, slowly, over coffee.

That night, Mozart's Requiem was echoing in my mind.

Et lux perpetua
Luceat eis
Cum santis tuis
In aeternum
Quia pius est.

Other professors were more understanding, for I was very attentive when I managed to come to their classes, always had ready answers and passed all the tests, practicums and written ones, successfully.

Sometimes, a professor or an assistant was cross with me, or maybe simply ill-disposed that day, and would lecture me on how it was too bad I couldn't always attend the classes or was late for them, so how would I learn this or that. I would have liked to tell them to mind their own business, for I was determined to learn everything and pass all the exams anyway, but I chose the line of least resistance, the one of silence and a bowed head.

Ms. Professor Jagoda (her name means 'strawberry' in Serbian; lots of Serbian female names are derived from those of fruits or flowers, like Raspberry, Quince, Marigold or Tulip) seemed to have just stepped out of the dance podium after a crazy Charleston night in the 1920s, in terms of her current attire and make up. She taught English and was one of those sweet little ladies who could sometimes sting you sneakily.

Veronica and I were sitting next to each other, just the two of us in front of the heavily powdered professor, answering her innumerable questions. The English she was teaching us had no purpose or function in normal life. She would spend ten minutes explaining how to hold your hand when being introduced to someone belonging to a high class society and how to breathe between words in a specific, 'English' way. Veronica and I were sure nobody in the UK could understand a single word of hers.

It bugged her that I was a good student, and a bit unusual for her taste. I liked to talk to her in her own voice and with her identical accent. I'm a musician after all.

The conversation would go on like this:

"Nikola, (sigh, eyes directed upwards, the index finger up) why are you late this evening?" (Very long eeevening.)

Turning her gaze towards me she would pause and make a no-no sign.

"Professor, (sigh, eyes directed upwards, the index finger up) I am late because there were no buses for quite a long time." (Very long, looong.)

Turning my gaze towards her I would pause and imitate her no-no.

That was our established dialogue.

Professor Strawberry was ancient but sort of cute, with all the makeup she was wearing. She was especially fond of the blush. Two big red spots were splashed on her cheeks, unevenly. We found out she lived with her two sisters and several cats.

Exhausted after two hours spent with her, Veronica and I would go for some beer to a bar at the Yugoslav Drama Theater next door, guessing what Strawberry's apartment looked like.

"There are lots of paintings," Veronica said.

"Yes, and they're all landscapes," I added.

"Porcelain figurines all over the place."

"Also, tons of small varnished boxes, full of valuable trinkets."

"Her tables are overflowing with doilies."

"And her armchairs protected by slip covers, to last for the next four hundred years."

"Her curtains must be thick and heavy, so the reality never enters."

"The windows are always closed."

"Men?"

"Fashion style?"

We laughed at the recurring topic every Monday.

At the school on the hill outside of the city, I was the youngest of teachers, conscientious and dedicated to my work. I liked all the children and the colleagues, and my days there unrolled pleasantly.

Nora was getting increasingly sad. Nora liked neither teaching nor the children.

Her deep dark eyes would look for consolation in mine after each class, in the teachers' room. She was on the edge of desperation, disgusted by the school, the kids, the colleagues, and most of all by the bus ride. She was thrown into that whirlwind by her father's decision.

Nora was getting unhappier day by day.

I tried to help her, but apparently in an inappropriate way. I didn't know then that Nora couldn't be tied to a work place, or to any place for that matter. I gave her advice regarding children from the pedagogical point of view, which was useless to her, because Nora didn't want to know about any of that.

Nora's Impressions

"It's a shame you have to work, it's too soon for you, you're so young and pretty," Iva says as I leave her bohemian apartment after a consultation on the planets transiting my sun sign this week. "You should be enjoying life more!"

I contemplate on that on the way to my modeling sessions with a wonderful old painter.

Just how on earth did the job happen?

While settling into the pose in the artist's studio, I slowly rewind the movie in my mind's eye.

It's spinning, it's sprinting up!

The employment office calls at my parents' house, I am to present myself at a certain school, right away. My father bursts into my place. I'm dragged to the bus stop. Pushed into a voyage to the unknown. Rushed into the classroom by the principal. No interview, no orientation training. Grab the register book and go! The bell rings. The class is about to start. Standing in front of thirty kids. Clueless as to what I'm supposed to do.

Just why the hell do I accept to be treated like a sacrificial lamb?

Why don't I say: "No! No way you're making me do this! I am the one who decides!"

No comment. I am shocked at my docility.

Men, stupid fucking men! The majority of the ones I got the misfortune to deal with, at any rate, including a succession of abusive ex-boyfriends, and pardon my French. I hate to hate, but honest to God, those manipulating idiots deserve all the wrath of a woman outraged!

Wake up, Nora, once and for all! Never ever again a pompous macho is going to dictate your life! You are the stronger one, spit on their slimy faces, scratch them with your sharp nails till they bleed, kick them in their filthy balls, c'mon, you are a fighter, so fight!

So now I have a job I haven't even applied for and maybe I should simply stay in it for the time being, since it came unasked for, like a touch of destiny and all that.

OK, everybody, myself included, can see I'm a lousy teacher. I can't get the children disciplined and don't interact with colleagues. My stomach turns upside down at the smells of the bus and of the school.

Well, for one thing, I definitely don't want to lose Nikola (he's not macho, so he's OK).

Also, there's that kid with bushy eyebrows growing at awkward angles over his sparkling green eyes, has articulation problems, and absorbs every word I say. I put my hands on his throat and chest and his on mine and work on making his speech clear. Eventually he starts picking up English pronunciation and is able to make simple conversations, to the disbelief of his class mates.

You are my sunshine,
My only sunshine.
You make me happy
When skies are gray...

That's the kids singing at choir rehearsals in the basement, which is actually the school kitchen and cafeteria but doubles as a music hall most days after the classes. With Nikola as a conductor, kids sing all kinds of songs: Yugoslav folk, archaic Serbian (enchanting lyrics, invigorating rhythms), lovely Polish and international and not so lovely revolutionary socialist (that's a must, but Nikola picks some palatable ones).

My mornings start pleasantly enough in the school's womb (the basement that is) that gives birth to gossips, multiplying like rabbits. I sip my coffee, smoke, look at, and listen to Nikola. I am deaf to all the chit-chat and tongue washing around. Gossiping has always been the least comprehensible of all human leisure activities to me. Like:

Why don't you just mind your own business?

Why do you have to stick your nose into what's none of your concern whatsoever?

Worst of all, why are you dying to spread your 'freshly acquired piece of information' about other people to every single soul in your surroundings, changing the original story along the way?

What good does it do to you to know what your next door neighbor is cooking for dinner?

Is guessing that her husband is having a love affair going to enrich your life?

Whenever one of the colleagues brings up a family, health, political or any other issue, Dara the cook's signature comment is:

"Shhh... it can only get worse."

Right, everything can theoretically always get worse, but reversely, also get better. There's absolutely no reason to be contented with an unfavorable situation! How about things looking up?

Normally I simply observe other teachers attacking the freshly baked pastries and pies produced in the subterranean kitchen, but make an exception one day. Happens that I have one hour window between the classes and that I'm hungry, so I take a cheese bun and eat it while leafing through a fashion magazine. Somehow it gets unnoticed, otherwise it would have been spectacular news in the whole village area, above and beyond, talked over for days on end.

The basement also provides the stage for a very important annual event: School Day, which is a socialist invention to honor the name a particular school bears, usually one of a national hero from World War II, but in reality it's just an excuse for opportunist shoulder tapping and gargantuan eating.

Luckily, the school in the village is named after Vuk Karadžić, 19th century linguist and creator of the reformed Serbian Cyrillic alphabet (the guy travels the world, hopping on one leg, settles down in Vienna, Austria, is a close friend of Goethe, a famous German poet, collects tons of old Serbian folk poems for Goethe to translate and puts some order in how Serbs should talk and write). So the mandatory repertoire of the revolution-inspired poems and songs is allowed to be diluted by literature.

A multitude of guests from other schools and political dignitaries invited for the occasion yawn through the children's performance (the poor little devils have worked so hard in anticipation of the Big Day), eagerly awaiting the 'real' thing. That being tables sagging under huge quantities of food, with Dara's intestine pie featuring the favorite and devoured plate after plate.

After a year and a half of basically fooling around playing a teacher, I finally say farewell to the village in the mountains, for I have got a new job. Actually the same one, also in an elementary school, just that it's in the city, and I found it myself!

Zora

On my professional music field, the most inspiring, imposing, and influential person was Professor Zora.

I took a liking to her at my entry exam to the university. I didn't know anybody there, just wished to God to give me a chance and a bit of luck. There were over four hundred of us, out of which only thirty-four would be accepted. There was no option for me not to be accepted. I had excellent grades in the High School of Music and anyway, I had already decided never to go back to that town in the South, even if I had to clean the streets of Belgrade.

Exams were getting more difficult as they progressed, stress and nervousness intensified. Lots of sweaty fingers slipped on the wrong piano keys. My Beethoven hovered above the hall and my Chopin's waltz echoed in the professors' gray heads nodding appreciation.

Then I met Professor Zora for the first time.

The room was packed, we were all ready with sheets of music paper to write down a melody she was going to present us with. Our oral exam depended on that. If you fail the written test, there's no oral for you.

The door opened and a middle-aged woman with ruffly ginger hair, cigarette in one hand and a cup of yogurt in another, walked in and started singing:

> *Ah, my daughter dear, why is your bodice undone?*
> *He who put a smear, let be seen by everyone...*

She kept singing the ancient folk song, stopped only to take a sip of yogurt and a drag of the cigarette, walked slowly along the rows of students. When she sat down at the cathedral, some ignorants started applauding. She looked at us with an icy glaze in her honey-colored eyes and said:

"Give in your papers, this was a test."

Shell-shocked prospective students cried out in despair because they thought the professor was just making a performance and that her singing had nothing to do with the exam.

A Higher Power helped me by having granted me good music memory, so I wrote down everything, even the moments when she took drags of her cigarette which I marked as 'breathing pauses'.

I passed the most difficult of exams.

She came to me and asked which town and music school I came from.

I answered.

She wasn't happy with the answer.

"Hmm, lots of morons come from that school," she said.

It was love at first sight.

And then came the D-Day.

The results.

I didn't sleep the night before, but deep in my heart, I knew everything would be fine since all the exams went flawlessly.

I was sure of that.

I am very self-critical, so I was sure.

Destiny, however, wanted to put me on trial. My name was nowhere to be found on the acceptance list. My sorrow was endless. So was my despair.

Mom was by my side, heartbroken, trying to comfort me.

"But I know I did all the exams perfectly, I passed them all!"

"I believe you," she resolutely started going upstairs.

"Where are you going, Mom?"

"To the administration office to ask them where the error occurred."

Mom and I climbed the stairs together. We entered a smoky office. The woman behind the desk was nice and said that of course, we were allowed to see the result papers. She looked genuinely sorry for me and for Mom. She opened one, then another, then the third drawer of the filing cabinet. Confusion was written all over her face.

At that moment, Professor Zora walked in and having recognized me exclaimed:

"Hey, you, Southern guy, I can't wait to have you in my class, you did the exam brilliantly!" She was all in smiles.

"Professor, it looks like I didn't get accepted, since I'm not on the list."

She introduced herself to my mom and marched across the room to the secretary.

"Do you have the files?" she demanded.

"I have them all except one."

"How come?"

"I don't know, it got lost."

"Leave the office," said the professor to my mom and me.

We left.

About ten minutes later, she came out waving with some papers in her hand.

"We found your 'lost' documents. With such points, you are not just accepted, you are one of the top three!"

I cried of happiness.

The doors of the big city weren't closed to me after all!

My professor Zora took the side of truth and justice.

Many years later, our paths parted, but my respect and love for her remained unwavering.

She is somewhere in the sky with Angels now and still in my thoughts.

Is It a Pie or Is It Not a Pie?

Since there wasn't a local bakery where students of the school on the hill could buy some fresh pastry or a sandwich for breakfast or lunch, the school provided snack services with two cooks, Rosa and Dara in charge.

While rolling the dough, making fillings and baking, they argued. Not loudly, just in whispering and inquisitive tones. Their arguments regularly revolved around the accuracies of a specific gossip and its source.

Rosa lived at the far end of the village and Dara in the valley. They would bring lots of stories to be discussed, compared and cross referenced the first thing in the morning, and elaborated throughout the day.

What intrigued them most were us commuters, because they knew next to nothing about us. We were like nomads, came to teach the classes and then disappeared, carried by the bus to the city. They were eager to reveal our weaknesses and secrets. The only time they could squeeze them out of us was in the mornings, when we sleepily arrived at the school at 7:10 a.m. Thirty-five minutes before the first class were just enough for the two of them to systematically sieve through each one of us, asking innumerable questions.

They were fuming about Nora, because other than "Can I get a coffee?" Nora didn't make them worthy of any other utterance of hers. Even though she would sit with us in the basement, instead of chatting Nora would read her book without paying any attention to human words, comments or Dara's and Rosa's remarks.

By a cunning women's sense, they intuited that Nora I were getting close and that became their new food for the soul, like a love story in the making.

Needless to say that within ten minutes, the whole village, including all the children, teachers, tellers in the bank and the post office, cashiers at the variety store and bus drivers knew that Nora and I were dating. Some of them 'knew' more, some less, and the news ranged from casual friendship to imminent marriage.

"Teacher, what do you think about the new English teacher?" That was the first question I was asked in each and every class those days.

"Teacher, do you like that teacher with long black hair?" The children pushed.

Nora took no notice of any of that, faithful to her principles:

- Don't talk.
- Don't have eye contact.
- Don't give out any sign of life.

On the other hand, when we were alone, Nora had a very interesting personality that shined only then and vanished in the school. She hated that school and all the people in it (myself excluded).

The snack menu wasn't the most eclectic in the world, but it wasn't bad either. The children and the teachers had options to eat:

- Bread with pâté spread
- Bread with Nutella
- Pastry with jam
- Pastry with cheese
- Meat pie

Meat pie was my favorite. It smelled so nice and warm, especially in the winter, when we commuters, with frozen hands and ears, walked into the basement. It was the perfect accompaniment to the first morning coffee. The most delicious pie I had ever tasted! Dara and Rosa would bring an extra plate of it to the teachers' room for me, during the recesses.

"Only for you, our boy. You love our pie," they used to say.

And I indulged in it during the three years that I worked in that school.

The turnover of colleagues was frequent. Everybody's dream was to teach in the city rather than stay in a village school, so everybody was looking for a better position.

Mira most of all. She was trying to find connections, small or big, asking and running around, in order to get a job closer to the city, so she could spend more time with her two little daughters who were growing up nicely, protected by her love and my frequent visits and phone calls. Ever since those first days after her husband left her, I felt a part of that family and that was like a responsibility I couldn't and didn't want to relinquish.

My students loved choir. Every day after the classes, about twenty of them stayed and sang. We were preparing programs for various public performances, social happenings in the village, and for all the holidays.

At the time we were getting ready to welcome The Relay of Youth in honor of President Tito's birthday in 1986, six years after his death. For the first time in local history, it was to run through the very center of the village. The Relay of Youth was an annual event, with young people running from the North West and the South East of Yugoslavia, carrying an Olympics like torch just without flame, to present to the president on May 25 at the biggest foot-ball stadium in Belgrade, after a spectacular gymnastic parade of thousands of soldiers and children.

That May, tons of exams, the Relay, and an intense sexual affair fell like a hammer on my head.

It was a Sunday and we had to be at the school at 8 a.m. sharp. The only thing I remembered was the phone ringing and Nora's voice:

"Don't tell me you're still sleeping."

"Aaah, what's the time?"

"After eight."

I got out of bed as if scalded. The mirror on my dressing table reflected the night's intoxication with vodka, white wine, kissing, and sex.

"Right, I'm coming, I'll take a cab," I said. "Please tell the children to wait for me in front of the school, just make sure they're properly dressed."

"I will," Nora said.

With a trembling hand, I called a cab. It cost me an arm and a leg, but I could have lost my job if I hadn't shown up that morning for 'the historic event'.

Everything was going smoothly. Everything except the Relay.

It was late.

A lot.

All of us were waiting on the little square, my choir, teachers, village dignitaries, the president of the village, his secretary, politicians invited for the occasion, the school principal, and GMs of local factories, and retail stores. Most of them looked like stuffed turkeys squished into suit jackets.

The principal came to me and said in panic:

"Come on, play, sing something to cheer up people!"

I turned to my children and they started singing with all their hearts, their voices echoing on the hills and in the valleys of the village.

At one point, the principal gave me a serious look and proclaimed:

"The Relay is coming!"

So the highlight of the day finally arrived. I was already exhausted. The midday sun that had been scorching me for hours, fermented all the residue of the previous night's alcohol in my brain. I was about to faint. People started applauding, entranced by the passage of the Relay. At that moment, I turned to the children and started conducting.

The song was running faster and easier than ever. Everybody's gaze was fixed on the Relay, except Nora's. She was looking at the choir and me with a curious expression.

The Relay passed by.

People were leaving slowly. The commuting teachers waited for the bus back to Belgrade.

Nora came to me. She laughed. She was so beautiful when she laughed.

"Are you aware of what you've done?" she asked me with a glint in her eyes.

"What do you mean?" I was puzzled.

"Hey, man, you're lucky nobody paid any attention to your song. I could have died of laughter, just that I bit my lips and kept silent."

"Why?"

She looked at me simply not believing I was so confused or tired that I didn't realize what had happened.

"OK, when the relay came and all the brown noses gathered around it, you gave the signal to the kids to sing:

Bumblebees got together
And attacked the bees.
All the honey you're making
We should lick at ease!"

Oh. I got the association, lazy bumblebees and lazy fat politicians.

Oh, it was good I barely listened to what the children were singing.

Nora laughed all the way to the city.

"Ha, ha, bumblebees got together to wait for the Relay!"

I was carried away by some unexplainable forces of hangover or whatever that morning. How it came that out of all the songs I chose that one, I didn't know.

Nora was the first one to leave. She found a school in the city. Nobody cried when she left, for she wasn't really friendly to anybody, except to me.

Nora lived close to the commuter bus terminal and I would often drop by after work for a coffee and heart to heart talk with her.

Our friendship was growing and developing.

On the political scene of the then Yugoslavia, not much was happening. Although dead, Tito was still present as a framed picture on the walls in factories, offices, classrooms, and teachers' rooms.

Socialism endured with all its weak and strong points.

The most common way of shopping for big things, like: furniture, electronics or piles of books, was paying by installments, which I used abundantly. I bought a freezer for my mom and lots of good books for both mom and me. It was easy to pay with post-dated checks and the interest fee was ridiculous.

And then I, too, got a job in Belgrade.

Mira stayed in the village school for a few more months without me, the last one to leave.

It was so hard to say goodbye to that school. It hurt a lot to walk out of the teachers' room that had become my second home.

Still, I knew, just like all my colleagues did, that the new opportunity was much better for me. Also, the time spent on the buses would be reduced, so I could focus more on my studies.

On my last day there, Rosa and Dara, both red-eyed, came to the teachers' room carrying a big plate of freshly baked meat pie.

"We made it especially for you," Rosa said.

"We know how much you enjoy our intestine pie," Dara added. "Just be careful, it's piping hot."

Intestine pie? That's what it was? My favorite pie, all those years, wasn't made of meat and spices as I thought, but of pig's intestines?

To reassure my scared thoughts, I asked quietly:

"You mean, this isn't minced meat?" I looked at them pleadingly. Don't ruin my dreams, I prayed. Please don't make me feel disgusted at all those times I devoured this delicious pie!

"It is minced meat, love. It's minced intestines."

Oh. I didn't want to hear that.

If they hadn't said it, I wouldn't have known.

Oh, ignorance, blissful ignorance!

Images of children's and my colleagues' faces, random situations, everything flickered before my eyes as I slowly walked out of the school and down the hill. I cried on the bus all the way to Belgrade. Luckily it was half empty, smoothly navigating the curves of Avala Mountain, taking me to the city where a new school would open new horizons for me.

It was so hard to leave that village.

It had become a part of me.

Act III
Transformations

- **Socialism at Its Best**
- **Nora's Impressions**
- **The Times of Ante Marković**
- **Nora's Impressions**
- **The Best 37 Bus**
- **Cinderella**
- **Nora's Impressions**
- **You Will Marry Well**
- **Nora's Impressions**

Socialism at Its Best

It is hard to write about something that does not exist anymore. Instead of one country, there are six now, the seventh one in the making. Without going into political debates as to who and what caused the fall of Yugoslavia, it was definitely a difficult, troublesome, and painstaking process in which everybody paid dearly. Some lost life, some all of their possessions, and some were left with a deep wound in the heart.

The Yugoslav myth lasted for a long time, from the end of World War Two till the late 1980s.

I am a child of Yugoslavia, like many others I know, but not all of them. Nora, for example, has always known that Serbia also used to be a great country in the course of history. She learnt a lot about it from her grandfather.

My generation and I were totally blinded by the imposing image and words of Tito. The past simply didn't exist for us. We were growing up and living under Tito's wing, under his power and authority. In his era, there were free apartments for everyone, supermarkets, and department stores full of various goods. We could afford winter and summer vacations. Life was really marvelous. As a young pioneer, I was happy to live in such a beautiful country that was stronger and better than all the other countries in the world, as they taught us at school. Yugoslavia rated well above the communist countries governed by dictatorial regimes, where everybody had just a little bit of something, but not freedom. We were also told that our country was better than the capitalist ones, because in those they could do whatever they wanted to you. Only money was important, not a human being.

That's why socialism was, according to its advocates, the best of all systems, for it gave everybody personal liberty and rights, while keeping people in a happy unity.

As one of the political writers put it:

"Socialism is a system in which it is unthinkable that some people sleep under bridges in cardboard boxes, while others live in palaces on picturesque hills. When we say 'apartment', we refer to state apartments that are being built from solidarity funds (a propos, solidarity should be one of the most precious values in socialism), since everybody has a right to a roof over their head."

His next explanation was just the way I felt it:

"Socialism is a society in which health is not the privilege of the rich and sickness punishment for the poor, but a society where the health system is public and accessible to everyone. Socialism is a system in which people don't go to their graves after their working age, but to a well-deserved retirement that entitles them to a dignified life. Socialism is not a system in which the so-called extended living age is an excuse for prolonging the age limit for retirement, but a society in which the demographic explosion in the last half of the century has affected the decrease of that age limit, thus vacating the job positions for younger generations.

This is socialism in a nutshell. Socialism is a system in which one lives from one's work and not from rent; society in which one's work is the only source of well-being, not stock exchange speculations or lotto games."

After Tito's death, everything somehow went downhill. Problems we had never had before started to show up, shortages of all kinds, increased prices, and fights among politicians.

The harmony that had existed and reigned for such a long time was being broken by atonal sounds of a nation falling apart.

In my mind, the flames of Yugoslavia were still burning bright. In my heart, there were still thousands of revolutionary songs I had sung and later conducted and performed with my choirs.

Revolutionary songs are, according to me, an incredible marketing tool. Too bad I wasn't born some twenty years earlier, or I could have been the composer of them. I'm sure I would have been the best! Ever since my earliest childhood, those songs had an intense emotional impact on me and would always strike my patriotic cord.

When I became an active choir singer, and sang them almost every day in various circumstances and political settings, sometimes mocking the lyrics, I realized that lots of them were written in a simple harmonic cliché, not as deep as I had thought.

Still, I loved them.

On a bus or a tram, I would occasionally hear a voice saying something against Tito and his and my Yugoslavia, at first quietly, then some other voices would rise up.

It was all so totally strange to me. My comprehension of Yugoslavia was innocent, clean, transparent, and virginal. My Yugoslavia was a wonderful fraternal unity of Slovenians, Croats, Bosnians, Macedonians, Serbs and Montenegrins (in the six republics); and of Hungarians, Romanians, Slovaks, Albanians and Turks in Vojvodina and Kosovo (the two autonomous provinces). Those were enchanting treasuries for me, eight treasure boxes filled with such a variety of songs, different in melodies, languages, and dialects. Each nation and nationality had their own traditional music that the other ones enjoyed listening to because it so differed from theirs, on the rhythmic, harmonic and melodic planes.

It had always been so pleasurable for me and my students to travel through Yugoslavia, by playing and singing songs from all parts of it!

My Yugoslavia was an ideal country of working people, honest, good, and patriotic.

It took me more than twenty years to realize my delusion and the total ideological darkness I had lived in. Even in the times when Yugoslavia was at its peak, there were apparently some people in each republic who dreamed of its fall and wanted to proclaim their independent countries. It had always been incomprehensible to me and will always be.

The Yugoslavia in the late 1980s was still strong. Without Tito and without coffee, sugar, gas, laundry detergent and cooking oil, but still Yugoslavia.

I was riding on Niš Express bus southbound. Mom welcomed me with a freshly baked cheese pie, my favorite. She looked better than before. When God smiled at me, when I got the job, He smiled at her as well. She still knitted, but less now. Her face resumed its natural healthy glow, for the first time in the last two years.

During the dinner I asked her about the situation in the South.

"There's nothing in the supermarkets, nothing," she sighed. "It's all empty shelves."

It was almost the same in Belgrade, just not that bad. The south always suffers more than the north, it's an unwritten rule of the world, it seems, regardless of a country or a century.

I opened my suitcase and gave mom a few packets of coffee that I got from Mira (she had a connection and managed to obtain one of the unavailable items in stores). There was some smoked meat, also from Mira, from her home village in Vojvodina.

Mom was overwhelmed. I brought her some cooking oil and two cartons of cigarettes. The latter was the most important.

Mom has always been a passionate smoker. Her daily routine is divided by and revolving around cigarette breaks, like:

"Now I'll peel these roasted peppers and then have a cigarette. I'll chop the onions and carrots for soup and sit down for a smoke. While the soup is cooking, I might just as well light up..." And it goes on and on in the same pattern, whether she is cleaning the house, doing laundry or gardening. A puff is her synonym for a break. The shortage of cigarettes affected her a lot.

According to her:

"Smokers are the coolest people. The best stories are told when we all smoke."

We watched the 8 p.m. News together, sipping coffee and smoking.

Scarceness of food, electricity and water restrictions, driving on even-odd days, forgeries in factories... All sad gray news.

Two days later, I returned to Belgrade. I was happy to see Nora waiting for me at the bus station. There were a few jars of ajvar, fresh and delicious, in my suitcase. Ajvar is a vegetable spread made of roasted red peppers and eggplants. It requires a lot of work to fill up even a small jar. Mom made it herself and dedicated it to Nora, Mira, Marko, and Lela.

To my dear friends.

Nora's Impressions

Yugoslavia has been such a charming mélange of cultures, traditions, and languages for decades. The more various, the merrier! I can't decide which nation or nationality I belong to, having Croatian, Hungarian, and Serbian blood in my veins. My favorite part of the country is the Adriatic Sea, along Croatian and Slovenian shores.

Still, ever since a kid, I've had a strong urge to get out of there, out of the makeshift country.

Yes, life in Tito's creation is comfortable, everybody gets apartments for free, there's a lot of stuff in the stores you can easily buy with money you haven't actually earned, since you can't be fired from a job in which you pleasantly spend time drinking coffee and gossiping; you can travel all over the world without visas… And you can eat pineapples every day!

Of course, a fairy tale like this can't last forever.

Especially if you mix too many kinds of apples and oranges originating from different soils into unfertilized ground. The people of Yugoslavia have lived their own histories for centuries. King Alexander tried to unite them, in the 1920s, then Tito in 1945.

The King's efforts ended with World War II; Tito's resulted in the civil war after his death.

From my elementary school history books, I figured out that all dictatorial regimes, be it fascism or socialism/communism, are essentially the same and eventually die out.

From my grandpa, who fought in two Balkan Wars (to get rid of the remnants of the Ottoman occupation in Macedonia and some parts of Serbia at the very beginning of the 20th century) and then in World War I and II, and was all over Europe in the turbulent years of 1920s to 1940s and is literally a piece of living history, I learn that things come and go and that you survive by keeping your centered, integral self. My grandpa was my best playmate in my kid years, by the way. We sat in his old armchair for hours while he read to me lovely stories with lively illustrations, and it's him who introduced me to the world of word and picture, the only world I belong to.

Back to the reality of Yugoslavia in the late 1980s and early 1990s, when the unfounded economy starts shaking a lot and the civil war follows. The 'paradise' is lost, there's no water for hours, and electricity only every second day. You have to wake up at like, 4 a.m. to join the already long line in front of a corner store that opens at 6 a.m., so you can get a loaf of bread or a carton of milk, if you're lucky. Most of the foodstuff is usually gone by the time you get a chance to come to the counter.

A serious economic crisis always precedes political upheavals and often inevitably leads to wars. Stands to reason, why would people fight in an economically healthy and stable society? Just think of Germany in the early 1930s, how did Hitler come into power?

The 'socialism' we have been brainwashed at school was based on Karl Marx' 19th century theory, sort of appropriate if applied to the living conditions of England's working class at the time, just that Yugoslav politicians purposely decided to ignore the century and the country, so they could stuff their already fat wallets by more empty talking.

The cause of the fall of Yugoslavia, therefore, lies in the castles in the air kind of economy, rather than in the historical, cultural, religious or whatever differences among its nations. The people of now ex-Yugoslavia are just the same as they've always been: honest, warm, and friendly. It's the greedy politicians who made the bloody mess!

Think about it; in Canada, hundreds of nations with most diversified backgrounds live in peace. Why? Because everybody is entitled to a decent life (strong economic foundation), so they can simply enjoy and enlarge their horizons with people from other parts of the world. Maybe that's the kind of society Karl Marx envisioned when he wrote that the basic, existential needs, like food, clothing, and adequate living conditions had to be satisfied first, before you turn to education, science, culture, arts, etc.

The Times of Ante Marković

Even after so many years, I can't put together two meaningful sentences about him.

A wizard or a scarecrow?

A savior or a destroyer?

At any rate, a man of Yugoslav background came from The States with an intention to rescue this country and its peoples. He won our hearts instantly, which wasn't hard, since we were sinking into poverty really fast.

He showed up neat and sleek, in an elegant suit and with a clear goal: to fix our monetary system. What he didn't count on was corruption, our mentality (which he apparently forgot about after all those years in the West), and current politics that always had a final say in all money matters.

To us mere mortals, what he was saying sounded convincing. Overnight, Yugoslav's currency dinar that was worth next to nothing, became convertible and could be exchanged for US dollars, Austrian shillings, French or Swiss francs, and German marks. That was all before euro appeared on the EU monetary scene.

Overnight, empty stores became full of everything and overflowing with goods. Supermarkets glowed with Austrian chocolates, Italian pasta, Swiss cheeses, Hungarian salami, and tropical fruits. After the denomination of dinar, when some sort of a balance with other currencies was established, people all of a sudden had money for going out and for things they had been wishfully thinking about in the previous few years.

Nora and I clapped our hands and exclaimed in unison:

"Trips, trips!"

We planned by the speed of light, ran to the travel agency, to the airlines company, worked out the details and here we are at the airport!

We organized an amazing long trip that was truly enjoyable soul, body and shopping wise, in equal parts. We flew to Zagreb, had a great time there, inhaling deeply the scents of the dignified and gorgeous city, as if we had sensed that the whirlwind of the civil war, in the years to come, would take us apart from it. We ate enormous quantities of Kraš chocolates (Croatian brand, the best in the world!) on the park benches or strolled on Ilica, Zagreb's main street. The funicular took us up over the treetops to the Upper Town and down to the cobbled streets of Lower Town, where the open market spread out, vibrant and colorful; embraced by St. Mark's Church and the Cathedral.

Then, we took off to a romantic old castle – oh, such a fairy tale castle of Trakošćan – settled on a hill above a lake, hugged by the woods. What a beauty! What pure nature of Zagorje! Nora and I were walking along the frozen lake in the January morning mist. I did a pirouette on the ice and it was excellently performed, just that my jump on was too hard, so the ice cracked and swallowed me up to the waist. The freezing water was harsh on my genital organs, but I didn't pay any attention to it because Nora was folding over with laughter and so was I! Sipping hot tea in the salon of the hotel where we stayed, just across from the castle, we were still laughing. Then we went to the sauna, where we melted together with the chocolate we had brought and licked afterwards in our room.

Trakošćan was a wonderful experience. We couldn't sleep in the castle itself, unfortunately, but we explored it inside out: its basements with armory, living rooms with pianos, easels, and needlework left on soft armchairs and the art gallery full of paintings by Julijana Drašković, once the countess of Trakošćan.

A few days later, Nora and I ventured to another castle, this one converted into a hotel. It took us some time to get there from the part of Zagorje we were in. We changed several buses, interspersed with footwork, to arrive to the border of Croatia and Slovenia, to the fabulous Mokrice Castle.

It was already getting dark when the two of us, dragging two big suitcases, started to climb the steep path to the castle hotel. We were tired and hungry. There was a sharp turn on the path and the hotel was supposed to appear.

To our utter astonishment, we saw the neon sign USA MILITARY BASE and hundreds of American soldiers running around. Nora surveyed the scene. I turned to her breathlessly,

"Nora, Americans attacked our country while we were wandering Croatian villages and now they've conquered us!"

Nora was silent. Like always, she would first think before she spoke, unlike me who was inclined to jump to conclusions.

"Impossible," was all she said.

We proceeded with unsteady steps to the entrance. Hypotheses and theories about what and how all of that had happened were swarming in my head. Maybe Americans made a pact with Croatians so they could occupy Slovenia together? Maybe Slovenians voluntarily gave away their small republic to Americans so it could grow economically stronger?

My brain was bursting with possible explanations.

We walked in.

Inside, everything looked like a hotel.

"A very good evening to you," a groomed receptionist greeted us. "Are madame and monsieur staying at our hotel tonight?"

"Yes," I said, hesitantly, turning to the entrance gate. "Is this still Slovenia and Yugoslavia?"

He followed my glance and smiled politely.

"Sir, it is those Italians shooting a movie of some kind. It is less expensive to do it here."

"Oh."

Nora laughed.

So did I.

American occupation? Croatian/ Slovenian pact?

It was just a movie.

Our suitcases were brought to our suite and we were guided to a regal dining room, where a pretty, rose-cheeked waitress made sure we were well-fed with roast turkey on a bed of soft noodles, accompanied by fresh dandelion salad and home-made wine.

Our suite featured the four poster canopied bed, paintings and artifacts, dream-like. A real castle and the two of us there. A local dog, Munja, befriended us and followed in our footsteps during our walks through the woods. We treated her to some delicacies from the substantial castle cuisine.

One night, I got out of bed for a drink of water. A strange light was shining through the thick drapes. I thought it was already morning and opened the window. To my surprise, dozens of eyes were looking at me, naked, with flashlights pointing in my direction. They were shooting the night scene of the movie on the window next to ours and probably had to repeat it because of my 'intrusion', but I couldn't have cared less!

We left Mokrice Castle and crossed the Austrian border on our way to Villach, a romantic little town where we listened to vivacious melodies played by street musicians, while we enjoyed strudels, smoked sausages, and beer. The hotel we stayed at was small, with only ten rooms, but so very Austrian, pleasant and impeccably clean; with geraniums in full bloom cascading over the balconies. They were all neatly planted, safe and healthy in the fresh soil.

Our days were unrolling smoothly, along with kilometers we passed. From Austria, we went to Italy. First to Tarvisio, on the slopes of the Alps, admiring the snow-crowned mountain peaks, and then, slowly, by a night train, we arrived to dreamy, tranquil Venice.

La Serenissima welcomed us warmly, opened her palace windows, lit up her street lanterns, and gently pushed the gondolieri to take us through the canals of the laguna to our destination. The Luna Hotel was more than we could have imagined. Our room window was over the water, the magical water of Venice. We had our breakfasts in the serenity of the top floor of the hotel, in a hidden garden viewing the roofs of palaces, the domes of basilicas and the spires of churches.

Nora put her glasses on and said:
"Are you ready?"
"Yes!"

And we started our typical sightseeing. Nora was an expert at finding the most secluded lanes where a human step hadn't been heard for hundreds of years. She could easily discover buildings that had been destroyed, vanished, and then reappeared in front of our eyes. She had archeology and art history at her fingertips. Tiny squares, Ponte dei Sospiri, galleries in Pallazzo Ducale, the island of Murano, and the Venetian cemetery stayed imprinted in the brain book of her memories.

We left Venice by ship one night, so that we could for some more instants experience the glittering lights reflected on the water, storing each glitter for the future. Venice was melting away from the view. The deep waters of the Adriatic Sea were calm. Our ship was gliding us to Rijeka, the biggest port in Croatia. After a few fabulous days in the nearby Scott Bay, named after Sir Walter Scott, who spent some time there and enjoyed it a lot, we decided to visit some islands before going back home.

The islands of Rab, Pag, Korčula, Hvar... Like pearls on a necklace, each one more resplendent than the other. Nora's skin was getting very tanned while mine retained its usual color of a boiled lobster. Nora's hair was bleached by the sun, her body like dark chocolate, while I remained white and red, like the Polish flag.

We swam a lot and had candlelit dinners by the sea.

We bought dried lavender flowers on Hvar and hand-pressed olive oil on Korčula, lace made of agave leaves on Pag and home-made cheese on Rab.

We walked the cobbled narrow winding streets, visited abandoned ruins and secluded coves.

The summer couldn't have been better.

We sent postcards to our moms, to my aunts, to my elementary school teacher, to Lela, Marko, and Mira.

We traveled.

After the poverty of the previous few years, it was easy to get used to abundance. Ante Marković knew what he was doing, or so it seemed to us. The stores were full, smiles came back to people's faces. Everybody could afford whatever they wanted. My salary had a completely different value with this new dinar and I liked it very much that way. Money dealers, who had been exchanging dinars for German marks, disappeared from the street corners, like mice from an empty church.

Nora was blossoming because she quit her job and started a new course at the University.

The winds of the Adriatic Sea were blowing in her hair.

On each air trip she laughed at my envy of flight attendants. I had always dreamed of becoming one of them. I knew the timetables of JAT (Yugoslav Air Transport) and of all the major international airlines by heart. I could always tell from my little apartment in the garage which plane type was flying over my roof, where it took off, and where it would land.

All my friends were amazed at that passion of mine.

A kind flight attendant gave me a bottle of air freshener from the plane once, and I sprayed it sparingly in my apartment, only for special occasions.

Nora and I flew to Budapest where, for the first and last time, we decided to stay in a private accommodation; in an old house on Buda hill, owned by an ancient lady Gabriella. Ever since the first morning, newly-posted signs would dawn in our lodgings:

'No smoking in the room, only in the hall.'

'No loud speaking after 10 p.m.'

'No eating in the room.'

'No taking drinks into the room.'

Those three days were fantastic in terms of the city and the sightseeing, but the landlady was a pain in the neck. She kept reminding us of this and that in Hungarian, pointing to the signs in German written by her son. Nora acted as an interpreter. We were allowed to take a shower only once a day (the water was heated by a gas boiler with an open flame and the hag apparently wanted to save on gas), to which Nora said:

"No way!"

And the old Gabriella couldn't do anything to prevent Nora's frequent showers, other than blabber on and on.

Budapest opened up her chest wide for us, with its gorgeous architecture, monuments, parks, and promenades. Spicy goulash in Matias Pince restaurant and an unforgettable visit to Szentendre, a picturesque village just outside of the city. The legendary Vaci Street and great shopping. Late evening piano recitals at the Faculty of Music.

Coffee and cake.

Another coffee and cake (apple strudel).

Oh, one more coffee and cake (Zacher tort).

We strolled the wide flat streets of Pest, looking up at the hilly Buda over the impressive bridges across the Danube River. We marched the cobblestones of Buda resting our eyes on the spread out Pest.

Our days were filling up with delights and souvenirs.

Traveling was so good in those times and we enjoyed it to our hearts' content.

Ships, planes, buses and trains...

Then we returned to Belgrade.

Nora's Impressions

In one of the conversation classes during my Italian studies at the university, the professor asks us to think ourselves as obscenely rich and present the tale of our imaginary lives to other students. While every single one of them is into mansions with swimming pools, at least two cars, designer clothing and never-ending parties, the Great Gatsby style, my answer is simple:

'Si avessi molti soldi, potrei viaggiare tutto il mondo.' ("If I had a lot of money, I could travel the world"). And then I elaborate my point.

In all honesty, I would be absolutely the happiest person on earth if I could wake up every morning in another city, in another part of the globe!

There's nothing better that traveling! People, places, customs, traditions, history, constant movement. It's like being in a movie, ever-changing scenery, scents of seas, rivers and woods, tastes of local food and drinks, eyes energized by architecture and arts, ears picking up different languages, fingers touching new clothing items… Aaah!

Above all, traveling gives you the real sense of freedom, opens up and liberates your mind, body, and soul even more effectively than Yoga does, and I'm sort of a Yoga addict, by the way.

Traveling teaches you to observe things as they are and not to worry if they don't run smoothly, for everything is a part of experience. Like, so what if your baggage gets delayed every time you land at Oslo Airport? Better they bring it to your hotel than you drag it across the city! And so what if they overcharge you for beer on Piazza Venezia in Rome? You enjoy the view and can even discern the outlines of Foro Romano in the background, which comes as a bonus!

You discover that the energy of some places, actually of some very specific spots, is palpably compatible with your own. You feel so light, almost levitating, while your spirit is soaring with a sense of power so immense, like you can conquer the world! The vast space in front of the National Theater and the Opera House in Warsaw, the promenade along the Danube River, at Lanczhid bridge in Pest, with the view of the Citadel in Buda and the neoclassical square with a sculpture in the middle; a fountain and flowers around it in Grünerløkka area of Oslo are such spots for me, my centering and gravitation points.

The charming south Serbian town of Niš doesn't provide me with such revelations, but I love its provincial peacefulness nevertheless.

At any rate, my thanks go to Ante Marković who makes it possible for us to travel easily and relatively inexpensively in the years preceding the collapse of Yugoslavia. It's too good to be true and I know it, so carpe diem, seize the day I say!

Nikola and I spend a day in Dubrovnik, the most unique city in Dalmatia and probably in the world, just the earliest plane to and the latest one back to Belgrade kind of thing. We see Lela and her husband on their honeymoon there, climb the Old Town walls and fortresses, stroll the marble-paved Stradun, the main street, hop on and off churches with Masses in full swing (Catholic and Orthodox Easter happens to be on the same date that Sunday in 1987), and eat fresh figs on the rocks while dipping our toes into the sea.

We attend Puccini's opera Turandot in Arena di Verona. The spectacle starts at sunset and we all turn our lit candles to the setting sun as the powerful voices from the magnificent stage resonate in the air. At the end of the marvelous performance, we throw cushions at singers and the orchestra, to show our appreciation, as is the custom.

We take pictures of Giulietta's balcony before going back to our hotel on Lago di Garda where ricotta, tomato, basil-filled manicotti, and white wine lull us to sleep as we dine on the lakeshore.

Then we head on to Padova, admire the park studded with sculptures of writers and scientists from the Renaissance times and make our wishes on the tomb of St. Anthony, who turns out to be our patron saint, in the impressive basilica glorifying his name, as is the custom.

A lovely summer vacation in Ostia, on the Tyrrhenian Sea, swimming in the warm water and walking on the soft sand in the mornings. We visit the archeological site of Ostia Antica, the ancient Roman port. Every day, a twenty-minute train ride takes us to Rome and we enjoy some more ruins, extensive shopping streets, beer and pizzas and a taped mass running round the clock in Chiesa del Gesù, conveniently located just across from Piazza Venezia, where tourists, exhausted after a hard day's footwork in the heat, seek its shady sanctuary. Via del Popolo, Via Nazionale, the softest shoes, the most stylish clothes and the most amazing makeup in the world, triumphal arches and obelisks, Parco Borghese, Campidoglio, Piazza di Spagna, Fontana di Trevi… we throw some coins over our left shoulders into the fountain, to come back to Rome, as is the custom.

We are denied entry into Basilica di San Pietro in the Vatican by the colorfully-attired Swiss guards, on account of Nikola's shorts and my mini skirt. Just what else do you wear in Rome in July, in 50 °C!

In Florence, we pay our tributes to the tombs of Michelangelo, Galileo, Machiavelli, Rossini, Puccini, and Dante (his tomb is empty, for he was buried in Ravenna, having been exiled from his hometown to which he gave some of the most beautiful poetry ever written on earth and a lot of political commitment, just proves that politics always has to mess up everything) in Chiesa di Santa Croce; window shop the jewelry display along Ponte Vecchio, bridge that connects the literary, artistic, and business core of the town with the gentle green slopes of Fiesole, across the Arno river. We licked the real Italian gelato on the steps of Basilica Santa Maria del Fiore (Brunelleschi's masterpiece!) and sip overpriced espressos on Piazza della Signoria, with Galleria Uffici in front of us and the sculpture of Michelangelo's David (well, the copy of it) behind us.

Wherever we go, we always somehow end up in Venice. The unreally real magical place. Memories of my first Tizian and my first pizza. Carnivals on Piazza San Marco, too many pidgins.

Reflections on Shakespeare and Thomas Mann. Coconut slices on Ponte Rialto. Water and the sky and some more of both.

We also spend a fabulous week on Malta, a tiny island huddled between Sicily and Tunisia, so packed with history. We visit the megalithic temples, learn about the knights of the Maltese Cross, buy some woven and leather goods at the Sunday bazaar by the medieval walls of the capital La Valetta, climb the cacti hills; and stand in awe of the huge white-crested waves of the Mediterranean Sea breaking with their full force against the rocks in the strong winds of January. We refuse to eat the national dish, which is a rabbit stew, for rabbits are such lovely cuddly animals, preferring local sweet delicious bagels.

We can even afford to go to China, on one of our summer vacations! We walk on the Great Wall and visit the Temple of Heaven, the Summer Palace, and the newly born panda in the Beijing Zoo. We take a peek into huntungs, just to see how people actually live there, sit in the pagoda in Beihai Park, attend the Beijing Opera and eat ourselves nuts on Vang Fu Jing Street, where all the food is prepared right in front of you and you consume it in a very relaxing squat posture; it's much better for your digestion than sitting on a chair!

My grandma says that times come and go, one day you might be filthy rich, only to find yourself a beggar overnight. And that the only real wealth you carry on throughout your life, is your trips, the experiences, and memories of them and that's something nobody can rob you of!

The Best 37 Bus

Out of all the buses, trams, and trolley buses in Belgrade, my favorite was the 37 bus. It ran from Dunav station in downtown, close to the Danube River, through the outskirts of the city, right to where I lived. Since it had been proved and confirmed (by my own opinion) that I was quite adventurous and a bit crazy, the 37 bus was my most preferred place for meeting unusual people, making some casual acquaintances and for occasional quickies, just in passing.

The paradoxical part was that even though I was super busy and with no extra time for anything more on top, I was always in a panic, searching for new faces in my life.

Honestly, all my long-standing friends were quite irritated by this urge of mine – some more, some less – but every single one of them definitely hated those moments when I presented a new person and said:

"Hey, let me introduce you to..."

The new person usually lasted three to five days and then disappeared.

My food for the soul was to have lots of people around me. I have never been narcissistic. Not even when my career started to skyrocket – to the extent I had never thought it possible – did I feel famous. Not even when people recognized me from my TV shows – on the streets or buses – was my heart filled with pride.

The 37 bus was my playful hunting ground for easy victims.

I would always stand at the back of the bus.

With the discerning eye of a professional, I always knew who the most suitable 'prey' was.

I was right eight times out of ten.

My story always ran along the same lines:

"I'm not from Belgrade, I'm so lonely." ('Lonely' indeed, with about a hundred and fifty friends!).

"I've always wanted to try this..."

"Can you tell me where (this or that) street is?"

"I live close by," (at least ten more bus stops to my place). "Would you like to come over for some coffee?"

Needless to say, I felt awful after all that, but just briefly. A few sonatas, a glass of pure peach juice, some cigarettes, and a short restorative sleep later, and here I am on the 37 bus again!

Parades of blond, black, and brown heads passed through my bed. Fast sex, a few phony phrases, and the polite closure:

"Keep in touch," with a wrong phone number on the piece of paper in their hands.

Guilty conscience?

No, I didn't have it – why should I?

Out of my precious time for sleep, piano playing, and getting together with my dear friends, I spared and stole moments to give myself to people from the 37 bus, so it was give and take and vice versa, and everybody was happy.

I met Milan by chance. He stayed in my life for a long time: after my military service, my voluntary exile in the Homolje Mountains, and my leaving for Poland, all until our friendship was dissolved by my decision, in the spring of 2000 – when I felt very hurt by his part.

Our companionship was built slowly but on firm foundations and I thought I was his best friend, maybe the only one – for he never mentioned a single name of another friend. He was lonely and I believe that a large part of his explicit or implicit egotism stemmed from there, from simple loneliness. Most of the times we talked on the phone, but every once in a while we would get-together and chat over coffee.

Milan was out of ordinary looking, the way Mother Nature made him: big and overweight, but with beautiful warm eyes and a soft voice. He cost the company he worked for millions of dinars for the phone bills, talking to people all over the world, until he was found out and fired. Then he got an even better job; as a night security guard in an embassy, with easy access to the phone.

An expert in his 'job', he found a way to squeeze dry people who had never met him, but kept sending him money on a regular basis. Being lonely, he now had some company, while making a lot of money along the line.

Nora liked him in her way, as he did her. He managed to get rich in an impossibly ridiculous way, known only to him; at the time when castles were falling apart, dreams faded and people became poverty-stricken all over Yugoslavia.

On our last get-together, I was throat deep in financial problems. Yes, I was already living in Canada, in the country of endless paradise, but because of my unusual way of life and my naïveté, I lost a lot of money and was penniless. For family reasons, I had to go to Serbia.

I met him in a café and we chatted. I was glad to see him after several years.

He was telling me about the huge quantities of money he had, I was telling him about money I didn't have. He had known me for 15 years by then and could have been certain that I would have paid him back as soon as I could, that I wasn't a cheater or a liar. He didn't offer me one single dinar. As a gift, he gave me a small pack of coffee, already opened, and a half-used bottle of a body lotion.

That was the last straw.

After an hour of listening to his boasting about his richness, the bill came. The assumption was that I should pay. I had coffee, while he ordered cakes, cappuccino, and juice for himself. I said to the waitress:

"Separate bills, please."

He didn't react, didn't say a word. We parted there, at the café across from the National Theater in Belgrade and walked away in two opposite directions.

I have lots of friends and take care of every one of them. The balance of the Universe doesn't reflect only in the order of the planets and their revolutions and pathways. Strong friendships are also very important, maybe even more important than the Universe.

Sometimes, I wonder how he is doing now. I wonder what he is up to in these modern times of high technology and emails, smart phones and all the electronic gadgets imaginable. When I decided to put an end to our friendship, he was still managing his strange affairs, barely comprehensible to me, through phone and letters, for computers didn't exist in those times in Yugoslavia.

Sava was the manager of a supermarket on Kanarevo Brdo, one of the seven hills of Belgrade. Walking down a steep street after a private lesson, I reminded myself to renew my supplies of biscuits, crackers and coffee, for Nora and Veronica were coming over that evening. I walked into the supermarket and was surprised to see the coffee racks empty.

"Isn't there any coffee?" I asked a man who was arranging some stuff on the shelves.

He turned to me. He was tall and broad-shouldered. He looked at me with dark-green eyes and in a deep velvety voice said:

"Where do you come from? There hasn't been any coffee for a month."

"I've been traveling all over Europe in the past few weeks," I explained without taking my eyes off his face.

"I'm sorry I can't help you," he said, not letting go of my glance for a second.

We were standing in the laundry detergent and dish liquid row. Smells of artificial roses, lilacs, and who knows what else were permeating my nostrils and tickled me. I was wondering if I looked good in my light burgundy sweater knitted by Mom and the white starched shirt from Austria and whether my hair was all over my head from the wind that was blowing with its full force that day.

"Do you live abroad?" he interrupted the silence.

"No, I've just been on some trips. I live on Cerak hill, here..." I made a movement with my arm in the eastbound direction, as if Cerak was right there, next to the supermarket.

I started feeling uncomfortable because we hadn't moved for at least five minutes. We kept looking at each other as if seeking something in each other's eyes. He held on to some papers in his hand.

"I have to say that you smell very nice," he said.

"Oh, thank you. It's Lapidus."

"Smells really nice."

I felt myself blushing. Me? Impossible!

I, the king of sweet little stories and fairy tales, the king of the 37 bus!

Timid all of a sudden.

"Thank you," I said. "I'll come by again, maybe I'll be luckier next time."

"Thank you and sorry," he said.

We didn't move an inch. Housewives were pushing through us, looking for the laundry detergent. They needed it right now? Couldn't they see how tense and hard this moment was?

I eventually walked out and made for the bus stop. He ran after me and in that wild wind on a bright sunny day, he looked even more handsome than in the dull supermarket.

"Here's my phone number, here at the office," he said out of breath. "Ring me up tomorrow, or better, tonight around 8, before closing, so I can keep some coffee for you if there's a delivery."

"Oh, thank you so much! I'm Nikola."

"Sava."

"Nice to meet you."

"Nice to meet you, too."

We shared a strong and warm handshake.

That evening, Sava came to my little apartment in the garage, bringing several packets of coffee. He was in a hurry, his wife and children were waiting for him at home for dinner. I had already made a sandwich for him, for he must be hungry after a long day at work. I put on some cream cheese, a sprinkle of Mom's ajvar, a few slices of chicken salami and covered it with shredded caciocavallo. He swallowed it gratefully.

He left.

Then he came back.

He came the next day after work and the day after.

Then there was Saturday and Sunday, so I didn't see him.

During the following weeks we got together regularly, sometimes at my place, but more often in the park behind the military garrison in the Voždovac part of the city.

Some months later, I was sitting with Sava on the sofa in his cottage, drinking home-made sweet wine, when he told me what had been going on in his head at that moment at the supermarket.

I laughed, because the very same thoughts had crossed my mind as well. I didn't want to leave without a contact sign, something that would make it possible to meet him again.

Over the course of several years, the 37 bus brought me tons of acquaintances, some enjoyable, fantastic even, some dumb and completely useless. I met a gorgeous ballet dancer and we got close right away. He was crazy in his own way, but so, so good-looking! At about the same time I met Jasmina, also on the bus. She was sitting and frowning at the notes, trying to write, on the old rickety bus, her homework in harmony.

I can't stand it when people on the bus look at what I read or write and breathe in my face, but this time I did exactly the same thing. I felt sorry for a pretty girl who didn't understand harmony.

"Pardon me for the intrusion," I said, "but you made a mistake in the second bar."

She looked at me as if I had asked her to strip herself naked (which wasn't actually hard for her as I later discovered).

"See, the soprano can't jump up like this, because it's in disaccord with the tenor here –" I went on, pointing to the music sheet.

She smiled.

"You're a genius, sent from God!" she said. "If I don't do this test right, I'll fail the year."

"Ugh, that changes the perspective. Do you have fifteen minutes to spare?"

"No, ten at the most."

I took her work in my hands and sighed. Wrong, everything was totally wrong and badly done. There was no comprehensible melody you could follow. I was writing by the speed of light, somehow managing to finish the piece in ten minutes.

"My name is Jasmina," she said. "Here's my phone number, call me tonight, please. I'll tell you how it all went and thanks a million!"

"You're welcome, I'll call you."

I rang her up later that evening while the ballet dancer was making me tea – because I had sore throat. Jasmina got a high mark and after all the bad ones she had accumulated, she was allowed to continue her studies at the music school. She cried of happiness, thanking me over and over again. Her mother suggested she should be taking harmony and piano lessons from me twice a week, to make it smoothly through the following school year.

She was young, exuberant and even more nuts than I was. She had a Dalmatian with exactly the same expression as hers, they looked like two identical eggs (no offense, Jasmina was really good-looking and so was the dog). Lessons with her were anything but serious music analysis, but I found a way to make her listen, learn, and do her homework. I would fetch her from discotheques and send her home to study. She would tell me about her sexual affairs and wanted to hear about mine. She introduced me to some weird people, even more foolish than herself, with whom everything was possible when intoxicated by rum. My ballet dancer attracted her a lot, but he preferred men, so couldn't help her there. She asked him how about her kissing him while he was held in the arms of a man. He accepted wholeheartedly.

It was really insane. Some mad times. Maybe there was something in the air, who knows.

Nora was impartial to Jasmina, while Mira and Lela openly disapproved of her. They would never miss to remind me of Jasmina's bad influence on me, while Nora stayed quiet and sweet in her own way. Marko didn't know anything about it because he was in the military.

Jasmina was passionate and exuberant. Her laughter would shake up the sleepy geraniums from their pots on the balconies of apartment buildings. She smoked, drank, was a party animal, and totally enjoyed her youth. We had a very unusual teacher-student relationship.

She exasperated me by interrupting the classes, eager to talk about her latest adventures. I was intent on teaching her patiently all she needed to know in order to be prepared for the exams, so that she didn't fail the semester.

Every so often, she would look at me with dog-like eyes and say:

"Oh, this is all so boring, so terribly boring! Have I told you I met a soldier yesterday?"

"No, you haven't, but let's first finish at least this part," I pointed at the score she was to analyze.

"Aaah..." she yawned. "So, I met him in a supermarket and he walked me home. Kept talking about being the best macho in his village; like all the girls fall for him. I was really into his sexuality and was getting horny, you know what I mean, so I brought him to my place. All those stories turned me on – I was hot, man! I wanted him naked, to see and feel all of him!" She took a drag of the cigarette.

"At first, I thought I was imagining things. Like, there was that huge round thick bush on his crotch and something small, crooked and tight sort of sticking out of it. THAT was the famous 'love muscle' he boasted so much about!?" She took another drag, frantically searching for the glass by the piano that was filled with water and spat out its contents.

"I told him to get dressed, like I was having cramps in the stomach and my period's coming, so couldn't have sex. Like, I didn't want to hurt his self-confidence, you know. So eventually, he left and said the next time we meet, he'd fuck me senseless. Just WHAT with, I wonder!"

I listened. That was typical of her. Only she could do that. The story about the postman was along the same lines, he brought a letter that had to be signed and while she was signing with one hand, she took a firm grip of his genitals with the other, took him inside, sucked him and then kicked him out half naked. That's Jasmina to you.

"OK, right," I stopped her. "Now, in this second bar, what is the leading melody and how do we harmonize it with the supporting voices?"

"Ugh... You've no idea how much I hate this," she was forcing herself back to music analysis. "Just why did all those composers have to work so hard to write boring sonatas and stuff? Why didn't they enjoy life a bit?"

I smiled at that.

"If Bach could hear you, he wouldn't have agreed," I said. "Just for your reference, he had twenty children produced by two women, on top of all his compositions, so he was obviously very busy in both fields."

She shrugged her shoulders.

"Can you make me another coffee, strong and black please? And lace it with some alcohol?"

"Of course."

Jasmina fluttered away from my life with the same speed she entered it, having passed the exams I had been preparing her for, accompanied by liters of coffee, tons of cigarettes, some whiskey, and endless sexual stories. Mira and Lela were ecstatic. Nora took it calmly, as if no dramatic change occurred.

One evening, the 37 bus brought me surprise and pleasure in the form of Sergei Nestorov, symbol of a true Russian beauty: tall and blond, with the deepest blue eyes I had ever seen (Many years later, my life torrents took me to Canadian waters where I met a pair of more beautiful and even deeper blue eyes).

We spoke Russian. He said he was staying for a few more days, was here with some colleagues, worked on a construction site, came from Leningrad (now St. Petersburg), showed me the picture of his wife and his two little daughters, as gorgeous looking as their dad.

I introduced myself as the editor of a men's fashion magazine and said he should definitely be a model, given his heavenly looks.

I lied a lot more, later in the restaurant, fueled by good food and glass after glass of white wine. He didn't say much. He responded courteously, in refined phrases and a soft voice.

Then it was time to leave.

I wanted to see him again. I wanted to ask him for a contact phone or address. I was afraid of losing him. Sergei was something special. Ignoring the fast flow of my words, uttered and unuttered, there, just in front of the restaurant, he motioned his arm towards the nearby park.

A fine mist covered the passing trams and seeped through the paths. The bench we sat on was wet. The fog swallowed us.

And kept the secret.

The next morning, Sergei and I had breakfast in a bistro, listening to the music from the radio. He was still mysterious, quiet, and sparse with words. On our way out, he waved his hand to call the cab that took us to his hotel.

It rained all day.

The evening before his return to Russia, we got together for a beer.

He wore a blue shirt, the same shade as his eyes.

The fog was still spinning its magic silvery web over Belgrade. You couldn't see a finger in front of the nose.

We walked to the same park.

Sat down on the same bench.

Caressed by an opaque veil, mingling in my mind with Rachmaninoff's Concerto No. 2 in C-minor. Adagio sostenuto.

Every time I listen to it now, at the moment when the deep tones of the second movement start cuddling the dreamy strings, I recall that night and the fog.

We parted at the edge of the park.

I took one path, he another.

I had some ready sentences in good Russian. I wanted to tell him something really very important.

He looked at me soulfully, smiled, touched his lips with his finger and...

Disappeared in the dense evening fog.

Cinderella

Lela had a new boyfriend. She was in a stable relationship, after lots of shaky ones, having finally found the 'right guy', as Nora and I sincerely hoped. He was born and raised in an old Belgrade family and loaded with money. She looked happy.

Marko was done with the military and started looking for a job.

Mira's daughters were growing fast. Sonja, the elder, was an excellent student at school, winning prizes at all sorts of competitions, one after another. Ana, the younger, was very spoilt, but a lovely little ballerina. Ever since she was a tiny kid, she knew she would become a ballet dancer. Her eyes were dark and deep. She always knew what she wanted and how, using all the means to achieve her goals.

A typical scene from her early teens –

Ana gets back home after her classes and is ready to go out. Mira is in the kitchen. Dresses, tops, shirts, skirts, pants, jackets, and scarves cover every conceivable surface in the apartment. The little one is looking for something, rumbling through the bursting wardrobes.

"Mom, Mooom!"

"What is it?"

"I've nothing to wear!" she starts crying.

I have to pinch myself to make sure I'm not dreaming. Everywhere around me, in all the rooms, tons of various clothing items hang from chairs and table corners or are strewn on the floors.

"What d'you mean you've nothing to wear?" Mira asks.

"Nothing I like! I want a black top!"

I pinch myself again, this time harder, because most of the tops around me are black.

"Shhh, don't cry, here's some money, go buy something nice for yourself."

The little one comes back ten minutes later in a new skinny top. The best part is that she doesn't actually like it, so she takes it off, puts on something dangling from the armchair and goes out.

On the other hand, Ana was a hard-working, conscientious young dancer, sweet and smiley to everybody. She had always been very fond of me as I was of her. She behaved as a spoiled brat only with Mira, because she allowed her to.

I had always been protective of Sonja who Mira often scolded for no apparent reason and mistreated, not exactly like the step-mother from Cinderella, but in a similar manner. Mira had those unexplainable outbursts of reproaching her elder daughter who was so polite and quiet, opening her mouth only if asked something directly. I would stand by Sonja's side, trying to break the code of Mira's brain, which was impossible. How come she was so permissive with one daughter and so strict with the other?

I felt them both like my own daughters. I loved them with a true fatherly love.

They were both growing up nicely.

They were good hearted and great looking girls, each in their own way. The elder one a natural long haired blonde with translucent skin, enchanting like a mermaid, silent and romantic. The younger one had a striking beauty that combined the body of Aphrodite with the eyes of a Moroccan dancer.

So, Lela was getting married.

She decided to tie the knot.

Nice.

Nora and I were in the South of Serbia, visiting my family, when Lela spilled the beans over the phone. We had a great time in Niš, were welcomed warmly, and treated like kings by everybody who invited us to their homes.

Nora enjoyed being there.

I didn't.

It took me twenty five years of being away from that town to forgive it, to let go of the past and look straight into its eyes, its streets, parks, and the river and say:

"This is a really nice town."

Lela's wedding was due in a week. Nora was contemplating what she was going to wear and how to style her hair. As for me, I already had my outfit done in my mind.

Talking about fashion style, there must be a molecule reserved for it in the brain, and like everything, in the course of evolution, it becomes more developed. My molecule probably worked on a slightly different basis, somehow. Ever since the elementary school, I liked to dress unlike everybody else. I had never had the least intention to attract attention, I actually tried to avoid it, but my urge to put on totally unusual clothes, especially all kinds of tops, was irresistible and stronger than any other power existing in the narrow-minded South Serbian world of those years.

My clothing frenzy started when I was eleven and wanted to look like Janice Joplin, wore faded jeans and tunics, bracelets like hers, a ring on every finger, smoked, and grew my hair long. I wasn't into drugs for the simple reason that it was a taboo in socialist times, in Niš at any rate. The first marijuana I tasted was when I was thirty. My 'drug' was clothing.

When I was fourteen, I had my hair colored blond, thus causing the biggest revolution ever recorded in that town. Never ever before had a man done that!

I narrowly escaped being stoned.

I survived.

I paid the most recent visit to my hometown a few weeks ago, thirty-five years after my hair coloring episode. Passing by my old elementary school, I noticed that half of the boys, aged eight to twelve, had highlights in their hair and earrings in their ears and noses.

I was a pioneer and am proud of that.

Beaten several times, with no bones broken.

Twice I left the battlefield with a swollen nose.

I wore the most original clothes in that town.

With the onset of the High School of Music, I left the hippy me behind and transformed into The New Wave style. My shirts, often sewn by myself, had thousands of frills interspersed with sequins. The moment I saw new models in imported fashion magazines, I would run to warehouses and get dirty and seemingly good-for-nothing fabrics for a bargain, wash, and iron them and then go to the workshop of a wonderful grandpa Vasa, a skillful retired military tailor who had all the patience of this world and was thrilled by my fashion ideas. I would explain to him exactly what I wanted and how it could be done. He didn't charge a lot, for he worked for pleasure, not for money.

His marvelous and outstanding creations were an eyesore to my high school teachers, especially to the old Pinky who taught Math and who on several occasions kicked me out of the classroom and sent me to the principal's office on the grounds of 'unsuitable and offensive clothing'. The principal would then call my mom who had to come to the school and repeat the same speech over and over:

"Is my son a good student?"

"Excellent."

"What are his marks in music subjects?"

"The highest."

"Then we have nothing to talk about."

Mom would leave his office lighting a cigarette in the corridor, on her way to chatting with my lovely lead teacher who was just about to finish the third fag on her ten minute break.

For the graduation ceremony, I wore an amazing combination of purple leather and white silk (both artificial) and had indigo highlights in my hair.

All my shirts, sweaters, and pants moved with me to Belgrade and followed me on my subsequent journeys that enriched my sense of fashion.

I remained faithful to my own dress code until I came to Canada.

For reasons unknown, I somehow settled in and became painfully normal. My lovely lead teacher would have said:

"You are too beige!"

Maybe because in Canada, there's such a huge selection of all sorts of clothing items and people can wear whatever they like and walk on the streets without having their looks commented on. The law protects everybody here, the ordinary and the un/extra ordinary. Everybody is allowed to make their fashion statements. The challenge of standing out lost its allure.

Lela's wedding was no different than any other: a parade of glamour, gossips, and kitsch. A mix of feelings, as is the way of all weddings.

She was glowing on the dance floor in an elaborately decorated pink satin dress over her protruding belly. Nora was wearing a silver pencil skirt with slits, a thin belt around her waist and a white blouse with frills falling over her shoulders. Her hair was wild, as usual. I was in wide black silk pants, fitted white shirt with high collar, necktie made of Austrian crystal and lacy purple sweater with bat sleeves, knitted artfully by Mom.

Lela's in-laws bought her an apartment and lots of expensive dresses. She deserved it. She had always been poor but with a huge heart. Now she was full of money. I hoped her heart would remain the same, for sometimes money can change people.

Nora's Impressions

Flying across the skies, beyond times and places, spinning and swirling through scenes and instances, I settle for a moment in a cozy crowded kitchen on the ground floor of a bit dilapidated building in the city center. The light flower-patterned curtains are rustling softly in the open window, its sill studded with African violets, ferns, geraniums, and miniature roses while the creepers from the small garden outside are making their way inside.

Nikola and I are having coffee in Mira's kitchen and there's barely any room for our cups, for the place is brimming to the brink with all kinds of objects, like dozens of teapots and sugar bowls (that hardly ever get used), ashtrays (the same goes for them), utensils, various cooking accessories, postcards, souvenirs from trips, costume jewelry, knick-knacks, trinkets, and trifles. The big aquarium is very busy with fish, sand, seashells, pebbles, plastic castles, plants, and multicolored neon lights. Yet, there's a sense of some sort of order in all that charming mess.

They say that a cluttered living space is a reflection of a cluttered mind, which is so totally not applicable to Mira. Like, she moves around at the approximate speed of 200 miles per hour, talks with loudspeakers attached to her vocal cords, is always all over the place, yet one of the most efficient and organized persons on the planet (Nikola still ranks #1). She always gets everything done! Her energy, vitality, and common sense are contagious and her physical strength in the fairly small frame is admirable! She's a true fighter, which is inspirational. Noisiness aside, Mira is a real, great friend!

So, as the three of us are comfortably chatting, Ana rushes in from her ballet school, only to rush out minutes later to meet some friends, throwing a tantrum regarding the lack of anything to wear and refusing to put anything into her mouth.

Sonja gets back from her high school with a friend, talks with us in her nice, polite way for a bit, then grabs a sandwich, and heads for the swimming pool.

Some neighbors and acquaintances drop by and Mira calls some others to come fix her kitchen cabinets, making a lot of fuss along the way. The phone keeps ringing all the time, Mira is making all kinds of arrangements for this and that, simultaneously talking to everybody in the kitchen from the top of her lungs, making some more coffee, opening another beer and preparing snacks.

It takes only about half an hour for all these happenings to take place. Incredible!

It's a crazy house, but lovely crazy!

'Mens sana in corpore sano' ('Healthy mind in a healthy body'), a Latin saying goes. And Mira is the living example of this. Like, with all her aerobics, running, skiing, swimming, basket-ball or whatever playing, of course her mind is clear, she's just in a fast forward mode!

I take to Nikola instantly because he looks different from all the people I have ever met. Like, this is who I am. A fashion statement, if it comes from the inborn sense of your own personality style, is a reflection of yourself. If the neighbors or school teachers spit on you, their loss! They might slip on their own saliva in the process.

One of the things I most respect about Nikola's mom (I am still learning from her), is that you don't judge anybody's expression of themselves, as long as they're good people and that you always stand by your closest and dearest!

You Will Marry Well

I've been working in education for quite some time, I said to myself and counted: two years and five months in the village, almost three years in the élite downtown school, coupled with the High School of Music for exceptional talents, and then at the Faculty of Music.

"You are a teacher incarnated, like a guru," Nora used to say.

"You are a true pedagogue," my colleagues often said.

I was impartial to their comments. I simply loved doing my job with all my heart.

The educational system had been undergoing lots of changes. I sincerely hoped that some teachers and professors would change, too. Like, in life, you keep people who are good close to you and those who are not you get rid of.

Professor R. was always drunk, if not totally, then halfway. In his distant youth, he was an expert on music and that's when he got hold of the cathedra which he now used only as a prop to lean on so he didn't fall down. He stank of cheap brandy, was choleric, and spoke in bad language.

In the first year of my university studies, there was a beautiful transparent girl with light, almost white hair and eyelashes, and an angelic voice, from an established Belgrade family, highly-respected in cultural circles. She used to sit in the front row so she could see better from her thick glasses.

Professor R. bore a grudge against her for no reason.

"Do you have a piano at home, Miss?" he asked.

"Yes, sir," she said quietly.

"Good, good for you," he coughed and went on. "So you'll marry well, for you can't count on your looks."

We were listening to him, astonished.

"You know what, miss?" he turned to her, breathing into her face. "It makes no difference to you what you look like, since you can't see yourself in the mirror anyway."

I got up and left the room.

I went to the administration office and reported the professor's remark which I found very disrespectful and inappropriate. They couldn't do anything about it. At the time, a university professor was regarded as a god-like creature and had all the authority. I was very glad when my colleague changed the department so she didn't have to attend his classes any more. Shortly afterwards, the professor left the Faculty of Music and retired.

Professor Ms. B. was a top-class specialist in her subject, but had an absent-minded way of communicating with her students.

She was very forgetful and her train of thoughts changed from one note to another.

My favorite episodes were when she was sitting at the piano, with nine of us around her. She played with lots of technical mistakes but harmonically perfectly, humming along the way. All of a sudden she would turn to one of us:

"You, you sir, what's your name?"

"My name is..."

"Tell me," turning to another student, "how did you experience the last two bars of this sonata?"

"It's a classical work, composed in ..."

"I am not asking you about music history, on the contrary, I want you to give me your own impressions of this piece."

Silence.

"You will fail the exam," her finger pointed in the direction of that person. "You, you will fail."

She would resume playing, then stop, turn once again towards the unfortunate victim and repeat:

"You, you will fail."

Of course, she wouldn't remember that student later, so if you attended her classes and studied regularly, there was no chance to fail the exam. She was very strict but fair and sweet in her own way.

January, the depths of the winter.

The classroom big and cold, with high ceilings.

Silence.
We were listening to Mozart's Requiem.
Lacrimosa.
Violoncellos softly permeated all the corners of the room. Voices joined them:

Lacrimosa dies illa
Qua resurget ex favilla
Judicandus homo reus.
Huic ergo parce, Deus
Pie Jesu Domine
Dona eis requiem, Amen.

One of the most poignant melodies ever composed.
Even the winds outside stopped howling, listening to the dialog between the choir and the orchestra.

Bang!
Boom!
Bing!

The door shook, the old parquet squeaked and two maintenance men walked in, carrying four buckets of coal to fill up the burning stove.
The moment was forever lost in that noise.
They used to do that during the exams, distracting us deeply absorbed in harmonic and melodic riddles.
Professor Zora was, like always, full of life, energy and love for music. She had a wide-open heart, ready to give out to everybody. Some students took advantage of it, I'm afraid.
She was my dearest professor and I her dearest student, I believe.
Depending on her mood, she would completely change her image and we got familiar with her transformations over time. Whenever she entered the classroom in a coat and with a walking stick, it was a danger sign. When the door opened and Professor Zora appeared with a cup of coffee in one hand, a tub of yogurt

in another, cigarette in her mouth and wearing a vibrantly colored tunic, we knew the paradise was awaiting us.

She was a fighter.

She was strong and brave.

After two years of being her demonstrator, just before my graduation exam, she said she would take me as her assistant if I did my Master's.

"Of course I will!" I said, overwhelmed with happiness and hugged her.

Oh, if everybody could be like her!

The magic of music entranced us all, each in their own way. I was carried away by the spring waters of authentic folk music and started diving deep into them. My school choirs embraced with their pure children's hearts the songs that had always been a part of them. I was so proud to hear my little singers perform centuries old songs so naturally.

Music brings people together.

Music opens up new paths.

Music doesn't know of boundaries, hatred or wars.

Nora's Impressions

I'm crying out loud to the Heavens, bursting with anger because of injustice! What kind of order on earth is this? Why do people who are 'different' have to be chastised by the 'normal' society standards?

The beautiful white-haired colleague of Nikola's, with extraordinary music talent, pissed off by a drunk professor, just because she's an albino. So what?

So what if Nikola looks and dresses out of the prescribed code?

So what if my favorite private student has Down syndrome and the kids mock him, yet he's so much smarter than all of them!

So what if I act, in all kinds of circumstances, by listening to my heart and intuition rather than complying with politics!

Why does it always have to get back to us, people who are merely maintaining our own integrities?

Aargh...! Fuck the norms (pardon my French) and be yourself, that's what I say!

OK, moving on to the lighter notes. I speak several languages, used to be a strong believer in Esperanto, only to see it totally overshadowed by English, so bye-bye Latin roots that once upon a time were lingua franca in all Europe. But the language of arts is universal, as Nikola keeps reminding me, especially the one of music. Music literally breaks all the barriers and resonates throughout your body long after the last accords have been played. It simply stays within you, and the music and you blend.

Another kind of blending is watching a ballet performance, if you are into movement. I tend to ignore the sets, lights, and costumes, focusing entirely on the synchronization of ballet dancers' bodies with the music. Pliés, pirouettes, pas de deux, grand battements, strong leg muscles floating above the stage, port de bras, graceful arm arches flowing through time and space. I will say again and again that ballet is absolutely the most elevated of all arts (and the most demanding on its performers!).

Yet another way of catching the essence of universality is by painting and sculpturing, be it by yourself or by letting the work of other artists do the 'magic'. It's 'The Object Stares Back' effect, as is the title of James Elkins' marvelous book on the nature of seeing. The interaction between a piece of art and us is such a subtle yet powerful energy exchange, the process in which we both get metamorphosed.

If there's any chance of this world being re-created, I'll personally bug the Great Creator until he consents to populate it entirely with artists!

Act IV
Who Turned off the Light?

- The End of an Idyll
- Nora's Impressions
- Thunder from the Clear Skies
- The Keeper of the Blackboard and Chalk
- Nora's Impressions
- Days Are Going By
- Nora's Impressions

The End of an Idyll

I attended the lectures at the Faculty of Music and studied for my exams conscientiously. Also worked in the elementary school five days a week, rehearsed the choir for two hours after the classes, featured on the TV music show every week, and spent my Saturdays at the university as a demonstrator. Thrown in that pot were private students (to pay the bills) and getting together with my friends, so I really didn't have much time left to myself.

Mira was active in the Union and moved the mountains to get us some meat, quartered pigs, and chickens.

The economic crisis started to slowly dominate all spheres of life, seeping under our skin. As much as I was disgusted carrying a half-plucked skinny chicken in a garbage bag on the way home, the urge for survival was stronger than anything.

The Union also provided us with potatoes and sometimes with soap. It was laughable when once they distributed tooth brushes but no toothpaste! Toothpaste was a luxury.

At that time, I somehow developed a practice of expertly getting old people off the buses and trams so that I could get on. This was the usual scene: 7 o'clock in the morning, all working people waiting at the stops in long lines, trying to make it to their respective jobs or schools, for there was work to be done. An invasion of retirees equipped with shopping bags, leisurely on their way to the market or wherever, would push through the crowd, intent on securing their place on the public transport. Well, somebody had to put a stop at that!

The doors of a bus or tram would open, exhaling a sticky stench of sweat. In a fraction of a second, I would overview the situation, focus on a 65+ group, take them by the sleeves one by one, and gently throw them out.

"What are you doing, idiot?" they cried.

"The idiot is kicking you out of the tram!" I retorted.

"You'll see how it is when you get old!" they mumbled.

"When I get old, I won't use the public transport in rush hours, promise!"

Most passengers laughed and cheered, some frowned slightly.

My life path was wide and forked in its way, but it invariably pointed at one direction: music. No matter how things went, this way or that, with more or less favorable outcome, deep down it all came to the realization that music meant everything to me. Still, during the recesses at schools where I taught I noticed that my colleagues didn't talk about sales, travel plans or exchange recipes any more. They discussed politics instead. Politics had a way of sneaking even into our teachers' rooms.

Studying my music books on trams and buses, I would overhear people whispering and mentioning some names, unfamiliar to me.

Politics, politics.

The least important thing in my life; in the same rank with the Ball. My life was fast, beautiful and complete, without any politicians out there.

I visited the Filharmony, the National Theater, and the National Museum on a regular basis. Each new performance or exhibition was a must for me, professionally and personally. I lacked time for reading non-university books, the ones that were not part of the curriculum. I just wanted to read 'ordinary' books.

During the choir rehearsal breaks, while the children rested and drank fruit juices, I would hear some of them mention a politician and something about him. I couldn't believe my ears. Even the kids started being involved in all that!

I'm the only one who doesn't know anything, I thought.

That evening I called Nora and we talked at length about what was going on around us. Nora hated politics, but she knew everything. She had a first-hand knowledge, from her grandma and grandpa, about political stirrings preceding World War I, the period between the two wars, the causes of World War II and the after-war period.

As for me, the creation of the world happened in 1945, with partisans, liberators, and Tito; beloved Tito leading them into victory. I was educated that way while growing up in a socialist climate, and as a musician with a sensitive soul, I took all the revolution celebrating movies, songs, and literature very seriously to heart.

Bloodstained Fairytale, a poem written by one of the most eminent Yugoslav women poets, Desanka Maksimović, soaked my pillows with sorrowful tears in the days of my youth. The scene from Sutjeska movie, so deep and utterly sad, the underground trenches where a father puts the palm of his hand against a German rifle pointed to his son's head, hoping that the Nazi couldn't tell the difference between the soil and the flesh and would go away. The scene from Neretva movie, where Milena Dravić, one of the most prominent actresses at the time, dying from typhus, begs to have her hair back, in her velvety voice. All that lived deep inside me. As well as the emotionally-charged scene from Užice Republic movie, where a little starving orphan boy with wide-open eyes asks the baker: "Is all this bread yours? Can I take a bite?" In the same movie, Božidarka Freit, another great actress at the time, enthusiastically urges women, mothers, sisters, and wives to take charge.

There were lots of war movies and series in the same vein, and like an addictive medication, they added up to my feeling safe and protected in my Yugoslavia.

Yugoslavia has always been such a beautiful country with a variety of souls living peacefully under the same roof.

What is happening now, I asked myself, listening to the comments on the streets.

Nora said that people were awakening to their own national consciousness, depressed for so many decades. I didn't understand a word of it. Nationalism?

We are all happy Yugoslavs, loving and respecting each other!

Nora's Impressions

Nikola is studying for his exam in Music History while I'm indulging in volume after volume of Alan Ford comics. We are cozily cuddled by his cute garage apartment.

At one point he looks up from his books.

"Hey, Nora, why aren't there any examples of Renaissance and Baroque music in Serbia, or any such influence in visual arts, for that matter?"

"Right, who was Serbia occupied by in those times?"

"Occupied?"

"Well, it was under Turkish domination, part of the Ottoman Empire, from the late 1300s till the second half of the 19th century."

"It was?"

OK, Nikola is so smart and knowledgeable about almost everything under the sun and is actually quite familiar with the world history, but when it comes to national history, I can only smile at his blessed ignorance. It's as if he has consciously blotted it out.

Hey, Great Creator, are your ears pricked up to hear this? See how our 'little project' can easily become a reality? A world populated entirely by artists, just to remind You, creatures of pure hearts and souls. A world devoid of politics and wars. An earthly paradise for every living being, as easy as that!

Aargh...! Nobody's listening to me.

Anyway.

What is happening in Eastern European countries in the late 1980s and early 1990s, sort of resembles Italian Risorgimento, but in reverse. In both instances, it's about the awakening of nations. In the case of Italy, it's always been one geographical unit, one nation speaking the same language (in a variety of dialects), sharing the same religion and more or less the same culture. Just that the country itself was divided for centuries into numerous small kingdoms, duchies, aristocratic republics, and independent cities, so Italians naturally wanted to unite at one point, which happened in the second half of the 19th century.

On the other hand, Eastern Europeans, so many different nations gathered under the same umbrella of socialism/communism, want to separate and go their own ways. They've been suffocating for decades and now simply want to breathe, stands to reason. Besides, the mammoth of the Soviet Union is dying at any rate, in a similar way that Austro-Hungarian Empire passed away with World War I.

The Baltic Republics, Lithuania, Latvia, and Estonia are the first ones who raise their voices. Poland, led by Lech Wałęsa, is the first one who gains the independence the hard way. Hungary and Czechoslovakia (in its 'velvet revolution') do the thing elegantly and smoothly. Events leading to the liberation of Romania are a bit more dramatic, but people are finally free. Bulgarians follow suit.

So, only Yugoslavia, which has never officially been under 'the iron curtain', remains the last staple of a regime that doesn't exist anymore. Being such a mixture of nations, nationalities, religions, languages, cultures, and traditions (so lovely and colorful), it has to cut its Gordian knot and throw out its Sisyphus stone in the most drastic of ways – by war.

It's so totally obvious, from the TV news and the general social climate in the city, that the once peaceful and comfortable country is on the brink of a civil war. It's quite scary waiting for it to inevitably break out, like being inside a horror movie when the introductory creepy music starts and you can only guess what comes next.

All those socio-realistic movies and songs have been lulling us into an illusion of safety.

Now we have to face the reality.

When the ever increasing crowds start gathering on the streets with a terrifying frequency, it's a sure sign that things are taking the turn for the worse. Especially when these crowds emanate the stench skunks can die from. Yes, the country is in a serious economic and political crisis, but that's not an excuse for holding on to your three-week old sweat, for God's sake! Like, water is still available and there's still some soap in the stores, so wash people, wash, try at least to keep up the appearance of human dignity!

Also, it seems that about two thirds of Belgrade population has just been released from geriatric wards. With all due respect, where are all these old people heading to, milling around like an invasion of yellow ants? I mean, there are so many more pleasurable ways to spend your retirement days, like reading a book in the quiet of your home, taking care of your grandchildren, or planting flowers in your garden or strolling in a park, than adding up to the mass confusion out there.

Just what does this fat guy with Stalin-like features think he's doing? I'm simply trying to get to my university classes on time and he's talking some nonsense in front of the National Assembly to the herds that have been pulled out of factories and driven by special buses so they can give their wholehearted support to the iron hand of the new leader!

How can they even listen to his voice, so unpleasant and unnatural!

Besides, his party is blocking the traffic in the downtown core and I'll miss my classes because of the stupid bastard!

If I spit, like real hard, into his pig face (no insult to pigs intended), he'll choke like there's no air left in his bacon lungs, and if I hammer my bony fist into his fleshy ox neck (sorry, oxen), he'll belch his last breath away, like, fucking hell!

During the demonstrations of the opposition (which also turns out to suck big time) in the years to come, he'll be equaled to Saddam Hussein from Iraq. I don't know about that guy, but this one's just garbage and belongs to a dustbin! That's all I say.

For once, somebody listens to me, when he's brought to the High Court of the Hague, accused of genocide and violation of human rights, imprisoned for life and eventually dies there.

Ha!

Great Creator, we might still be doing business together, after all!

Thunder from the Clear Skies

That evening on October 13 1989, I didn't have anything much to do, so I was switching channels on TV, looking for something nice to watch. It was too early for the rerun of one of my favorite series and there were no movies on. My glance fell on a meeting at an assembly. It was in Ljubljana, Slovenia, its president Milan Kučan and all the politicians dead serious, wearing badges with a green leaf on their lapels.

He was talking about Serbian attacks on Albanians in Kosovo, about complete disrespect of human rights and how Slovenia didn't want to be a part of the country in which one nation mistreated another.

I was struck like by a thunderbolt.

They were publicly renouncing our beautiful Yugoslavia!

As a matter of fact, there had been some stirrings a bit earlier. I remembered scenes from a live TV show reporting the celebration of the 600th Anniversary of the Battle of Kosovo, in Gazimestan, and masses of people – Serbs with their flags, songs, and national costumes. There was a lot of talk about Kosovo as the cradle of the medieval Kingdom of Serbia and Albanians now destroying Serbian monasteries.

That was the first time I saw such a huge gathering that was clearly political, but not Yugoslav oriented.

On the badge the Slovenian politicians wore it said: "Kosovo My Country", a phrase that made lots of hearts angry the following morning. Slovenian products weren't popular in supermarkets in Serbia that day.

I was sitting with Nora over our early morning coffee.

"But why do they want the confrontation, why do they want to separate?" I asked, unable to believe.

"They look somewhat differently on that, Nikola," Nora said. "They don't have that strong socialist-Yugoslav sense you do."

"Why?"

"Because they were a part of the Austro-Hungarian Empire for a long time and have been in this country for only a few decades," Nora sighed. "I'm pretty much sure they feel nostalgic about the class system, about Austria that used to be and what it is now."

"Isn't it better like this?" I was trying to convince Nora. "We have no worries in a one-party-non-class society, no opposition, everything nice and honest!"

Nora wanted to utter one of her 'poisonous' sentences reserved for very specific occasions and the words were just about to slide down her freshly-painted lips the color of ripe cherry, when she paused, looked at me and said:

"Nikola, don't change, I beg you."

She hugged me.

I hugged her.

"Just remain as you are," she said.

I listened to her advice as much as I could.

"Son, don't change and don't meddle into politics," Mom said a week later when I went to see her.

Autumnal colors painted an amazing picture over my rain-soaked hometown. Chestnut Street glowed in the flames of orange and yellow leaves. I ran its length holding my hand over my head. In October, chestnuts were falling from thick fronds, spilling into sidewalks. They were cocooned in spiky green shells. If they fell from higher branches, they could hit you really hard, even make you bleed.

The mouth-watering scent of just-baked moussaka wafted from the kitchen window, making my steps lighter as I climbed the long staircase to the house.

"Good evening, Mom," I said cheerfully.

"Good evening," she said somberly.

"What are you doing, Mom?"

"Watching the news."

That was out of character. Mom would read a book or watch a movie rather than the news. There must be something really hard boiling in the pot of politics, if my mom was sitting in front of the TV.

I sat down beside her.

The Keeper of Blackboard and Chalk

Once upon a time, people fell into categories of good or bad, tall or short. Distinctions could be broken down in multitudes of ways: beautiful or ugly, funny or boring, rabbits or turtles. Some new winds differentiated people by sectioning them into political parts. That was beyond my comprehension.

During the intermissions at the National Theater, the conversations were only about politics, not about the opera or the ballet we were attending. All of a sudden, everybody had an opinion and wanted to voice it. I had never felt more like I was dropped down from Mars or any other planet than in those days and months.

Wherever I went, murmurs and whispers in the style: "Have you heard that this or that one said this or that?" followed me on each step. Something was cooking and it didn't smell nice.

Slobodan Milošević went to Kosovska Mitrovica to find a total chaos going on between Serbs and Albanians. The situation threatened to escalate even more, so he stood up in front of the Serbian people and with a microphone in his hand, uttered the sentence: "Nobody is going to beat you!" which, by the speed of light, brought him to the throne of the government and in the center of political events in 1989.

In the course of the following weeks, some weird things started happening to us living in the capital. All of a sudden, on my way to work, a bus driver would stop, turn towards the passengers and say:

"The ride is over, everything's blocked."

Masses of people were standing on the streets or rushing from all directions towards the National Assembly building. Serbs from Kosovo were arriving by trains, in smaller or bigger groups, to share with the public, in front of the Parliament, their hardships and sufferings, as they put it.

Milošević would come to the podium and talk to them. More and more people were coming every day. I got used to walking to work for about an hour, from where I continued on foot to the university. The square in front of the National Assembly looked like a fairground: tons of people, music, placards, and flags.

I sprinted into the school one day, sweating all over. Right on time, one minute before my first class.

"From now on, you'll be on night duty until further notice," the principal announced while I was preparing the program for my choir.

"Night duty?" I was bewildered. "Where?"

"Right here," she said. "Another teacher will replace you and you'll be on duty from 10 p.m. to 6 a.m."

"But what needs to be watched and secured here?" I asked. "This is a school, nobody is going to steal blackboards or pieces of chalk!"

She looked at me angrily. She was a communist and a viper of a woman who wouldn't take 'No' for an answer.

"I said what I had to say," she seethed.

And disappeared into her office.

Starting from that evening and during the following two months, I acted as a security guard in the elementary school from 10 p.m. to 6 a.m. There was a TV in one of the classrooms, so time went by somehow. The worst part was that there were so many things I wanted to teach children, I had to rehearse my choir, for the competitions were just around the corner. It was important only to me, it seemed. Nobody else cared.

I lingered there night after night, studied for my exams, phoned my friends, talked to them at length. Nora would come to the school just after 6 a.m. We used to go for a quiet walk in Kalemegdan Park, at sunrise, arm in arm, get some breakfast, and then I would take off to the university. I was over-exhausted in those days, getting very little sleep.

Yugoslavia was facing cornerstone exams, just like me at the university. The difference being that mine were Mozart and Beethoven related, while the Yugoslav ones were to decide on the survival of a country and its nations.

Trains kept running to Belgrade, bringing more and more unsatisfied people. Serbs from Kosovo, steadily arriving several times a week, were joined by groups of residents of small towns, unhappy with their salaries or the way their bosses treated them. Then came farmers with their concerns about prices on the markets, fertilizers and tools of trade, for there wasn't enough gas for the tractors and the fields waited to be harvested.

People would come to the podium, sharing with others their sad stories, one after another.

Belgradians started 'going out' to the National Assembly, the same way they used to go out to concerts or art exhibitions. The square in front of the building became the center of all happenings, without traffic, always crowded with people.

Nobody could stay indifferent. In factories, offices, schools and on the streets, there were whispers about the war, about Slovenia wanting to separate – about Kosovo. Murmurs about Krajina, Serbian enclave in Croatia, started.

Like an ostrich, I was trying to bury my head into books, notes, and the piano. I did my best to hear nothing but music, but that was impossible.

The orchestra of human disappointment was deafening.

I started watching the news. Started to listen to people on the streets.

I started to realize that was a journey of no return.

Nora's Impressions

It's the crack of dawn, maybe 5 a.m. or even earlier, the sun hasn't risen yet. I drag myself out of bed and get into cold shower, like to wake up (there's no warm water, anyway). Only to realize I'm stuffing mascara in my mouth and smearing lipstick on my eyelids. Alright, reverse, eyes are up, lips are down. See, the upside down state of my country, even though I'm not particularly fond of it, is getting to me.

I put on some casual clothes and go on a quest to unbolt the chains of Nikola's night duty imprisonment in the cells of the elementary school. How I get there is an odyssey, like changing all the means of transportation that don't run properly, and basically relying on my feet.

But it's all well worth the effort! We walk at our own pace, hand in hand, in companionable silence, in Kalemegdan Park, a vast grassy area resonating with Celtic roots from the west and vibrations of Ilyric and Trachian tribes from the east, where the remnants of Roman and Turkish fortifications are still standing, all with wishing wells, towers, gates and draw bridges.

We watch the sun rise right over the confluence of two rivers, the Sava and the Danube, standing at the very spot where the Celtic Singidunum was founded and Slavic settlement later established, when Slavs descended the Carpathian mountains, followed the river and exclaimed at the sight of the place on the hill: "It's a white town!" which gave the city its present name Beograd = beo (white) + grad (town).

If nothing else, I pay tribute to my hometown then and there, which doesn't mean I don't want to get out of there as soon as possible!

These sun-risen mornings are our little oasis of peace and quiet in the otherwise very noisy surroundings, they are like real magical moments. After the walk, we dig into burek (oil-drenched thick phyllo pastry cheese pie, delicious!) in the nearby bakery and go to our respective universities or private lessons.

Impending war or whatever, life goes on!

Days Are Going By

My professor Zora was embittered by the situation in the country, but remained focused on her work, music, and writing books. One day, I was sitting in her kitchen, helping her to remove stones from sour cherries that a friend of hers had brought from a village. I had never been assigned such a task before, so I was clumsy and ended up staining myself from head to toe. The sour cherries were lovely, but de-stoning them was a hard work, even though I was sharing it with my dear professor.

We talked about my exams and about future. Sitting by the window on the fifth floor of her apartment building in the downtown core, we could see people passing on the megaphone to one another and hear what they were talking about on the main city square. Streets were overflowing with people. At that time, everybody had something to say and to criticize; everybody wanted to voice publicly what bothered them in the everyday reality, at work, in the country, on the political plan, on and on, all day and most of the night.

I was preparing for my final exams, played the piano a lot and worked in an élite school just across from Kalemegdan Park. As always, I had tons of private students. Nora was studying Italian and went to the university mostly on foot, since the public transport was virtually non-existent. Marko was playing the guitar in my garage apartment while I was away on short trips with my children's choir, or longer ones with Nora. Lela was married and about to give birth.

Mira was doing fine and her small children were growing up. Their apartment was close to the National Assembly and they could hear the echoes of demonstrators until late into the nights, between the noise of the rickety trams passing by. Mira now worked in a school just two blocks away from home, so she could spend more time with her daughters.

The younger one attended a ballet school and practiced with all her heart. Her talent was obvious, we all knew she would be great. Her ballet dancer friends were so sweet, especially one young guy, always smiling and bonded to her by genuine friendship. I enjoyed seeing them cuddled in front of the TV, watching videos of Nureyev, Baryshnikov and especially those of Maya Pliseckaya. They watched them breathlessly, discussing every movement vigorously afterwards. I knew the doors of success would open up for them one day; and so they did!

The elder one looked like the spitting image of Mira physically, but not mentally. She was quiet, focused, and extraordinarily smart, winning all the school awards that could be won. I loved being in their company, in that colorful, small kitchen with the big aquarium. Mira would concoct a meal on the spur of the moment and open a cold beer for the two of us.

Mira has always been a great fighter and that she will remain in all the years to come.

Nora was immersed in her world of Italian Literature, in Dante's Inferno, Purgatorio, and Paradiso. I learnt a lot from her in those days. On planes and buses during our trips, I asked her to tell me more about Dante's Divine Comedy. I loved her interpretation of the verses and many years later, I read a book, The Last Cato, inspired by the second part of Dante's trilogy.

Nora lived by herself on the fourth floor of a new building outside of the city center. Her apartment was spacious and decorated with style. We enjoyed sitting on her balcony full of plants and flowers and talking over innumerable coffees and sweets. Oftentimes, to my delight, Nora's mom would drop by, bringing us a pack of cigarettes and the food she had just cooked that morning. It was so nice being there, the three of us, chatting about everything: Nora's studies, my studies, this and that, anything really.

Nora's mom was entering deeply into my heart. She was a woman simply made of love, gentleness, kindness, smile, and beauty. Madame Violetta was a symbol of calm and balance. She had learned, during the long years of living with Nora's father, a hard-headed man with obsessive character and bad habits, to hide the suffering deep inside herself. Her smile never revealed the pain that was engraved in her heart.

If she had somehow made it to be the UN President, there would be no wars or conflicts in this world and the deserts of Sahara would be turned into rich fertile fields!

Nora's father was a cruel man, without a tinge of compassion. He was full of vices, without the tiniest of virtues. He couldn't stand me, neither could I him.

Nora's mom and mine clicked instantly and the two of them created a paradise for themselves in a spa where they spent a couple of weeks together every year, tucked into the warmth of their room, long walks in the parks and their 'sisterhood'.

Nora and I visited them once and in just one day we could see how so completely at ease they were, enjoying each other's company. We had the privilege to sit on the benches they claimed to be their own, ate ćevapčići (barbecued minced meat in the shape of a thumb) that were done 'just to the point' and 'the best in the spa', according to them.

They took us shopping to the local market.

They toured us through their kingdom.

Nora's mom was reading novels, my mom was knitting.

In the evenings, they would go out to listen to live music over some red wine.

Our moms were happy.

We were happy watching them enjoy life.

On the way back to the bus station, Nora said:

"I had an impression we were disturbing them, like they're having a super great time without us," she laughed.

"I had the very same impression," I agreed.

As I passed my exams at the university, one by one, with honors, burden was lifted from my shoulders. Some exams were more difficult than the others. More comprehensive subjects like Music History, I studied in sequences, divided by composers or periods, while waiting in long lines for the public transportation. My new piano professor was wonderful and approved of my selection of pieces to play for the finals.

On the other side of the universe, only a few blocks away, masses of tired, angry, and sad people still occupied the streets around the National Assembly. 'Depressed and oppressed' Serbs from Kosovo continued to arrive by trains, but it now became an everyday scene, so it had less impact on us, living and working in Belgrade. Still, I listened attentively to what was going on around me, for my military service was getting closer.

The conflicts in Kosovo worried me.

The Kosovo I knew was the one from the songs, ancient and enchanting. I had been in Priština, its capital, a few times, but since there wasn't even a tiniest doubt in my brain that somebody might not like to live in Yugoslavia, it had never occurred to me that Serbs and Albanians in Kosovo could be having a problem. Every time I visited Priština, Peć, and especially the mesmerizing Prizren, I met wonderful Serbs and wonderful Albanians. Walking on the stone cobbled streets of the old town of Prizren, I could feel the two worlds merging into one in the beauty of the place. The feeling was especially strong while climbing Kaljaja hill that keeps the secrets of centuries' old walls of the medieval Serbian castle. Even though it's just piles of stones now, those piles could tell long stories from the past. From the hill, there was a breathtaking view on Prizren in which, until recent times, two cultures had lived peacefully with each other. Actually, more than two – side by side with Albanians and Serbs, there were Goranians, people of the mountains, and Turks. The harmony of Prizren looked ideal to me, at least during my few days there.

Later, when Serbian refugees started coming to Belgrade, with their stories about burned-down homes, demolished churches, and ruined cemeteries, I didn't know how to react. I believe in the goodness of the human heart. I believe there is a spark within every single person that can easily transpire if we make just a little bit of an effort. The reality, however, wasn't on my side. It seemed that in the deep essence of human beings, hatred was more strongly rooted than love. All history was written by wars of nations against nations and attempts of one nation to convince the other that their beliefs were the only true ones, ignoring the other side.

From the South of Serbia, news was coming from my dear high school teacher about life being increasingly difficult, without money, foodstuff, and electricity more off than on. That saddened me a lot, for my teacher had always been so vibrant and full of lovely funny stories and her apartment a cultural oasis, untouched by politics or street gossips. Her daughter, Yvette, enrolled at a university far away from home. That was hard for her mom and grandma. Their baroque apartment was now void of Yvette's solo singing and piano playing. Silence entered one day, made its nest, and remained there forever. The cigarette smoke lingered above the dining room table at which the two women sat quietly, waiting for Yvette's phone call.

I always dropped by, every time I went to the South to see my mom. They were so dear to my heart. I would sit with them and tell them all about my exams, performances, and projects at the school where I was teaching. They would tell me how Yvette was doing great with her studies. She had lots of friends and they all loved her. I wasn't surprised, for she was a hard-working, sweet-natured girl, open-hearted, and giving. We would drink coffee after coffee and smoke tons of cigarettes, just like in good old golden days.

Politics never entered their magical place, but the inescapable reality of everyday shortages did. The political powers stayed outside of their wide windows, in the wind. That day, my wonderful teacher made, in my honor, hot sandwiches with sheep cheese and prosciutto that I loved so much.

That night. I slept in my old room in the house on Chestnut Street, in my hometown. Mom was washing the dishes after dinner she had prepared for the two of us: breaded roasted red peppers, soft white cheese, home-made bread, and coconut cookies. Mom has always been a great cook. She can make a royal feast out of nothing. She is always ready to exchange recipes and try something new, being a firm believer that "Health enters through the mouth" (a Serbian saying).

Surrounded by books from school reading lists and those of my early youth, and by the atmosphere of the past, I couldn't easily fall asleep, so I started leafing through scores, hoping to find some nice songs to perform with my children's choir at one of the upcoming festivals or competitions. Songs about Tito were popping up in front of my eyes, scores and scores of them, so much music dedicated to Tito.

Nostalgically, I put them aside.

I missed those times.

On May 4th 1980 at 3:05 p.m., Josip Broz Tito passed away. A legend of a man who was the head of Yugoslavia. A man who managed to put together and unite so many different nations and make a strong and beautiful country.

Now, there is no more Tito and there is no more Yugoslavia. Slovenia, Croatia, Bosnia Herzegovina, Macedonia, Montenegro, Serbia, and Kosovo became independent countries, separated from its core and went on their own ways. History will have the final word on the price they paid for that journey; we mere mortals are too small and insignificant in that matter.

The afternoon Tito died I was in my room, chatting with my best friend from the High School of Music over juice and cigarettes, when somebody knocked at the door.

"Oh, that must be Iron," I said to my friend.

That was the next door neighbor and sort of a poet. His verses were incredibly boring and made no sense, but I felt sorry for him and whenever he had one of his poetry readings, I would go with him and accompany his poems with some soft piano music. On one of those occasions, he sounded totally chaotic, like:

Iron – electricity
Charge – iron
Passion – iron pressed passion…

It dragged on in the same style. On our way back home, my best friend and I nicknamed him Iron.

He was standing on the threshold, his face swollen.

"Are you alone?" He asked.

"No, Voja is here," I said.

He walked into the room leaving the door open behind him.

"Young men!" he shouted like crazy. "It is time you understood what lies ahead of you, because," he started sobbing, "Tito has passed away."

Voja and I looked at each other.

Iron was crying loudly and inconsolably, jerking every once in a while to say:

"Our future is upon you!"

"Independence and self-management have to be defended!"

"Everything depends on young generations now!"

Left alone, Voja and I cried as well. The whole country cried. Mom just got back from my aunt Kankica's house, with red eyes.

What is ahead of us now, I asked myself that night in bed. Is this the end of the world as I knew it? All my childhood and my school days were marked by Tito. On the first day at the elementary school, the teacher said that Tito was watching over us from the picture above the blackboard and that he loved all of us equally. She also said we were not to believe in God, that was superstition; for how could there be God if nobody had ever seen Him?

When I repeated those words to Mom, she made the sign of the cross and apologized to God for what I said. She sat down beside me and explained simply and in a nutshell the whole philosophy of socialism, totalitarianism, and religion. Mom made me understand that in specific life situations, you have to lie a bit, for the sake of your own soul and heart. She said that Tito was a good man and a great leader of the country, but also that sometimes ideologies rush too fast towards the new, ignoring, neglecting or breaking up with the old completely.

"Son," she said, "the day you were born was the happiest day of my life. I worked in a tobacco factory then and was an active communist. I went to all the meetings and was full of ideas, so I soon got noticed and promoted. I was a good worker and a good communist, believed in every word that was said or written. I understood everything and respected everybody, but there was one thing I could never deny or give up – God."

"Weren't you afraid somebody would see you go to church?" I asked her.

She smiled at first and then got a bit more serious.

"Son, going to church isn't the only way to show faith in God. You carry God deep inside your heart, He is a part of me, you, of all the people who are honest and believe in Him."

She looked straight into my eyes.

"God gave me twins and by a doctor's error, I lost one child. You are the one left to me. You have been saved for me by Him. I had you baptized secretly. When I was at a communist meeting, far from you and our town, your auntie Kankica took you to the cathedral."

Thus, I found out that I was baptized.

Ever since then, I have accepted the fact that God is somewhere here around us, that we can feel Him more than we can see Him. On the other hand, I really liked the idealistic picture that the one-dimensional Tito's reality was offering.

Tito was a symbol of peace. Tito pacified some big countries and was one of the founders of the Non-Aligned Movement that was initiated by Jawaharlal Nehru and created in Colombo, Sri Lanka in 1954. The movement had as its goal the unity of the countries supporting one another and together, providing help where it was needed most, where people lived in total poverty. The first Conference was held in Belgrade in 1961 and was attended by representatives of twenty-five countries. The original five Principles of the Non-Aligned Movement were:

- Mutual respect for territorial integrity and sovereignty.
- Non-aggression.
- Non-interference in internal affairs.
- Equality and mutual benefit.
- Peaceful co-existence.

What a pride it was for all of us when Tito's dignified walk on the runways of far-away, exotic countries was broadcasted in the 8 o'clock evening news on TV1. His gorgeous wife Jovanka walked slowly by his side, elegantly dressed and made up, with a big bun on her head and a warm smile on her face.

The Non-Aligned Movement basically had a very reasonable idea. In the late 1970s, it started weakening internally because the expansion of oil in some of the member countries made them very rich, and also because of the external accusations that it was 'pro-Russian'. One part of the world apparently didn't want that movement to get stronger. Slowly but steadily, it was extinguishing. The last conference was held in Havana in 2006, without much publicity.

Tito was no more.

The chains of sorrow tightened around us.

The High School of Music looked sad, Tito's pictures on the walls were lined with black ribbon as a sign of grief. Then, our choir started performing ten to fifteen times a day, singing songs about Tito at all the imaginable commemorative sessions in the South of Serbia. I guess it must have brought a lot of money to the school and to our conductor, but in that moment, it was irrelevant.

Tito was no more.

The first big concert we gave was on the main town square in Niš. The podium was constructed to hold several united choirs, about three hundred of us singers. The sky was angry, crying bitterly over Tito's death. When we started singing, the rain poured over us and the orchestra. I was singing and proudly stayed drenched, feeling I was doing that for Tito. Day after day we performed in various factories, offices, and schools, listened to speeches about Tito, his deeds, words, and actions. If somebody had said to me then that only about ten years later Yugoslavia would find itself on the very edge of an abyss, I would have told them they were just big liars.

We were stronger than ever, I was sure of that. Tito's ideas lived within us.

My whole generation and the previous ones were raised and grew up under the umbrella of Tito's socialist paradise and we found it really hard to accept the end of a dream.

Tito was blamed for everything that was happening to us after his death, as if it was all his fault.

All those inspiring songs that were running in my veins became good for nothing. Tito's pictures were eventually removed from the walls of all the classrooms, offices, government institutions, and universities. Nobody said that he was watching over all of us anymore.

Nobody, nobody was watching over us.

Nobody cared about us.

I went to his grave several times to pay my respects.

Criticism of him and his time was getting stronger and sharper. Some newspapers wrote about his international loans, to explain the huge debt Yugoslavia was in, some others about his wasting money on trips to the Non-Aligned countries. He remained a target for attacks long after his death.

It's easy to criticize those who are not there.

And he was not there anymore.

Nora's Impressions

The everyday realities don't bother me too much as long as I have my Italian books around me. Nikola and I talk about Dante's Divina Commedia as I draw pictures of the circles of Inferno, Purgatorio, and Paradiso, cross referencing them with mythological, historical, and religious characters' associations. We enjoy Petrarca's sonnets and Boccaccio's Decameron, move on to Machiavelli, Ariosto, Tasso, Marino, Goldoni, Foscolo, Leopardi, Manzoni, D'Annunzio, Pascoli, Montale, Svevo, Pavese, Pasolini, Sciascia, Calvino, Cassola, Deledda, Ginzburg, Moravia, and wrap it all up with Eco.

He and I have been student and teacher to each other for like, forever, and so is everybody in this world to everybody else. That's what life is all about deep down – a never-ending learning process.

My mom and Nikola's have been sisters in spirit from times immemorial.

My mom is an Angel, just dropped from the Heavens, where she returns.

Nikola's mom is a true sage woman, spreading her wings on this plane.

They are both our moms.

Fatherly love never flows in my direction. There's not an inch of a common ground that the man who happens to be my father and I share, so I try to avoid him whenever possible and shake him off like an annoying bug or a speck of dust off my feet if it's absolutely necessary to make a contact. He's done a lot of bad things to all the people around him, especially to Mom and to Nikola: turned my healthy mom into a diabetic by his constant brain washings (the guy is a doctor, for crying out loud!), purposely sent Nikola to the Army and then accused him for Mom's heart attack when the war started (does a sane mind come into the picture here?).

There's no pardon for things like that! Without another word wasted on him, I'm mentally sending him directly to the 9th circle of Dante's Inferno, let him freeze deep down there in the eternal ice in the company of Lucifer where he belongs, and may he enjoy! Ha!

The day Tito dies, Mom and I have just got back from touring The Netherlands, after a fabulous week of visiting Rembrandt and Van Gogh, reveling in boat cruises along the canals and the architecture of tall narrow gabled houses, Dam Square, and a peek into the Red Light District in Amsterdam. Then we go to the open-air tulip exhibition in Keukenhof, experience the busyness of Rotterdam and the graveness of The Hague, stroll on the North Sea beaches of Scheveningen, see the miniature town of Madurodam, and indulge in creamed coffees and pastries and Edam cheese along the way. We meet some friendly people in the village of Marken who take us to their bedrooms to show us the built-in-the-wall beds and finally collapse on our own beds in the hotel across from the Artis Zoo, loaded with bags after a good big shopping at the Sunday flea market on Waterlooplein.

That's the thing about Mom – she travels the world, moving swiftly and smoothly from one point of interest or pleasure to another and always knows her way around without a map!

OK, she studied geography, but still, how can you have the layout of every single city and town with all the landmarks like imprinted in your brain?

Bugs me. I'm pretty good at orientating myself in new places, but she has all the itineraries neatly figured out like, beforehand!

So, Tito dies, but he was old and sick so naturally expected to die one day.

Mom looks just a tiny bit worried as the 8 p.m. News announces the news, and we go on unpacking our suitcases while sipping a nice creamy coffee.

In the course of the following week, relatives from outside of Belgrade start coming to our house like they want to attend Tito's funeral. I have to attend it, too, involuntarily, because we don't go to school that day but have to walk in organized miles to bow to his coffin displayed in the National Assembly. Mom and I were obliged to do the same to the mummified Lenin in the Kremlin on our trip to the Soviet Union a couple of years ago. I put a black ribbon in my hair for this occasion, like to pay my respects.

One of the relatives, stumbling over our doorstep, almost blinded by tears, wails inconsolably:

"I never had a father; Tito was like a father to me. What is going to happen to us now?"

Well, whatever is meant to happen, will – Tito or no Tito. Hey, it's just a president of a country that died, it's not the end of the world!

Tito was very smart in formulating his ideas and making them catchy. Really, who on earth would have any objections to the whole planet, not only the multicultural microcosm of Yugoslavia, but the macrocosm of the world at large – becoming one loving, peaceful brotherhood of nations, like the Non-Aligned Movement he co-founded; the globe being at the time divided between the strict West and the even stricter East, with cold war in full swing. He picked 'the middle way', as in Buddhism. Yes, the guy was super smart, I have to give him that; just that he knew it wouldn't last forever, but intentionally kept us in the belief it would. There's no pardon for that!

So now the 'living god' is dead and we are left to ourselves. But that's exactly what God has always wanted us to be, by giving us the very special gift of free will, to be our own true selves, strong and centered, coming from Him; and what the hack if an old man died!

People can fall into categories of nationality, language, religion, tradition, culture and whatnot. These are all artificial divisions, invented by politicians and statistics offices. The only true difference between people falls into good – bad category.

I tend to look at the world from the Yin-Yang perspective. In the black, there's a dot of white; and in the white, there's a dot of black and they form a perfect circle. Dualities unified is what makes the world go round. Just ignore the gray area.

Another thing that transpires on the scene is love versus hatred. As a believer in Universal love, I can't overlook the downside of the wheel.

My Sociology professor tells us a little story in one of his lectures.

An old lonely woman is sick and dying and wants to commit suicide. Her therapist asks her:

"Is there anybody you love and would want to live for?"

"No, there's nobody."

'"Is there anybody you hate?"

"Yes, lots of them. I hate them so much I'll live to see my revenge!"'

There's a simple way to avoid all misunderstandings, conflicts, fights or wars between people, to erase all kinds of boundaries and prejudices, and to make everybody peaceful and happy. It's so easy to do, you don't even have to think about it.

So don't think, just do it.

Put the palms of your hands together in front of your heart, lean your head graciously towards a person in front of you and say the 'magic' word: 'Namaste'. It translates from Sanskrit loosely as 'The light of me bows to the light of you' and is the most beautiful, all-encompassing greeting ever invented!

Prejudice leads to discrimination, and discrimination can have much more subtle manifestations than direct oppression.

There's an Indian family, living on the same street, just a few houses away from ours. None of the neighbors want to mingle with them, like they carry some strange diseases and viruses; like you'll catch cholera if you just look at them. Well, look at them: the father is a diplomat at the Indian Embassy in Belgrade, the mother wears the most elaborate saris and a green dot between her eyebrows, and the boys are brimming with peaceful energy.

Mom takes the two-year-old me to their house to welcome the new family into the neighborhood. Mom is fluent in Hungarian, German, French, and Serbo-Croatian, and the Indian lady speaks Hindi and English. So Mom does her little performance of body language to communicate and the Indian lady simply puts her hands in front of her heart, bows to us and says: "Namaste". Mom and I do the same and are invited to her house for tea; and I play with the boys who become my absolutely best childhood friends. They're such fun to be with!

Over the course of years, we get regularly invited to all their lavish parties and celebrations, fireworks of vivid colors, artistically arranged food and exotic scents. We kids indulge in peppered new potatoes!

When Mom, at one point, ends up in hospital with a broken meniscus (too much careless running up and down the stairs, but then, that's Mom), the small boys take care of the little me like experienced nannies, and their parents visit Mom in the hospital every day, bringing her flowers and her favorite food: hotdogs. They are vegetarians, but manage to find the best hotdogs in the city for her!

Other kids avoid coming close to our terrace and garden when the boys Dippi and Nitou are there (as they almost always are), and I couldn't care less! Their loss!

Like Nikola, I also get baptized secretly. My father being a military doctor, communist, and atheist, Mom doesn't think it's right to have the baptism done like behind his back. Then my njanja, my grandma that is, takes the strings into her hands, brings the priest to the house, dresses me in white lace from head to toe, gets me a godfather who gives me a silver teaspoon (all that while my father is blissfully absent as he is most of the times), and voilà – I'm baptized!

My njanja and I don't have enough time on this earthly plane to get to know each other properly, but have always shared a very special bond. Every spring, she brings me the very first strawberries, deep red and fragrant, abundantly covered with sugar, in a mug with a nice picture of a little boy fishing by the river. Then, my dear njanja dies just a few days after my fourth birthday. Next spring, Mom brings me the first strawberries, but it's the wrong mug and the wrong amount of sugar and I refuse to touch them. Even today, strawberries are my least favorite berries (and I can live on berries alone), for they are not deep red, fragrant, and sugary any more.

Mom and I have a conversation similar to that of Nikola's and his mom's regarding religion, just that I'm a bit older than Nikola at the time. Like, we (Grandma, Grandpa, Mom, and I that is) celebrate Christmas and Easter and go to church whenever we feel like it. The teacher says there's no God, but I don't listen much to what he says anyway. I don't speculate on God's existence either, for I just feel He's everywhere and simply take Him in.

I recognize His presence when Teresz tanti (my great aunt Theresia Maria) arranges dolls in fancy dresses crocheted by her hand, complete with hats, gloves, slippers, and purses in lovely shades of pink interspersed by white, picture books and chocolate eggs along her long window sill before sunrise on Easter Sundays, saying the Easter Bunny has brought it all to me. I pretended I didn't see her doing all the work by herself at the crack of dawn.

I recognize His presence in Anus tanti (my great aunt Anna Maria), my dearest one, in her soft eyes clouded with tears when both my grandparents die and she takes up the role of replacing them, in the safety of her warm bosom whenever I need consolation. I know she'll always fix whatever kind of mess I somehow manage to get myself into, in the comfort of her cheese dumplings, specially made for me.

Mom explains scientifically how the Immaculate Conception is actually possible and how Jesus is a true revolutionary, with great ideas that people of his time were unable to understand. The baby Jesus of my Christmases transforms into a real man, the gentlest person who has ever trodden this earth, whose teachings about love and compassion are so beautiful and who gets crucified because he exposes stupidity and greed.

Two thousand years later, human race is no smarter.

They obviously have no ears to hear.

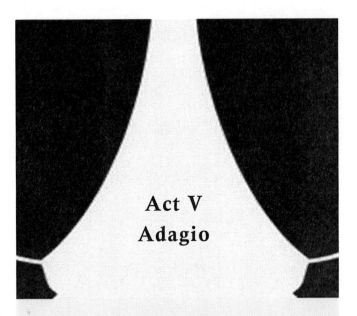

Act V
Adagio

- Ivica and Laura
- Nora's Impressions
- Flight Attendant Between the Earth and the Sky
- Nora's Impressions
- Nora's Impressions
- Frozen Warsaw and Hot Hearts
- Nora's Impressions
- Veronica
- Nora's Impressions

Ivica and Laura

Nora's birthday that year, in 1987, was coming closer and I was thinking of how to surprise her. I wanted something special, something that would make Nora overjoyed. So I decided on a weekend in Arandjelovac, a beautiful green spa in the West of Serbia, with a magnificent park and a dignified hotel called simply The Old House. The brochure promised canopy four poster beds and antique furniture. And it was exactly like that.

Our room was transported into another time and century. From the very entrance into the hotel that was built in 1843, we could immediately feel an out of ordinary warmth. Amazing canvases hung on the walls and crystal chandeliers glowed above us. Our room was luxurious and fabulous, with a view to the park. Nora stepped out on the balcony, inhaling deeply the evening air.

We were lying on the bed, smoking, eating chocolates, and watching TV. In one moment, I blinked hard, not believing my own eyes.

"Nora, look!" I cried. "It's In the Register!"

In the next forty-five minutes, we were immersed into the magical landscapes of Croatian Zagorje and into Laura's captivating eyes. That series has always been my absolute favorite. I have it on DVDs now and watch it from time to time. My passion for it may have cooled down over the course of the years and after watching it over and over again, but its charm remained.

Our room blended so perfectly with the series, with our canopied bed from the mid-19th century, which was exactly when the story in the series was taking place.

Then we walked in the park, looked at the sculptures, and analyzed them. Arandjelovac Park is fabulous, with marble sculptures, modern and classical on every step. The Marble and Sound Festival, where musicians perform in the vast green, is held there every summer. Some sculptures simply take your breath away, you want to sit down next to them and observe them for a long time.

The unpleasant part of the trip was that my paternal aunt lived in the same town.

"Nora, I don't feel like going to see her, I really don't." I hesitated.

"Don't be like that," Nora said. "She's your aunt, we're probably very close to her house, so we'll just drop by and say, 'Hi'. What's the matter with you now?"

Nora averaged 50/50 in succeeding to convince me to do something, which was a high score, for even though nice and polite, I have a reputation of being an extremely stubborn person. Visiting my aunt wasn't exactly my idea of a great evening out, but on the other hand Nora was right – the aunt, no matter what she was like, was part of a family.

Her house was indeed only a short walk away from The Old House. We bought flowers, a box of chocolates and Nora had brought some crystal figurines. Aunt's house was at the same spot as before, the same red one, on the corner of the street. A torrent of memories rushed in, almost blinding me. I stopped in front of the staircase, white as a sheet, as if I had seen ghosts.

"No, I can't go in," I said, frightened.

"Come on, we won't stay long," Nora was persistent.

Throughout my childhood and early adolescent years, I had to spend at least one month every summer at my aunt's, in this red house. That was a duty, something that inevitably had to happen, like the change of the seasons. Summers meant going to the aunt's in Arandjelovac. She was a tall big woman with pitch black hair, always in a house gown, married to a quiet, good-natured man with a thick mustache.

Their marriage was peaceful and comfortable except that they didn't have children. Being the youngest child in the whole extended family and my father being her first cousin and respecting her a lot, I would be sent to stay with her every single summer, until I was fourteen and said "No!" which caused a thunderstorm of shouting on my father's part. I was at the age when he couldn't beat me anymore. Even if he had tried to, I wouldn't have let him.

My aunt was a good woman in many ways, but like all of us, she had her downsides. She was so nice to me, played with me, was filled with pure kindness all day, until the evening when the phone rang, bringing my mom's voice from the other end of the line. That long month of separation was very hard for Mom. It was hard for me, too, but I didn't want anybody to notice it and hid my feelings deep inside me. The aunt always changed after the conversation with Mom and became cold, almost cruel. She was jealous of my mom because Mom had me. She was envious because Mom was educated, painted her eyelids, had a lipstick on her lips, and was elegantly dressed. Mom's hair was always nicely styled and she wore shoes on platforms and high heels, as was the fashion at the time.

She hated the way my mom talked, in a paced, cultured tone, using sophisticated expressions, the way Mom would put her hand over her mouth if she accidentally yawned. She couldn't stand Mom talking about theater performances and the latest movies.

My aunt was an ordinary woman, but she purposely made herself even more ordinary. Some women in Serbia decided to take that path in life. Once they got married, they would start wearing the same worn out dresses day in day out, put broken slippers on their calloused feet or men's socks and wore their husbands' old shoes when they went outside. They stopped caring about themselves and eventually didn't look like female human beings anymore. Then some years later they would wonder why their husbands went away with another woman, leaving them in sorrow and misery.

My aunt and I used to go for 'our adventures' in the huge park that was a museum in itself. I have been an art lover since my early childhood. The aunt would pack a few sandwiches or donuts – freshly fried that morning, and we would slowly make for the park. There were eight fish ponds there and I liked to look at the fish swimming and enjoying the sunny day. I had my favorite sculptures and would stand in front of them for a long time, or sit down if there was a bench nearby and gaze at them.

Each bore a plaque with the title, name of the artist, the year in which it was sculpted, and the country the sculptor came from.

Mom usually came at the end of July, stayed for a maximum of three days, and took me back to the South of Serbia. Oh, what joy to travel with her back to my house, my room, my bed, and library! The aunt always cried bitterly at the bus station and in those moments, I was really sorry for her. She was a lonely woman, longing for a child.

I had been her child for about ten summers, when she got pregnant and gave birth to a little boy. Since she knew nothing about babies, my mom was sent, by my father's orders, to spend a few months with her and help her out.

Whether because of the childbirth or who-knows-what, my aunt changed drastically and became a monster of a woman. When she didn't yell at my mom, she cried and freaked out about everything. If she saw me sitting quietly in the room, drawing and painting, she would scream from the top of her lungs:

"Your son's goin' to destroy my whole house, he's goin' to ruin everything I have, so let it, let it, so, so, poor me, poor me…" She would wail.

Her husband stood it all stoically, like a stone. Our meals turned into her incessant crying and shouting at me and Mom. Whatever my mom or I did, it was so bad to the extent that she would run out of the house and loudly gossip about us to the neighbors gathered on the street, listening to what was going on.

"Calm down, Andja, have you gone nuts, that woman's all to you, where'd you be without her? You crazy-head!" they said.

"What's got into you, Andja? Have you gone blind? That woman's doing all your washing an' cleaning an' cooking an' is tending the baby an' you just sleep. What's got into you, stupid?" they asked.

My mom had already had more than enough of that torture, but there was no way out. My father had sent her on this 'mission' and she couldn't back off. If I had had the brain and the knowledge I have now, I would have said to Mom to divorce my father, go somewhere far-away and simply to disappear from his grip. I would have lived with her in a jungle or in a desert, just as far as possible from him who maltreated us constantly, her in one, me in another way.

Since the aunt was aware of the fear father imposed on my mom, she purposely tormented her, knowing Mom couldn't strike back. My father was her cousin and that very fact would make only her side of the story credible, regardless of what Mom and I had to say.

My father's role in my youth was aimed at creating the deepest complexes, tension, and pressure in me. His egotism and hatefulness for his own family hurt a lot in the first few years, until the emotional pain transformed into a constant wound that occasionally bled. For a long time, I thought I was somebody else's son, that maybe Mom had got pregnant by somebody else and then married him, but that wasn't the case, for I was the spitting image of him. He chose a wrong life path, the one of hatred, and on that path, my mom and I had to tread every day.

Orthodox religion honors the sentence from the New Testament: "If someone throws a stone at you, offer them bread." My mom has always strictly observed it. Not even the tiniest trembling could be seen on her face while the aunt was firing poisoned arrows in her and my directions. Mom listened motionlessly to the ugly words from the mouth of that unwashed woman with unbrushed hair. All of a sudden, one very hot July evening, in the midst of aunt's screaming, crying, and cursing, my proverbially quiet uncle stood up from the dining room table, turned towards his wife, slapped her in the face as hard as he could and said:

"Shut up right now, you evil woman. Shut up, for God's sake, and fuck off!" And he left the room.

She wept a lot afterwards. Our faces were silhouetted in the darkness that caressed the silence. My mom was lighting one cigarette after another, her eyes focused on something far away, far beyond the open window, following the distances known only to her. I was proud of my uncle because he restored some order in that house. I wasn't sorry for the aunt at all. He should have hit her harder, I thought.

The baby cried some time later and woke us all up from our musings. As always, Mom immediately made for the nursery to change his diapers, wash, and feed him, but the aunt took her hand and said:

"I'll go."

We left the following day. The aunt didn't get up to say goodbye. She excused through her husband that she had a severe headache and couldn't get out of bed.

I had the image in my mind of her lying in that unattractive bedroom, furnished with a huge wardrobe and a big quilt-covered bed, with disgusting yellowish wallpaper, all in tears and furious because she had been humiliated in front of my mom. All the previous days, she had been a queen, ordering my mom around, now she was ashamed. I was secretly glad for her suffering because she was really evil to my mom all that time.

I hadn't seen her since then. Her son was my cousin, now probably an adolescent. I didn't want to meet that family again. No threats uttered by my father could make me go back to that place. I erased it from my itinerary map and the aunt from the list of my relatives.

"Where's the bell?" Nora's voice brought me back to reality.

"Here," I pointed to a white bell button hiding in the creeper.

The aunt opened the door wearing the same style of dress she used to years ago, a house gown made of cheap fabric, with buttons all along the front, wrinkled and of dubious cleanliness. Her hair was a thick dark mess with lots of grays. She was beyond surprised when she saw us. At first, she didn't recognize me:

"Oh, my dear, is it you? Aah, poor me, I can't believe it! Sweet God in Heavens, is it really you?"

She was cheerful like a little child. How could I ever hate her? Impossible. This woman had given me so many beautiful and warm summers, acting as my mom all those years. We used to go on trips to the woods, pick wild strawberries, and paint together in my coloring books. Even though I wanted to, I couldn't hate her because of what happened that last summer I was there. Women change when they give birth, everybody knows that. Some become very strange, as though they undergo a total transformation. She was now standing there, in front of us, all smiling and clapping her hands.

"Aah, what a happy woman I am! C'mon, love, c'mon in!"

She invited us inside and made coffee. She couldn't take her eyes off me. She was glad to meet Nora. Her son was on a school trip. The uncle worked the night shift, so we didn't see him. After the coffee, we talked some more and then left. Her dining room looked exactly the same as it did many years ago: varnished furniture, figurines, and photos in the glass display cabinet, the old wood burning stove, and the framed needle point work on the walls.

"See, it wasn't that bad." Nora said as we walked back to the hotel. "She was really happy to see you."

"It wasn't bad," I echoed.

Nora and I went for a cocktail to a nearby bar in the Šumadija Hotel. Then we took pictures of each other in the park, sitting at the piano made of marble.

"Let's go, we don't want to miss it!" Nora said, grabbing her bag.

We ran back to the hotel, to the room with the canopy.

Laura and Ivica series was just about to start, with its beckoning music introduction which has always stayed within me. When, about ten years later, I worked in a lovely restaurant Kuchcik in Warsaw as a pianist, every night from 8 p.m. till midnight, I always started my performances with that melody. Now, before warming up with scales or accords, those are the first notes I play.

It was the last episode, in which Laura dies. Exhausted by her passion and disrobed of her long curly hair, she gets shot. I cried my eyes out. Nora knew about my attachment to this series, she understood my tears.

Many years later, when one war ended and another started and then that one ended as well, I managed to get all the episodes of In the Register on DVDs from Croatia, from my dear friend Marjan. I still love this series, even though I know every word by heart and still cry when the beautiful Laura dies.

Nora's Impressions

It's a Saturday evening. Mom is entertaining, as usual. People are mingling, kids are playing. The TV is humming in the background. Suddenly, the opening accords announce the new episode of In the Register, and eight-year-old me abandons the game she's been into, runs and gets, like, literally glued to the screen.

"She's too young to be watching this."

"This stuff is too heavy for a little girl."

"Shouldn't she go to bed soon?"

That's the 'well-meaning' guests, making remarks that Mom chooses to ignore. Even if she reacts, it won't shake my determination to absorb every scene and word, each fold of Laura's dress. I'm entranced, enchanted by life in olden times and by this huge love going on. I'm so positive that Laura is absolutely the most gorgeous woman in the world! Everything looks so dreamlike to my child's eyes; I'm living a fairy tale through this series, with characters good and bad.

A little boy, hundreds of kilometers away, is experiencing the same thing at the same time, just that I don't know it yet.

The teenage-me reads the book by Ante Kovačić that the series was based on and discovers the heavy undertones of obsession and the underlying dark sides of a human soul. It doesn't undermine the visual impressions stored in my memory, though.

Many years later, the little boy, who has grown up quite a bit in the meantime, just as I have, and I watch the same series together in the most perfect of ambiances.

It's my birthday. Nikola is treating me to a special weekend in Arandjelovac, a town where Prince Miloš, ruler of Serbia finally liberated from Turks, around the middle of the 19th century, built a summer palace for himself and his family, which has been converted into a hotel.

It opens up to a spacious sculpture park, tons of sculptures in white marble, spaced out thoughtfully so each one dwells in its proper place under a tree, or on a clearing and we visit them all, greeted into their homes which we're invited to explore. November leaves are settling on the sculptures, us, and the yellowing grass, with a splash of vivid colors.

On the restaurant's terrace, we eat some barbecued meat (that was in my carnivore days), accompanied by freshly-baked bread and tomato salad topped with cheese crumbs, while writing postcards to our moms and friends.

Somebody's lighting firecrackers out there and the park is ablaze with all the shades of pink, blue, yellow, and purple. We take some pictures. There's a local painter, displaying his work in the park. He's very good, actually. We buy from him an oil painting of poppy flowers just about to jump out of the canvas and a portrait of a woman in aquarelle that is now looking at me from the wall of my study.

We luxuriate in our suite, in the huge soft four-poster canopy bed and in the salon with the authentic sofa, chairs, and coffee table that once were used by the Prince himself. As we munch orange-flavored chocolates and idly switch TV channels, the re-run of our favorite childhood series, the story about Ivica and Laura, is on!

Just goes to show how everyone and everything is interconnected. What starts in the past continues in the future if it's meant to. Like, Nikola and I have known each other forever, are kindred souls, and one of the links that brings us closest to each other is our fascination with this series.

There's a question that's been bugging me for a very long time and I still haven't found an answer to it.

What is fatherly love?

Every day I see kids on the streets running happily into their fathers' arms, fathers lifting them high in the air and placing them on their strong, reliable shoulders, playing and laughing with them. Fathers protectively hugging the kids, and moms and carrying their grocery bags. Every time I see such an expression of affection, which is probably the most natural thing in normal families, I'm genuinely amazed and like in awe. I never got to experience something like that as a kid, and neither did Nikola.

Hey, fathers, Nikola's and mine! Why are we denied and deprived of your warmth, understanding, and love? Why is it we never ask you for help and advice when we need them, preferring to run away from you? Do we ever go willingly into your embrace on the rare occasions when you're in a good mood? No, because being close to you means more physical or psychological pain to us.

Are you satisfied with what you've done to us and to our moms, playing your pater familias role the way you think it should be played? Where's your heart been in all that?

Anyway, you are forgiven, your wives are free of you and your kids have better things to turn to. Just that Nikola and I would have liked to have had a chance to cuddle in your laps, interlace our fingers around your necks, kiss you loudly on the cheeks and feel safe, when we were little. An occasional heart to heart conversation would have been appreciated when we grew up, but apparently, neither of you has been made of that kind of material, so it's a let go.

Our strong, independent, self-sufficient moms, like prototypes of Viking women, make up for our fathers' shortcomings and thanks to them, Nikola and I become independent fairly early in life, in our respective ways.

There's a strange phenomenon happening to some people when they are sad, in the blues, depressed, grieving, or faced with situations beyond their control. It manifests in neglecting your personal self, usually on the body plan, thus victimizing yourself for something that's not your fault at all; like 'culpa mea' kind of thing. 'Fault' and 'fear' are the inventions of a human mind, they don't exist. Like, why should I bother brushing my teeth when my whole world is falling apart, right? Wrong, totally! You are the center of the world in your own microcosm and so is everybody else; just that people tend to forget it. The more we take care of our intimate temples, our bodies that is, the happier we will be and everybody around us and eventually the world at large.

An example of the downside:

An uncle of mine dies. My aunt, his sister, is so overwhelmed by grief that she lets her hair hang limply over her shoulders in greasy stripes for days and obstinately avoids the shower, as if it's been infested by plague. Her husband tries at one point, like five days later when the body odor starts to permeate the apartment, to tactfully draw her attention to some basic hygiene, to which she bursts out hysterically:

"For Heaven's sake, man! How dare you mention something like that in such a tragic moment? My brother has just died, how on earth can I even think about washing my hair!"

Well, we're all allowed to be sad every once in a while and terrible things can happen, like a part of an experience, but none of them can justify the neglect of our appearance! We want to stand proud and clean, as dignified human beings (who can actually learn a lot from animals), in whatever kind of circumstances, we owe it to ourselves!

At least I do. OK, I freak out when I notice that my left eyebrow has been plucked a hair too many compared to my right one and if one of my nails gets slightly chipped it equals the dimensions of a natural disaster. Remove the nail polish from all the nails, cut them evenly, file and buff them, polish them anew in two coats, not to forget the base and the top coat, is what I do in such a case, which might be taking the whole thing a bit too to the extreme.

Still, there's an easy, pleasurable, and accessible-to-all way to overcome everything that bothers you. You'll feel so uplifted after following this simple procedure.

An example of the upside:

Get rid of that old cracked nail polish (if you are wearing any) from your fingernails and toenails. Cleanse your face thoroughly, brush and floss your teeth meticulously, exfoliate the face, run the neti pot through your nostrils, clean your ears and gurgle the mouthwash. Wash it all off, give your face a few good splashes of cold water or run an ice cube over it. Apply a face mask (bought in a pharmacy or made in your kitchen from oats, honey, and a few drops of lemon juice). Play your favorite music, lie down, and unwind while the bathtub is filling up with warm water. Take off the mask. Throw some Epsom salts, bath oil, and bubble bath in the tub, sprinkle the water with rose petals, rosemary, mint, and lavender leaves, not necessarily all of the above. Light some tea candles, give yourself a good water massage with a sponge and then simply float. Wash your hair properly, use a hair pack and the conditioner.

When you are ready, empty the bathtub but stay in it while the water is flowing away. Watch all your problems and troubles disappear down the drain. Shed the callus from your feet and cut the cuticles around your nails. Take a long shower, alternating warm and cold water. Towel yourself dry vigorously. Apply your eye cream and face moisturizer (also infusions, serums, and line minimizers if using any). Concentrate on the areas along the chin, the temples, and the forehead. Treat your body to liberal amounts of a nourishing cream, paying special attention to neck and décolleté area. Perfume yourself profusely. Style your hair. Do your complete makeup, even if you're not going out. Polish your nails.

Make yourself a nice drink, you've deserved it!

By the time you do all this, you'll forget what the original problem was and your self-confidence will get a tremendous boost!

When you look good, you feel good and the whole world feels like a so much better place to live in! Has been proven so many times in practice; take it from me!

Wars and catastrophes may happen, your own world may be shattered to pieces, but hey, here's the beautiful you: cleansed and centered, ready to tackle every unpleasantness that might come your way!

People can hurt one another so many times, in so many ways, unintentionally or purposely.

As the time passes, even the most painful wounds will eventually heal physically or emotionally, yet they stay somehow more vivid in our memories.

The longer we bear grudge against somebody, the longer we carry the unnecessary burden on our shoulders.

So – pardon them and let go!

Flight Attendant Between the Earth and the Sky

Nora and I traveled like crazy, every weekend and whenever it was possible. The monetary system made it affordable for us, even though the economic and political crisis was palpable, or maybe just because of it. Everything you wished to buy, you could, paying by post-dated checks. Trips that up till then had existed just in dreams now became a reality.

For Nora's birthday in 1988, my idea was to spend the day in Sarajevo. Tickets were purchased and the flowers too. Unfortunately, the plane had a mechanical complication, so we decided to enjoy Belgrade instead, went for walks, to cafés, had a nice lunch, and bought a little white finch bird that we named Cleopatra. Out of all our flights, only the one to Sarajevo didn't happen, maybe as a sign not to go there, for it would be very hard for us to watch the destruction of that city on TV a few years later.

Ante Marković gave a nice try to tame the inflation and make the Yugoslav currency dinar convertible, but it didn't really work out, so the inflation was slowly but steadily increasing. For us, the middle-class, it was paradise on earth. Everything, literally everything could be bought on lots of installments. Whatever the cost, only the first installment was what you actually paid, the rest of them burnt under the fire of inflation which, at the time, was still like a kid in a kindergarten: young and innocent.

Traveling has always been a part of me, ever since my childhood. When I say traveling, I also mean day trips by bicycle to nearby villages or hiking in the mountains, supplied with a couple of Tetra Pak fruit juices, a coconut chocolate bar, and sandwiches that Mom invariably made like this:

- white bread with a spread of cream cheese
- ajvar (hot) sprinkled over
- a few slices of sausage
- pickled cucumber rings on top

And so, I used to travel by myself, with my backpack, on my green bicycle, to some picturesque places outside of the town. I met people who ploughed the fields and learnt from them how to plant peppers and how to weed around tomato stalks.

Some sweet village women waited for me when I let them know I was coming, welcoming me with a freshly-baked spinach pie or still-hot donuts. Their sons and grandsons were playing foot-ball with the likes of them, never having a kind word for their mothers or grandmothers. I praised them, told them their eyes were beautiful, but their hands were dry and cracked. I was secretly stealing the glycerin hand cream from my mom and brought it to these women. They were so happy. So was I.

One summer in the late 1970s, about ten kilometers south from my hometown, I was out in the fields, with my two dearest acquaintances: Živka and Radulka. Živka was a mother of four, married to a policeman, the only one in charge of the security of the village and its surroundings. His name was Milovan and he would drop by in the police car every so often to see how she was doing. He was always glad to see me there. On a hot July day, I said to him:

"Uncle Milovan, I don't know why, but I like police uniform a lot."

"So you'll be a policeman when you grow up," he smiled.

"No, I won't. I don't like what the police do, I don't like fighting. I just like the uniform, only that."

Milovan laughed softly, not wanting to hurt my feelings.

"Well, that's fine then, next time when you come leave your bicycle here in the field, I'll give you a ride to the village and a police uniform to try on, deal?"

"Of course, of course!" I was ecstatic.

When he left, Živka turned to me:

"Honey, my Milovan loves you a lot, like you're his own son."

"Maybe because you have four daughters, Aunt Živka."

"Maybe, honey."

The two women went on digging and planting and after a while, I made my way back home. I never told Mom about my friends in the fields just outside of the town. She wouldn't understand it and would be afraid. Always afraid of what might happen to me. Too much!

The D-day came.

Radulka was already in the field. She was a small woman, with deep blue eyes. She had two sons and a husband who liked to drink. He wasn't angry, violent or anything like that, on the contrary, he was a very nice and quiet man. His 'love affair' with alcohol sort of filled in some gap in his otherwise calm and ordered life. He was a good father and a hard worker in the village bakery. He would wake up before the first morning cock-a-doodle-doo to spend his working day, naked to the waist, by the burning stove, surrounded by the wafting scents of the freshly-baked bread. Then, in the evenings, after chatting with the children, dinner and affections given to his wife, he would withdraw into his room to drink silently. He drank only rakija, Serbian brandy, strong and yellow, that he made himself. Radulka loved him a lot and he loved her a lot.

"Aah, there's Živka comin'," she pointed her finger at the approaching figure.

Živka was carrying two big bags. I ran to her to give her a hand. The bags were heavy.

"What ever is it, woman?" Radulka asked.

"Aah, just them seeds for that garden down there," she waved.

I helped them as much as I could with my young hands. The earth smelled of health. Then we sat down in the shade of a big walnut tree, on a white and green blanket that Radulka always had with her. They spilled out the contents of their baskets: phyllo pastry pies, corn bread, smoked meat, and lard fritters. I brought some fluffy donuts that Mom had made the night before.

We simply enjoyed, mesmerized by the soft summer breeze that was so gentle, you could barely feel it in your hair. The silence was broken by the most beautiful sound I had ever heard.

Radulka stood up, straightened herself, and started singing:

A lass fell asleep,
Eeej, a lass fell asleep...

What a beauty! I was a kid, didn't know I would study Ethnomusicology one day, the treasure of forgotten tones and melodies. At the time, I was just a witness to a wonderful song unfolding its primordial harmony, etching deep grooves in my brain.

Živka came close to Radulka and repeated the lines, but in a different voice:

A lass fell asleep,
Oj, ejjj, a lass fell asleep...

I watched them enchanted as they hugged each other and went on:

By the roots of the oak tree,
Oj, by the roots,
Eeej!

Their voices were meeting each other in search of the best duet, interval or a constellation of tones. They were a symbol of beauty and music.

I was mesmerized.

I melted.

The last tones were still lingering somewhere between my ears and the high fronds of the walnut tree, when a sound of a car broke the spell. It was Milovan. He got out of his small police car, smiling, in a freshly-washed and ironed uniform.

"Hey kid, shall we go?"

"Yes, yes, Uncle Milovan!" I said happily.

The small police car was speeding on the dusty road to the nearby village. We got to his and Živka's house. It looked exactly the way I had imagined it, a real love nest. It was a cottage all in flowers. Creeper roses, white as snow, climbed all the way up to the roof, giving an illusion of winter in July.

Once inside, he offered me a coke which I gratefully accepted. I didn't ask for ice, for I knew the answer in advance: "There's none." Everywhere in the South of Serbia, soft drinks were consumed lukewarm or slightly coldish, never over ice cubes. The animosity between Southerners and ice was like a primal instinct. Being always a black sheep and a white crow, I liked my fruit juices and coke with lots of ice, in spite of my mom wrinkling her nose:

"You'll see how it feels when you get a sore throat after this," she used to grunt.

We were sitting in a nice kitchen. It was spotlessly clean and full of Živka's crocheted handworks.

"Let's try the uniform," he said.

He was undressing slowly, first the belt with all the accessories, rubber stick, gun, whatever. Then he took off his shirt, leaving the undershirt on. I looked in admiration at his arms and chest, covered by thick black hair. I had always wanted to have a lot of body hair when I grew up, but that didn't happen. My father was bald as an egg, body-wise, and I picked up his genes.

As if reading my thoughts, Milovan smiled:

"Živka says I'm her hairy monkey."

"Oh, Uncle Milovan, I would so much love to look like that when I grow up."

He roared with laughter.

"C'mon, try the shirt," he said throwing it to me.

It felt wonderful when I put it on. The shirt was too big for me, of course, but still suited me fine. While buttoning it, I sensed a strong scent emanating from it. I couldn't say whether it was pleasant or unpleasant, I only knew that the scent was powerful, filling me with an unknown sensation, the most unknown of sensations I had experienced till then.

He clapped me on the shoulder and took his pants off.

"Here, try these, too."

Now I was almost completely dressed in the police uniform. Milovan rolled up the legs of the pants for they were too long for me, put the belt around my waist and the cap on my head, and took me to the bedroom to look at myself in the big mirror with a beautiful dark-brown wood frame.

"I'm telling you, you'll be a policeman when you grow up," he said lighting a cigarette. "It suits you."

I liked my reflection in the mirror. I love the uniform, I was thinking. Maybe I'll become a policeman. That didn't happen, but in the course of my life, I always looked good in a uniform: soldier's in 1990 and then in flight attendant's in 2000.

I was posing to myself in front of the mirror, at the same time admiring Milovan's legs, muscular and hairy. He was most hairy on his belly. Whether a rising sexuality had something to do with this moment, whether I was hit by some cosmic power, I didn't know. I was listening to my voice realizing it was coming from me, but somehow it wasn't me who was talking. I was too young to know about intoxication by drugs or about trance, but I guess that in that moment, I was in a sort of trance. I was listening to my voice not believing what it was saying:

"Uncle Milovan, can I just touch that hair on your belly?"

"Aah, what are you talking about? I'm not a gay."

"What is gay?" I asked, for I had never heard the word before.

"It's..." he started and then stopped. "Never mind."

"Is it something bad?"

I was sorry I had spoiled the moment. I felt I had messed up something and didn't like the feeling. He noticed that I became ill at ease and came to me. He hugged me and we sat down on the bed. He looked into my eyes and said:

"Listen, Son," his voice was deep and velvety.

His breath smelled of cigarettes, sweetly and soothingly.

"Listen to me now," he repeated. "Men don't show their bodies to other men, but to women, because it's women who like to touch them, got it?"

"Yes."

I was so uncomfortable, the blood was rushing up to my face. I was most irritated by something I couldn't put my finger on. Without my permission, my lips blurted out:

"I didn't mean to be rude, Uncle Milovan, I don't know what's got over me. It's like I'm going to be sick, it's the first time I'm feeling like this now, like a fever."

He gave me a worried look, a look of someone who really cared.

"What is it? Does it hurt somewhere?"

"Yes."

"Where?"

I pointed with my head to the lower part of my body. Even though his pants were too wide for me, my stiff masculinity was clearly visible. It was the first time I consciously knew I was having an erection. It was strong and painful. The worst part was that I felt it wasn't the end of it, as though there was something deep inside, tightening and hurting.

"You're having a hard on," he started laughing. "It's fine, it's normal."

"It is?"

"Yes," he took a sip of coke. "All men have a hard on when they need it and sometimes when they don't." He looked at me down there. "Yours is big for a young guy, you'll make lots of girls happy when you grow up. They like it big and hard."

He stood up. I was still sitting. He took me by the arms to push me up.

"Let's go now, you've tried the uniform."

I started unbuttoning the shirt.

"Aah, fuck, now you're all sad, c'mon, give me your hand," he said.

I opened my palm, he directed it towards his belly, pulled up his undershirt and gently ran it over his thick hair.

The heat of his body, the feel of thick hair caressing my palm and fingertips, did who-knows-what kind of a miracle. I leant towards him, afraid I would faint and hugged him with all my strength. At that moment, I came. It was my first orgasm. I was dizzy, wanted to disappear, to be out of that room, that village...

He held me in his arms, patting me. There was nothing sexual about it, just comforting. He realized what had happened and didn't want to spoil my moment. Then, he gently took the shirt and the pants off me and sent me to the bathroom to wash myself down there, for there was a big wet stain on my underwear.

We went back to the field.

"So, how's the young policeman doing?" Živka asked.

"Super, I look great in the uniform!"

Biking back home, I rewound the movie, every single minute and detail of it. It felt good contemplating about it. That night, I made one more stain, on my pajamas.

My trips into the fields continued, get-togethers with Živka and Radulka, and sometimes with Milovan. Whatever had happened, stayed hidden in the silence of the bedroom, filled with the scent of quinces nicely arranged along the top of the wardrobe.

Traveling always awakens a certain power and strength within me. I am like a different person on trips, short or long. I enjoy the movement, by car, train, bus, but most of all, by plane. My love for flying has always been stronger than sexuality; stronger even than the love for chocolates, very pronounced in my case.

In the late 1980s, when the monetary system in my country was screaming under the burden of inflation and everything was upside down, I was buying plane tickets on installments. Their price eventually came to nothing, having been swallowed by the above mentioned inflation. It just took someone smart, like me, to figure it out.

At that time, JAT (Yugoslav Airlines) started to operate regular Niš–Belgrade flights. My mom was the very first passenger. She had the whole plane for herself. The 737 Boeing contained three crew members, the pilot, and my mom.

She lit a cigarette and took a sip of coke, looking at the sky and clouds from the window seat. As she was putting the cigarette out, a flight attendant came to her to say they were about to land. The flight took only fifteen minutes!

I waited for her at Belgrade Airport.

Then Nora and I took a plane to Niš to visit Mom the following week.

The two of us flew innumerable times to Pula, Rijeka, or Zagreb, just to have a good espresso, eat pizza or calamari and come back. As the inflation progressed, the paradoxes followed. At one point, the airport tax in Pula was higher than the cost of our return tickets. No logic at all!

What a cigarette is to a smoker or a drink to a drunkard, that's what a plane is to me, in a way. Not as an addiction, more like gravitation. It has nothing to do with music or children's choirs or anything else I've been doing. It has always been there as pure affection. The way the sound of the machines in a casino inebriate those who like to gamble, so have I been inebriated by the sounds and smell of planes; and I got the air freshener they used on JAT airplanes!

The very entrance to Belgrade Airport would make my heart beat faster.

"Last call for Yugoslav Airlines flight 702 destination Dubrovnik, gate A7."

To say nothing about the actual plane.

Window, always the window seat. I loved DC9 and its 2/3 configuration and Boeing 727-200, nowadays less used, for it's getting old.

I enjoyed the small Adria Airways propeller Dash 7 and the latest JAT Boeing 737-400.

My thirst for take offs and landings was unquenchable. My bookshelves were filled with timetables of almost all air companies in the world. I studied the airport codes attentively, learnt them by heart.

Nora often accompanied me to the airport. We would sit there in a café, sipping overpriced espressos, just so I could fill up myself with the 'music' of the flight announcements.

My passion for planes and the whole air industry and business was simply so enormously huge. Flying with Nora all over Europe, I was telling her about the types of planes, their seat capacity, and their strong and weak points.

I loved all planes and all their crews. I would enviously look at the crew, envisioning myself as a flight attendant one day. That has always been one of my strongest, innermost wishes.

I prayed to God every night to give me a chance and open up a way to my dream job. I prayed to the Omniscient to let me be a flight attendant, for I would do that job earnestly and proudly, taking care of every single passenger on board, especially of the weak, the elderly, and the children.

Like always, God listens to those who believe in Him. He listened to my prayers.

Much later, but not too late, I did become a flight attendant.

Nora's Impressions

Liberation, at least temporary, is anything that makes you feel at ease with yourself

In my case, it translates into:

- Waxing my body completely (getting rid of what I don't need, left with nice smooth skin).
- Walking for miles in parks and woods, preferably barefoot.
- Swimming, preferably skinny dip.
- Hugging the trees (ribboning my arms and legs around their trunks, letting their barks caress my cheeks, aaah... ecstasy!).
- Traveling!!!

Traveling is such a wonderful mind opener, brain stimulator and muscle enhancer. You learn geography, history, archeology, arts, all first hand, no need to dig into books. You learn about such a variety of customs and traditions, mythologies, and religions.

You are so much more enriched after every single trip, be it to a nearby village or overseas.

To paraphrase my grandma: "The more you travel, the richer you are."

To paraphrase my grandpa: "The more languages you speak, the freer you are."

So you visit places, see the sights, and listen to languages and dialects. You eat local food and chat with locals, using body language when necessary. Some of my most fulfilling conversations have been with rickshaw drivers in Beijing, China, them speaking no English and me just a few words of Chinese, sharing the same oil cloth covered table with flies landing on it at a street bar, quenching our thirst with tasty lukewarm beer during the monsoon season. You simply blend and go with the flow. Surrender. Feels... well, it just feels so peacefully natural in whatever country, city, town, or village you happen to be. All the time your legs are working like crazy to support the cravings of your senses. So much more to see, hear, smell, taste, and touch.

Energized and truly richer in your soul (the amount of money you have spent on the trip is totally irrelevant), you come back home, to whichever part of the world where your home is (my physical one is in Montréal, Québec, Canada, my grounding one in Budapest, Hungary, my emotional one in Warsaw, Poland, my spiritual one in Oslo, Norway and my inherited one in Belgrade, Serbia).

Sometimes I get confused as to which one I should come back to,

What airplanes are to Nikola, ships are to me.

I like the speed of the planes to transport me fast from one place to another. But I'm always so bored on board, like, "Are we there yet?" The structure of a plane trip is so predictable: announcements, snack, drink, flipping through music/TV channels, hot towels, meal, drink, movie, sleep, snack, coffee. Love to look at the fluffy clouds across the immense skies, though. Adore the take offs and landings: you leave a place so that you can experience a new one. If there are two or three stops on your trip to the destination, this becomes sort of addictive.

Boats and sailing ships are my thing.

I could live my entire life on one of them (envy those lucky people in Amsterdam of their floating homes along the canals, with flowers overflowing the outside window sills) simply being, watering and having a free swim any time I want it!

Never ever will I set foot in one of those luxury cruise ships! They are so artificial, they actually break the connection between water, man, and the sky.

You have attained liberation. Just say a heartfelt "Thank you!" to the stars shining brightly above you and to the glittering waters under you and hug yourself for a good measure!

High above the clouds

Thousands of fires burn inside me,
Glowing flames melt the frost,
Your heart and mine waiting to meet
There in Warsaw...

These are my lyrics to Nikola's accords. He will sing this song on the Polish radio and perform it on numerous occasions in Warsaw, but that is still to come.

A few years after Nikola's first visit to Poland, Warsaw is still gray, but has retained its dignity, the old times noblesse and a very specific Polish charm.

Everybody's here: Nikola, his mom and mine, Lela (pregnant with her first child), Marko's mom (Marko doing the military) and Nikola's colleagues from the University. We are spending one week of our winter vacations in Warsaw and Nikola is playing a tour guide. He shows us the Old Town with its Royal Castle and Park Łazienki where Chopin's Monument is. As we pass by the residential areas, the dullness of communist apartment blocks is mollified by the whirlwinds of snowflakes.

As much as Nikola's audience is grateful for the historical and cultural insight, they can hardly wait to go on shopping expeditions, for everything is so incredibly cheap! Purchase thirsty hordes of tourists invade the half empty stores, plundering every visible thing from the racks, shelves and cases, from furs, silver, cutlery, bed linen, to underwear,

Lela and I buy real cool black leather knee high boots, pointed and with six inch stiletto heels (very practical for walking on the ice covered cobblestone streets of Warsaw), some hand sewn silky frilly blouses from a sweet sore handed woman in a small side street shop who makes them herself, and YSL perfumes and Golden American cigarettes in stores exclusively for foreigners.

I splurge $20 on an absolutely stunning evening dress in layers of black satin, lace, and tulle, embedded with sequins and rhinestones, custom fitted for me, and feel a pang of guilty conscience at the sight of modestly yet somehow tastefully dressed and made up Polish women who have to save on food in order to buy even the least expensive clothing or cosmetics item.

Food is scarce for Poles in the late 1980s and what little there is can be bought with coupons, in restricted quantities. By contrast, we indulge in lavish meals in luxurious restaurants decorated in Old Polish style. One late afternoon, Nikola's mom and mine, exhausted from walking and shopping, decide to treat themselves to a five course dinner, for something like $5!

Some University colleagues of Nikola take a horse-drawn carriage from the Opera, where we attend a magnificent performance of Lucia di Lammermoor, to the hotel, even though it's a five minute walking distance. Just because we are all so full of money and are spending it extravagantly and arrogantly.

Not too long afterwards the situation will turn upside down, but none of us could envision it then.

Neither can I intuit that in a few short years Poland will become my new country and that I'll spend the best years of my life in Warsaw.

Frozen Warsaw and Hot Hearts

Right after the Christmas of 1989, Nora and I decided to go to Poland. That was our second time there together. The first time was a couple of years before, with so many people that it remained as a misty memory in my mind. I organized the trip to Warsaw then, and as a tour guide traveled for free, but it cost me a lot of nerves. On the positive side, some of my friends were in the group and Nora's and my mom as well. Lela was there, Stoja, my dear ex colleague, math teacher at the village school and Veronica, my dearest friend from the Faculty of Music.

Those seven days passed in sightseeing and shopping, in a chaos of faces, questions, objections, remarks, criticism, and occasional praises. I could hardly wait to get on the plane back to Belgrade.

The brightest moment of that trip was when Nora and I, dead tired after an unsuccessful thorough search for our moms in every single corner of the hotel, finally decided to go out and have a nice dinner at the upscale Forum Hotel. While the waiter was taking us to a séparé, we heard familiar voices. Our moms were there! Tucked in their own séparé by the window, they were enjoying Polish cuisine: duck stuffed with apples, potato cakes, beets, and carrot salads. Wide smiles spread across their faces when they saw us, but they didn't actually invite us to join them. The two of them had really wonderful moments together, those two women different from each other, like the north from the south, yet the same in the love they were giving out. Nora and I had our dinner by ourselves. We simply loved Polish dishes. At about that time I discovered I liked wódka with ice and lemon a lot.

The Poland we were exploring now looked pretty much the same shade of gray as the very first time I visited it, but it was only ours. Nora looked lovely in her white fur coat with the matching cap. She blended into the Polish atmosphere even more with the addition of Pani Walewska perfume which smelled deliciously on her. The story behind the perfume is this: Mademoiselle Walewska was leisurely walking, hand in hand with Napoleon, in the lush green fields of France, full of wild flowers, and when she took a carriage back to her homeland, Poland, her skirts, blouses and shawls emanated the scents of those wild flowers and grasses. The most pervading one was the scent of violets. That's the perfume's top note.

Nora was inhaling the hidden beauty of Warsaw with wide-open eyes. Since Warsaw was a part of my heart and soul, just like Nora. It was my responsibility to introduce them properly, to make sure love was flowing between them.

We spent pleasurable hours in Chopin Museum settled in the palace of Ostrocky family on Okolnik Street. We strolled the grand rooms and halls, looking at Chopin's manuscripts and listening to his pieces performed on the very same piano he used to give music lessons to Ostrocky's children. Heaven on earth!

On our way out, it started snowing, somehow setting us apart from the city, the streets, from everything. We were standing there, at that magnificent building, on the top of the staircase smooth with white freezing drops of water that wanted to surprise us, turning into snowflakes on my black coat and on Nora's white fur.

We went to see my old friend Alfred and met some of his friends. Alfred had a special place in my heart and I was happy to introduce him to Nora. We stayed at the luxury Europejski Hotel, in a beautiful spacious room with baroque furniture.

The wind was whipping our faces with the icy breath of the North and the humidity from the Vistula River, but our hearts were too hot to feel the frosty bites. We were regular visitors to The Warsaw Opera and Ballet. We dined at the most exclusive restaurants on The Old Town Square. Nora preferred obwarzanki, Polish bagels, freshly baked, that women from the villages were selling at street corners. I liked zapiekanki, a full taste open sandwich with wild mushrooms, melted cheese, and a stripe of ketchup. We inhaled the mysterious scents of cathedrals, admired their statues and stained glass windows, and wondered at how they were always so full of people.

Warsaw welcomed us with all the love and warmth it could offer us, since it was winter and poverty in the country. One evening, we had salmon in sauce prepared the traditional way in the romantic Literacka Restaurant, in the womb of the Old Town, by candle light and violin music. Even the almost empty department stores had a certain charm then. We walked lightly on the wide long streets, through unremoved snow and sad, depressed faces.

We took a train to Kraków, a magical city, so far away in time. Narrow streets were pushing through the walls of cathedrals and universities, trying to find a place for themselves. The street lamps looked like transported from a fairy tale and so did the horses and carriages. Snow covered parks were waiting for our steps to explore them and lonely cafés were ready to offer us shelter and hot tea.

The dignified Kraków was spreading regally in its beauty, from the center towards the south. Nora was fascinated by its squares, museums, and amber. We found out that Kraków housed the greatest school of art in amber. We admired the artifacts encased in silver. I wanted to buy them all, every single one of them, for Nora. Amber is usually golden yellow, but there we also saw Baltic milky ochre and green, rare and very expensive.

Kraków hid its best restaurants in the catacombs. They were so beautiful, with huge crystal chandeliers, deep green velvet curtains and armchairs, and the 16th century porcelain, that it was no wonder they were hiding from the tourists. Coveted by those in the know.

On the way back to Warsaw, we were sipping champagne and looking through the window of the first class train compartment. Poland was proudly showing us its fields covered by snow. Corn and wheat were asleep deep under the icy cover. Impressive landscapes were shining before our eyes.

The next day, we had dinner with my dear friend, Alfred. He aged a lot in a year since I last saw him and his vision was getting weaker. He was still active at work, the owner of a big export-import company specializing in antiques. His apartment, suspended like Christmas lights on the tree, was on the 27th floor of a gray building in the center of Warsaw.

Alfred had always been surrounded by people who took advantage of him. In terms of poor living conditions in Poland at the time, he was a millionaire and knew how to enjoy his wealth. I was glad that his best friend Pani Maria joined us for dinner, to meet Nora. She was a single elderly woman with cheerful spirit and sharp tongue. Pani Maria used to be a judge, a very important one in the country, for thirty years, and now she retired, with plenty of money. She enjoyed spending good times in company, with lots of drinks.

Poles had an ongoing love affair with alcohol. Nora and I were trying to follow their rhythm of emptying wódka glasses, but there was no chance anybody could compete with them.

Adam, a ballet dancer, was there, and Darek, a taxi driver. Adam was Alfred's close friend, whether because of money or some other reasons, I didn't know. I only knew that Alfred got him a job at the National Theater through influential political connections and that Adam had slept with many people on his thorny path to success. Darek was young and handsome, with clear blue eyes. He was so kind and innocent looking that he won the hearts of everybody who met him. Nora and I said we wanted to take a plane to Gdańsk, a city in the North of Poland, on the Baltic Sea. Darek managed to convince us, after quite a few wódkas and a lot of talking, that it would be better to pay him half of the money we would otherwise spend on the plane tickets and take a taxi instead.

"Przecież, to tylko pare godzin," he said. ("It's only a few hour drive.")

We agreed.

In the morning, at the crack of dawn, we went down the balustraded staircase of our hotel to find Darek waiting for us in his Lada taxi. We set off, without the slightest idea that a big snow storm was about to hit the very part of Poland we were heading to. It never occurred to us to listen to the news. Like always on the trips, Nora and I proved once again that, although mature, we didn't have an ounce of brain in our heads, just followed our hearts.

The highway was getting increasingly difficult to navigate. Darek was sweating and cursing the terrible weather. Snow drifts were so big and north winds so strong that every now and then he had to stop at the side of the road and wait for them to subside. Nothing could be seen except whiteness. Nora and I were so excited about going to Gdańsk that we didn't fully realize how serious the situation was. Finally, six and a half hours later we entered an amazing city featuring a mix of German, Scandinavian, and Polish architecture. The façades of the buildings on the main street were in pastel colors and the windows high, with reliefs and coats of arms above them. We went for lunch to a ship converted into a restaurant. Darek was dead tired. We wondered if he would be able to get us back to Warsaw in one piece.

After lunch, he took us to Sopot, a high class residential area on the shores of the Baltic Sea and a seaside resort. He said he would take a nap in the car while we walked around. Nora and I went to the Metropol Hotel, one of the oldest in Poland. We admired the huge imposing building. Seagulls were picking up scraps of food from the beach. The sea was the color of deep gray lead and the sand darker than the sea. We walked along the beach, sprinkled with snowflakes, breathing in the smell of the sea, the smell of the Baltic. Then we had tea at the hotel, taking in the beauty of the velvet walls and high chandeliers of the majestic hall. We imagined what it must have looked like in the golden days of Poland, during the kingdoms of the past. The building was magnificent, its windows, façade details, the roof: feast for the eyes. The Baltic Sea was tired that day, trying to absorb the color of the sky full of snow.

"This is where I would love to retire and live till the end of my life," I said to Nora.

"Me too," she said quietly.

We didn't know then that Poland would one day become our sanctuary, our hope, and salvation from the whirlwinds of the war that pulled our Yugoslavia apart. We didn't know any of it then.

Darek was taking a nap in his taxi. We let him rest a bit more, but then had to wake him up because it started snowing again, heavier by the minute.

He was driving carefully, for the gusts of wind were about to turn the car over any second. The wipers were working at maximum speed, to no effect. It was getting from bad to worse. At one moment, Nora cried:

"Nikola, he's fallen asleep!"

Darek's head was lolling back and forth and his eyes were closed. I shook him up and saw that he was on the edge of exhaustion and desperation. Fortunately, the light from a road side café could be discerned through the darkness and the dense snow. We stopped.

Darek had a couple of strong black coffees and ice-cold cokes to come around and pull himself together. So did Nora and I. We were scared for him, scared for us.

Our verbal communication wasn't the greatest, since Nora and I knew only a few Polish phrases and Darek didn't speak our language, English or French. Still, the graveness of the situation made us understand one another perfectly.

Continuing slowly towards Warsaw, in a better mood, we made some more stops along the way, for refreshments. We stacked a few bottles of coke, for its caffeine helped Darek's concentration.

We arrived to our hotel room at about 4 a.m., totally worn out. Safely in bed, we were bringing back the memories of the beautiful Sopot, the beach and the sea.

In the end we decided to pay Darek the full price of the plane tickets, had we taken the plane to Gdańsk (which would have been impossible, considering the weather conditions). He got a lot of money. When we told Alfred about it, he said it was the equivalent of Darek's two years' salary, but he was glad we did so, for Darek had a wife who didn't work and two small children.

Before leaving Warsaw we stopped at a Pewex store, for foreigners only, and bought chocolates, candies, cheese, salami, and foie gras for Darek's family. He was crying tears of gratitude when he received the gift. And over the following years, until the situation in our country worsened, Nora and I regularly sent letters to Darek with a $20 note wrapped in aluminum foil. A few days later we would get a postcard from him with:

"*Dziękuje bardzo.*" ("Thank you very much.")

Now let's jump into the future, to the still far-away year of 1994 when I was living in Warsaw with Nora, jobless and penniless, but also warless. I met with Darek. He became the owner of a huge parking lot in downtown. He wore expensive clothes, got very fat, and lost all the innocence and kindness he used to have. He supervised over twenty taxi drivers and was arrogant and merciless to them. I was certain he could help us find any kind of job, after everything we had done for him. He said that the economic situation in Poland was tough, there were no jobs for foreigners. He wondered why we had come here, yes, he had heard about the war in Yugoslavia, by the way. He didn't want to waste his time with us. He offered me to watch the parking lot from midnight till morning, illegally, without papers, paid less per night than the cost of a cup of coffee. I said I was afraid, if the authorities caught me working illegally they would immediately send me back to the war chained Yugoslavia. His answer was in the 'take it or leave it' style.

So he left Nora's life and mine.

Back to our winter Warsaw and our last day. Pani Maria and Alfred took us to a fabulous Belvedere Restaurant, a rococo green house with palm trees leaning over the tables, nested in the vast Łazienki Park where Chopin Monument stood in all its glory immortalized by ice. We simply enjoyed.

That last evening we spent at The National Theater, attending an amazing performance of The Swan Lake. Then we walked around the Theater Square. Snow was falling on us. It was quiet and unreal. The street lamps cast yellow light, making the snow glittery, like fairy dust. A touch of destiny happened then, that evening in the cold Warsaw.

Nora was silent. She was walking slowly, looking around. She turned to me and said:

"Nikola, look at these ugly communist buildings around the Theater. People who live in them are so lucky, their windows have the front view to all this beauty…"

"So they can come to a performance at the last minute," I continued.

"Yes!" she said.

Let me briefly take you again to the year of 1994. Our first apartment in Warsaw was in one of those communist buildings. As if destiny had already planned it all for us then, that evening, under the cover of snow and Nora's words:

"People who live in them are so lucky…"

That last night we walked in the Old Town. We were saying our good-byes to the narrow stone cobbled streets and colorful houses. Street musicians were playing mazurkas and polonaises which Nora and I absorbed with all our pores.

The next morning we flew to Belgrade by LOT Airlines, on an old Russian Tupolev 154 aircraft, with noisy motors and wonderful service (needless to say how much I envied the flight attendants on their job).

We got back to Belgrade.

At the Faculty of Music, my colleague and friend Veronica said she had broken up with her taxi driver, a boyfriend of hers for over eight years. She realized he wasn't for her.

I was really sorry.

Nora's Impressions

Cześć, Hi there, my birthday happens to be on November (11th month of the year) 11, which coincides with the Polish National Holiday (Święto Niepodległości – Independence Day), and 1+1 is 2, a number of balance in numerology and multiplied by 2 gives 4, a number of creation and organization, and stands for foundation and stability in Tarot and we were both (Poland and me, that is) born/reborn under the sign of Scorpio whose symbol is eagle, and the white eagle with gold crown is on the Polish coat of arms and the Polish National Anthem (that ex-Yugoslavia borrowed the music from) is Mazurek Dąbrowskiego (Dąbrowski being a Polish general in Napoleon's Army in Italy in the late 18th and the early 19th century, at the time when Poland was virtually non-existing on the map of Europe). I love dancing mazurka, and our best friend Emil, yet to appear in our lives, lives on Plac Dąbrowskiego in downtown Warsaw, and my mom's name, when translated from Serbian, is Violetta and violets from the woods of France are the main ingredient of Pani Walewska perfume that smells so nice on me; and I'm in love with Nikola who loves playing Chopin and Chopin was buried at Père-Lachaise cemetery in Paris but his heart is in Kościół Świętokrzyski (the Church of the Holy Cross) in Warsaw, in a marble case on which Nikola and I lay a white rose and his heart is beating for us...

OK, if you are intent on looking for signs, you can find symbolism in literally everything.

Also, when you are in love, even the dreariest place on earth will look like paradise if you are there with your beloved.

The fact is, however, that our visits to Poland in general and Warsaw in particular have a fairytale-like quality, which implies that not everything flows smoothly, just the way it doesn't in fairy tales, there's a lot of struggle until you reach the happy ending, but somehow all works out perfectly for us there.

There's something almost karmic about this city, about this country, like some unfinished business carried over from our separate who knows how many lives, blending into this land of genuine nobility, no matter the title, no matter the circumstances.

Poorly dressed Poles at the time bow elegantly before a lady and kiss her hand. You are served tea and cheap herbatniki (tea biscuits), when there's nothing else to offer to a guest, in delicate porcelain cups and on little crystal plates, inherited from past generations.

If there is one expression to epitomize the Slavic soul of Poles, it would be: 'the spirit of national dignity'. Warsaw gets reduced to ashes in World War II and then rebuilt, brick by brick, so the Medieval Old Town now stands proudly in all its splendor and glory, complete with the Royal Castle; to tell the stories of the past, provide enjoyment at present and be an inspiration for the future.

Poland talks to me, even though I speak very little of her language yet. We communicate intuitively.

Dear old Alfred in his like 20 square meter gingerbread castle is preparing hot bubble baths for his young lovers while chatting with his close friend, Pani Maria. Nikola is posing in front of Wilanów, Sobieski's palace (Jan III Sobieski was the King of Poland in the 17th century and a great general, defended Vienna, Austria, and most of Europe from Turkish invasions), as if having stepped out of his bedroom, in a long black coat and a white scarf around his neck. There's something truly aristocratic about Nikola. The almost empty department stores Wars and Sawa are named after the young man and woman who made the first dwelling on the bank of the Vistula River, in bygone times, loving each other and fishing for survival (that's how Warsaw got her name – Wars + Sawa = Warszawa). I'm firmly holding Nikola's arm so I don't slip on the snow covered streets with ice underneath that nobody cares to clear, neither do we care.

The tapestries in Wawel Castle in Kraków are weaving the stories of kingdoms past. My mom's best friend ever, Krystyna, had been sending her postcards from this noble city, her hometown, until the day she died from an overdose, too depressed by the communist Poland. She also sent to mom a figurine of Chopin's Monument in Park Łazienki in Warsaw and an amber necklace, and I eventually broke both for they were my favorite toys as a kid. I'm mentally hugging Leonardo da Vinci's Lady with an Ermine in Museum Czartorijski, a hug longed for years, ever since I saw its reproduction in an art history book.

The snow is covering the seas of the Baltic and the seagulls are whispering into my left ear: "You'll come back home, come back home..." And the tea is so fragrant and soothing in the hotel as we look at the beach and the sea and the amber earrings that Nikola bought for me are so warm in my earlobes.

Nikola is playing Walse Brillante on Chopin's own piano in the arts infused salon of the great composer's home in Żelazova Wola, just outside of Warsaw, where Darek takes us. Nikola and I are standing on the little bridge in the woods over the frozen stream and snowflakes are dancing their heavenly dance upon us and I'm following the flight of the seagulls, far up north, to Sopot, listening to what they are telling me:

"You'll come back home, come back home…"

Veronica

We met in our first university year. She was a year older and more mature. We were taking baby steps towards each other, timid at first, until we started getting together on a regular basis. Veronica was a gorgeous girl, with an extraordinarily beautiful face and body, tall and stylishly attired. She always wore high heels and lots of makeup, both of which suited her so well.

She was dating a handsome, athletically built Zvonimir, a taxi driver, hiding it from her very strict father, who would never allow his daughter to date somebody 'so low on the social scale', so she had to lie and make up excuses. It's a pity it was like that, because Zvonimir was a good, honest guy, and loved her with all his heart. I believe their marriage would have been splendid, had it ever happened.

It didn't happen.

On the other hand, I was warmly welcomed by Veronica's parents. I didn't know whether her father was counting on me as a future son-in-law, but at any rate he showed a lot of respect for me and was always glad to see me in their house. Her mother was a simply wonderful woman of quiet words, soft movements and a big heart. Their home was open to me at all times.

When you are poor and somebody invites you to their rich house and treats you as their equal, without prejudices, without pretending – that means a lot. Her mother sensed that I didn't have much food to put on my table, so she did all her possible to make every moment I spent in their dining room feel regal. She was one of the best cooks I had ever met in my life.

On yet another hand, I meant a lot to Veronica's parents because I studied conscientiously and devotedly, and she and I together prepared for exams with all our might and power. We distributed exams into 'hers' and 'mine' and helped each other in a compatible way. When I got a job at the village school and started missing lectures, her notebook was always there, ready for me, and in return I would explain to her some not so easy to solve musical problems that were not her strongest point.

We were inseparable.

We were like one person, which reflected in our final exam grades.

We were drinking coffee like crazy.

The amounts of coffee that passed through our bodies could be measured by thousands of gallons. We both liked it black, strong Turkish coffee drunk from big mugs. We smoked a lot, too, during our sessions, totally immersed in and dedicated to the study of music.

She also found a job in a school, one day a week, which provided her with some pocket money (not that she needed it) and most importantly with an excuse to get out of the house, meet with her taxi driver and spend a couple of hours in his passionate embrace. He was something really special, Robert Redford look-alike from his early days, somewhere around The Way We Were.

Veronica and I sang together, conducted, practiced the most boring subject in the world – Choir Partiture, and then decided to change the department, driven by the youthful rebellion against two professors who were so very unfair to us, clearly letting us know that no matter how hard we worked, we would never be in their mercy. One of them was old, the other young, both bad. For unexplained reasons, they sort of hated Veronica and me. Maybe because we had jobs on the side and were not brown noses.

None of our colleagues believed we could make it to another department. It was Sisyphus' work, involving lots of additional exams and very little time to prepare for. Still, we made it!

I would go to Veronica's house after a long day of teaching in the village school, tired but ready for studying. Her mother, with a caring glance, would bring sandwiches and coffee to the study and say the cookies baking in the oven were for us. I would stay until very late at night.

Our efforts paid back.

They brought fruit.

We managed to pass with honors all the second year exams, including the additional ones. Our colleagues with their eyes wide-open, were pinching themselves.

"Bravo, my children!" Professor Zora, who had been supporting us in our endeavors, was ecstatic.

So were we.

We treated ourselves to a trip to a distant, almost forgotten Island of Lastovo on the Adriatic, about six hour ship ride from the port of Split. We were listening to Beethoven on the deck, looking at the sea. Lastovo welcomed us with its untouched nature and the Solitudo (Lonely) Hotel.

A brilliant place.

Silence.

Real silent silence.

The sky was clear, cloudless, windless. The sea crystal blue and very deep, calm. Balmy nights, not a breath of a breeze. Above our heads – billions of dispersed stars.

Silence.

And some more of it.

We spent seven days in that oasis of peace, so quiet that it was sometimes too much to take in. The beaches were hidden, all in the coves, and although there were lots of guests in the hotel, we never came across a single soul, except at breakfasts and dinners.

The passage of time was marked by our swimming, our stories, and coffees from the thermos. I got to know Veronica better than ever and savored everything she was telling me. Our friendship was deep as the sea and serene as the sky.

Despite all that tranquility, we went through quite an adventure on the day before the last. Somehow, we miscalculated the money we had, for the hotel and the return ship tickets turned out to be more expensive than we had expected. There was no internet at the time to search for the best prices and information. Debit or credit cards didn't exist then. It was all cash or check. At any rate, we needed cash.

We were on a far-away island with a population of about 150 people, mostly old, bent over their small dry fields barricaded by stone walls that kept the soil from sliding into the sea by sudden heavy rains.

We had no option but to go to the island's capital, also called Lastovo. It was tiny, situated on a steep hill, turned towards the endless sea, charming and basking in the radiant July sun. The bank and the post office, both smaller than our hotel room, were closed. Our steps were wandering the narrowest streets you can imagine. Some of them were so narrow we could barely pass through.

"Greetings," said a guy in front of a small shop.

"Greetings," we replied.

He was young, tanned and with deep eyes the color of the Adriatic Sea. His smiley face added even more sun to that resplendent day.

I told him about our problem we couldn't figure out a solution to since we were leaving the next morning.

He was listening.

He was wearing a blue T shirt and faded jeans reaching just below his knees. He had the face of Apollo, the Sun God.

I felt his unblinking intent gaze on me and was a bit uncomfortable, for he never once glanced at Veronica nor did he address her. Men would normally glue their eyes to her wherever we happened to be. He didn't. I was his center of the Universe at that moment.

"Where are you staying at?" He asked.

"Solitudo Hotel," I said.

"I'll do a little something for you," he looked straight into my eyes. "I'll come to the hotel tonight and bring the money, you can give me checks. I'll cash them when you say it's OK."

I was speechless.

"Thank you!" I said.

"Thank you," Veronica said.

He left.

We were standing in the middle of the main street, on a scorching summer day, in the middle of the town of Lastovo on the island of Lastovo. The hotel was more than ten kilometers away.

"We'll hitchhike," I said. "The same way we got here."

We got there in a van that was transporting some stuff from the hotel area to the town.

We started walking slowly down the road.

Veronica's legs were getting tired. Nobody passed by in an hour. Not even a cart or a donkey.

Then we heard the sound of a motorbike.

It was him, Mate, the guy from the shop, on a small red motorbike.

"I thought you'd be crazy enough to walk all the way to the hotel," he smiled.

"How else?" Veronica said.

"There's a boat that runs every hour from the port to your place."

We didn't know that.

He first gave a lift to Veronica. I rested on a rock in the shade, waiting for him to come back and pick me up. When he returned, I sat down behind him and took him around the waist.

Mate was driving very fast, but I have always liked speed and wasn't afraid. We were rushing into sharp curves, there were Russian roulette moments, for an occasional vehicle, sheep or cow passed by. Chances were 50/50 that we would hit into something or somebody at every curve and get killed. Then, close to the hotel, he stopped.

"I want to show you this," he said.

He walked into thick shrubs intertwined with slender trees spreading their leafy branches. Wild roses were scratching my sunburnt skin, but I followed him. At one point a vista opened, like out of this world. We were standing on a flat rock, about meter and a half long, protruding above the abyss, with the sea frothing and fighting with cliffs, sharp and black, below us. I was breathless with amazement.

He was right behind me.

The rock was slim and the cliffs high. I had a sensation of hovering above the sea, above the island, closer to birds than to the earth. I had never been dizzy before, but somehow my legs started shaking a bit and I might have fallen down if Mate hadn't gently pulled me towards him. We sat down. In silence.

He turned to me:

"Will you ever come to Lastovo again?"

"I don't know," I said honestly. "Why?"

"I can't explain," he scratched behind his ear. "I like you a lot."

I couldn't believe my ears.

"You know, here on the island there's eight of us guys and six girls. They will leave for Split or Germany, but I have to stay because I'm the oldest and have to take care of grandpa. I've always dreamed about a boy, a boy like you, so beautiful, to be only mine."

I wanted to tell him something but couldn't find a proper word. Years of music, composing and analyzing washed my brain from ordinary words.

"I'd like to keep you for myself only," he went on. "To lock you up and have you every night until death sets us apart."

Silence fell.

The waves were breaking against the cliffs with renewed strength below us. I was thinking about Veronica, probably worried where I had been so far. I was thinking what to tell him without hurting him.

"Mate, I'll write to you, promise," I said.

He gave me a soulful look and hugged me. I wasn't ready for this kind of affection, especially not on a slippery rock sticking out above the foaming sea and ragged cliffs. He simply held me in his embrace. I could feel his heartbeat, fast, much faster than mine. Then he kissed me on the cheek, brotherly, friendly, tenderly and only once.

"You are the most beautiful one in the world," he said.

We got up.

He gave me a lift to the hotel.

In the evening he brought the money. I gave him four postdated checks. He stayed for dinner with Veronica and me, was so kind and gentle. We were telling him about our weird professors, their strange habits, and bizarre ways. He was laughing to tears and every now and then asked us to stop, for he would pee of laughter. It was a pleasant evening. We were also feeling special because at the table next to ours was a singer of a very popular rock band at the time, with his family. Mate was delighted.

Then we settled on the balcony of our room, drinking wine. The sunset was softly penetrating our gazes. Veronica left us alone, said she had to go for a walk for her butt was getting numb from sitting. We were grateful to her. I think she did it on purpose, but we never talked about it later.

Mate and I were sipping wine. I white, he red. And smoking. I light, he strong cigarettes.

"I've fallen in love with you," he said. "I don't know how I'll ever forget you."

"You can't fall in love with somebody you've known for only half a day and besides, I'm a man," I said.

He smiled.

"You're either dumb or pretending. But it doesn't matter, I still love you so much."

The night now reigned over our balcony. We were talking about Lastovo, about his family. He lost his mother and father as a little boy. Grandpa and he ran successfully that little shop. He had been to Split a few times but didn't like it. People were arrogant and guys good-looking but haughty.

He left quietly, with tears in his eyes.

I was very sorry that he felt that way but couldn't do anything about it, for I wasn't in love with him.

A big white ship took Veronica and me to Split the next day. Mate didn't come to say goodbye, but I knew he was there somewhere, hiding on the docks. Then the wings of JAT DC9 airplane brought us to Belgrade.

Mate never cashed the checks I gave him. I believe that was a secret gift from him to me. He wrote me love letters to which I regularly responded, not in love terms. I sent him tapes with the music I composed or performed with my choir. He sent me lavender flowers, rose petals or just a small green leaf, a part of Lastovo and a part of him.

The letters stopped when I went to the Army and were never resumed. I wrote to him several times afterwards, but every single letter was returned to me, stamped with 'Unknown Address'. Who knows what the war did to him, to his grandpa and the shop. I didn't want to think about the worst, choosing instead to finish the story with the idea that he managed to move to Germany with grandpa, opened a new shop, and found happiness.

My dear Mate.

Veronica and I were heading into the next academic year when Nora appeared in my life. My love for Nora was strong, still unclear, but certainly strong. Nora didn't like Veronica. Veronica didn't like Nora.

If at any point in life you happen to be in such a situation, please take my advice and don't tear yourself apart. Jesus Christ was crucified to bring us salvation, your crucifixion or mine won't make the same effect. It was getting very difficult for me to balance the two of them. Jealousy was burning on both sides: on Veronica's, because Nora was taking away the time I would otherwise be spending with her, studying and talking, and on Nora's, whose instinctive female nature feared that something might happen between Veronica and me.

The torture was unbearable and long-lasting. I was fighting both of them in order to find a solution, but there was none. Then we all went on vacation together. At the time Veronica was dating a guy who doesn't deserve a name in this book, even this mention is too much. As if he had put a spell on her, who knows how, I'm not going into that. She changed a lot and little by little we parted and broke up a wonderful friendship.

It hurt.

A lot.

And then it came to pass, like everything does when a deeper hurt arrives.

War was in the air.

Veronica and I are still the symbol of friendship in the memories of our colleagues from the Faculty of Music. Her father passed away and her mother got some deep lines on her lovely face. Veronica has never found the love of her life, that right man who is there simply for her. She is doing great on the professional plan, though. We met three times in the last eighteen years and had a nice time. I wanted to stay in touch, asked her to learn e-mailing, for it's easy and fast and can get us together within seconds. She hasn't learnt it, couldn't or didn't want to.

Let it stay like this.

Our friendship cannot disappear, for it was grooved into our University years and sealed on the beaches in the silence of Lastovo. It was preserved in her mom's ajvar and conserved in our oversized coffee mugs.

Nora's Impressions

You know those stunning tall women with long slender limbs and all parts of their bodies so perfectly proportioned, who make a statement with their very appearance? Well, that's Veronica to you. Like, she walks on the streets, along the University halls, into a party, and everybody forgets to breathe at the sight of her!

She looks so totally, absolutely amazing, fabulous, and fantastic! Her body is like chiseled in white marble by ancient Greek sculptors. Her heart-shaped face, featuring prominent cheek bones, slightly slanted bright chestnut eyes under artfully shaped eyebrows, sensual nostrils and luscious lips easily spreadable into wide brilliant smiles, on the background of silky skin, is framed by a mane of wavy reddish hair. She combines sophistication with sex appeal, for she is gorgeous, witty and very intelligent.

On top of everything, she's bursting out with self-confidence!

The exact opposite of the small shy me in every respect.

Whoever it is distributing the gifts of physical beauty and mental capacities to people is doing it unequally and unfairly!

Naturally, I'm jealous of Veronica, or rather I'm shit scared she'll snatch Nikola from me. Like, rationally I know that's not going to happen, but still, fear knows no reason. And besides, every time I look at her, I can only see a fox or a lioness.

Nikola tells me all about their study sessions: a tradition – ritual more like it – so pure and wonderful, established a long time before he met me. Imagine two young people who are dealing with their respective everyday issues, ups and downs, but when they are together, they're like encapsulated, nothing else exists, just the piano and scores to analyze and music history to be studied and pieces to listen to and they stay up all night, dedicated to their God: Music. Can anything in the world be more pristine, especially with their God smiling at them?

There's a legendary quality about these sessions and legends never die. I hope that both Veronica and Nicola can go back to that time wrap of theirs, whenever they need to draw strength for challenges on their current paths. They have proved, then and there, that nothing is impossible, as long as you put all your heart into it!

Veronica and I meet every now and then, at concerts or at Nikola's place (that lovely garage apartment), politely seething at each other. She makes a step towards reconciling the two of us, I have to give her that, by inviting Nikola and me to her house for relaxed chatting over oversized coffee mugs, just that it turns out strained for all three parties concerned.

We go on a couple of trips together (Veronica, Nikola and I that is), to Verona, Italy, to attend the Opera Festival at the Arena and then to the Island of Hvar, on the Adriatic Sea, with her future husband. We are civil to each other, but far from what you can call on friendly terms.

She seems calculating and somewhat artificial to me. Only on her wedding day do I catch a glimpse of a layer of emotional and vulnerable Veronica. I get an intuitive understanding of her, but don't show it. Guess we're both hiding under our self-defense shells.

I see her two more times afterwards. She's walking in the neighborhood park, a new born baby boy in her arms. A few months later, she's standing on the highway, in the cold wind, waiting for the bus to take her to work.

She strikes me as a strong, independent woman, still as gorgeous looking as ever!

In retrospect, what was it about jealousy and fear and non-friendliness?

After all, Veronica and I have so many things in common:
Love for

- Make up
- Clothes & accessories

- High heels

So we're right on the spot.
Passion for

- Music (she)
- Visual arts (me)

So we're complementary here.
Relaxed mode

- Coffee
- Cigarettes

So now we can chat.

Just why don't I ever chat with her about our loves and passions? Maybe because we don't actually need it.

Maybe because Veronica and I are just incidental passers-by on our separate life paths that cross at one point, enriching us with experience of whatever kind, and then go on in diverse directions.

Maybe that's been her role in Nikola's life or Nikola's role in hers, just experienced on a deeper level.

There's been no need, really, for Nikola to metaphorically crucify himself over the two of us, who, again, are just passing by his path, in different degrees though.

Of course, Nikola being truthful and honest to himself, wants to make the whole world move smoothly and harmoniously (harmony being his key word), but hey, not even gods have managed to do that!

Take it easy, you wonderful human being!

Act VI
The Sound of Freedom

- **The Last Moments Before the Army**
- **Nora's Impressions**
- **Army**
- **Nora's Impressions**
- **The House of the Rising Sun**
- **Nora's Impressions**
- **Students and 'Students'**
- **Nora's Impressions**
- **Freedom**

The Last Moments Before the Army

- Get a haircut, very short.
- Have as much sex as possible
- Inquire about all the ins and outs of military service.
- Say good bye to my little garage apartment.
- Say good bye to my piano.
- Finish the first part of my Master's thesis.
- Go to the South and visit all the relatives before the Army, as is appropriate.
- Buy the bus ticket to Petrovac upon Mlava.
- Put my brain into the freezer, so it doesn't go bad in a year.
- Cry my eyes out before leaving.

The military service was coming dangerously closer. There were only about two more months to go and my fear attacks increased in frequency. At the time I was working on the first part of my Master's, often with Professor Zora and also with Nora, who was typing my thesis, being faster and much neater than me. Notes, songs, music, writing, concerts, full head, full days and nights, only not to think about the approaching Army.

Fear is weird.

It can make you do things you have never imagined you could.

It seeps into the bones.

My fear was enormous, but I tried to come to terms with it.

Why was I so scared?

The very idea of being separated from the ordinary everyday life didn't appeal to me, and then there was the issue of living in a group. I don't like groups. I couldn't picture myself confined to one group of people day in day out, and that's exactly what was awaiting me. It will be composed of young men from every possible village, from the boonies. What am I going to talk about with them? Then there will be guns and rifles. I hate fire arms but will be forced to dismantle them piece by piece and put them together again for days on end. And to shoot, the horror of horrors!

I can't stand stupidity.

I can't stand nonsensical orders.

The very thought of the military service caused shiver shocks throughout my body.

Cold sweat sometimes ran down my spine.

On the brighter side, Nora and I were so occupied by music and my thesis, so that the Army, even though really close, somehow still seemed far away.

I used to wake up just like that, in the middle of the night, and look around: my lovely apartment, my piano, paintings on the walls, clothes strewn all over the place.

"I'm still here!" I would say happily.

The summer was beaming with sunshine. Days followed each other, every next one more brilliant than the one before. The school year was over and my students, my choir singers, were vacationing in the Mediterranean with their parents. September was approaching inevitably and with it, my going to the army.

It happened that just before the Army I had so many musical ideas in my head, so many works in progress I could see the fruition of, but all of that was pointless for I was leaving for a year.

I had my hair cut very short.

I looked like an idiot.

Moving from the garage hurt a lot.

More than moving forever from my hometown in the South of Serbia. I could feel a part of me left there, contained within the walls of my beautiful garage apartment, in my green and white curtains, in my unfinished stories and unplayed sonatas. As I watched my piano go through the window, for it couldn't through the narrow door, tears were burning my cheeks.

Everybody was feeling my pain, Nora, Mira, Marko, my friends and colleagues. Everybody. Lela was busy as a full time mother and a part-time helper in her mother in law's office. Her mother in law was one of those people you never want to meet or have anything to do with. That's exactly what I did, stayed away from her and didn't want to see, hear, or feel her presence.

Lela had her choice, as all of us have at certain points in life. Hers was to be well off, including that woman breathing down her neck, or to stay in poverty. She chose money and I didn't blame her. Her husband wasn't particularly fond of me. Deep in his heart he was probably an honest man, loving, and full of goodness. You couldn't see it on the outside, for he was spoilt, bad mannered, narrow-minded and with shallow brain waves, always ready to argue about things he didn't know about. I never asked nor wanted to know if he was faithful to Lela, my dear friend.

As for her, she was changing dramatically. She was the one to whom I owed my first Belgrade days, she was the muse who brought warmth into my bitter cold tiny basement room and I will never ever forget it. Her transformation hurt a lot at first, and then the pain ceased. I saw her happy in expensive outfits. Some of them suited her, some really didn't. Her body wasn't made to the measure of fitted designer clothes, she looked like a squished potato sack in them; but in flowing dresses she was gorgeous.

I saw her glowing in her five bedroom, ultra-modern apartment. She still kept her old habits and had a cat, a dog, birds, hamsters, fishes, and turtles. If there was a garden, she would have a horse, too.

There was less and less space for me in her life and I respected that. With the same love for her and her first born son, I was slowly going away from that family, especially from the political opinions of her husband and his mother.

One of the last phone calls before the Army I made to Veronica.

Her icy voice froze for a couple of seconds my wish to talk to her.

She sounded artificial and wanted the conversation to be over as soon as possible.

Oh, Veronica, please, let's not lose everything, hold on.
So we didn't – lose everything.

Veronica is happy in her world and I am in mine. If she had learnt how to send emails, we could be in contact every day now, after almost twenty years, but she obviously decided not to, or not for me.

She will forever stay in my heart and, I deeply believe, I in hers.

Nora's Impressions

This is not happening, no, it simply can't be! Nikola has to finish his Master's and there are so many new projects: concerts to perform with his children's choirs, ballets to be choreographed for the little dancers, TV shows to bring the magic of music to the audience every Friday night!

The bees are buzzing and swarming in that beehive head of his and in my mind's eye, I can see all these ideas made real, like materialized right now. Please God, don't interrupt the flow, it's so palpable, an artist's first and foremost duty is to create, don't send him away from creating, to a place where he doesn't belong!

Well, God is obviously not listening to me. He/She appears to be deaf, anyway, to all the pleas I have ever made, like directly from my heart. So much about an honest soul asking a loving, divine parent for help when it's most needed.

So, left to my own resources (hey, maybe that's always been God's plan, to simply bring me back to myself), I come up with:

- OK, it's not the end of the world, a year will come to pass.
- You'll visit Nikola in the Army, he'll come home on leaves.
- He'll survive (if anybody, he's capable of finding beauty in the direst of circumstances).
- Use the year to finish your Italian studies.
- Cry to your heart's content, you'll pee less.

But oh, my God, he can't be wearing that rigid uniform and his pianist hands are not made for guns and rifles!

And what about all the candles I have lit in churches and prayers to the brightest star in the night sky?

I'm crying out to the Heavens, once again, for good measure. No answer.

When all the effort fails, you just surrender; there's nothing else to do.

Right, let's enjoy the time we have left, Nikola and I, our way!

We have the whole summer ahead of us!

So we go to China and get totally immersed in the experience, like see all the sights as prescribed by tour guides, but basically hang out with locals, give the early morning Tai Chi a try, walk in parks and roll the singing metal balls on the palms of our hands like everybody else, play pandaminton (Chinese version of badminton, just more elaborated) and squat to eat on the street after a busy day of visiting temples and quaint shops.

Then, we bring a part of China to Niš, to the South of Serbia, where we spend a fabulous month in the loving embrace of Nikola's mom and his two aunts. These three graces are the most warmth-emanating humans on earth! We prepare spicy pork cubes with mango and chicken stripes, with pineapple and a lot of steamed rice and show them how to eat with chopsticks and they like it all!

We also do a lot of clubbing with Nikola's cousins till the wee hours, shifting from one place to another, more drinks, more music, more talk, more… just being there, alive and vibrant! Southerners really know how to enjoy life to the fullest!

Then, totally exhausted, we slump on the bench under the pear tree in Nikola's mom's garden, where she's waiting for us, smoking in the silence and fragrance of her flowering bushes and we're instantly invigorated and want the night never to end.

So, now we are empowered for whatever is in store for us.

And there's a lot in store.

The contents of the loveliest and the most soulful apartment in the world are neatly packed in boxes, all of Nikola's dearest possessions ready to be transported to another place, patiently waiting for his return.

The moving operation is skillfully organized and supervised by Nikola, Marko, Neško (Nikola's cousin from Niš, great one for clubbing) and Lela's husband and successfully executed with the wholehearted help of dozens of friends and neighbors.

Nikola's apartment gets transplanted into mine. Incidentally, the most precious of his belongings: the piano, is the last thing that leaves his apartment and the first one that enters mine, occupying now the place of honor in my conventional dining room, which it transforms into a real salon.

Boxes are all over my place and I open them with sort of a reverence, one by one, like Christmas gifts. They are going to be my solace in the long days of Nikola's absence and I want to savor every single thing that's in there before incorporating it into my living space, which suddenly gets illuminated with each new addition.

Still, there's a lot of work to do. Flattening the boxes and taking them out to the recycling bin is my least favorite part of the process, like there's nothing creative about it, right? That's when Mom comes to rescue, like an Angel simply dropped from the Heavens – just that she doesn't look like one – for she's fully equipped for the job of a cleaning lady: loose pants, sweatshirt and running shoes, brooms, brushes and dust cloths. It's only the polka dot scarf on her head, which she wears on occasions of floor-to-ceiling spring and fall cleanings, to protect her freshly-done hair, by which I recognize the stranger who marches into the apartment with the firm intention that a job is to be done.

In parenthesis, Mom is normally all into classy outfits softly accentuating her curves, elegant shoes matching her handbags and into furs. Accessories, such as belts, gloves, and jewelry understatedly blend in.

Anyway, she empties the boxes, leaving me to play with all that wonderful stuff and while I'm still debating about the best spot for this trinket or that, she's already back from the trip to the recycling bin, four flights of stairs later. And so it goes on like that, all night, both of us fulfilled with what we are doing.

I sense what's going on here. Mom is helping her daughter while wishing her spiritual son well.

The finch birds, Caesar and Cleopatra, are cheerfully chirping on my dining room table, loaded with dictionaries and books to be translated.

Nikola's piano is hugging the chair I'm sitting on.

We're heading into a new adventure.

Army

And so it came.

That day, Marko and I, going slowly down the street to the bus station. Nora stayed in her apartment, in tears.

If it had been possible to exchange 40 years of my life for that one year, I would have gladly done it, but there was nobody to take the offer.

So I left.

I thought I would go crazy on the bus. The hour and a half ride was too short and too long. I hated in advance everything that was awaiting me.

Petrovac upon Mlava, a tiny town in Eastern Serbia on the banks of a small river, wasn't ready for my arrival. The autumnal rain splashed dust over it. There was the main street with a few shops and the bridge. I went to the first café and ordered a coke. I lit a cigarette and looked around. Everything was drab and dreary. This place was going to be my reality for a year ahead, unless I got sent somewhere else.

It was about ten at night when I finally had to show up at the barracks. With heavy steps, I made my way and gingerly came to the gate. I was told where to go. I entered a huge room with dozens of beds, most of them already occupied by recruits coming that day from all over Yugoslavia. It stank of sweat. Senior soldiers were bullying somebody at the far end of the room. We were told to go to bed just as we were; we would get the uniform and all the rest the next day and send our civilian clothing home.

There was a variety of faces: handsome, less so, dumb, scared, confused, expectant, a bit of everything, a real melting pot.

Fear left me for I surrendered to the course of time, to the inevitable clock of destiny that had decided it was my time for the Army now, so here I am and whatever it is, it is.

Later on, they turned off the lights. Several young men wept quietly. Sleep overcame me. A strong light woke me up, stinging my eyes. In the middle of the room, there were three senior soldiers, totally drunk. The shortest and drunkest of them was screaming from the top of his lungs:

"I'll fuck your mothers, you idiots!"

"I'll destroy you!" another one was yelling.

"You'll obey us, we're your gods now!" shouted the third.

They were laughing and shrieking like they were insane. The alcohol in their blood was more active than any other element, and since they were brainless, you could tell right away that they were very aggressive. They started removing the blankets from our bodies, sneering at the exposed underwear and pajamas.

"Who bought you these pajamas, son of a bitch?" they asked a youth sleeping next to me.

"My mom," he said.

"Fuck her, all three of us!"

Zoran, as I later learnt his name, started crying. That made them even more hyper, so they went on mocking him. Then they got tired of it and left. Darkness fell on the room.

Somewhere in the distance, a dog's barking blended with sighs of despair.

The morning was quite eventful. Everybody with longish hair was sheared (my hair had fortunately already been clipped short), then we had to pack up our civilian clothing and put the 'send to' address on the box. I sent mine to Nora. I envisioned her opening the box, probably very sadly, looking at my shirt and jeans.

They took pictures of us. Horror. Apart from being non photogenic, I looked like a prisoner, with dark circles around my eyes and a sheet-white face.

Then they started distributing us into groups and subgroups. I was in A2, whatever it stood for. The first day went by fast and in a blink, it was time for sleep.

The dormitory was enormous and shabby, with beds stacked one above the other, spread out all over the place. I was assigned to the upper bed, in the left corner, right by the window. I was so happy, for I always loved being close to a window. In the bed under mine was Zoran, from Montenegro, so sweet and honest and somehow always the laughing stock of senior soldiers. I figured out it was because he was scared of them. Those who are in a position to control people can smell fear, which makes them hyper.

Days were following each other in the wreath of the most imbecilic moments and 'teachings' in the world, humiliating, degrading, and just plain stupid. Still, I didn't allow myself, not for second, to give way to sadness or melancholy, to become a target for the seniors.

We were sitting at desks for hours, studying how to address different ranks. Then we exercised the most ridiculous movements of approaching and taking leave from the officers by clicking the heels. After lunch we were taught how to clean our boots and shoes. The most ludicrous thing was that the new boots and shoes we got the first morning would invariably be replaced every afternoon by old and worn out ones, who knew whose, and ours stolen by senior soldiers. We were practicing the shoe cleaning process for hours on end and while doing it we had to sing some moronic songs.

Brainwashing rated very high in the job description of our teachers who qualified by various degrees of stupidity, so they could wash brains (that they didn't know a single thing about) better.

I wasn't disturbed by anything, for I decided not to be. I was learning how to address an officer.

"Comrade Captain, allow me to report," you had to say.

The captain would retort:

"Report, soldier."

There was the procedure of two and a half steps and saluting with the right hand on the brim of the cap.

Then a modification if addressing a lieutenant, general or whichever rank in the Army. Then the ending of the 'conversation' and the whole thing all over again.

It was ridiculous, it was beyond any common sense, but it was true. The Army was still deep in the waters of fat socialism, rigid and without the slightest changes or adjustments. The military authorities stayed on the level of previous decades, blind and deaf to rebellions that were happening in the country. None of them noticed that the Army was becoming decreasingly 'people's' and increasingly the Party's. It all fell back on their heads in the upcoming years.

Then there were night guard duties. Everybody tried to avoid them but I actually liked them, if there was one likable thing about the Army. When you do the night, you don't have daytime 'lectures'. You are on duty for 24 hours, guard the barracks for 4 hours, sleep for 4 hours and so it goes. There was more satisfaction in watching over worn out boots and the empty corridor than in 'learning' how to wash my hands before and after eating.

Sometimes, during the night, suddenly, one of the ranks would come to check if everything was alright. Then the procedure followed:

Two and a half steps, the salute.

"Comrade Captain, soldier Nikola on duty, Second Division, Brigade A2."

The captain would do a tour, make sure everything was in order, all the boots in neat rows and the corridor floor clean, nod, and go.

I often wrote letters to Nora during those nights, even though there wasn't much to write about.

I missed her a lot.

I missed my piano.

I missed all of my friends.

My non-soldier's life.

My beautiful life, somewhere far away from that corridor.

When you are forced to face unpleasant circumstances in a space you're trapped into, you wonder if life outside of that place still flows, naturally and normally. I made an oath to myself that from that moment on I would fully enjoy and cherish every single day of life in freedom.

Other than the Almighty who is in charge of the whole of existence, there are some staples in our lives that help us come to this point or that, to eventually achieve what we have been meant to. In my case, that was music. It gave solace to my early adulthood, its gentle tones softening the sounds from the room next to mine, where my father yelled at my mom, regularly, punctually, as if by the clock, for no reason whatsoever. Music brought me away from my hometown, saving me from the emotional disaster.

My music won again.

My music was my salvation.

We were standing in strictly ordered rows when the only military person in civilian clothing was introduced to us. He was the Manager of the YPA (Yugoslav People's Army) Home, a separate building that had proper bedrooms, like a mini hotel for higher ranks passing through the town, with all the facilities, a bar and a small cinema. To get there was a soldier's dream. You don't sleep in the barracks, but in a real bed in a beautiful house. The YPA Manager looked groomed, like a real gentleman, and had a velvety voice.

"Dear soldiers," he said. "Your Oath Day is coming and I would like to know if there are some musicians here, so that we can organize a nice event for your parents and friends. Who can play an instrument or sing?"

Lots of hand were raised, mine among them.

Everybody explained briefly what they could do. When it was my turn, I said:

"I have a B.A. Degree in Music and have completed the first part of my Master's. I work as a conductor and professor."

Hundreds of faces turned towards me. In the whole place there were maybe two soldiers with a University Degree. During the past few days nobody ever asked me what I did for living or what my profession was. Needless to say, from that moment I was nicknamed 'Prof' which wasn't bad at all, for nicknames in my country were usually pejorative and degrading. 'Prof' sounded neutral and clear.

The next morning the twelve of us chosen were marching to the YPA Home, on the gray and dusty streets of Petrovac. That was the first time I was outside, after twelve days of 'prison'. We were walking two by two, in the same rhythm. People were going to the market or chatting with neighbors in front of their garden gates. It was an ordinary day for everybody except for me, for all the soldiers in fact. It's a heavy feeling when you are there but you are not there, for I couldn't leave my group, couldn't simply walk away and do what and when I wanted to. For a year I had to be a robot and take orders. We turned from the main road into a side street.

The building was old and dilapidated, the passage of time left deep traces on it. Still, it was imposing. Dark-yellow, with a bay window over the entrance door, it stood proudly, embraced by trees.

We went inside. Two soldiers were guarding the building. I envied them. One wore a wrinkled uniform, had a snotty nose and so totally didn't belong there, to that dignified house. The other one was short, with a handsome face, full of himself, and puffed up, as if he were a general. He gave us a glance 'from above', even though he was shorter than any of us. He paced a bit, then turned on his heels and said:

"I am the boss here!"

Having finished picking at his nose, the other soldier approached us:

"I'm also the boss."

Oh, God, please have mercy!

"We don't sleep in the barracks," they boasted.

"We bring girls here and fuck them," they went on.

"We don't have to eat in the canteen, we buy what we want."

"When the manager goes home at three in the afternoon, we're the kings, don't do anything, just sleep."

They prattled on and on, until their voices drowned into the hum of a cow's intestines digesting her food.

I looked around.

Three steps from the main entrance lead to an oval-shaped hall that could have been so impressive were it not so badly neglected and turned into a big garbage bin. The vaulted, four meter high windows viewing fir, oak and birch trees were stained inside and out, and on top of everything covered with the dirtiest curtains ever, the color of a dead olive. The curtains were at a weird angle, stiffened by dust, just hanging there like a corpse.

I could picture myself working on that place, bringing air, freshness and beauty to it, making it look gorgeous, I wouldn't sleep if need be, but I would do it! My thoughts were swirling only in that direction during the music rehearsals that week.

"Good morning, guys!" The YPA Home Manager greeted us running from the second floor.

He took us to the store room where drums, guitars, keyboard, and the sound system were kept. I was fully in charge, for he graciously let me do the audition of the long listed soldiers in order to find the best ones. Some of them sang, some played an instrument. Everybody was doing their best to show what they could do. It lasted for two days and eventually, I had my band:

Predrag K., drums.

Dejan B., bass guitar.

Cale M., solo guitar.

Me, keyboard and solo singer, which was great.

Predrag and Cale sang well and knew how to hold the supporting voices. Dejan was hopeless singing wise, but was good at keeping the rhythm on the bass guitar.

At any rate, we were exempt from lots of stupid military exercises while getting ready for the Oath Day, on which occasion we were to perform a few songs. Life was getting a tiny little bit of a shade brighter.

Still, living in the barracks was terrible, disgusting, and simply unbearable. Senior soldiers would burst into our dormitory almost every night, yelling, threatening, grinning, doing whatever they wanted, totally drunk. We would wake up at the crack of dawn and make our beds. Goes without saying that they were always 'badly' made and we had to repeat the process four or five times. That was a part of the drill, a way to break the spirit of an individual so it could become a part of the group.

Sometimes, just because, without any announcements, there was an emergency alarm in the middle of the night. We had to get up immediately, run outside as fast as possible, and stand in orderly rows, one behind the other. The officer on duty would step on the podium, scowling and screaming, because he had found a boot with a dirty sole. Until then I had never heard of cleaning your shoe-wear upside down. Then, at 1:30 a.m., 350 soldiers were cleaning boots until each one of them shone spotlessly clean, polished from top to bottom, with a special attention to the soles.

The torture finished, we were allowed to go back to bed for an hour and a half of sleep.

One day brought interviews with the lieutenant. We were told it was very important and that each of us was allowed fifteen minutes. We also heard from senior soldiers that he was a shit of a man and was there only temporarily, until the captain in charge of our brigade got back from sick leave. Each of us got a list with allotted times.

While waiting for that interview, we were dusting the furniture in the room leading to his office. The room was falling apart, with lots of wooden beams, rotten and full of holes. We had to clean them with dirty rags until we fell down on our noses from exhaustion. Every once in a while a senior soldier would come and order us to scrub this or that part again.

It was my time for the interview.

I entered the office in which the lieutenant was sitting behind the desk and did the loathful ritual of introduction followed by heel clicking. He told me to sit down in front of him.

Lieutenant Željko was very good-looking for 'a shit of a man'. He really had the evil gleam in his penetrating eyes framed by curved eyebrows. His hair and sideburns were black as ebony. He had something of a movie star, like a mix of Alain Delon and Sylvester Stallone from their young days.

His most striking, actually beautiful feature was that face, the expression, with eyes darker than coal and deeper than the Lake of Baikal.

He stood up and walked around the room. Short and stout, all firm muscle. He walked self-confidently and his glance was too strong for me, so I gazed down. I wasn't afraid of him, but that look was too powerful to hold on.

"Where are you from, soldier?" he asked. His voice sounded cold and cruel.

"From the South of Serbia, Lieutenant," I said.

"What do you do?"

"I am a musician, I teach music."

"Soldier, speak up, I lost my ears at maneuvers," he said almost angrily.

"Yes, Comrade Lieutenant," I said in a louder voice.

"What do you do?" he repeated the question.

"Music, I teach music," I said from the top of my lungs.

"That's good," he said.

He asked me about my fears, my past, and allergies, my family and what I thought about a suicide. He wanted to know everything, among other things, if I had a girlfriend. When I said I did, he asked if I missed her.

"Of course I miss her."

"But not enough that you cry for her."

I didn't know what to say to that, for each answer would be a wrong one.

He sat down. He was writing something on a piece of paper. Then he stood up again and cast me a glance that pierced my stomach in a second.

Then he told me I could go.

Many a soldier left that office crying, sweating, and shaking. I didn't have any of that, leaving with the impression that our conversation went alright. I couldn't tell anyone that I actually liked Lieutenant Željko quite a lot, because he was incredibly handsome, strict but fair.

The following few days were spent almost entirely outside of the barracks, except for going back there to sleep, for I was busy preparing the program for the Oath Day. It consisted of three revolutionary songs, two poems written by soldiers, accompanied by music and a popular ballad that had always been a great hit at all patriotic gatherings:

With fire in our hearts
Remembering the battles past
Count on us...

The Oath Day came and went. The music was super, my band played professionally and everybody enjoyed our performance. Then we were allowed to leave the barracks for the rest of the day and be with our families. That was one of the most difficult moments in my life. My family and relatives were there, and Nora. I was wearing the uniform, looked and felt terrible. They were on the other side of the line, for they were free, and we didn't have much to talk about, so we were simply looking at one another. I could only tell them that it was horrible, that we were maltreated, that it was all stupid and without any sense, but I didn't want to talk about it, to bring more worries into their lives.

For the people in Yugoslavia the Oath Day used to be one of the most important events in the world. The military service was regarded as a symbol of masculinity and meant everything to parents who had sons. In some parts of the country, going to the Army was celebrated more than a wedding. At that time, in that country, there was no chance for me not to do my 'patriotic duty'. If I had been miraculously saved from it, my mother would have been spat on by the whole lot of her neighbors, friends, and acquaintances.

Later, when Nora or mom came to visit me, it was different, nice and relaxing, but that day, the Day of the Oath, it didn't feel good to see them. They were free and I wasn't. I knew that at the end of the day I would witness another attack of senior soldiers who were well aware that we, the juniors, would get money, food, cakes, whatnot, so they were in the 'Ready, Set, Go!' mode to steal and destroy everything that came their way. As luck would have it, I was on duty that night, from midnight to four in the morning.

Drained out, I went to bed at ten, knowing that Zoran would wake me up at midnight (he was on duty until then). Looking at the raindrops slowly running down the dirty window pane, I felt a deep longing for mom, Nora and everybody who came that day.

Zoran woke me up at 11:40 p.m. He always did that, woke me up earlier so he could sleep a bit longer. Each time I promised to myself I would also wake him up earlier, when it was my turn, but never did it, for I was sorry for him. I washed, got dressed, and started to guard shoes, boots, toilets, and walls. While washing my face, I took stock of my bloodshot eyes, tired and puffy, from the lack of sleep. I didn't look myself, not at all.

The silence of the night was disturbed only by snoring of some soldiers in the adjacent dormitory. I was so sleepy, but had to be on guard and pace up and down the corridor lit by a pale light of a single bulb. I heard steps, unsteady yet firm, and turned towards the entrance door.

Lieutenant Željko was standing there, heavily imbibed, barely supported by his legs.

"Comrade Lieuten...," I started the routine introduction, when he shushed me up.

"Shhh, quiet," he said with a heavy tongue. "D'you want everybody to see me drunk?"

I kept quiet.

He came closer to me. A strong stench of alcohol wafted from him.

"Soldier, I forgot your name." He was looking at me intently.

"Nikola."

"Take me to my room, Nikola, that's the order!"

"Yes, sir!"

He tried to put his left arm around my shoulder, but since he was shorter, it was easier for him to hold me around the waist. I helped him walk slowly on the wet slippery path to the next building where his room was. We went inside. I turned on the light and barely made it to sit him on the bed. He was very heavy for such a short man.

"Soldier," he rolled his tongue.

"At service, Comrade Lieutenant," I answered the way I had to.

"Fuck that lieutenant, here, help me undress and let me sleep, lock the door when you leave."

"Yes, sir."

It was hard to undress him because he was groggy, jerking and mumbling something every now and then. It was both sad and comical to see him in such a state. Lieutenant Željko had a sculptured body. In his early thirties, he started losing his hair (probably from the helmet he had to wear on frequent maneuvers) but even that suited him. He had sort of a savage beauty. A mix of a Muslim father and a Serbian mother, he inherited glistening dark eyes and light complexion. He looked gorgeous. The rumor went that he wasn't married because he loved whores too much and would spend his paychecks immediately, taking three or four of them at the same time, paying for a night of pleasure. Zoran heard from somebody that once, at the maneuvers, he fucked a local hooker on sand sacks, in plain view of about hundred soldiers.

He was now lying on the bed helpless, like a little child. What a difference from his shouting at us, his hard glance and cruel voice and this man in front of me, naked to the waist. I was trying to take off his pants but it wasn't easy, for they were tight. He came around a bit and made an attempt to help me, but I gently pushed him back for his movements were in the way. When I eventually managed to remove his pants, shoes and socks, he was left only in his underwear. To my astonishment, his masculinity was so clearly outlined, huge, like a horse's and stiff hard. The lieutenant had an erection charged like a thunderbolt. No wonder he took four whores per night, with such a tool he could shag senseless the whole of Petrovac upon Mlava and all the surrounding villages.

I was slowly taking my leave when he woke up and asked for some water. He was gulping it, gazing at me with sleepy eyes.

"Thank you, soldier."

"You are very welcome, sir."

"I remember you, you're a musician."

"Yes, indeed."

He removed the blanket and took hold of his masculinity. He looked at me in such a strange way that a few drops of cold sweat ran down my spine, all the way to my butt.

"You see this?"

"Yes."

"This is the biggest cock in the barracks, I'm telling you, but there's nothing to fuck. If you were a woman, I'd screw you right now, tear you apart."

I didn't know what to say to that, so I was still standing between him and the door.

He cast me an inquisitive look.

"Come here."

I came closer.

"Sit down."

I sat down next to him.

He patted my hand and said in a low voice:

"If you're gay, I'll fuck you every night when you're on duty."

He was serious. Dead drunk but dead serious.

"No, Comrade Lieutenant, I am not," I muttered.

He whipped me with his eyes.

"Sure?"

"Sure."

He mumbled something, went back to bed, then got up and took my hand.

"Musician?"

"Yes."

"I want you to sing something for me now, softly, in the ear, so I can go to sleep. I'll discharge you of all the unpleasant tasks for a day if you do me this favor."

"Which song?"

"*Ibar water, flow slowly.*"

"I know it."

That was one of my most favorite folk songs. The Ibar is a fast river running through the South West of Serbia and you ask it to slow down, to relieve you of everything that's bothering you, while you contemplate on its banks.

I sat down beside the lieutenant, singing sottovoce. He listened and breathed deeply. His eyelids were closing slowly, carried away by the quiet melody coming from my soul. The silence woke him up for a moment. He looked at me. His eyes were soft.

"Go now, I want to sleep."

"Yes, sir."

I closed the door and went out into the crisp night. I looked at my watch. It was time to wake up Zoran, to take over the guarding duty.

Days were dragging on. After that great music performance on the Oath Day, I expected to be established in the role of the official musician and transferred to the YPA Home, but it wasn't like that. The YPA Home Manager stopped coming to the barracks. The boot camp exercises we had to undergo were too harsh for my physical condition. I started breaking down a bit, for I was waiting for something to happen, but nothing did.

In sad nights, just before sleep, I thought about those two soldiers who lived in the YPA Home undeservingly. They slept in nice clean beds, had a bath every day, and could do whatever they wanted. I envied them. I prayed to God to help me be there, instead of having to learn how to take apart every single kind of rifle or gun and put the pieces back together. I prayed to all the Saints and apologized for not going to church often enough.

The barracks was getting fuller and fuller.

The exercises were getting increasingly demanding and complex. We started training for a sort of a tank, some stupid vehicle that could take up to eight soldiers, called FVI (Fight Vehicle of Infantry), even though IFV (Infantry Fucking Vehicle) would have been more appropriate. I could never digest the disgusting thing. Endless instructions and practice as to how to get on and off that useless piece of machinery were destroying us all slowly, hour after hour, day after day.

"15 seconds, not bad, girls," a senior soldier, not the sharpest knife in the drawer, would say. "You can do better, girls!"

15 seconds got reduced to 10 and then to 8 seconds, which was a record.

The hateful thing was hitting us from all sides, for it was full of metal bars and various hooks, so we constantly bumped into them, especially when all eight of us rushed inside and out like crazy. I could smell the stench of my own sweat and that almost killed me, for never ever before had I felt it.

Whenever Lieutenant Željko came to supervise the procedure, he looked at me somehow differently than at other soldiers. I thought he was remembering that night and was uncomfortable about what he had said to me. Maybe he was ashamed. He came to me one day and said he wanted to keep the promise he had given me that night.

"What is it you least like to do, soldier?"

"Getting in and out of this vehicle, Comrade Lieutenant."

"At 9 a.m. tomorrow you'll be at my office. I want you to type some documents for me, I'll leave them on the left side of the desk. Go out in the afternoon, I'll inform the officer on duty."

"Yes, sir."

He was fair and honest to his word. I liked him a lot at that moment. 'A free afternoon' was an abstract adjective noun combination for all of us. I could barely sleep that night from excitement.

The next day, at his office, I typed everything he had asked me to and then went out to the town. My first stop was a bakery where I bought burek (a thick phyllo pastry pie soaked with ripened cheese). Next, I ordered pljeskavica (Serbian style hamburger, minced meat with chopped onions and spices, grilled on the spot) from a nearby kiosk. Then I sat down at a bistro by the river, sipping beer. Hours were ticking like minutes and minutes like seconds.

We were about to leave for a maneuver somewhere far, into some distant fields. It had been raining insanely for days and I could visualize the hell waiting for us in those fields, shooting, sleeping on cold mud and all the evil breaking loose. I hated shooting from the very first day. The rifle didn't suit my shoulder, nor the trigger my fingers. My arms and fingers were made for piano keys and conductor's stick. I was disgusted by the smell of gun powder. I abhorred the moment of firing, especially when it had to be in a succession of bullets. I hated all of that but had to do it, for it was a part of my life at that point.

Fortune came in the shape of misfortune. We were standing in orderly rows in the early morning, the dumb commander of the barracks droning some stupidities, when I almost fainted from a sharp pain. Blood was leaking through my boots. As if all my blisters burst out in a second.

I was secretly glad for that, hoping that might be my ticket for escaping the maneuver. Lieutenant Željko was standing next to me when I asked his permission to go to the military hospital.

When the doctor examined me, he said I had to stay in the barracks, couldn't possibly go to a maneuver. I was so happy I could fly!

I was lying in bed with my feet wrapped up for a few days and felt so much better. My mate soldiers came back, dirty as pigs from the mud and dust. They said it had been all terrible and horrible. I shivered at the thought that I might have been there.

"What are you thinking about, Prof?" a familiar voice woke me up from daydreaming.

"Nothing really, Kuki, how are you doing?"

"It's going, Prof, it's going somehow," he said lengthening each word. "I'm thinking about my cows and the meadows in my Zagorje."

Kuki, as I called him, Davor Kukica in fact, was a wonderful young man from a small remote village on the river Drava, cuddled by green pastures on the gentle slopes of Zagorje, in Croatia. He grew up in the fields, surrounded by cows and sheep, enchanted by the music of the birds, by the young shots of grains and the silence of the woods. Army wasn't for him, the same way it wasn't for me.

Unfortunately, nature didn't match his soul to his looks: big ears, narrow head, spiky hair, and a shrilly voice to go with that. He was the laughing stock from the first to the last day of the Army. In his extraordinary way, Kuki bore it all with a smile. He obeyed the senior soldiers and did whatever they told him to, like:

"Go see if I'm outside."

Kuki would step out and come back dead serious:

"Comrade, you are not outside."

They mocked and tortured him and he stood it all like a stoic, often laughing to himself. Any other soldier in the same set of circumstances would be on the brink of a suicide, but Kuki survived. I marveled at how he did that.

He was telling us about Čakovec, a small-town where he was born, about beautiful lush valleys around the village he lived in, about the birds' song in the trees. He liked Nora a lot and Nora liked him a lot. Every time she came to visit me, she had a big chocolate bar for him. He felt very important in those moments.

I often wonder now, after more than twenty years after the Army, how he is doing. I sincerely hope that the madness of the Serbian-Croatian war didn't take him away to some battlefield and extinguished his young life. I visualize him happy, married, with lots of children, in his green fields, surrounded by cows, sheep, birds' song in the trees and grains sprouting from the fertile soil.

One day Nora and I will go to Čakovec and to the Small Village on Drava to experience the beauty from Kuki's stories and maybe meet him One day, when there's no war any more.

Not a trace of it.

Not the tiniest trace of it.

When time heals the wounds.

If time can heal the wounds.

That night, like every night, I prayed to God to watch over all the people I knew and didn't know, to keep the peace in the country and to give good health and happiness to my family and friends. I was lying in bed, with eyes wide-open towards the ceiling. Zoran was snoring loudly in the bed under mine. Siniša, to my left, was playing with his winkie, as usually. He was funny in his own way, with hands constantly deep in his pockets, fiddling with his genitals. We all laughed when one of the soldiers accidentally noticed that his front pockets were always torn, so he could have unlimited access to his intimate organs.

Through the small window of my dormitory the light from the adjacent building was entering. Another soldier was on night duty.

I was gazing at the ceiling, praying for a better day.

The second month was slowly coming to its end, rolling into the first day of my third month in the Army.

The power of my being was still strong, but I could feel it seeping away. As the exercises were getting more strenuous, as the days became filled with shooting, targets and simulated attacks, I was feeling worse by a bullet, losing bit by bit my composure and courage. I knew there was no way around it. I had to do the Army and I would, come what may.

I was looking through the ceiling and saw the galaxies of the Universe and secluded places where God lives. I asked Him to give me the strength to go through all this.

"Amen," I said quietly and turned to my right, towards the wall.

Brought by my sudden movement or by the flight of Angels, a small white feather landed on my nose. I caught it carefully and held it between my fingers. I knew that something was about to change.

For the better.

Nora's Impressions

Army is the most abominable of all the men invented organizations ever!

What is the purpose of it anyway? Who wants to fight? Who wants wars? It blows my mind. Like, if you were born into this world, you're supposed to live in it and let others live, not get trained for potential or real killing (and maybe get killed yourself in the process).

OK, some people don't know where to go, so they go to the army, like it's straightforward, you do what you're told to, brain goes to sleep, easy. Just don't make it mandatory for people who know where to go and whose brains are very active!

The animalistic side of humans (a distorted form of pure animals' instincts) finds its full scope in torturing its fellow mates. Are you happier with yourselves after you have maltreated people around you? I bet you aren't. So why do it?

How about living in peace with yourselves and all the people surrounding you? Where did the loving kindness go?

Just before Marko comes on the day that didn't need to come, Nikola produces a long paper roll, tapes it on the inside of my closet and writes on top of it: 365. The number of days he is to spend outside of himself, in 'another country'. My first early morning task is to cross the days, one by one, until they come to 0, which will mark his freedom.

I watch my love unwillingly departing into an unknown future, supported by a firm shoulder of his best friend. The view from my wide-open bedroom window isn't large enough to encompass all that's transpiring. All I feel is that a part of myself is going away with every single step of Nikola's.

So, I pour myself a large brandy, which I hate, but gulp it in one shot, just to sooth my tingling nerves and my aching heart.

Thus encouraged, I start writing a letter to Nikola, one of the many. His letters come to me multifold, filling up the picnic baskets which we normally use for our outings into nature, woods, parks and walks by the river.

The first morning without him I wake up to the scent of his skin on my pillowcase and everything's fine with the world, just that it isn't. Nikola's not here!

For God's sake, he's somewhere out there, where no real human wants to be, in the cold, deprived of sleep, obeying the orders of some imbeciles! No!

Please God modify his path, for this is so totally plain stupid! I'm desperate!

Mom comes to lift up my spirits. She makes tons of open sandwiches, all artistically decorated, to prompt me to put something into my stomach, and gallons of coffee. We're chatting like casually, never mind we're silently crying our hearts out to Heavens.

"Nikola is safe, don't worry, he is going to make it. Now, how about a nice walk or some shopping, you want to look pretty on his Oath Day, right?" Mom is soothing as always.

My best friend Lina, a cosmetician, gives me a special face & body treatment, basically treating me as if I were recovering from a near death experience, and as we sip coffee (into which she secretly pours some fiery liquid) and smoke, she shuffles the cards that happen to be on the side table and says, like by the way:

"Hey, you'll get married sometime soon."

My friend Iva, an astrologer, analyzes Nikola's progressive chart, transits and all, and proclaims:

"The path is clear, the bumps are negligible."

My dearest Italian professor greets me as I run along the University corridors to my classes:

"You look like a little girl!"

That's what physical activity, like playing with moving boxes and placing their contents at appropriate spots does to you.

So that's it, I have my staple. Study the beautiful language and literature, assured that my love will come out of all the hardships, purified.

In the interim, I give tons of private lessons which relax my mind and my students bring me gifts of flowers and small tokens.

Anyway, the Oath Day comes, Nikola's mom, his aunt Paki, his cousin Neško, some more relatives, and I are going to see him again after more than a month! We are all so excited, while Nikola is standing in the front row, waiting for the official ceremony to be over, so he can play his music and sing! My parents don't come, my father because he doesn't care about what befalls my beloved, and my mom because she cares too much.

I meet the guys from Nikola's band, they're so cool! I guess it's the music that guides them through the involuntary service.

I also meet Dean, a great guy from Zagreb, Nikola's close friend then, always keeping in touch with him in the years to come, and we enjoy beer at the YPA Home garden with his parents.

There's a tall blond guy, with a head that sort of resembles cubist paintings. He comes from a small village in Croatian Zagorje. He's the only one really grounded there, totally centered, like come what may, my fields and cows are waiting for me when this is all over. He's my absolute favorite, like how on earth does he do it?

Never judge a book by the cover or a person by the appearance.

By the end of the day I'm in a philosophical mood. Life has its ups and downs. Good times and bad times. Day and night. The Sun and the Moon. Crocuses, daffodils, tulips, and hyacinths rejoice in the first spring sunrays. Bare tree branches and dry grass blades sway to the late autumn winds. And so it goes on, the circle of life, death, and rebirth.

If you're not down, how do you know when you're up, or vice versa. Then Yin and Yang comes to mind again. In the black oval, there's a white dot, and in the white oval, there's a black dot and they form a perfect circle.

"There is a fortune in every misfortune," my grandma used to say. A blessing in disguise, just that the expression is sort of worn out, so people don't fully comprehend its meaning.

Human beings tend to shift from one polarity to another, often not recognizing the little white or black dot.

Also, there's A Time for Everything, if you read the Ecclesiastes.

Time for me to leave Nikola to his duty, however unpleasant it may be and go home to tell mom everything about the day.

House of the Rising Sun

My prayers were granted one morning. I didn't know there were three soldiers at the YPA Home, not just those two I had met. The third one was a constantly drunk, out of control bully. While on duty one night, he got totally drunk, took off his uniform, and showed up only in his underwear when an exhausted superior officer from out of town knocked at the door, in dire need of a bed and some rest. Then, of course, he was kicked out of the Home and sent back to the barracks. I couldn't figure out how he had managed to get there in the first place. In my mind the Home was reserved for special soldiers, those who could represent it properly.

One man's misfortune is another man's fortune, you could say. Lieutenant Željko was told to let me move into the Home the next day. I was with my group, in the action of dissembling big machine guns to their minutest parts, cleaning them and putting them all back together. That particular 'operation' was absolutely the most irrational thing in my soldier's life so far, totally absurd and irritating. I couldn't understand any of it. I was the worst in my group, which was actually a good thing, for it gave the opportunity to my companions to be better than Prof in something, which made some sort of a life balance. Nobody can be good at everything.

My dear, always smiling Kuki was helping me with all his heart, showing me how to do it and encouraging me.

"See, Prof, it's easy: you unscrew, pull out and close there, then slowly put that small part inside, right here, c'mon, it's a piece of cake for a professor like you!"

"I just don't get it, my friend. It's all Spanish to me," I said.

"Ah, don't play daft now, Prof. You've read so many books, have University diplomas, you can do this, too, trust me!"

"Right, Kuki. I'm trying, see?"

Time stood still. Seconds were dragging like minutes and minutes were endless. On the positive side, the ten of us were at that moment far from any reality, in some strange time pocket. We were sitting, talking quietly about parts of rifles and machine guns while clocks were ticking imperceptibly. There was no TV, not even a radio, just the half open window bringing the sound of rustling leaves, ready to part from the trees and fall on the ground.

Suddenly, the door opened.

Lieutenant Željko walked in and we all stood up quickly and saluted him. The leader of our group approached him and briefly reported what we were doing. The lieutenant approved of the report, then turned to me and said:

"Soldier, follow me."

"Yes, sir."

I didn't know what was in store for me, but I didn't have any forebodings, because I hadn't done anything wrong other than having spent a few days in hospital, which wasn't my fault. My boots got stolen one night and replaced by much smaller and tighter ones, and as luck would have it, we marched for kilometers that day, so my feet were all in blisters that broke and my heels bled.

He was walking very fast, I could barely keep up with him. He didn't say anything, so we strode in silence.

We entered his office.

"Sit down, soldier," he said.

I sat down on a chair in front of him. I couldn't get out of my head the image of his half naked body from a few weeks ago. I guessed the same thought crossed his mind, because he smiled (which he did on very rare occasions) and said:

"Remember how drunk I was that night?"

I kept quiet, not daring to say "Yes" or "No".

"Don't be afraid of me, soldier, I'm not as dangerous as everybody says."

He was still smiling, for more than two minutes, simply impossible for him, for the fearsome Lieutenant Željko. His smile brought light to that small gray room –, which was a pleasant experience. He had dazzling white teeth and lips like Richard Burton from Cleopatra, with divine Elizabeth Taylor, forever remembered in the hearts of millions of her fans.

"I am not afraid, Comrade Lieutenant," I said. "Yes, I remember that you were drunk that night, it's true, but not too much," I added hastily.

The smile never left his handsome face. I wished I could have looked at him intently, but that wouldn't be polite and besides his mood might change in the fraction of a second and he may start yelling, as was his way. He went by the nickname 'H', for Horrible.

As if reading my mind, he looked straight into the pupils of my eyes, lit a cigarette, and said through the dense smoke:

"Listen to me, it's good news you are being transferred to the YPA Home, sign here."

The Heavens had been listening to my prayers.

Angels came to my aid, I was certain.

"Yes, Comrade Lieutenant," I said with a trembling voice.

The sky and the earth blended into one, they became paradise. A new door was opening before me, inviting me to come in. I knew that from that moment on everything would take a turn for the better. I was secretly scared that something might happen in the next hour or two, outbreak of World War Three or a natural disaster, so I wouldn't be allowed to move from the barracks to the YPA Home. I was shit scared as a matter of fact. Please God, no earthquakes, floodings or alien attacks in the meantime.

With a shaking hand I signed the document that stated my transfer as well as duties and responsibilities at the Home. I couldn't see the words clearly, for the Home building, surrounded by beautiful fir, oak and birch trees was in front of my eyes.

The lieutenant stood up and we shook hands. Then, to my astonishment, he hugged me tightly, unexpectedly. I was caught up in the moment, all the air was pushed out of my chest. I was sure he interpreted my cry for oxygen as weeping without tears. He took me by the shoulders, shook them, and hugged me again. This time, for just half a second, I felt his sharp stubble scratch my sensitive face skin.

"I'll miss you, soldier," he said.

I really had nothing to say to that, because I wouldn't miss anything about this disgusting barracks.

"You are a good young man, the best of all," he said. "I'm sorry that you're leaving. Your group needs you as a role model of a soldier and a great friend. They will miss you, too."

I panicked. What if he does something to prevent the coming true of my biggest dream?

"Comrade Lieutenant, I know you will be visiting the YPA Home and I will often come here for lunch or dinner and to see my mates and you..." I was talking nonsense. Then I asked:

"May I have your permission to leave and pack?"

"You are free to leave, soldier," he said.

I made to the door, then retraced my steps and turned to him.

"Thank you for everything, Comrade Lieutenant," I said.

As expected, he hugged me again, tightly.

I went out into the cold November afternoon, running at high speed from the office building to my dormitory. The soldier on duty was a newbie, only a couple of weeks in the army. He got taken aback by the way I flew in, but I calmed him down.

"Sorry, I'm in a hurry."

I grabbed my military bag and stuffed all my 'treasures' inside:

    4 pairs of socks
    4 pieces of underwear
    4 white undershirts
    3 long sleeved shirts
    2 short sleeved shirts
    1 uniform for special occasions
    4 pairs of pants
    1 belt
    Shoes
    Boots

A bundle of letters from Nora and Mom.

I was racing up towards the main gate of the barracks. Dean was passing by. He was lucky to become the secretary of the commander in chief and moved into the command building, where it was so much better for him. He was my closest friend, so sweet, with such a great soul. I told him my news. He was ecstatic:

"You deserved it, bravo!"

Dean could go out to town whenever he asked, he didn't need passes. I knew that he would often come to the Home and that we would be actually seeing much more of each other there than in the barracks.

"Godspeed, may luck always be with you!" he wished me as I was running out.

I walked on the same dusty road as on the first day of the Army, just that now I levitated, my steps light with happiness.

As I entered the Home, the staleness of an unaired place almost suffocated me. To the left there was some sort of a bistro. The owner apparently rented the space from the Home. An ugly skinny old woman with filthy hair and a cigarette dangling from her mouth was standing a bit unsteadily behind the counter sporting dead flies in the thick layer of dust.

"Who the fuck are you?" she asked.

"Good afternoon, my name is Nikola, I am a new soldier here. And you are?"

"I'm Draginja, head waitress in this mother fucker in the ass bistro."

"Nice to meet you," I said and turned toward the reception desk.

The hatred in the eyes of the guy at the reception was so thick, you could slice if with a knife.

"What do you want?" he snapped.

"From today I am here at the Home with you," I said.

"You?"

He looked at me as if I had three noses or green hair.

"Yes, me."

"I haven't been informed, but since you're here, I'll show you to the room."

We climbed the stairs to the first floor.

The building was old and dilapidated, but that staircase stayed forever in my memory as a scene from Gone with the Wind. I was Scarlett O'Hara and going up. The room was tiny, but it had a decent bed by the window and I had it all for myself! The luxury of having privacy in the Army!

The next morning I was in high spirits. I went downstairs and saw the other soldier at the reception desk. He was looking at me with the same loathing as the previous one. I realized they blamed me for the departure of their companion who was from their part of the country and spoke their language. It wasn't my fault that he was a drunkard and I couldn't care less about the whole thing.

At 8 a.m. the YPA Home Manager came, in an elegant suit and an impeccable white shirt.

"Welcome, Nikola," he greeted me.

"Thank you, sir."

"Make yourself comfortable here, you have the whole morning to settle in. We'll talk about music and events in the afternoon."

"Yes, sir."

"Relax, Nikola, I don't need military formalities, OK?"

"OK, boss."

He smiled and went upstairs. I liked him a lot then, and to this day, some twenty years later, I still bow to this man and his heart. I will never forget the way he welcomed me and everything he did for me later. May he have all the best of life, each day more prosperous than the previous one.

My first week passed in getting familiar with various duties and the building itself. It was situated on the crossroads, where the center of the small town gave way to villages. On the ground floor there was a huge space, equipped with chairs, stage, and a big screen, made for concerts and movies. Also potentially beautiful hall, currently unappealing, never cleaned, with dirt stiffened curtains swinging like corpses when the strong winds blew through numerous holes in the huge windows. It must have made a bad first impression to everyone who came in: to the left an old drunk woman, to the right a dark entrance hall. In the center the rotting reception desk cluttered with food leftovers, newspapers, porn magazines, and overflowing ashtrays.

On the second floor were the manager's office, two guest rooms ready for superior officers in case they needed to overnight, soldiers' rooms, and a nice conference hall, full of light that shone through the white curtains.

The main roles at the Home were distributed to the manager, his secretary (a sweetheart of a woman) and the cleaning lady (good hearted but often moody). I loved to hear her laugh and always tried to transform her pain and sadness into joke and laughter. Who knows what happened in her life who knows when, for her distress was sometimes palpable. The three of them were there from 8 a.m. to 3 p.m. every day except on Saturdays and Sundays.

The notoriously drunk 'head waitress', the only one at the bistro as it turned out, played the supporting role. Every once in a while she would utter something profoundly wise, but basically blabbered incessantly, like an empty windmill. On a good day there was a max of four guests. She spent most of her time bent over the table, sipping her drink and chain smoking. It was impossible to follow the train of her thoughts, because at one moment she was all smiley and vibrant with life, only to switch to disgusting swearing and cursing the next, vowing she would never ever come back to work again. She was so alone, withered and deep into alcohol, that she often mixed reality with dream. My fellow soldiers found it very funny and often mocked her, saying "Hi!" to her like twenty times a day and then pretending it wasn't them who were coming to the bistro, just to confuse her even more and clog the membranes of consciousness in her brain.

The rest of the cast consisted of three soldiers: two from Kosovo, from the same village, and myself. Those two had only three months left to serve in the Army and acted as if the whole world belonged to them. I didn't blame them, at least not too much. That was probably the highlight of their lives, let them enjoy, for what was waiting for them back in their village? Their petty remarks and sneaky stings couldn't reach my nervous system or my emotions, I just let them pass. Their comments were always based on comparison of the clean and splendid people they came from and bad, very bad people and habits here in Serbia.

"Shame on this hag drinking brandy, a woman to drink, no woman could ever do it in our parts," one of them would say. "If she was my mother, sister, or wife, I'd beat her to death, right away!"

"Uh, see this shame, the girls on the streets dressed like this, a sin, we don't allow that," the other one would add. "If she was my sister I'd kill her on the spot, by gun or axe!"

I wanted to stand up for women's rights and explain that here in Serbia we don't kill our mothers, sisters and wives if they wear short skirts or drink a glass or two, but that would have initiated a long discussion and no good would come out of it.

I didn't want to meddle into cultural differences. I always respected everybody's opinion, no matter how opposed it might be to mine. With all my willpower I tried to bridge the gap between our cultures and avoid disagreements, like let's talk about the beautiful music of Kosovo, impressive old buildings and cobblestoned streets. Sometimes it worked, sometimes not.

We divided the duties in the Home more or less equally, just that the night duty always somehow fell on me. I actually didn't mind it, because I found an old typewriter in the basement and typed letters to Nora, to her wonderful mom, to my mom and to my friends. I made the envelopes from pages of fashion magazines and believe that Nora still has hundreds of letters written during those long nights.

November swept over Petrovac, swishing the last leaves from the trees around the Home. We started heating. I switched my jackets, the winter one I liked better, for it filled up my emaciated body. I weighed 120 pounds then. Nights were infused with long, heavy rains. Sometimes it rained for three days on end, incessantly. I wrote letters by the window in the entrance hall, listening to the rhythm of the rain. I loved the music of the drops falling from the sky. Strong winds from Homolje Mountains were blowing, shifting the curtains.

With the Home Manager's permission, I went to an elementary school twice a week and taught children choir singing, rehearsing them for upcoming events. It was wonderful, I felt myself again, a musician, not a soldier. We sang both traditional and military songs that we later presented to 400 soldiers of our battalion.

I often called Dean before going to the school and we would get together. Our friendship was genuine and beautiful. We were both apprehensive about the conferences of the presidents of all Yugoslav republics, where they disputed and fought a lot. Dean was Croatian and their president was very much against the unity of Yugoslavia. Dean and I were scared of every next day. There were rumors about mobilization, about war. It didn't sound good, not at all.

We used to sit in a small café, just off the main street, over coffee and fizzy water, chatting about fellow soldiers, our superiors, the Home, and the barracks. Occasionally, to release the fear, we mentioned the possibility of a war.

"I'm afraid the worst might happen," I would say to Dean.

He would shrug his shoulders.

The presidents and leaders of our republics at the time were having their meetings in magnificent old castles and luxurious rooms in opulent villas all over the country, discussing and fighting over vintage champagne and most sophisticated food. A multitude of various representatives and advisors and God knows what not from abroad was with them. It was a humongous ratatouille, with chopped human pain and disaster as main ingredients. They were 'trying to save Yugoslavia', which was a downright lie, simultaneously acquiring fire arms and building up their respective armies, at first secretly and then more and more openly.

Attacks on Serbian villages by Croatian para-military formations were getting increasingly frequent, as well as attacks of Serbs on Muslim villages, Muslims on Serbian villages, a vicious circle. The TV news were more disturbing day by day.

On top of everything, I was in the Army.

The Yugoslav People's Army had already been declared enemy in Slovenia and Croatia and Bosnia followed suit. We were soldiers captured in the Army, scared of what the next day might bring. Dean and I shifted our conversations to music and arts,

Petrovac upon Mlava and its people, to anecdotes and jokes. We both wanted to shake the dust of politics off our feet, but that wasn't always possible.

We would finish our coffees and go – he to the barracks, me to the school for the choir rehearsal.

My colleague at the school, Julia, was studying at the College of Music in Skoplje, Macedonia. She was sweet and eager to learn as much as possible about music, so I often helped her prepare for some difficult exams. I felt needed and that made me happy.

One gray November evening my fellow soldiers at the Home were, for no specific reason, extremely irate, punching their fists into the walls, the reception desk and the railings. They were freaking out all day. The add-on was the old waitress, also for unexplained reasons incredibly loud in expressing her opinion against Croatians, Albanians and all the other nations. She was swearing to no end. I was caught up in the middle: on one side the two of them raging about her and the whole world and on the other her, the way God made her.

And then, somebody knocked at the door. It was Julia. Her exam was in a couple of days and she needed help.

I welcomed her in and we sat down at the table. The moment she opened her harmony book and my eyes glimpsed the wonderful landscapes of accords and notes, the angry soldiers and the drunk woman became a past. Music was the present, right here, in front of me. I gave Julia some useful tips for the written part of the exam, but also made sure she thoroughly understood the subject, so she could smoothly pass the oral.

She made it, with a high mark.

Days were passing by.

Nora often came to see me, telling me about her studies, about Lela, Marko and Mira and about her mom's fragile health. Her visits were a real pleasure.

She was also telling me about the political parties in Serbia, the newly formed opposition and their goals against the current government and the regime. It all sounded so irrational, so tangled up, so full of hatred. The world went crazy and the craziness was spreading high speed.

My world was this building with nine rooms.

The autumn was slowly ending, already in a passionate embrace with the approaching winter. Nights were getting darker and colder. On one of those nights, while on duty, I composed a song. It came quietly, almost imperceptibly, like a tender bud opening its music petals in my head. I was writing notes and harmonies all night, hearing duos and trios, main and supporting voices, in a polyphony of a choir. I could barely wait for the morning to bring it to the children at the school, to see their reaction.

The children loved the song. We rehearsed for a couple of weeks until I decided to present it to the Home Manager. He was ecstatic and suggested we send it to 'At ease, soldier', one-hour series on TV1 every Sunday morning, about lives of soldiers.

We sent a letter and the tape I recorded with the children's choir in the hall of the Home. The response came swiftly. The TV team was coming to Petrovac, to make shots of the barracks and especially of the YPA Home, of me, my choir, and the band.

I was bursting with happiness, as were all the soldiers and the officers. The barracks would be on TV for the first time in its history and it was all my doing!

I was sincerely looking forward to it, for I wanted all the best things to happen to this small town. I wanted music, at least temporarily, to be the center of attention. Dean called me that evening to congratulate me.

"You rock, old chum, everybody's talking about it!"

A week later, the TV team showed up at the entrance door. There were six of them and they set up the cameras, lights and everything.

Needless to say how much we cleaned to make sure the Home looked presentable. A few days before their arrival, I decided to take charge of the interior decoration and turn the spacious room on the ground floor with curtains that had never been washed, filthy windows and floor full of stains, into something really appealing. I asked the manager to give me some money to buy a few things and to get me about ten soldiers to help with cleaning. He agreed. That man had a big heart and respect for me. He trusted me and knew I wouldn't do anything unreasonable.

When the soldiers came, I split them up into groups and distributed tasks: floor cleaning, window washing, then painting the woodwork around the windows. I chose olive green, the color of our uniforms, but the inside of the window frames was painted white. The stiff old curtains went into the garbage, replaced by light translucent ones, swaying in the wind that was coming through the open windows. The soldiers were happy to be at the Home with me and not in the barracks, so they worked with great enthusiasm.

Two days later, the manager was presented with a room he couldn't take his eyes off. The floor was scrubbed and the white and black tiles shone. The four huge windows were sparkling clean and the freshly painted white and green frames added to their beauty. The curtains were spread out and tied at the bottom of each side with white ribbon, and dark-green pots with geraniums were arranged along the windowsills. The geraniums were not in flower yet and I could hardly wait for them to come into full bloom in the spring to bring warmth and vibrancy. I brought some tables and chairs from the storeroom, polished them, and made nice white table runners rimmed with green. The hall looked amazing. We even managed to unhook the big old chandelier, gave it a proper cleaning and fixing, and sprayed with gold bronze all the once rusted chains and details, so now it looked like new.

It was a job really well done and we were delighted. I wanted to thank the soldiers who made it all happen, so I ordered ćevapčići (minced meat rolls) from the restaurant across the street and they were brought promptly, with freshly baked focaccia-style bread and finely chopped onions. We were all in high spirits and enjoyed our well-deserved dinner, after a tiring but fulfilling day.

Among the soldiers who helped me most was Kuki. I specifically asked for him, for I wanted him to see a bit of the world outside the barracks gates. He respected that. I could hear him explaining to the new, just arrived soldiers, the importance of their tasks:

"C'mon, guys, don't you fool around, we don't want to be ashamed in front of the cameras! Our Prof. is bringing the TV here; what's it going to look like if everything's dirty and messy. C'mon, push harder!"

He was 'ordering' them while pushing hardest of all, and pulling out big rotting roots of the trees around the Home.

That night, before he was due to go back to the barracks, I said I had something for him.

"What is it?"

I gave him two large chocolate bars, one from Nora, one from my mom. His face was glowing with happiness and gratitude.

The TV team came and sat down at the tables, admiring the hall while we were serving them coffee and juices. The manager and I were basking in contentment.

My little choir was very excited about the show. I was telling them there was no reason for a stage fright, they were good singers and everything would be fine. Their parents were there, too. That Saturday, the weather resolved to give up rain and wind and presented us with a gorgeous day. We recorded three songs in an hour, smoothly. My band was in great shape. There were lots of people that day around the small marble podium in the patio behind the Home. Parents came to watch their children, soon joined by curious passers-by who wondered what the TV cameras were doing in that yard. The sun made its appearance from behind the clouds and decided to stay, to keep us company. The shooting went flawlessly.

When the TV team left, the manager congratulated me and said:

"Nikola, how about organizing the New Year's Eve here, at the Home? Now that we have everything, the music band and this beautiful hall," he motioned to the space lit by pale yellow light.

"That would be fabulous, sir," I said.

"You decide on the selection of songs, just include some folk dances, people here love to dance."

"Of course!"

I was ecstatic.

I started making a list of songs that everybody would enjoy singing, adding some waltzes and traditional dances. I called mom to give me some more suggestions, for she had an incredible repertoire in her head. She loved music and sang with all her heart in her wonderful voice, virtually all the time. From all the remote memories of my childhood I remember most distinctly mom's voice when I was getting back home from school. She was singing while cooking, cleaning the house, ironing, tending to flowers in the garden or knitting sweaters, scarves, and gloves for the winter.

I asked the commander of the barracks to let my musicians come to rehearsals three times a week. To my astonishment, he agreed. We practiced a lot and we sounded better than ever. Like always in life, whenever it's nice something has to go a bit astray. My musicians started arguing among themselves. Whether it was because new soldiers were coming, so living in the barracks became easier for them, whether it was all the fault of the political climate that pervaded the general mood that rainy autumn, I couldn't tell, but I often had to calm them down, bring them to their senses and focus them on music and singing. We had an excellent selection of pop, folk, and patriotic songs and we also played beautiful Viennese Waltzes and authentic folk dances, like Kolo, a typical Serbian dance in a very fast rhythm, a bit similar to Riverdance, where all the dancers hold each other's hands in a circle that opens and closes and moves from right to left and vice versa, in intricate legwork.

Song after song, accord after accord, our program was complete. Two days before New Year's Eve, I told them not to come to rehearsals any more, just to relax in the barracks. They had practiced more than enough, everything possible, and we sounded really great. Before the performance it's never good to over-practice, I knew it from experience.

"The night before the piano exam, don't play," my favorite, dearest piano teacher used to say. "Just look at the score, read the notes as you would a book."

I took her advice and discovered she was totally right. The exams went easily, melodies simply flowing through my fingers. My teacher was the most beautiful one at the High School of

Music, with long blond hair, dressed like from Paris fashion magazines. The whirlwind of life brought her a tempest of love and a thunderstorm of passion, rushed decisions at inappropriate moments that separated her from music, the school and from me. When I was seventeen she left the school quietly clicking her high heels. She left for a hard life, full of disappointments and tearsome days.

My new piano teacher was a tired old woman without a single sparkle of joy. She criticized everything she could about my technique and forced me to play pieces I didn't have the slightest affinity for. One winter morning, when half of my schoolmates were absent because of the snow storm, unusual for the South of Serbia, I was sitting in her secluded studio on the third floor, playing Chopin's Nocturne Op.72, No.1 in e minor, my choice for a change. I finished the piece and braced myself for the gunfire of criticism. The teacher was looking through the window, deep in thought. She came back from her reverie for a moment:

"Graveyards are beautiful today, clean and white."

I was silent.

She gave me a sad look of a woman who has no love waiting for her at home and said:

"If you play like this at the entry exam for the University, you'll make it. It was excellent."

And so it was one day in June, in the Grand Hall of the Faculty of Music in Belgrade. I remembered her words as I gently touched the piano keys and started bringing the soul of this melody with the strength of my fingers.

The New Year's Eve came to the YPA Home, resplendent in its exuberance. Hundreds of candles were glowing on the tables, formally dressed waiters were moving fast, serving drinks and food. The élite of Petrovac upon Mlava was here: senior officers with their wives, fresh from beauty salons, their friends, people from cultural circles. The atmosphere was festive.

I spotted Lieutenant Željko beside a mature woman with beautiful, but over made up eyes, probably his new lover. He congratulated me on the TV show that he liked a lot. I was glad. The royal blue shirt he was wearing that evening suited him perfectly. I had always seen him in the uniform, never in civilian clothing before, and now he looked even more handsome. Captain Miha was also there, back from sick leave and in charge of my unit, with his amazing wife. He was a symbol of goodness, a man with a huge soul. A conscientious soldier, an excellent leader, and a wonderful person. I got to know him much better a year later when the course of destiny brought me back to this town, the way it often happens in life: you leave something only to come back to it and then leave again so you can make a fresh new start.

The evening was unrolling, we were playing and singing. Roasted peppers with garlic, hard boiled eggs, white cheese, and smoked ham were replaced by steaming soup in big bowls. The waiters were serving the guests at a leisurely pace while we were playing soft romantic music. Dishes were appearing from the kitchen, one more delicious than the other, filling the whole ambience with mouthwatering aromas.

Cale, my solo guitarist, was sipping beer after beer and I could see him getting red in the face. He was still playing very well, but sometimes losing rhythm. Predrag, the drummer, was all smiles and superb, like always. Alcohol didn't get into his veins or mine, even though we had a few drinks. Sometime after midnight we sat down to rest, have supper, and listen to the replacement back up group. Alcohol went a bit deeper into Dejan's, my bass guitarist, and Cale's bodies, so they had to argue, even on that night, not too loud though, because we were not the only ones at the table. Their heated discussions on Bosnian-Croatian political issues were boring and pointless. It was hot, too hot. I was boiling under my soldier's shirt and the jacket, so I went outside to change air and get refreshed.

I walked on the path behind the Home, to the woods. The night was freezing. I could feel the icy humid air stick to my uniform. Somebody's silhouette with a lit cigarette was outlined against a tree. I looked closer and recognized Lieutenant Željko. He was totally drunk. I felt really sorry for him. He was standing there so vulnerable, in the unbuttoned shirt, in deep cold, on that snow covered New Year's Eve.

"Sir, you'll freeze," I said.

He smiled drunkenly.

"Come closer."

I came closer to him. He hugged me with his right arm. With his left hand he was trying to bring the cigarette to his lips.

"I'm not cold," he muttered.

I disentangled from his embrace and ran inside, climbed the staircase up to my room and took out of the drawer my warm burgundy sweater that mom had knitted for me some years ago. Rushing outside, I somehow managed to pull the sweater over the lieutenant's head. He protested, but I didn't pay any attention. I wanted to help him. I didn't want him to get sick. What's the point of getting sick when you don't need to?

He was trying to say something.

"The cunt left," he finally uttered.

"I don't understand what you are saying."

"That shit of a woman, the cunt – left."

"Sir, she's not the only woman in the world, don't get so disturbed about it."

He was silent. Inhaling the smoke to the top of his lungs.

"She said she'd let me screw her tonight, fuck her stupid!"

"Maybe you hurt her somehow or did something to make her angry."

He turned to me abruptly.

"Me? How? I bought the tickets for this night, we danced. Then I said we'll go to my place for a shag, and what happened? She got mad. Why? No idea."

Actually, it was very clear what had happened, but I couldn't quite blame the lieutenant. He looked gorgeous, women were pulling up their skirts for him on the streets, so he was used to having them all available for shagging at all times. Maybe this woman was more reasonable or just different, but at any rate, she didn't like the way he treated her, so she left.

"Sir, I have a plan how to win her back."

"For real?"

"Yes. Tonight you will sleep here at the Home because you are very drunk and I don't want to see your picture in obituaries stuck to the lamp posts of Petrovac."

"I can drive even more drunk."

"No, you are not going to, you will stay here tonight," I was adamant.

He mumbled something I didn't get.

"Then, tomorrow morning, after a good sleep, you will go home to tidy yourself up. Since everything is closed because of the holidays, I'll give you a nice bunch of flowers I have upstairs in my room, you'll bring it to her door and say you're sorry. She will definitely fall for it."

He nodded, but stayed outside for at least one more hour. I went back inside to go on with singing and playing.

There was a lot of dancing and singing that night. At least for that one night, there was no Evening News on TV announcing nothing good. Satisfied guests were leaving slowly, some of them stumbling. The hall was emptying.

The night came to an end. Exhausted waiters were cleaning up, barely able to walk, with half closed eyes and swollen legs. As for our music instruments, it was agreed we would clear everything up the next day in the afternoon. My musicians went to the barracks to sleep. My two fellow soldiers at the Home had gone to bed a few hours earlier and locked my room so that I couldn't get any sleep. As much as I banged at the door, they didn't hear, or didn't want to. I had been awake for more than thirty hours, arranging the stage, playing and singing and now it seemed I had to be on duty that night. Passing by the mirror, I saw my drained face and red, puffy eyes. I laughed to myself and thought things were not that bad after all. I'll be on duty, so what? I'm not in the barracks, the world is beautiful, life is beautiful. Around me, everything was messed up, plates, glasses, unburnt candles. The stench of cigarettes from the unemptied ashtrays was disgusting.

I went to the bathroom, washed my face with cold water and instantly felt better. Then I made a strong, black coffee.

I heard him come in. Lieutenant Željko was tumbling, his face frost bitten. I firmly gripped his waist and led him along the staircase to the room on the second floor. The room had already been warmed up for him. The lit lamp radiated soft yellow light. A bottle of water was on the bedside table in case he got thirsty. While we were climbing the stairs he came around a bit and said he had to go to the washroom. I was waiting for him on the other side of the door. He must have been running his fingers through his hair with cold water. Drunk as he was, he had never looked better. His shirt was unbuttoned and my sweater that I had pulled over him earlier that night to protect him from the icy air was turned upside down, hanging on one shoulder. His hair was wild, all over his head. His half-closed intoxicated eyes were shining in the mild light of the corridor.

"Now to bed, sir," I said.

"Yes... yes," he mumbled.

I covered him with a bed sheet and a blanket, didn't want to put a duvet on, for he would be too hot.

"Sleep well," I said turning off the lamp. The darkness that fell in that moment made the lamp post bulb shine through, right there in front of the window. Its light outlined the room and the lieutenant's face, half asleep but with eyes open.

"Good night." I was on my way out.

He motioned to me to come closer to him.

"Yes?" I said quietly.

"Lie down next to me, just for a minute." His voice sounded strange.

I knew he was drunk, I knew he was sad. I was sorry for him. And compassionate. I also knew that what he said was nonsense and that it would be even more nonsense if I did what he asked for, but I couldn't deny the favor, for there was something about him that I liked.

I lay down next to him.

What ensued was more funny than erotic.

The lieutenant turned towards me, grabbed my butt really hard, took me close to him, and kissed me full on the mouth with all his strength. Once. That was it. The next moment he was snoring deeply.

I left the room. Sipped the coffee.

I sat down at the reception desk. Dawn was making its appearance through the windows of the Home.

Everybody was sleeping.

'Happy New Year,' I sent a mental message, 'to all of you I love.'

Happy New Year.

Then I went upstairs to brush my teeth.

I made some more coffee in the kitchen and lit a cigarette.

Another day, January 1 1991 was unfolding before me.

Ice was playfully creating artistic images on the huge windows, making me smile every time I looked at them. I was enthralled by the icicles descending from the roof of the Home.

Lieutenant Željko woke up in the early afternoon, took the flowers I had ready for him and made for the door.

"Thank you, Nikola," he said.

"You are welcome, sir."

He turned, looked at me, opened his mouth as if to say something, then left.

As I had predicted, the lady was glad for the flowers, invited him in, offered some drinks and made dinner, so they spent a pleasant evening filled with sex.

I met him a week later. On my way back from the post office to pick up mail and bills, I saw him with a suitcase, in full uniform. He waved to me to come over.

We went to a café next to the bus station.

"I got transferred," he said. "To Monte Negro."

"Forever?"

"In the Army nothing is forever, who knows?"

"That's true."

We were drinking coke and chatting. Then he got up for it was time to leave. We said our good byes like really good friends. He hugged me and whispered in my ear:

"Don't be mad at me for that night."

"I won't."

"I'd like to have you always close to me," he said. "Fuck it, I have no idea why, but I feel something for you," he whispered in a bit different tone of voice.

I was silent. What can you say to that?

"Nikola," he looked at me. "I know I'm not just a lieutenant for you."

"You are right," I said. "Honestly, I think you are the most handsome man I have ever seen, and it's always a pleasure to look at you, even though I prefer looking at girls."

He smiled.

"I'm not handsome, Nikola."

"No, you are gorgeous."

"I won't forget you," he winked.

He turned, went towards the bus, and disappeared like my footprints in the snow covered by new snowflakes.

I wished him happiness. I wished him a good woman to love and respect him.

The two guys from Kosovo, my fellow soldiers at the Home, were leaving. Their military service was over. I was envious, because they were going home, but happy when they left. There were two spare beds now and I had to decide who to bring here from the barracks. My picks were Dejan, bass guitarist, and a guy from Vojvodina, polite and quiet.

Since I had been there for quite some time and was entitled to a certain degree of authority, I made it clear to both of them what had to be done every day and how, to avoid possible problems. There were none. The Home was well maintained. Geraniums on the window sills were growing nicely. Visits by superior officers always provided feedback in form of letters of appreciation regarding cleanliness and service provided by me and my soldiers.

Everything was picture perfect – nothing was.

While life within the Home walls was flourishing, the political situation in the country was getting out of control. There were real shootings now, with lots of dead on all sides. Muslims against Croats and Serbs, Serbs against Muslims and Croats, Croats against Serbs and Muslims. A chaos. Serbs from Krajina and those from Lika (regions within Croatia), against Croats and vice versa, all from bad to worse. Pop music stars, loved by all of us Yugoslavs, started to declare publicly their political opinions, verbally attacking this or that nation. One of them, adored diva of our music scene, appeared on a TV show where she spat all the possible insults on Serbs, even though her LPs were cherished in every Serbian home, which contributed to her success. All of a sudden, everything became ugly and sickening.

The Home Manager's face was a darker shade of gray each day he came to work. His secretary grew silent and the atmosphere at the Home changed. The cleaning lady didn't laugh anymore. She would clean quietly, then go home without a 'Good bye'. The secretary's husband, a junior officer, would come at 3 p.m. sharp to take her home. He was a cheerful young man, all in smiles, with dimples and long eyelashes framing his clear green eyes. He smiled less and less. His eyes lost their sparkles. Everybody was waiting for the worst.

So did I.

So did Nora.

So did all our friends and relatives.

We were all waiting for the next step and the next day.

It sounded like a countdown, a moment from a requiem, a moment of silence.

Saint-Saëns' Requiem was in my ears.

Agnus Dei

And the beauty of the pause.

And the words of my Harmony professor, a wonderful woman:

"In every piece of music, be it the shortest, for one instrument, or the most complex, for orchestra, choir and soloists, pause is the most important."

Agnus (pause) *Dei* (pause)
Qui tollis (pause)
Peccata mundi (pause)

The music of silence is powerful.

The same is in life. Unuttered words hurt most. Like nettles, unfinished sentences can singe and burn us.

'The Balkan Requiem' started with the ouverture of disputes in the National Assembly of the still so called 'Yugoslavia' and then picked up a deep harmony line, chosen to be the one of aggression, with no pauses whatsoever.

Slovenians were the first who decided to step out of Yugoslavia. They didn't want to live under the same umbrella.

Everybody had to be present at the barracks the next morning, myself included, to attend to an impossibly long monologue by the commander in chief about Slovenia, in the style "How is it possible that something like that happened?" peppered with lots of nonsense and spiced with big word quotations from some political books he himself didn't understand. Then all Slovenians were released from the Army. We were so envious! Radio and TV News were all about the withdrawal of the Yugoslav People's Army from the territory of Slovenia. So, it started. The break up started.

Then the night fell. The News was very bad that evening and the announcers' voices trembled with apprehension. I knew something was up, I could sense something boiling in Satan's pot.

'The Balkan Requiem' was adding up darker and more sinister tones.

Mobilization!

That was my first thought when I saw soldiers running on the streets, that night when I was on duty. The worst thing that can happen to a city, town, village, to civilization. The soldiers were sprinting from house to house, mobilizing all males aged 16-60 and sending them to the barracks where they were to undergo a hasty training before being sent to the front. Which front? Nobody knew nor understood anything. Masses of men were streaming towards the barracks.

The next few days were shrouded in News from hell, one worse than the other, from all parts of the country. An innocent retreating soldier was attacked and almost killed in Split, Croatia, where animosity for the Yugoslav People's Army was strongly pronounced.

My dear Nora's mom, the woman I respected and loved with all my heart, with the same unwavering love I have for my mom, watched those TV News and worried a lot about me, for I was in the Army and now everybody was against soldiers. Her huge heart, full of gentleness, was too small to bear the burden of the war.

She went to hospital.

It was my birthday and her last day. The dawn was coming slowly. I was on duty, sitting on a chair with my head in my hands. My thoughts were in the hospital, with Nora's mom. An unusual knocking sound diverted me from my prayers. I lifted my head and saw a bird on the outside window sill. I came to her and she wasn't afraid of me. She was looking at me, pecking with her beak at the window. As if she wanted to greet me, to say something in her language.

I don't know if all of that exists, if there is something waiting for us after this life, but I know it was the soul of Nora's mom that came to say her farewell. We were looking at each other in silence, the beautiful little bird and me, until she pecked at the window pane one last time, looked at me and flew away.

Soon after that, the phone rang. Nora's mom left for a better place, without wars.

My best friend parted from me. She was a part of my being. Her love had been warming my soul for years.

It was a Sunday. The barracks was full of soldiers and mobilized civilians, now soldiers as well. I was called and ordered to go there right away, organize my band and play and sing, to boost the morale.

The order was clear and without any possibility not to obey. With tears in my eyes I played and sang all the songs I could think of, with the help of my band, dedicating one after another to Nora's mom. It was a sad singing on that sad day, Sunday May 12 1991.

Then it was worse and worse. Soldiers were sent to newly formed fronts on the borders of Serbia and Croatia and to some others. The war was getting fiercer, the News more soaked in blood. Bus after bus was leaving with mobilized men. Women were crying. The barracks became smaller and emptier. Mobilization was going on. Those who could, fled abroad. Those who couldn't were forced to go to the war.

A civil war, brother against brother.

A pointless, senseless war.

There were only about twenty of us left when the decision was made that everybody, to the last soldier, had to go to the frontline. The order came by phone. Dean called me a second later and said in a shaky voice that the bus would pick me up in half an hour.

I got ready, took the rifle, gun and all of my possessions. My heart went to my heels. The only thing in my life I had always tried to avoid was to be a soldier. I didn't want to fight. I never hated anybody and couldn't bring myself to kill a living being. The politicians concocted all this mass and common people were being shot.

Desperate, I was standing in front of the Home, with my bag and rifle. The little town was very quiet.

I was waiting in silence.

Waiting to be sent to a slaughterhouse.

My knees were shaking. Then I took a deep breath and decided not to be scared any more. I sent love from my heart to faraway places where my mom, Nora, Nora's mom, and my dearest friends were peacefully asleep. I sent all of my loving thoughts to all of them, in that moment.

I decided to accept the reality, for whatever it was meant to be. I wasn't afraid of anything anymore, I felt the only way to live was to embrace every next second the way it was.

Am I alive?

Yes!

Fine, let's go on.

It was around 4 a.m. when the bus came.

As it turned into the side street I saw ice glittering on it in the lamp post light. Freezing rain was descending from the skies, not a good sign in the spring.

It smelt of cold and wet.

It smelt of disaster.

Captain Miha got off the bus and asked me how many of us were there at the Home. I said there had been three, but two of them were pulled out a couple of days ago, so I was the only one left.

"Wait a second!" he said.

That was the longest second of my life. Reasonable and smart Captain Miha figured out he had to keep at least one soldier at the Home for the backup, mail, and communication between the headquarters and Petrovac.

He decided I should stay.

"You stay here. Take care."

The bus door closed.

"You take care, too," I said and waved my hand, but the bus was already leaving. Through its misty windows I could discern the silhouettes of my mates. I couldn't see their faces, but I felt sorrow in their eyes.

The bus left with all the remaining soldiers of that little town.

I opened the door of the Home, walked in quietly, put the rifle and the gun to rest and then in a slow pace went to the storeroom, down in the basement, sat on an old dusty chair and cried. I was shedding tears over Nora's mom, over Yugoslavia. I was weeping incessantly and inconsolably until there were no tears anymore and the morning almost there. I splashed my face with ice-cold water, smoothed my wrinkled uniform and went back to my duty, to guard the Home.

I was the only soldier left.

The Little Prince on his meteorite, on his planet, with my rose withered and the active volcano destroying my world.

Nora's Impressions

All living beings have a way of adjusting to even the most unpleasant of circumstances. It's survival instinct, I guess, that brings a bit of good luck along the way, because when you focus your energy, the Universe naturally responds.

"Find the beauty necessary, find the necessity beautiful" writes Anne Michaels in Fugitive Pieces, thus encapsulating the essence of human existence on earth.

Nikola instinctively sticks to this principle, like, by the book.

The weather beaten, negligence infested YPA Home, turns into a Polish palace under the ruling Prince. And I know he'll put geraniums, out of all plants, on the window sills! There's sturdiness and vibrancy about them, just as it is about him.

I visit him on a weekly basis, running from my Friday afternoon Italian classes to the bus station, to get the early Saturday ticket to the Temple of Music for the weekend.

Bringing some home-made food, to the best of my abilities, for I'm basically a lousy cook, but Mom adds her touch so it turns out delicious, to all the people Nikola is surrounded with.

And so, I sit in the spacious luminous concert hall, listening to the music rehearsals of Nikola's band. They are a funny mismatched bunch that somehow works out smoothly, God knows how. Actually, I know how: they're all musicians, by education, inclination, soul, heart, or all of the above. Like, they get into heated arguments regarding supporting voices, rhythm or melody lines, but once they come back to just playing and singing, the verbal fights get erased. Music does it all!

I meet the YPA Home Manager whose gentlemanly manners are at odds with the strict army discipline. Yes, duties have to be done, but the 'orders' are delivered in a nice and polite way. On top of it, the guy is into music, esthetics, and organizing entertaining events, which makes him a perfect supporter of billions of ideas that Nikola's buzzing head and tingling fingers can hardly wait to put into practice. Also, he sometimes allows me to sleep at the YPA Home, in a comfortable guest room reserved for generals and such, all with crisp linen and a private bathroom. I'm probably the only woman who enters these premises 'officially'!

One Saturday morning, Lieutenant Željko shows up in the grand salon, which is entrée to the concert hall, with cushioned chairs, polished tables, tea candles, and bud vases on the white table runners rimmed with green. The guy looks absolutely stunning! One of those stout, all muscle human specimen, with nature given good looks and a quizzical mind that doesn't want to admit what his spirit is searching for. I treat him to my signature chocolate cookies with walnuts on top (I invent the recipe!) and he likes them, so I'm not such a bad cook after all.

Every once in a while I get Kuki and Dean out of the barracks for the whole day, for a breath of fresh air, acting as their girlfriend.

Nikola's school kids rehearse Freedom for Yugoslavia, a lovely soulful song he writes the music and lyrics for.

So everything is fine with the world. Nikola is playing his music, entouraged by good people. I'm enjoying my Italian studies, reading and translating like crazy.

In the intermezzo of my university lectures, I go out with the girls to a nearby café to discuss the finer points of Manzoni's Promessi sposi, Verga's Malatesta, and D'Annunzio's Pioggia nel pineto.

The TV News are getting sort of disturbing, like Slovenia is separating for real, and Croatia as well, while Serbian politicians wave a clutched fist, Russian way, to their neighbors. So I switch the channel to a local version of MTV.

My private students learn better and faster in the music background, and after the sessions, I rest my fingers on Nikola's piano, retrieving adagios and staccatos from my childhood piano classes.

The kiosks display a variety of political magazines, mostly by the opposition to the current government and I devour them all, just out of curiosity.

When I need to stretch out and feel my body alive, I get together with Mira, who's an expert on all kinds of exercises.

When I need to play, I get together with Lela and her adorable, now five-year-old son.

Nikola's letters come in twos or threes every day, in artistic envelopes cut out of fashion magazines' pages. He's doing fine and is safe.

I know I'm living in a bubble, but life feels good, nevertheless. Every night I look at the starlit sky, pick the brightest star, and say my mantra: "Peace, health, love", while rubbing the silver ring with a crystal blue stone I got from Nikola on our first trip together, just for a good measure.

Mom's enigmatic, though. On one hand, she's all into Nikola, but on the other, she doesn't want to go see him. Like, she's sort of a globe trotter, wants to explore every single place on earth, so why not Petrovac upon Mlava? I tell her about the romantic park along the river bank, I tell her about the charming place Nikola has settled in, yet she's not tempted.

Early April arrives and lily of the valley is budding under the rose bushes in the large garden of my grandparents' house, where I move back temporarily. I'm going nuts about the upcoming exams and need to recharge my batteries at my old desk by the window, overlooking the greenery. Mom looks a bit weak, but she's happy I'm here. As I endlessly pace up and down the piano room that used to be my bedroom, reading aloud from my books, she slows the tempo by bringing me ham and cucumber sandwiches, and making me sit down for short breaks of chatting over a cup of strong coffee. She gets her grounding from my njanja, my grandma, the strongest woman on earth, and in fractions of seconds the two of them blend into one in my mind's eye.

Early May arrives and lilacs are in full bloom. I somehow always associate them with Nikola, for they are so exuberant and have such a clean scent. They overflow the vase on my dining room table, back at my place, where the finch bird Caesar is chirping cheerfully through his red beak and the fluffy white Cleopatra is laying eggs, while I'm absorbed in translating an Italian short story,

The phone rings. I contemplate ignoring it, so as not to disturb the perfect setting and the creative flow.

The ringing goes on forever and I eventually answer the annoying machine.

"Nora, can you come, I'm not feeling well." It's mom, sounding desperate, for the first time in her life!

I grab my book, notebook, and dictionary and catch the first available cab to get me as fast as possible to my grandparents' house. As I rush in, Mom stands proudly on the terrace door, the way my njanja does on the last day I see her, when she decides to leave the hospital because doctors are just stupid assholes, my father included.

Mom is white as a sheet. She needs to lie down. I take her to the bathroom and back to bed. My old childhood bed by the piano. The pallor of her face scares me. I call 911.

In the interim, I translate.

The ambulance takes Mom and me to the hospital where I was born. We wait for a GP to examine her. Mom keeps phoning my father, doctor in another hospital, but he's nowhere to be found. A few hours later I find out that he's been busy screwing women around, by the guilty look on his face when I tell him about mom. Not that it matters.

What matters is this the kind knowledgeable GP sends mom immediately to the Cardiology Ward and a sweetheart of a nurse promptly brings a wheelchair and asks me if I would like to wheel my mom to her room.

And then it happens! If a picture is worth thousands of words, a glance is worth millions! My mom's soul spills out of her beautiful expressive chestnut eyes, rimmed with tears not shed, for there's no crying from this point on. The moment our eyes meet, we both know that she's leaving for a place of peace. A heavenly place where my father's brainwashings can't reach her anymore. A place where my njanja and deka are waiting for her. A place from where she can watch over me, day and night.

On the way back home, I'm inexplicably calm. I finish my short story translation and now it's ready for publishing. Everything's fine with the world, right?

I bring red gladiolas, Mom's favorite gold encrusted Indian vase, her soft pink Italian terry robe, and a fashion magazine to the hospital the next day.

"Nora, Nikola's birthday is coming up, go get a nice birthday card and write it on my behalf." That's her only preoccupation.

"Mom, you're getting out of here, you'll pick the card and write it yourself!"

"No, you do it."

"No, I'm not doing it because you will!"

But she won't. She chooses to become our guardian angel.

The next thing I know is mom Vera, Nikola's mom, stepping out of the express bus from Niš to Belgrade, hugging me the way her spiritual sister would.

We enter the house full of people, neighbors, acquaintances, relatives, friends, and old family friends, saying condolences and wondering why I'm not crying. Like, they're all paying tribute to a marvelous woman and her daughter is cool as a cucumber.

"We have to cook žito," one of the female relatives insists. That's boiled wheat grains, minced with ground walnuts and icing sugar, you take one teaspoonful of it, according to the Orthodox tradition, when somebody dies. On its own, žito is a delicious desert, topped with whipped cream, the way njanja and mom do it. It takes hours to cook and mom Vera and I are so much more into my mom at the moment than into žito.

The woman is pestering us, as if accusing us of lack of respect.

Mom Vera and I stare at her blankly.

Like, Mom is both Catholic and Orthodox by birth, totally at ease in Protestant churches, mosques, synagogues, Hindu and Buddhist temples. She doesn't care about prescribed rites, because –

She's right here, a slim transparent figure hovering above my left shoulder, laughing at the procession of people who think her dead when she's more alive than ever! We telepathically wink at each other.

I call Nikola at the YPA Home. He already knows everything even before I do.

My dear aunts and uncles from my father's village come in tears, bringing freshly baked pies, soft white cheese, and just-plucked chicken. They revere my mom who is a saint to them, for her own merit and especially for having to put up with my father for years.

Lilika, Nushi, and Kato, my aunts on the Hungarian side, envelop me in melancholic violin tones and csárdás rhythm of their voices while reminiscing mom.

Marko, currently working at a funeral home, offers the best selection of wreaths and flowers for free, to my shell-shocked father and takes me out of the crowd for a long walk and a good laugh.

Lela and her husband come on the day of the funeral, even though I don't tell them what happened.

Mom Vera and I are chilling out with booze and smoke, back at my place. We're celebrating my Italian Literature exam that earlier in the day I passed with honors.

And Mom joins us from above.

Students and 'Students'

We were all panic stricken when we heard that, due to the unstable political situation, our military service would be extended for three more months. That was very bad news. We were already fed up with everything. I was still at the YPA Home. The buses were coming back from the front with soldiers and mobilized civilians, coming back with lots of empty seats, for unfortunately too many had given their lives for a totally absurd war.

The little town of Petrovac was getting ready for the belated spring. Gardens were waiting to be weeded, orchards to be pruned, and fields to be prepared for sowing. Life seemed to be back to some sort of normality, even though everybody was just going through the motions. I went less frequently to the elementary school to rehearse the choir, for the children were busy studying for the final tests at the end of the school year, trying hard to get the best grades.

The YPA Home looked pretty much the same as before. The geraniums were now in full bloom in the pots on the windowsills of the main hall. The drunk waitress was still sitting at the table or leaning against the bar, barely able to hold herself straight, indulging in long political discussions with the only guest, an elderly man who wasn't allowed to drink quietly at home, so he kept coming to this small bistro at the end of the world, enduring her dull, senseless blabbering.

The soldiers from Croatia were now released from the Army. The rumor was that the remaining republics would soon withdraw their soldiers as well. News was coming through grapevine that each of the republics had been strengthening its own military power. In the official news, unfamiliar faces, men who had kept low during the times of Tito, appeared now and talked loudly against everything that used to be good. Craziness conquered the Balkans.

Somewhere outside of our borders, people were leading ordinary lives, doing their jobs, going home after work, relaxing with their families or going out, attending concerts, theater performances or exhibitions, simply – living.

Our people were blindfolded by the TV News. Like all the media, television had a deep impact on the general public and kept kindling the already-lit fire of hatred. The same way our news were pro-Serbian, the Croatian news were pro-Croatian and everything was pushing towards something beyond control. It was all completely nonsensical.

The date of my release from the Army was to be July 6, for I hadn't taken any leaves, except once, or any of the allowed days off. I had collected them all so I could sooner get out of that hell. With this new order extending our service for three more months, it meant I would have to stay there till October.

The only time I took leave and went to Belgrade was in March, on the day of the biggest opposition demonstrations against the Serbian government, as it happened. In addition to tear guns, shootings, and demolition of the city, tanks were sent from all the barracks to downtown. Astonished as I was, I realized now that all hell broke loose. I clearly saw the lunacy of it all. Serbs started killing each other, party against party, father against son, because one supported Milošević and the other Vuk Drašković, the opposition leader. In the insanity of those days lots of political parties were formed, all with the aim to destroy our reasoning even more.

Because of the events in Belgrade, the military action, and all that commotion, I was summoned to return to Petrovac one day earlier, so instead of three, I spent only two days with Nora, Nora's mom, and her father (unfortunately him, too). My mom also came to join us and be with me for this short time.

Nora's father did everything possible to destroy the beautiful moments of our getting together, the communion of our moms and us. He was unbearable, boring to death, and evil. His veins trickled with blood poisoned by jealousy, and sickening possessiveness. I admired Nora's mom (as did all the cultural and social circles in Belgrade) and wondered how she survived the years she did with such a monster of a man.

Other than sexually harassing my mom and all the women he came across, he was obsessed with collecting stupid, totally unnecessary things. He collected corks, egg shells, broken glass, rusty nails, and buttons. He was buying the worst quality stuff if it was on sale.

His most annoying feature was his monotonous nasal voice that went on endlessly:

"Sweetheart (talking to Nora), don't smoke, smoking is harmful. See this encyclopedia." Nora rolled her eyes as he showed her the pictures of lung cancer, only to give her two cartons of cigarettes because they were at a reduced price.

"Sweetheart (again to Nora), don't wash the coffee cups in the sink, it will cause clogging, and the dregs can be dried to make a fertilizer that I'll bring to my sister in the village."

"Don't drink so much water."

"It's not good not to drink plenty of water."

"Don't eat sweets, they are bad for the teeth."

"Take some of this sweet preserves, I got it for free from one of the patients."

"It's not healthy to sit in the draft." (The window is half open to let the breeze in)

"Don't forget to keep the corks."

"All rags have to be saved, you never know when they may come handy."

He was a doctor, acting as a poor homeless person. He hated me from the first time we met and the feeling was mutual. Those two days were lovely because I spent them with Nora and my two mothers, but at the same time, exhausting, for he was constantly pestering us, always having his say, incessantly prattling nonsense minute after minute, hour after hour. Like he could sew better than a tailor and knit more skillfully than my mom, competently give advice to shoemakers, butchers or philosophy professors, and driving instructions to everybody, for he was the best driver in the world. For every single word each of us uttered, he had dozens in store and would then elaborate on the subject, while we were simply chatting over coffee, walking in the garden or enjoying our meal. The man was literally breathing down our necks!

Still, I have to say that many years later, in 2011, my boss at the company I worked for surpassed even him in grudging, nagging, collecting stupid things, as well as in telling lies, making up stories to suit her purposes and manipulating people. It was hard to believe there existed another person in the world more arrogant than Nora's father, like his female counterpart.

The two days passed in the blink of an eye and when I turned around, I was already on the bus, and an hour and a half later at the YPA Home.

From all that tension I got some skin infection, on a psychological basis of course, but since I couldn't sleep from itchiness; I had to go see a doctor.

"It's just the nerves," said the dermatologist and prescribed an ointment.

It stank terribly when I put it on, so I didn't know anymore if I was more annoyed by my itchy skin or the unbearable stench of the cream. A couple of weeks later, that too came to pass, even though I had hard times between scratching myself and applying the obnoxious ointment.

The lady doctor and I developed a friendship. A single mother, she lived with her young son in a tastefully furnished spacious apartment and was a respectable specialist at the only clinic in Petrovac.

Nora called me frightened every day, to tell me what was happening in Belgrade, and to update me on the political situation. One of the magazines published my lyrics for the song I composed and performed for the TV show with my children's choir a few months ago.

> *Traveler, come to my country,*
> *Dance in kolo, waltz or oro*
> *These people fought with all their heart*
> *To create this beauty of art.*
> *Some men are angry now*
> *And don't want our joy to last*
> *But they can't do us a thing,*

For love they cannot grasp.
In Ljubljana, Osijek and Šid
Working people are proud and free
For freedom binds places big and small,
Freedom binds all Yugoslavs.

How sad my song sounded now, for Yugoslavia was no more. Ljubljana became the capital city of an independent country, now separated from us, and Osijek was being heavily bombarded. My song was a ballad about a non-existent unity. I felt cheated.

Summer heats came, dry and scorching. Fortunately, the Home was surrounded by trees, so it was always cool inside. My two fellow soldiers there, Dejan and the guy from Vojvodina, argued round the clock and got on my nerves. They could never agree about anything. Even though younger than me, they were not children and I expected more mature behavior from them. I started going to the barracks almost every day for lunch and dinner. Normally I would buy some food and eat at the Home, but the two of them irritated me so much that I preferred to walk to the barracks, have a meal there and a chat with few friends left. Darko was as cheerful and easy going as ever. I didn't know then that I would meet him in Toronto, more than twenty years later. I missed many of them who were not there anymore. I missed Dean most of all and our get-togethers at the café by the river. Slovenians and Croatians left for their respective armies and some of them died. It was getting sadder and darker.

New soldiers were arriving, I played on their Oath Days with my band, to the young men coming only from Serbia and Monte Negro now. The Republic of Macedonia stopped sending recruits. Bosnia and Hercegovina as well, being in a turmoil. The new soldiers were scared by the reality and uncertainty of every next morning.

On my way back from the barracks, after lunch or dinner, I used to go for a long walk, street after street, looking at the town. I felt as if I hadn't given it any kind of support, even though I had been living there for almost ten months. I would stop on the bridge across the Mlava and gaze at the river. Slowing my pace in front of the old High School to look at the façades around it: weather-beaten, but still imposing, from the turn of the century. A little town, leaning against the Homolje mountains, steep and green. The charm of that town was its people, and they were Serbs and Vlachs, authentic people of Romania and Eastern Serbia. I knew nothing about Vlachs before. Petrovac taught me some new things.

Back at the Home, I would wait for Nora's phone call. Her sorrow was immense. She missed her mom a lot and how wouldn't she, for her mother was such a wonderful woman!

In the mornings, when I went to the post office to pick up the mail or send what was ready to go out, I always stopped at the phone booth and called mom, to hear her voice, to see how she was doing and what was happening around her.

"Take care of yourself, Son, please," she kept saying.

"I will, Mom, I will."

In the evenings, when Nora called, she always said:

"Take care of yourself, Nikola."

"I will, Nora, I will."

There was a lot of talk about a new mobilization. Overwhelmed by fear, people were contacting their relatives abroad and leaving hastily. One after another, young men were disappearing overnight.

In Belgrade, the media war was in full swing among the political parties. Ferocious verbal fights, spitting on one another and on top of everything, demonstrations almost every day, organized by one party or the other. Milošević had absolute power at the time and huge support especially from the South of Serbia. It was incredible to see so many women parading on the streets carrying his picture. They were spellbound by him and his ideology. The seed of hatred germinated in each family. It was very often the case of parents being in favor of SSP (Serbian Socialist Party) led by 'Sloba' (Milošević), and children of SRM (Serbian Renewal Movement) and Vuk (Drašković), its charismatic leader.

My days were good if there were no calls from the barracks for mobilization. As my military service was slowly coming to an end, I was more and more afraid that the release from the

Army may never happen and I would get stuck there forever. I started re-reading my music books to get back to the point where I was before all of this. I tried to compose, to listen to symphonies, but none of that could stay in my thoughts, nothing. Fear was stronger.

And then, it happened.

A law came in vigor that soldiers who had been enrolled at the University, starting the academic year in September, didn't have to stay in the Army for the extra three months. The downside of it was that it referred to freshmen, and I had only one more year of my Master's studies ahead, so it didn't apply to me. Desperate, I talked to Nora and asked her to find a way to 'enroll' me to any of the faculties in Belgrade, just to get me out of the Army.

It was chaotic in Belgrade. Everybody was providing 'documents' for the university, everybody was becoming a 'student' all of a sudden.

Nora managed to get me accepted by the Faculty of Economic Studies. It could have been the Faculty of Farting for all I cared, it was my passport to freedom. Scared to lose every precious moment, Nora took a cab all the way to Petrovac and gave me the enrollment papers, signed and stamped, right on time to be handed over to the barracks.

"From tomorrow you are free," the commander in chief said. "Come here at 7 a.m. for the raising of the flag and then go home."

It was too good to be true.

Nora overnighted in a house close to the Home Manager's, in a village on the outskirts of Petrovac. The owners lived in France and he had the keys, so he let Nora sleep there that one night, till the morning.

My night was sleepless.

There was no chance I could go to bed. I counted seconds, counted minutes, rejoiced in every hour that passed, it was getting closer to the morning. I was afraid of any kind of sound that might bring who-knows-what bad news and prevent me from going home tomorrow.

I walked the YPA Home that I made look so beautiful, back and forth, up and down. Opening and closing the doors of the rooms, one after another.

Checking on the empty hall, watering the flowers already watered, and thinking:

"What if the whole country gets mobilized right now?"

"What if a big war breaks out suddenly and all the countries of the world get involved?"

"What if there's an earthquake and I don't live to be free again?"

Thought followed thought.

Then it dawned.

The sun appeared timidly at first, between the clouds wrapping the tree branches around the Home, then broke through and sent its rays to my face, glued to the window.

Suitcase in hand, I made for the barracks. The soldiers were standing in neat rows and the commander in chief was doing his habitual boring speech about our country falling apart, its enemies, etc. When the soldiers were "at ease" to go get some breakfast, he turned to me, shook my hand and wished me good luck. I thanked him and ran back to the Home.

Nora was standing at the front door, waiting for me.

The Home Manager came shortly.

The three of us sat down at a table together, sipping coffee. I was wearing jeans and a T shirt now. We chatted a bit and then it was time to leave. I looked deeply into the eyes of a great man.

"Thank you, thank you so much, sir, for everything you have done for me!"

"Thank you, Nikola! Call me whenever you can," he said.

"I will," I promised.

I didn't know then that I would come back to that little town less than three months later and start living there, all over again. Neither I nor Nora knew it then.

The bus was about to take us to Belgrade. Sadness overwhelmed me and I started crying. As if a burden, a heavy burden fell off my shoulders and chest and broke into pieces. As if my heart burst out at the same moment. The pain was strong. Tears were rolling down my cheeks. Leaning to the left side, I looked through the window.

The bridge...

The school...

The fabrics store, pastry shop, the café...

Then the trees and the outskirts.

And... the journey.

The journey back to Belgrade.

Tears were competing with each other over which one would fall faster from my eyes on my t-shirt or into my lap.

Somewhere after we passed the town of Požarevac, they stopped and turned into sorrow, then found a way into my heart and entered it quietly.

And stayed there.

Nora's Impressions

Just what the hell is going on?

The insanity of the political situation surpasses by far the surreal lines; complete lunacy is signing a pact with the darkest forces of the underworld. Irascible anger, unquenched greed, the blackest hatred, all the evils spring out of Pandora's box and spill out, jumping and sneering in a horrendous danse macabre.

Vade retro Satana!

But he's quite at home in the eternally turbulent Balkans, so of course he won't leave.

This is definitely the totally worst summer of my entire life!

There's no way of knowing when, and if ever, Nikola is getting out of the army of the non-existent country.

I stay up till 3 a.m. glued to the TV screen, following the developments in the war zones and reading political magazines during commercials, like forewarned is forearmed, not that it does me any good.

It's not enough that the civil war in the mess of a once beautiful country by the name of Yugoslavia, is raging and people are being sent to slaughterhouses, but Serbia itself is divided into like hundreds of political parties that mushroom overnight and there's a chance of blood shedding in every single family every single night, while watching the News.

Realistically, the opposition to the autocratic, dictatorial regime of Milošević would be a good thing, if only most of these parties were not so plainly nationalistic. So it's not safe to be a Croatian or a Slovenian, or anything other than Serbian in Belgrade anymore. Which makes me, with my Catholic/Orthodox/Croatian/Serbian/Hungarian background a potential target for any madman in my hometown.

The scenes from the fronts get increasingly sickening, to say the least.

Is there anybody out there to stop the wicked wheel of killing, its human beings being tortured by some other 'human beings', for Heaven's sake! I, for my part, am all too ready to punch the politicians' noses, kick their asses, and thrust my knees into their balls, but nobody's soliciting my heartfelt offer.

The only uplifting scene is when mothers, sisters, and wives of the soldiers, thousands of them, march firmly and decidedly, in their full right, to the National Assembly, crying out loud to Heaven and Hell:

"Stop the stupid war!"

Women always rock!

I still occasionally visit Nikola at the YPA Home, but the atmosphere around us is very tense now and we are frightened; holding on to every single moment fearing it might be our last together. Phone calls and letters feel safer for the time being.

In the end, I go to Niš for two weeks to put my mind and heart at rest in mom Vera's loving arms. We watch the News, just to be updated, but basically chat over coffee, go shopping, walk in the parks, get together with family, read books in the afternoons, and watch videos in the evenings. And talk to Nikola on the phone every day, of course. Sometimes we go to her lovely cottage in a village just outside of Niš, to pick up some ripe tomatoes, peppers and new potatoes, but mostly to enjoy the fast flow of the small river over the rocks and the gentle breeze in the tall poplar trees. Some nights I go out with Nikola's cousins for a beer or two, to a bar or a discotheque.

Life is so beautiful when it's simple. Why do assholes have to make it complicated? It's a recurring theme, all over the world, at all times: if things are going smoothly and serenely, there's always somebody or something to spoil it, just so you can't enjoy and I bet they're not enjoying what they're doing either.

Live and let live! Easy enough.

The project 'Get Nikola out of the Army' takes a full action-packed day. Strategically navigating various faculties, government, and military offices, I finally obtain the papers for his release, all officially stamped and signed. I play honest as long as

I can, and when I see it's not working I start cheating and that does the trick! A bit like 'effort-surrender' kind of thing, you do your best, and then watch and wait. A cab materializes in front of me at the highest point of my puffing and panting, and I mentally 'whip' the driver to get me to Petrovac ASAP.

I catch up with my breath just before reaching the YPA Home. I land the documents into Nikola's hands, and he, in a gesture of gratitude, drops a puppy, Jeremy, into my lap, as he rushes to the barracks to hand in the papers to his superiors. I gently stroke the shiny black fur of the tiny warm creature that keeps licking my hands and looking at me with teary eyes. The poor little guy seems convalescing.

Nikola is back from the barracks and tells me the story of Jeremy. He is named after a character in Alan Ford comics that has every imaginable disease. Nikola found a shivering starving puppy in the woods outside of the Home and decided to take care of it. He gave him a nice hot bath and fed him bread soaked in warm milk, bit by bit, from his hand to the puppy's mouth. The little guy couldn't swallow easily at first, but eventually he managed to keep some food in his stomach.

So, the revived Jeremy and I spend the night in a big house in a small village, two kilometers from Petrovac, waiting to see Nikola free in the morning. The first thing we encounter on our way out is:

A short, stout woman pointing a rifle right into my face, accompanied by a huge dog ready to tear us apart.

Jeremy smartly retreats behind my feet while I try to figure it all out. Has a new front been formed in Eastern Serbia overnight? Is the borderline this very house? How do I snap the rifle out of her hands? How do I pacify the dog?

Turns out the woman's name is Anita, she's a neighbor sharing the yard, vegetable garden, and orchard with the big house, concerned about some movements going on here. Her husband is an army officer, often away, hence the rifle, for her protection. The dog's name is Lilly and she's so peaceful, never mind her big size. I confidently leave Jeremy in her care.

Finally I get to see Nikola wearing jeans and a t-shirt as we head to Belgrade.

That first night at my place he wakes up abruptly, sits bolt upright on the bed and starts sobbing:

"Never again, never ever again!"

I put my arms around his shoulders to release the nightmare, but it's still there.

We treat ourselves to leisure time filled with cartoons, chocolates, getting together with friends, all easy going and relaxing, yet I'm sensing something's not quite right.

Nikola isn't happy here, like there's some unfinished business lingering in Petrovac. I can't get to the bottom of it and neither can any of our friends. It doesn't make any sense to me. Why would you want to go back to the place you've just been liberated from? Yes, there's his Master's thesis, and yes, Eastern Serbia is such a rich field for an ethnomusicologist, but still.

There's something unfathomable about it all.

So again, I surrender. Instead of thinking myself crazy, I wish him well into the new adventure.

Freedom

*Freedom's just another word for nothing left to lose
Nothin', I mean nothin', honey if it ain't free…*

Thus sang my high school love, Janis Joplin, cocooned forever in my soul, in her song 'Me and Bobby Mc Gee'.

It took me about a week to settle down and get used to the fact that I was free. Nightmares started visiting me on the first day of freedom and never left, to this day, more than twenty years later. It's always mobilization, always that same scene coming back, with the bus parked in front of the Home, waiting to take me to the front. It played in variations: I don't have the gun for I can't find it, I either get on the bus or stay behind, invariably in a heavy cloud of uncertainty. The trauma of that night has been following me ever since.

Nora was a sweetheart and did everything possible to make me feel comfortable at her place. My piano and all my possessions had been moved into her apartment.

I went to see all my friends.

Veronica had a baby now. We weren't close any more and I didn't want to interfere with her life.

I got together with Lela in her opulent apartment, crammed with furniture and all kinds of decorations, with barely space to walk, but lovely in its own way. We were sipping coffee and reminiscing our younger days.

"Remember how we dragged those lamp posts on the streets?" She said all of a sudden.

"What are you talking about, Lela?"

"Don't tell me you forgot about it! Your second apartment, before the garage, at that old hag's who had an imbecilic son. You forgot?"

"Hmmm..." I was thinking hard. "I really can't recall that."

She stood up, put her hands on her hips, and raised her voice:

"You remember you had that small heating stove that worked on coal, but there was no coal, so Marko, you and I went to Košutnjak, that huge park in the neighborhood and found those wooden lamp posts, pulled down and frozen, just left there, and we carried them for kilometers to your apartment, then borrowed a sea saw and cut them."

As if I had turned on the video, the movie started playing in front of my eyes: Lela, Marko, me, and a freezing winter day.

We were in search of wood to keep me warm and able to play the piano and study. At the time, I lived in the hilly part of Belgrade called Banovo Brdo, in a basement room of a big house, sharing my lodgings with two Arabic guys. The landlady was a weird old woman and her son a notorious drunkard. His role was to make her life bitter, and hers to maltreat her tenants.

There was no coal to be found. We went many times to the park to pick up thicker fallen branches. Lela and I would bring them behind the house and Marko would cut them into pieces that could fit into my heating stove. Then, on that freezing day, guided by the lucky hand of destiny, we came upon the lamp posts. There were four of them, lying in the deep snow. Lela and I went back to fetch Marko and we carried them one by one.

We must have looked like circus attractions, for just imagine the three of us, dragging a very long and heavy lamp post along the main street of Banovo Brdo. For the subsequent tours, we decided to take a roundabout by the side streets. When all the lamp posts were safely stored behind the house, we borrowed the electric saw from Lela's neighbor and cut them into chunks all that day and the next. I was supplied with wood for the whole winter!

How happy we were! How we celebrated our achievement! I made hot pea soup my way, Lela brought cookies she baked herself, and Marko came with home-made hamburgers his mom had grilled that morning. We had such a wonderful time.

Back to the present, the year of 1991.

Lela's lavish place in New Belgrade, strong black coffee and chatting.

She was smiling, sitting on a huge orange leather sofa. She lived in riches now. Dear sweet Lela, who spent her childhood in dire poverty, with an angry father and an alcoholic mother, taking care of her younger brother Mile and two cats, Rebica and Mikica. Now it was her time to enjoy life.

"Hey," she said, "give me that recipe for your famous pea soup, my mouth is watering at the very thought of it."

"With pleasure!"

Pea Soup Niš Way
A là Nikola

Finely chop 4 onions and one clove of garlic and sauté them on low heat. While they are slowly cooking (in sunflower oil, not olive), slice thinly one carrot and a parsnip and dice meat (pork or lamb), about 200 grams, into small cubes. Soak a few sprigs of fresh parsley in cold water.

Throw into the pot the carrot, parsnip, and meat, stir lightly and add half a glass of water. After about ten minutes, when the onions are golden brown and the meat isn't red, add 2 cans of peas or about 700 grams of fresh peas. If you're using canned peas, rinse them first. Add to the pot and stir. Then throw in two peeled, finely chopped tomatoes. It's important to also add a very hot red pepper, cut in thin rings. Season with the soaked parsley, salt, and pepper. Turn off the heat and let the soup cook down for about half an hour. That's all the "magic".

"I'll make it today!" Lela said, putting away the piece of paper on which she was writing down the recipe. "How's Nora doing?"

"Fine. She's doing great with her studies."

Lela and Nora were getting along nicely. Maybe not at the very beginning, there was a bit of jealousy, which was normal, for I had been a part of Lela's life a few years before Nora appeared, but they somehow found a way to each other and became friends. Lela loved the way Nora had with her son.

We talked a lot that day. Her husband was away, on a business trip with his mother. Her son was playing in his room. The birds were singing in their cages and the cocker spaniel was napping by our feet. Lela started chopping onions for the soup in her state of the art kitchen, talking. I was sitting in the adjacent dining room, listening to her.

"You know that Zorica became a real star? Her new album just came out," she said.

"Really?"

"Yes, she's very popular."

"Is she keeping in touch?"

"For God's sake, Nikola, of course not. She's a big fish now, she doesn't have time for us ordinary people."

In the remote 1985, Zorica was a student at the College of Pedagogy together with Lela, and they were friends. She looked gorgeous, tall, blonde, with deep purple eyes à la Elizabeth Taylor. Her physical beauty was striking, as was the capacity of her voice. Once she came to my little room at the old hag's place on Banovo Brdo and asked me to help her with the arrangement. She had a song in her head but didn't know how to put all the pieces together. I helped her with all my heart. We were singing, I was accompanying her on the piano while our dear Lela was making coffees for us, listening and making comments on the details. Lela had an extraordinary musical ear.

A few rehearsals later, the song was done. Her first stage performance was scheduled for the following week. The three of us were contentedly sitting and smoking, looking forward to her success.

"What are you going to wear?" I asked her.

"Whatever," she said. "Mom doesn't have any money to give me to buy something new, so I'll wear my jeans and the top," she motioned to what she had on.

"No, no!" Lela and I shouted in unison.

"So what do I do?"

Lela and I had the same idea. We headed to a nearby second-hand store, old and crumbling, where we bought meters and meters of various fabrics and accessories for peanuts. Then Lela went home, secretly took the sewing machine, and brought it over to my place. We spent all night working on the costume. I created a fancy skirt in Spanish style, with frills, overflowing tulle and sequins. It was wild, it was extraordinary and unique. Several metal rings holding tons of tulle and ribbons were attached to the slim sleeveless top. It was all in glittering, shining black. Zorica was in tears of joy when she looked at herself in the mirror.

"I'll never forget what you've done for me," she said quietly.

She forgot soon afterwards. Her performance was amazing and she got ovations. Then she recorded her first tape.

A couple of months after my get-together with Lela, in a small Fiat I was driving at the time, on the highway Belgrade-Požarevac I unwrapped the just bought tape and played it. Zorica's voice filled the interior of the car and intoxicated me with its exuberance. I was happy for her, but at the same time deeply hurt. Why didn't she put my name next to the song I did the arrangement for? I phoned Lela that evening. She couldn't believe it. We both felt lesser and it wasn't a pleasant feeling.

I met with Zorica one more time, briefly, to congratulate her after one of her concerts. She wasn't the same one. Now she was successful and a star and didn't need people like Lela and me any more.

On my fifth day after the Army I went to see Mira and my heart was singing when I heard that Sonja was the best student at her high school, and that Ana was fast progressing in ballet. They were 'my little daughters' and I loved them dearly. Mira was still without a man in her life, but still beautiful, without a wrinkle or a line on her face, like mummified. No man would be a match for her, anyway. She did have a short and passionate affair, though. She worked full time in an elementary school, taught aerobics classes in the evenings, and over the weekends took tour groups to skiing or seaside resorts. Lithe and trim, she had the energy of at least five strong women. She's still the same now, in her advanced age. I can't say how advanced, for she'd kill me.

Marko was in a new relationship, worked in downtown as a secretary of some obscure company, and was content.

Every now and then I called the Home Manager in Petrovac to hear how he was doing.

"It's not the same without you," he said. "These new soldiers are lazy and good for nothing."

I visualized the new soldiers who had to water the flowers and clean inside and around the Home, like by grass blades, every day. When somebody (me) sets up high standards, it's hard to maintain them.

Nora and I were watching cartoons we rented from a video store down the street, every evening. We made pancakes, hot sandwiches, or home-made pizzas to go with them.

Two weeks later, I called my professor Zora so that we could decide on the theme for the second part of my Master's thesis.

The memory of the Army was still very present and the nightmares wouldn't go away. Yet, the everyday life does miracles and my turbulent nights subsided a bit, just enough to let me have a couple of hours of peaceful sleep.

Nora and I often visited her mother's grave and sat there in silence. We always brought her freshly cut roses from Nora's grandparents' garden, in full bloom, fragrant and gentle, the way her mom was.

We were running out of money.

I started looking for a job.

There were no jobs to be found.

The budget for the Faculty of Music was drastically reduced, so even though I could get a position there, I wouldn't be paid. The schools I used to work in were restructured, so instead of choir rehearsals and teaching full time, they offered me only part-time teaching, no choir. At the unemployment office there was no help either, there were too many musicians. The war and the politicians did what they did. There was no place for me.

One day I brought budding gladiolas to my dear professor Zora as I stepped into her noble apartment. She was glad to see me. We talked about the Army and the economic situation in the country. She was bitter about the government and the sneaky ways of the political parties. At one moment she turned to me said:

"Why are we talking about all that crap? You and I have better topics to discuss."

I agreed totally.

She brought coffee and lemonade in a big jug and sat down next to me.

Then we set to work.

After a few hours of hard thinking and analyzing, we came up with the theme of children's musical improvisations, a comparative research of Vlach-Serbian music inheritance with children in Petrovac region and the same experiment with children in Belgrade coming from various ethnic backgrounds, all broken down to those who attended music schools and those who didn't. It was sort of a music parallel, with children from the city and a small-town, musicians' children and those who were talented but without formal music education. It was a huge project but my professor had confidence in me and gave me motivation and strength. I always loved her and admired her enthusiasm. She was a great woman, a legend in the music world.

That night, on the tram back home, I was thinking what to say to Nora and how she would take it.

"No, you can't possibly be going back to that village!" Nora was astonished and almost angry.

"Yes, I will. For a year."

"But why, why there?'

"I don't know, Nora, I don't know. Something is pulling me back to that place and besides, there are no jobs for me here. I'll establish a music school, have a decent salary and work on my Master's and everything will be super!"

She was suspicious.

She didn't like the concept at all.

Then she understood me totally. I could always count on her heart.

I called the Home Manager. I could hear joy in his voice when he realized it was me on the phone.

"Sir," I said, "I am coming back to Petrovac."

"Are you serious, Nikola?"

"Yes, I want to open a music school and work on my Master's, on the topic related to Eastern Serbia."

"Well, that's really great news! Is Nora coming with you?"

"No, she still has one more year at the University. By the way, do you know anybody who is renting an apartment?"

"My neighbor across the road would let you live in her house for home sitting. She and her family are in France, they all work there."

All the pieces of the puzzle were falling into place.

The next day the house owner called me from Paris. We talked at length and she said I could move in right away if I accepted to take care of the house. It was on two floors and I was free to use all of it except one room containing valuables that was locked, and to make myself comfortable. I was so happy! On top of everything, I wouldn't be paying rent! The house was in a small village, two kilometers from Petrovac. I said I would move in around mid-August.

And so I slowly started packing for the return, for a new beginning.

None of my friends liked the idea in the least.

"What on earth are you going to do in that village?" they were saying.

"It's not a village, it's a small town," I took it in defense.

"People are strange there, different mentality, nobody's going to be your friend."

"They're not Martians, I spent a year there and got to like them very much."

"You'll be alone."

"I'm never alone, besides, you'll come to visit me."

"It will be hard for you, you're not made for life in the country."

"Winters are terribly cold there."

"Those people are weird, you'd better take care. It's not for you."

"They believe in sorcery."

"People there are cunning and you're naïve, Nikola."

I listened and didn't listen. My decisions had always been mine only. As a Taurus in the Zodiac, I had often run with horns through a wall, sometimes even against myself.

It was no different this time.

I rushed into a new story full of whirlwinds, lies, and deceptions, but in the end I learnt a lot and now feel so much richer for having spent another year in that part of the world.

In the magic of the Homolje Mountains.
Where a beginning is the end.

Act VII
Enchanted by the Song Without Words

- A Little House in the Village
- Nora's Impressions
- How to Heat a Foot-ball Stadium
- Romanians
- Nora's Impressions
- Show me Yours, I'll Show You Mine
- Giselle in Krepoljin
- Winter
- Granny Jana's Song
- Nora's Impressions
- Each in Their Own Way
- The Month of Limburg

A Little House in the Village

My small Fiat was trudging on the winding road from Požarevac to Petrovac upon Mlava. The road itself wasn't that bad, but had lots of curves and was a bit scary to me; I was used to driving on the wide streets of a big city. Bach's Magnificat was pouring over the inside of the car and over my heart. I always loved to listen to that piece and to sing it. I remembered my student days, when we performed it at the Philharmonic Hall in Belgrade and Nora was in the audience, beaming with pride. Now, in this tiny car, the tones became stronger and somehow even more powerful, as I was venturing once again into the new and the unknown.

I was coming back to the town I had left only a few short months ago. I was returning to it not knowing why I had decided so. The heat was filling up the interior of the car, mingling with the notes written by the hand of Bach, centuries ago.

It was August and my to-do list was quite extensive:
- Obtain the documents necessary for the opening of a Music School.
- Move into a house I had heard about only over the phone and figure out what I need to make myself comfortable there.
- Buy wood or coal for the winter.
- Hire at least two more teachers for the school, also an accordionist and a guitarist for extra classes, for I can't do it all by myself.
- Start working on the second part of my Master's thesis, develop the plan of research.
- Get together with my dear YPA Home Manager, Captain Miha and the lady doctor.

- Bring a box of chocolates and flowers to that wonderful woman and her two daughters who live in the house next to the YPA Home, who always had a warm word for me and invited my mom and Nora over for coffee every time they came to visit me.

I started shaking with some unexplainable apprehension. I was going back to the town I didn't actually like, for I associated it with the hard days of my military service. I was going back to that town for a year.

The thoughts were swarming. The road was curving. Wheat and corn fields were caressing the edges of huge forests. The bright colors of the summer landscape tingled my eyes, but the tingle was pleasant. Birds were flying over the green fields, fearless of the scarecrows whose shirts were swaying in the gentle breeze that day.

The house was waiting for me, white, on two floors, freshly painted. In front of the house, a big yard. A vegetable garden without vegetables or flowers, with overgrown grass and weeds, to the left. A small shed at the far end of the garden. At the back of the house, big oaks, tall cherry trees, and a walnut tree. They were leaning against the house, creating a deep cool shade and also isolation from the noise of the road over which the house was perched. 'Noise' is an inadequate word for the traffic of maybe twenty vehicles a day, but still, the trees had their way to make the silence even more silent. They were higher than the house and seemed to reach up to the skies. The large balcony could be barely discerned from the outside, hidden by the spread out fronds.

The YPA Home Manager who lived across the road was delighted to see me again. He gave me the keys to the house and invited me over to his place for supper, as soon as I unpacked.

"You've just arrived, I guess you don't have any food prepared. My wife and I want to welcome you here."

"Thank you so much, sir."

I could never get used to call him by the first name and after numerous tries on his part to make me quit the habit, he eventually gave up.

I unlocked the door and looked around. The house was spacious, but crammed with a multitude of various objects, millions of lamps, toys, souvenirs, ceramic bowls, wooden boxes, evening gowns, fur coats and, elegant suits hanging around; hundreds of the most colorful ties ever seen, all blending into an unbearable chaos. There was so much stuff! In the living room alone, there were four standing fans and six huge crystal vases with plastic flowers. Too much, really. Not to mention that the windows were adorned with three layers of curtains, one more patterned than the other, all in clashing colors, proudly swishing in the wind.

Each room sported one, and the living room: two large display cabinets, overstuffed with knick-knacks, porcelain dolls and figurines of animals, ribbons and bows, candleholders, baskets with dried flowers, framed pictures of cats, dogs and birds, and a whole lot more of the least useful trinkets.

Lacking bright ideas as to how and from which spot to start clearing all that clutter, I went outside to get some fresh air. As I was slowly taking out my possessions from the car, I heard a door open in the house sharing the same yard. A plump, short young woman appeared, armored by an apron with millions of bright-red stains. In that moment, she looked as if she had just finished chopping her husband into thousands of tiny pieces. I wasn't scared, but backed off just in case.

She marched with determination and stopped right in front of me, her hands on her hips. Her expression was dead serious, but at the same time so very funny.

She cleared her throat and demanded a straightforward answer:

"What are you doing here, mister?"

"Good afternoon," I said. "I'll be staying here for a year as a tenant in this house."

She gave me a look all over. The stern glance lasted for a few more seconds before the cute woman hit her forehead with the palm of her hand:

"Oh, I forgot, the landlady from Paris mentioned she was renting to a professor."

She softened and shook my hand.

"Apologies, I'm in the middle of making strawberry preserves, I am such a mess," she said, motioning to her apron.

"No problem, that's actually very nice," I said with a relief. "I thought you were slaughtering your husband or a lover."

She laughed wholeheartedly. Her laughter was wonderful, sonorous, and contagious.

"C'mon, move in, I won't be bothering you, and besides I have to tend to the preserves. Don't want it to burn on the stove and good luck!"

"Thank you. I'm Nikola."

"Anita."

"Nice to meet you."

Going back inside, the TV set in my arms, I remembered who she was. Wife of an officer from the barracks, came from the border of Vojvodina and Croatia, with some German background as I recalled.

I realized that my moving in required an elaborate plan. First clear out the clutter, remove all the unnecessary things, i.e. everything. A staircase led to the basement fortunately equipped with lots of shelves and several rounds later I finally managed to make some room in the kitchen and the living room for my stuff.

After a sumptuous supper at the YPA Home Manager's lovely house, gingerly walking on the dark road, I was approaching my new home. Never before had I lived in a village, being a child of cities and concrete. The silence was piercing my ears, for it was deadly. Remote barks of dogs and howls of owls were the only sounds around, except for my footsteps.

Anita heard the gate clicking, peeked through her kitchen window and ran outside.

"How about a cup of coffee, Mister?" she asked.

"I'd love it, but please don't 'Mister' me, there's no need for that."

"A deal!" she smiled.

Her cozy kitchen was sweetly evaporating with the scent of strawberry preserves. We were sipping coffee, getting to know each other. Yes, she was an officer's wife and her husband was on the frontlines. He was allowed to come back home once in three weeks for a couple of days. She was alone, cooked and planted flowers. She was filling up her waiting with the most imaginative recipes.

"I don't like the people here," she said. "They're really weird."

'Why?"

"You know, they don't like newcomers. You'll see it for yourself."

"But I spent a year in the Army here and they were nice."

"That's different, like they knew you'd leave, but if you live here" – she shook her head –"you'll figure it out. I don't want to scare you in advance."

The night was conquering the village with pitch black darkness. I turned the lights on in all the rooms and on the balcony as well. I couldn't sleep because it was too quiet. I played the tape with Beethoven's Grosse Fugue Op.133, which, although full of fire and passion, always had that wonderful magic power to relax me and take me to sleep. That particular fugue has such divine, typical Beethovenesque tones, spinning and swirling in a perfect harmonic and melodic balance.

My eyes began to close slowly.

I dreamt that night about the barracks and the soldiers in it. The early morning formation in neat rows of olive green uniforms, and the orders of the commander in chief. The dormitory, my bed, and the broken glass on the window.

I dreamt about my Army.

The infant days of it, those without the war.

The morning found me on the balcony, accompanied by Anita, coffee, and the yesterday's strawberry preserves. She had just baked rolls sprinkled with sesame seeds and we indulged in the scent and flavor of the warm bread, and the fragrant preserves. Unable to refrain myself, I was eating more and more. Anita was a cheerful woman, full of laughter. I was glad we were neighbors.

As I locked the front door and ran to my car, she came back from her house and asked:

"What do you like to eat most? I'm bored here and enjoy cooking, just tell me."

"I don't want to bother you, Anita," I said.

"No bother, just tell me."

"Plum dumplings are my favorite, the way they make them in Vojvodina."

"Ah, I like it when people say what they want, I love those dumplings, too. They'll be waiting for you tonight."

The very thought of the delicious pastry filled with plums and walnuts or almonds and topped with fried breadcrumbs sent olfactory sensations through my stomach. I smiled and got into the car.

The day was starting.

Uncertainty sneaked somehow imperceptibly into my pocket and went with me.

The day lasted forever.

The day forgot to call the night and went on for eternity.

I was thinking, in the late afternoon hours, about plum dumplings Anita was probably making at that very moment, maybe now roasting almonds, peeled and slivered. I wondered if she would really welcome me back 'home' with this delicacy.

Time was dragging on with its boredom and the incomprehensible monologs of school principals and their sad looking secretaries.

After an exhausting day filled with meetings where I had the impression that nobody could understand what another person was talking about, and that everybody was speaking a foreign language, late in the evening the freshly-made plum dumplings were waiting for me on a nicely laid table in Anita's kitchen. She had the hands of a chef. The dumplings were melting in my mouth. Every single one of them smelled of plums, nuts, and breadcrumbs, of home-made dough, of warmth and home. I ate one, then another, and when I got to the ninth I declared I couldn't any more, not even with a knife under my throat.

Anita was happy I enjoyed them.

She put the coffee pot on the wood burning stove and pushed the platter with dumplings closer to me. I took one more.

It tasted so good.

I was telling her about the meetings I'd been in that day. First at the High School, where two classrooms were available. They agreed to rent them to a music school, but who was going to pay for the heating? They couldn't get it that I was simply a professor of piano and solfeggio and didn't know much about such technicalities. Since we didn't come to terms about anything, I went to the elementary school, the same one where I rehearsed children's choir as a soldier. It seemed it had been centuries, not just a few months ago. Walking through the main entrance I felt a bead of sweat slide down my spine. My body was coming back to that day, to that moment when I walked in here in the uniform, praying to God to give me a chance to work with a choir, teach, anything, just to be as far away as possible from the Army, guns and rifles.

The principal was very much in favor of opening a music school, so he found a way around the heating issue. Just when everything seemed to be on the right track, a new problem turned up, right in front of our noses.

"The school doesn't have a piano," he said lighting a cigarette.

"What do you mean, there's no piano?" I asked, shocked.

"Well, we don't have it and have no money to buy one."

"And how am I going to teach piano classes without a piano?"

"I don't know, my friend. Nobody wants to invest in education."

I was flabbergasted.

"Have you tried to contact the Music School in Požarevac, maybe they have a spare piano we can rent for a start."

"I have, but they declined."

"What about the Ministry of Education?"

He looked at me as if I had asked him about a NASA project for Mars or Jupiter.

"What's wrong with you, Belgrade guy?" He stood up. "Nobody in the Ministry gives a damn about a music school in this provincial town. Can't you understand that?"

"So what are we going to do now?"

"Don't know, maybe it's better not to open it."

That was the last straw. When I was here as a soldier it was all like come back when you're done with the Army, let's have a music school, so many children interested in playing and singing, suggestions and ideas flowing from well-meaning people and now – no heating, no budget and no piano.

What kind of a music school is it without a piano?

The Taurus in me arose, stimulated by the school principal's red tie.

"You know what, I'll bring MY piano!"

"Yours, from home?"

"Yes!" I said sharply. "And you will pay for the truck and moving expenses from Belgrade to here, for tuning and also for the trip back, upon my leaving."

"You have my word," he said.

Nora was aghast with the situation when I told her everything on the phone that night. She said she'd stay at home all next day and wait for the truck with movers to take my piano and bring it to the school.

"A music school without a piano," she said matter-of-factly.

"What kind of a music school is it without a piano!" Mira was raging when we talked on the phone later.

"Son, how are you going to teach in a music school without a piano?" Mom asked when she called me late that night and I told her about my tragedy.

My mom was doing fine, knitting less, and in spite of the war and the economic crisis she managed to find her inner peace in books. She was currently devouring Pearl Buck's Chinese trilogy: The Good Earth, Sons, and A House Divided.

Nora and I also enjoyed Pearl Buck's books, often reading them one after another. There is such understated beauty in those stories from the Far East.

No piano.

Then no job for me!

The decision has been made.

The piano will come.

My piano.

I went to see Julia who had just graduated from the College of Music and offered her a job which she enthusiastically accepted. She would teach accordion, four days a week. I would teach piano three days and night, singing once a week. The rest of the time I planned to work on my Master's, to start ethnomusicological explorations as soon as possible.

My piano, properly tuned, stood in a big classroom of the High School in the town center. There was apparently an agreement between the elementary school principal and the High School one who was stingy on heating. The view from the window revealed the main street, people milling around, horses, and cars. The birch trees were swaying in front of the high windows.

That's how the Music School started to live.

It became a reality.

The High School teachers sent letters to all the parents, telling them about us and the new school.

We got an extraordinary response from the very beginning. We were filled up to the last student.

Captain Miha's daughter was also in my class, a lovely, quiet, and exceptionally talented girl. Her dad and my ex superior, such a pure soul of a man, was at the front and seldom came home, while her mom was taking care of her and her younger sister, an adorable baby with beautiful eyes that smiled every time she saw me. Her mother was a wonderful woman with warm voice and a huge heart. I remembered her from my soldier's days. Now we established our twice a month 'ritual' of coffee, cakes, and chatting. Whenever I asked her about Miha and the situation on the frontline she would sigh deeply and shake her head. I knew how this woman must be feeling, alone in a 'foreign land', for she wasn't a native of Petrovac, with two small children and husband in the war zone. She kept herself brave in face of the circumstances, focusing on her two girls. She was very happy to hear that the elder one was nicely progressing in music.

September days were unusually warm, the town was melting under the hot sun. The fields adjusted to the heat and gave out generously, the markets were overflowing with fruits of the earth of all kinds, colors, and scents.

The evenings were mild and pleasant. Anita and I would sit on my balcony or hers, always over some just baked delicacies, and talked. Once she made meringues covered in dark chocolate and ground hazelnuts. That was the most delicious food ever created in the history of mankind! Being in her company felt good and natural. She liked to listen about classical music, Mozart's life, various composers, and their works. She enjoyed stories from my trips. We would usually get together around eight in the evening and stay up until very late at night, turning over coffee cups and trying to see in the coffee grounds the symbols that would predict our destinies, but without much success. One evening her husband called, he was coming the following week. He said he was glad I was there, close to her in the same yard, so she didn't feel lonely and afraid, and that he remembered me from my soldier's days as a good and honest guy.

A soft breeze was playing with my hair and hers, the evening was so delightful.

I was happy I was there.

Nora arrived on the same weekend as Anita's husband. She liked the house, the garden, and the trees. I took her to the Music School and to the best bakery in town where I had burek (pie made of thick phillo pastry) with cheese and yogurt every morning. Nora stayed for three days and then left. The wonderful scent of her perfume, a floral so full of spring, lingered after her. Anita's husband stayed for four days, then put on his uniform and got on the bus. She cried all afternoon. I didn't want to interrupt her, crying is sometimes necessary to purify the soul and clear the mind.

Nora's presence, her fantastic sense of space, and interior decoration helped a lot to rearrange things in the house and make it lighter and simpler for living.

Back from the bus station, after having seen Nora off, I passed by the post office. I suddenly felt cold and shivered. The post office reminded me of the Army, of all those mornings when I went there to pick up the mail and the bills, of all those days when I went there to send letters to Nora, Mom and to all my friends.

I crossed to the other side of the street.

It was better on the other side.

Days were following nights by the rhythm of my job. The Music School was functioning perfectly. I started thinking about my Master's and about getting wood or coal for the upcoming winter. I had no idea where to look for. I asked Anita and she said there was no coal, but directed me to a place where I could order wood. It was at the far end of Petrovac, beyond the barracks, in a part of the town I had never set foot before.

One night I had a dream: I was sitting in the middle of the village, everybody was looking at me while Anita was cutting my hair with big scissors used for shearing sheep. When I told her about it the next morning, she promptly opened the Dream Book, confirmed it was a good sign, and meant that she was taking my worries away.

"I'm here to make your life easier," she said.

"Thank you for that. It's true."

She laughed wholeheartedly while putting coffee cups on the table.

"I don't have time for coffee now, I'm in a hurry, really," I said.

She gave me a glance from the corner of her eyes.

"Nikola, being in a rush won't do you any good, so sit down, let's have a nice cup of coffee and then you'll be ready to start your day."

"Yes, Madam!" I sat down at her kitchen table.

All of a sudden, the day assumed a different dimension.

That September was one of the warmest ever, but the winter was coming inevitably, so the next day, I made for the place where Anita said I could get wood for heating.

Nora's Impressions

The original state of the house is so chaotic that even the sickly little puppy, Jeremy, now on the way to restoring his strength, runs away from it after having peed, like a lot, into the thick triple carpets, as Anita informs me.

Trust animal instincts and women's common sense, and sail safely through life.

Like, Nikola does an awesome mental and muscular job of clearing out the mess, but it's women who make the place livable.

If in anything, I have always believed in the feminine principle.

Mom Vera figures out there's electricity running through the water, due to incompetent wiring, since we all get electric shocks when taking our showers the first thing in the morning. She rewires the whole thing, fixes the plumbing system, and cleans the pipes.

I play with interior decoration.

Anita creates the most mouth-watering dishes presented artistically.

This is where she and I click, like totally. We share our Hungarian background (my German blood having been thinned over the centuries), liberally spilling over plum dumplings, spicy goulash, cheese noodles, stuffed tomatoes, and pastries right from the oven. She brings back the warm, comfortable feel of my njanja's kitchen and has the same spirit of a strong woman.

When her husband is forced to go to the war, she runs out on the dusty road and shouts to the Heavens:

"Don't shoot your brothers!"

When she decides to spend Christmas in her Baranja (north eastern part of Croatia, bordering Serbia), where the war is raging, she goes for it, never mind the difficulties of a long and life threatening journey. Before taking off, she knocks at the door of the neighboring house (no rifle this time) and says:

"I'd love to share the joy of trimming the Christmas tree with you!"

So Anita and I play like little kids, putting our hearts into it, in a foreign land where our existence is uncertain, but we're enjoying the moment, so what the heck!

Safely back from the war zone, Anita wants to treat Nikola and me to the authentic experience of fish paprikash, Hungarian style. Traditionally, you simmer it for hours in a huge pot hanging over the open fire outside, preferably by a river. There's no river running by Anita's house, so she makes log fire in the yard and the stand for the pot that she fills with various fish and vegetables. The slight inconvenience is that it's raining and she has to keep the fire going and stir the broth at the same time.

No problem for Anita! She puts on her husband's military hooded jacket, simultaneously blowing at the fire and adding more herbs and spices to the paprikash, running back and forth from the yard to her kitchen.

In the safe haven of her temporary home, Nikola and I devour the most delicious, finger licking dish sprinkled with raindrops.

Small and sparkling, always in action, the words 'obstacle' or 'impossible' non-existent in her vocabulary – that's Anita to you!

During Nikola's self-imposed exile in Eastern Serbia, Anita and I become genuine friends. We slowly sip our first morning coffees and drag on our cigarettes in our pajamas. We talk about everything on earth while pealing roasted peppers or chopping onions. Life is so easy with her!

She buys a real cool purple winter coat for her and immediately gets Nikola to buy the same one for me, just in a slimmer size, so now we look like sisters.

In the course of one of her spectacular dinners (all with smoked meat, stuffed hard boiled eggs, cheese, and pickles as a starter, chicken soup with home-made noodles, roasted pork, potatoes and trimmings, salads, piping hot pastry, and cakes), she presents me with an elegant thin golden chain with a tiny cross wishing that it never leaves my neck.

We both know what it means: remain centered in face of all circumstances.

Anita's heart shows that good people are always there when you need them.

How to Heat a Foot-ball Stadium

The way an elephant would feel in a china shop or a goldfish in the desert of Sahara, was exactly how I felt at the 'wood purchasing' place. It took forever to find it and then an eternity to get to the entrance gate that was barely discernible from tons of rusty iron pieces that covered it almost completely.

A large group of loud men was gathered there, in a heated discussion. As far as I could hear the words from the noise, the subject was politics. Politics was the main topic of conversation those days anyway, wherever you went, on every step of every city, town, or village.

I got out of the car and asked where I could buy wood. They motioned to a man, gray-haired and very tall. I approached him.

"Good morning," I said.

"Morning."

"Could you please tell me how to buy wood for the winter, I've been told I can get it here."

"Yeah, here," he mumbled.

I looked around. It was like a junk warehouse. There were lots of punctured tractor tires, all kinds of metal, broken pieces from who-knows-what, but there was no wood.

"Where is wood?" I asked.

"It's not a supermarket to you," he said. "You order, pay, an' we deliver it."

I let go of his remark remembering Anita's words that Petrovac people didn't like newcomers, and her advice to bite my tongue whenever I felt like retorting.

With a wide smile, I said in my most polite voice:

"That is fine, excellent. Could you please tell me how to buy wood?"

My question was overheard by some of the men from the crowd who were eager to know who I was with BG (Belgrade) license plates on my car. Since they couldn't find out much about me from mutual guessing, one of them turned to me and said:

"An' whose are you?"

I had no answer to that. Whose was I? Mom's and father's, but they didn't know my family, so it would be stupid to say that.

"I am a professor in the new Music School, just arrived to your lovely town," I said.

"Aaa, professor, professor..." They nodded and wrinkled their noses at the same time. It was as if I had said I was a professional fire or knife eater.

One of them, quite drunk, asked me through hoarse throat:

"An' wha' do professor, like you, teach children?"

"Music."

'Folk songs like, to sing?'

"No, classical music and piano."

"You know, I've never bought wood in my life, so I don't know in which measure or quantities to order. By kilograms maybe?"

Some of the men burst out laughing upon hearing my idea to buy wood by kilograms. The tall man also laughed, displaying his rotten teeth:

"Wood by kilos? Wha' on earth!"

"Youn' man," the 'boss' said, "wood's sold by meters, s'you know an' tell those in the city!"

Now it was my turn to laugh, silently though. I visualized myself telling Marko, Lela, Mira, Nora, my colleagues, and professors that you buy wood by meters, not by kilos and elaborating on the distinction while emphasizing the importance of it for the smooth functioning of a big city. Without that knowledge all of Paris and London population would freeze to death, for sure.

"Right, so I'll by it by meters," I shrugged my shoulders.

"Yeah, how many d'you want?"

"Well, I think about 300-400 meters would be enough for the winter."

Total silence.

Then roars of laughter, shrieking, a general chaos. The men were hitting one another on the backs so as not to choke

"You want to heat a foot-ball stadium or wha'?"

"No, just two rooms and a kitchen."

At this point, all the men were on the ground, rolling in guffaws.

My logic was correct, as far as my reasoning went. If wood was sold by meter, I'd need a lot of meters. I imagined a log 3-5 centimeters thick and one meter long. So, 3-4 of such logs a day, and since winter lasts for approximately 100 days, that equals to 300-400 meters of wood, easy calculation.

When they calmed down a bit, shooting glances in my direction just to make sure I wasn't joking, the youngest one of them came to me and said:

"Aaa, don't make a fool of yourself, listen: a meter of wood is a cubic meter, like meter by meter by meter, got it?"

"Yes."

"4-5 meters will be enough," he said.

I paid and left. The men's laughter trailed after me.

The wood saga wasn't finished, though. I expected those five meters to be delivered neatly packed, in nice even chunks, like on TV commercials, when they put them in the fireplace. Being an urban child I used wood for heating only in my early Belgrade years, when Marko chopped it. I didn't know how to kindle the fire, for Lela would do it. I had no idea where to store large quantities of wood. When the truck arrived and brought tons of roughly cut trunks all with branches, I got desperate. When they threw the whole lot into my yard, it was a mountain of wood in all shapes and sizes, big, smaller, gnarled, oval and rhomboid, full of roots and dry leaves. I looked at that mess wondering whose magic wand would turn it into logs suitable for feeding the stoves.

I heard the door of Anita's house opening. She was standing on the threshold, scanning the situation. The bright-yellow apron made her look like a radiant round sun that suddenly appeared in the yard.

"How am I going to cut all this?" I asked her.

She touched the wood, checking its quality.

"You'll have to hire a Romanian."

Romanian? To hire? She was speaking a language I didn't understand.

"Go to the market tomorrow morning and you'll see Romanians standing there. You'll hire one of them to cut this wood, it'll take a day or two, you'll pay him 100 dinars per day, plus provide him with food and drink."

The idea seemed interesting.

"Hey, let's put some tarpaulin over the wood, it's going to rain!"

"Why?"

"Because if the wood gets wet, you'll have no heating this winter, my professor!"

"As you say, Anita."

We covered the most part of the wood mountain with the tarpaulins she produced. I wasn't made for such a job and soon realized I wasn't helping her, rather getting in the way.

"Please go inside," Anita said. "I'll finish it, you really don't know how to do it."

I took her advice once again and made for her kitchen. She walked in shortly, breathing fast.

"How about crèpes with rosehip jam?"

"Of course!"

"Make some coffee, I'll quickly do the crèpes, a dozen or so."

We were sitting on my balcony. The crèpes were soft and thin, just the way I liked them, without milk. The rosehip jam was home-made by Anita a week before. It smelled of woods, of freshness. I brought a pitcher of lemonade with freshly-squeezed lemon juice and a few floating mint leaves, for the finishing touch and the added scent.

I told her all about my wood purchasing adventure.

Anita shrieked and doubled over with laughter. She was trying to calm down and stop, but couldn't. Picturing the men's reaction when I said how much wood I needed, she almost choked on tears that were rolling down her red cheeks. Frantically attempting to say something, she was laughing even harder instead.

"Ha, ha!" I said sarcastically. "Very funny indeed!"

'You'll be the talk of the whole town of Petrovac and beyond!" she finally managed to say.

"I don't care, let them talk!"

She quieted a bit and lit a cigarette. She was breathing normally now.

"You've made my life more beautiful, Nikola," she said.

"So have you mine, Anita."

Later that night Nora called and when I told her about my wood ordeal she didn't laugh. Being an urban child herself, she didn't have a slightest idea if wood should be bought by meters or kilograms or actually bought at all. When I told her I would be the laughing stock of the whole town and the surrounding villages, she simply said:

"Nikola, you have to make a distinction between what really matters in life and what is totally irrelevant."

She was right.

The following morning I walked into my favorite bakery to buy burek for breakfast, as usual. The owner and her husband had wider than usual smiles on their faces. They were trying hard to suppress their giggles whenever they looked in my direction.

"How're you doing, Professor?" They could barely refrain from bursting in laughter.

"Fine, thank you," I said, taking the burek. I didn't want to eat it there.

Anita was right, everybody knew.

So what!

With a raised chest, head up, I entered the Music School when the cleaning lady stopped me halfway up the narrow staircase. She was holding an envelope in her hand.

"Professor, I have something for you."

"What is it, Madame Rada?"

"Well, this letter was sent to the barracks and from there somebody sent it to the YPA Home, the manager brought it in this morning and said to give it to you, for it's addressed to you."

Who would send a letter to me to the barracks or the YPA Home? I was puzzled.

"Thank you very much."

"You are very welcome, Professor. Shall I make you a cup of coffee and bring it upstairs to your classroom?"

"Yes, please, I'd love a good strong coffee now."

A couple of minutes later, she knocked at my classroom door and brought the steaming coffee. I thanked her and gave her a nice silk shawl I had bought for myself in Italy, just before my Army days. She was always such a sweetheart.

"Oh, this is so beautiful, Professor!" Delight was visible in her eyes.

I lit a cigarette and took a sip of the coffee. It was twenty minutes before the first student would show up. An unfamiliar handwriting on the envelope, fast, nervous, almost illegible. I took a deep breath and opened it.

To my astonishment, it was from Lieutenant Željko.

How are you, Nikola?
How's the new job?
I'm writing to you from Danilovgrad, in Monte Negro, where I got transferred. It's a strange place and people are very different, but I hope it'll get better with time.

I tried to contact you at the Faculty of Music in Belgrade, but nobody knew where you were, so I called the barracks and found out from one of the soldiers that you returned to Petrovac and are working in the Music School. Congratulations, even though I don't understand why anybody would leave the capital and go to work in a provincial town.

Nights are very cold here and in my case usually sleepless. I'm writing this so you know that I very often think about you. You were a special soldier and a special friend. I regret that I didn't get an opportunity to be closer to you, to share with you my badge collection and my poetry books, to show you pictures of my family, my sisters, and parents. I have a lot of unfinished thoughts regarding you, that's why I'm writing this.

If there's a chance and if it makes any sense, I'd like you to come over here for a couple of days, I'll show you around this small town. Maybe it will be nicer with you here.

I'll understand if you decide not to come.
Still, I'd be very happy if you came.

I know that you don't like my swearing, so I promise not to swear even once in your presence.
Once again, thank you for everything.
All the best,
Lieutenant Željko.

A knock at the door awakened me from my musings. Maja, Captain Miha's daughter, was standing there, in a lovely white dress. She resembled a little angel.

"Good morning, Professor," she said.

"Good morning, pretty doll, have you practiced your Bach's Minuet nicely?"

"I have, a lot," she said quietly.

"Excellent, so make yourself comfortable and start when you are ready."

I went to the window.

The warm melody of Bach's Minuet in G major filled the classroom with its vibrations.

My thoughts were traveling to Lieutenant Željko. I didn't know what to do.

Maja was playing beautifully. Her strength was in conscientious practice combined with music talent.

She left.

The door closed and I took the letter in my hands again. I started re-reading it.

How are you, Nikola?

How am I?

"I used to be fine, now I don't know," I said aloud.

The letter was burning in my bag and its contents were singing my thoughts.

Romanians

Taking the advice of my dear neighbor Anita, I decided to hire a Romanian to help me with wood, not that I would be doing any work about it, rather to chop it all himself and stack the chunks in the shed at the end of the garden. The logic of heating on wood wasn't quite clear to me, but one gets used to anything, so why wouldn't I learn how to kindle the fire in the stove?

That morning I first went to the supermarket. My fridge was yawning, so I did a major grocery shopping, then sat down at the bakery and ate two wedges of an excellent burek with cheese. The supermarket, as I called it, was very unlike those in the capital, just a store in the town center, attached to the market, that sold basic foodstuff and household items. Then I went in search of a Romanian.

At the very end of the market, behind the last stalls, thirty or so men were standing, waiting to be offered a job. The setting reminded me a bit of a designated area in a park in the center of Belgrade, where young men from poorer parts of the country would sit on benches for hours, expecting to be hired as moving help and for all sorts of heavy duty physical jobs that involved storing coal, carrying bricks or cutting wood.

The Romanians were not aggressive like the men from the park in Belgrade. They didn't argue among themselves neither boldly approach prospective employers. They were simply waiting for someone to come to them and give them work. Since they all had the same 'price' of one 'red' (a banknote of 10.000 dinars at the time), which was really reasonable, and a meal per day, there was no need for fighting or jumping at people offering jobs.

There was field work on offer, for the autumn had just started and a lot had to be done before the winter. Most men had been mobilized and those who were left at homes were either too young or too old. The fields needed to be tended to nevertheless, as did the trees sagging under ripe fruits.

There were a few of us looking for workers that morning. An elderly red faced man, unshaven and dirty, was yelling:

"Strong I need, strong as mules, for the field!"

He walked around them, touching and checking their muscles, as if they were mules.

"Strong I want, strong, show me how strong you are!"

I couldn't stand the way he was treating them. I was just about to punch him right in the nose and lecture him on how he was a disgrace to all of us with his shameful conduct, but I didn't do or say anything because I didn't want to be in conflict with anybody. Besides, what would it look like if a professor got into a fight at the market with a drunken old man?

Then I spotted a young guy.

He was about my height, with short dark hair, blue eyes, and Apollonic body that delineated under the tight t-shirt and jeans. I decided to hire him.

"Can you work for two-three days?" I asked.

"What job, boss?"

"To chop wood."

"To sleep?"

I thought of "my" house with four rooms. He must have been sleeping in some hay for who knew how long. It would be inhuman not to offer him a proper bed.

"Yes, I have a room for you."

He looked at me to seal the deal:

"A red a day and a meal?"

"Of course, breakfast, lunch and dinner, no problem."

He smiled with brilliantly white teeth. Then he shook my hand as a sign of accepting the offer and came with me. We got into the car and in less than five minutes were in my yard. I took him to the kitchen, made coffee, put a plate of waffles, a glass of fruit juice, and a bottle of water on the table and explained I had to go to work. We communicated easily. He could understand some Serbian and I tried to talk in simple sentences, using body language.

I showed him the mountain of wood covered by the tarpaulin and the shed where to store it, once chopped. He figured it all out. Then he asked for an axe and a saw and when I brought them from the basement, he set to work right away. I said I would be back around noon, with some lunch for both of us.

On my way out, I knocked at Anita's window to tell her not to be afraid of a stranger in the yard.

"Just don't stick your little nose where it doesn't belong," I said jokingly.

"Me? No way!" She laughed.

I motioned with my finger towards the yard. Anita came closer, took a good look, and licked her lips.

"Wherever did you find him?" she said. "All lean meat, not a stripe of bacon."

I laughed in the car taking off to the town. I waved at him and he waved back. He was a really well built young man.

"All lean meat, not a stripe of bacon..." Anita's comment was echoing in my ears. She was always saying funny things.

The autumn was entering the town quietly, still dressed in summer days. My classroom was filled up with the bright sun. The children were inspired and played lovely. The piano music was often accompanied by the cheerful bird song coming from the birch and poplar trees in front of the school. Between the classes, I liked to watch the life unrolling in that little town. The classroom window offered a panoramic view. To the right – the market, always brimming with people, the bridge over the Mlava River and the park. To the left – the main square paved with concrete slabs (not nice at all), the bank, post office, and pharmacy. There was also a hotel, the only one in town, in business thanks to the barracks, to soldiers' families that came for a visit and over-nighted in it.

I got back home around one, with lunch for the Romanian and me. The table was laid with the roasted chicken I just bought in the town, tomato salad I had already prepared the night before, white cheese from the market that morning, and fresh bread from the bakery. I asked him if he would like a glass of beer or wine, and he explained he preferred Coca Cola. My fridge was full of coke cans, for I also liked to have it with lunch. I didn't speak any Romanian and his knowledge of my language was limited to a dozen or so words. We were eating in silence. Using more gesticulation than words, I asked him if the food was good, to which he replied with his hands, rubbing his belly, that it was delicious, so much of it, he was very happy and grateful.

I left soon afterwards, back to work. Coming home in the evening, I saw that he had gone through a good third of the wood mountain. Some pieces were too big and tough and it certainly required a lot of strength to cut and chop them.

He also washed the dishes, which was really nice on his part. For dinner, I brought barbecued minced meat rolls and French fries from a restaurant close to the school; they were still hot. He enjoyed each mouthful. I knew that the economic situation in Romania was very hard during the reign and after the fall of Chaushesku.

Later, I took him upstairs to the bathroom, gave him a clean towel, and showed him where the toiletries were. He was delighted, I could see it in his eyes. While he was taking his bath I was getting ready the scores and notes for the next day classes. Anita phoned me, asking about the Romanian. I said he was in the bathroom.

"I'll jump in through the window," she said. "And then I'll lock the door and stay there forever with him!"

"Why?"

"To soap him, to rub his back, and he'll do the same to me," she sounded coquettish.

"Slim chance, Anita, the bathroom is on the second floor and the window is tiny. By the size of you, my dear, no way you could squeeze in."

She laughed.

"Don't take all of him, leave some for me," she said.

"I won't."

The Romanian came downstairs freshly bathed and like reborn. He took a pack of cigarettes out of his pajamas pocket and lit up. I hadn't seen him smoke before. I offered him some beer and wine and he decided on beer. So we were drinking together, smoking and watching some stupid program on TV, when he pointed his finger to tons of video tapes on the shelf beside.

"That's films," I said. "Dramas, series, cartoons..."
He motioned to the videos again.
"Sex film, film sex?"

I got up from the sofa and showed him a few porno movies I had bought on my trips to Italy, superbly made and full of action. He picked one and I put the tape into the recorder.

While he was watching the movie I went to the kitchen and made some phone calls, to catch up with my friends, every once in a while casting a glance in his direction. He didn't move his eyes from the screen, neither his left hand from his crotch area.

When the movie was over, he got up and mimicked that he was sleepy. I showed him to a nice guest room upstairs, the bed already prepared for him. He took off his pajamas right away, even though I was still there. His winkie was in full erection, small and thin, barely visible from the pubic hair. Considering his perfect built, handsome face and the complete appearance, I would have imagined he were well-endowed, but, as we all know, nature has a way of playing with us, giving and taking in unequal proportions.

I ran downstairs to the living room, picked up the glasses, emptied the ashtrays, took a shower, and went to bed. I was thinking about the strange game of nature that sometimes gives everything to some people except one thing, and to some others gives only that one thing.

In the course of the following two days, all the wood was chopped and neatly stacked in the shed at the end of the garden. Only then the heavy rains started. I was so lucky!

My Romanian left happy since he had spent three days without overworking himself, and three nights with: hot baths, porno movies, and good food. I gave him a lift back to the market. He thanked me and explained that if I needed anything else to be done, just to look for him. I agreed. He was a decent and grateful young man.

I had half an hour to spare before starting the classes, so I drove to the elementary school where I used to teach children how to sing when I was a soldier and walked into the principal's office. I asked him about my salary. I had been working for five weeks already and was supposed to get paid, by all logic, standards, and criteria, which obviously weren't his.

"Ah, Professor," he said. "First we had to pay the High School for the classrooms."

"But they said the classrooms were free!"

"People say a lot of things and don't mean it. You don't understand anything; this is different, people."

I knew he was lying through his teeth.

"When am I going to get my salary? The parents pay regularly and I teach every day, all my classes!"

"I know, I know, but there's nothing left for you this month."

"Pay Julia at least! She is supporting her ailing mother."

"I'll pay her part-time, that's how much I have, and you next month."

I left his office fuming with rage. If Nora had been there, she would have kicked the principal in his balls, and would have turned to me and said:

"I told you so!"

But that evening on the phone she was quiet and full of understanding for me.

"Nikola, you know what you're best at and what always brings you money – private lessons! Start giving them again and everything's going to be fine. That principal can't break you. Nobody can break you except yourself," she added.

"You're right, Nora!"

I put down the receiver and smiled at her words. She was so right that evening and also many years later. I have always been my most dangerous adversary.

The next day I talked with Julia about private lessons. She said there were lots of children who didn't want to attend a music school, but to learn music from a private teacher. In the next couple of days, I got six students. They were all talented children who had their instruments at home, piano or a keyboard. I got paid after each class. It was going smoothly.

The lady doctor I first met in my soldier days became sort of a friend now. She phoned to say she was throwing a big dinner party the following evening and invited me to come, by all means. I accepted the invitation. She was an esteemed person in that town and I pictured the stage filled with the local élite. I immediately decided on what to wear: black pants and the floating deep purple silk shirt I bought with Nora in Budapest, on Vaci Street, a few years back, but had never worn.

The next morning, driving in reverse from the yard, I noticed that the gate and the whole fence were in a poor state. I thought it might be a good idea to have them painted before the winter, approaching fast with the winds from the Homolje Mountains.

I went to the market. Romanians were standing at the far end of it, as usual. I looked for the guy who had chopped my wood, but he wasn't there.

A well-built young man with tanned complexion came quietly to me and asked:

"You have job, boss? I need job."

There was sincerity and warmth in that voice and in his eyes.

"Yes, I need to have the gate and the fence painted."

"You pay a red a day?"

"Yes."

"Good, boss, good, I need job."

It was a done deal. He got into my car and we drove to a paint store where I chose a lovely pastel green. I left him in the house and explained what I wanted him to do, first to remove the old paint, put a coat of the new one, let it dry and then apply the second coat. It could all take a few days. He was speaking Serbian fairly fluently, good enough to be understood. I gave him a carton of yogurt and the puff pastry buns I had bought for my breakfast that morning. He smiled like a little kid when he saw a few chocolate bars at the bottom of the paper bag.

"I like chocolate," I said. "More than any other food in the world."

He laughed, approvingly.

He got the sandpaper and the thinner ready as I grabbed some scores I needed for that day's classes. He waved at me happily on my way out of the yard.

When I got back, sometime after five in the afternoon, a lot of work had been done. The old paint had been removed from the big gate and at least three quarters of the long fence. I congratulated him on a job well done and said it was time for him to take a bite.

I took him into the house, placed two baguette style hot sandwiches with ham and cheese from the bakery on the kitchen table, and said he was free to help himself with everything from the fridge, I was going to a dinner at a friend's place. Then I showed him where the TV, videos, the bathroom, clean towels, and his room were, when he wanted to relax.

"Will wait for you," he said.

I realized I hadn't changed the bed linen from the previous Romanian and ran upstairs to put the fresh one on the bed. On my way downstairs, I saw him sitting in the kitchen, enjoying the sandwiches.

"Thanks a lot, boss," he said through mouthfuls.

"Hey, call me Nikola, OK?"

"OK, boss... Nikola."

I looked at myself contentedly in the mirror. The purple shirt was falling freely over the black hand-made silk pants I bought in Beijing, China. I put some gel in my hair, ruffled it, sprayed the perfume Just Musk behind my ears and on my wrists, and was ready to go.

Perfumes have always been one of my passions. I had several bottles at all times, always hungry for some new ones. The company Krka, based in Slovenia, was the shiniest star in the cosmetics sky of Yugoslavia. They were representatives for the British Yardley fragrance collection and for Tokalon, Swiss skin care line. Luckily I had stashed quite a bit of those products before the Army, for now it was very hard to find Slovenian goods. I was using Tokalon day, night, and anti-wrinkle cream. I didn't have any wrinkles yet, but wanted to prevent them, so I regularly applied creams to my face every night and morning. The scents Krka Cosmetics offered were refined and so lovely. They were technically ladies' fragrances, but smelled very nice on me, not feminine at all, and besides, nobody could tell the difference between perfumes in the poor Yugoslavia at the time. My favorites were Just Musk and Reverie. They were also available as solid perfumes in little pots and you could dab some on whenever you needed to refresh, without spraying the alcohol around.

I went out of my room and passed by the kitchen where the Romanian was just finishing his dinner.

"This is nice on you," he said pointing at my shirt.

"Thank you!"

Before leaving for the dinner party, I dropped by Anita's house to get a final approval on my looks. Standing in her signature posture, with hands on hips, she gave me a critical all over.

"You are a bit overdressed for this God forsaken place," she said.

I laughed at her remark and got into the car.

After a ten minute drive I parked in front of the apartment building. All the windows in the doctor's apartment were lit by a bright light from the crystal candelabra. First I went to buy a box of chocolates and a bottle of wine for the hostess and a chocolate bar for her son. Then I bought a bouquet of chrysanthemums, golden yellow and red.

I rang the doorbell.

She opened the door.

She looked beautiful in the sleek navy evening gown. Her hair was pulled up, revealing expensive earrings. The place smelled of good food.

I went in.

At the large dining room table there was an empty place waiting for me. I introduced myself to everybody and sat down. As the hostess was bringing me a glass of white wine, I looked around.

The table was laid like in the times of the Russian Empire, with elaborate candleholders, tall candles rising from them, white porcelain plates, silver cutlery, and silk napkins.

Sitting next to me was the pharmacy lady, town expert in all prescriptions and medications. She had been working there for years, managing the store with her iron will and it worked out perfectly. She remembered me from my soldier days.

"I knew I had seen you before," she said. "Cheers!" She lifted her glass.

"Cheers!"

Next to her was a judge from Požarevac, an elderly gentleman in an elegant suit and his wife, a youngish woman, fashionably dressed, but with too much make up that was melting under the candlelight.

On the other side of the table, across from me, was a very handsome young man I didn't know. Next to him was one of my ex-superiors from the army with his wife, and the general manager of one of the local factories with his wife. There was also the owner of the most popular café in the town and her girlfriend.

We were talking about everything. The evening was flowing in a very pleasant atmosphere. The dishes had been prepared masterfully. For the starter there were all the imaginable cold cuts and smoked meat, breaded peppers, and roasted chili peppers stuffed with goat cheese. Then we were served baked turkey, cut into thin slices, with a mix of aubergines, potatoes, and mushrooms between each slice. There were also mini schnitzels, filled with caciocavallo cheese and topped with a sweet and sour sauce.

We were so full of all that excellent food, none of us had any place left for another bite when the hostess invited us to the salon for a glass of French brandy, cherry brandy or a cup of coffee before she brought the cakes.

So we got up from the table and made for a spacious room all in white and blue color combinations. We made ourselves comfortable on state of the art leather sofas and armchairs. The very handsome young man I didn't know sat down next to me.

"I don't think we've met," I said. "My name is Nikola, I teach piano in the newly opened Music School."

"Nice to meet you, I am Dragan."

The cakes arrived on nicely decorated crystal platters. There were èclairs, coconut squares, pies with wild berries, and Swiss rolls with chocolate. They all tasted so good with hot Turkish coffee, simply melted in the mouth!

The evening was a real success. Nobody talked about politics. Slowly, one by one, we were taking our leave. Dragan got up at the same moment I did. We left the doctor's apartment together and went downstairs.

"Where do you live?" he asked me.

"I rent a house, two kilometers from Petrovac, in the direction of Požarevac."

"Well, enjoy your stay here."

We said our good byes, I got into the car and saw him walking towards the town center. I stopped.

"Dragan, do you need a lift?"

"It's OK, my car broke this morning, it's in the garage now. I'll take a walk, it's not far, about twenty minutes," he said.

"Get in," I said. "I'll drive you home. Where to?"

"Behind the barracks."

Cold sweat ran down my spine as we passed by the barracks. I saw two soldiers on guard at the front gate. Dragan noticed that I shivered.

"Are you cold?" he asked.

"No, it's just that I did my military service here and freeze when I only think about it."

"I can understand you," he said. "I feel the same way. I'm going to the army in six months and am scared of it."

He showed me where to turn. I parked in front of a beautiful white house, new and luxurious. It was adorned with columns, bas reliefs on the façade and oval balconies.

"You have a gorgeous house," I said.

"That's my mother's and father's, they've been working in Austria for twenty years. I live with my grandma and grandpa," he motioned to another, as beautiful and even bigger house.

The front yard didn't look like ordinary yards in Eastern Serbia. It was clean and neat, with paved paths lined with bushes and shrubs and probably with lots of flowers in the spring and summer.

We agreed to get together again and exchanged our phone numbers.

Driving back home I was thinking about the kind of life Dragan was having, living with his grandparents, yet loaded with money. For somebody so rich, he was very quiet and polite, not in the least arrogant or snobbish. What made him special was his /r/ sound that he naturally pronounced in a French way. In some parts of Serbia, that was considered a speech defect, but I always liked to listen to people who had that gift.

Other than that, Dragan was one of the best looking young man I had ever seen, even in magazines. He was a bit shorter than me and perfectly built. Wavy chestnut hair framed his beautiful face, with deep green eyes. Nora would have probably said he could have modeled for Michelangelo's David.

I got back home and found my Romanian asleep on the sofa in the living room. I didn't want to wake him up, so I brought a pillow and a blanket and let him sleep peacefully. He didn't move.

I went outside, lit a cigarette, and ran over to Anita's house.

She was dying to hear how it all went at the dinner party with the élite.

I told her everything.

No matter how I described each of the guests, Anita had her comments:

"That one is all puffed up, like a turkey."

"Oh, don't tell me about him, a fat pig."

"Of course she had to be there, a stupid cow."

"And the pharmacist is still alive, I can't believe it, she must be at least two hundred years old!"

It was funny how she imitated everybody.

About Dragan she said:

"A cry baby, needs his diapers to be changed every day."

"Why diapers?" I asked.

"Because he's all like fragile. He's very rich, the parents already arranged a marriage to a Serbian girl in Italy; her family is millionaire. As soon as he's done with the army, he'll go there."

"Well, there's nothing bad about it."

"It's not, but why don't I have so much money, or you?"

"You know, Anita, everything is predestined in life, some people get bigger, some smaller chunks of the cake."

She sighed.

"Maybe, but anyway, you get on my nerves when you look at the world only from the positive perspective."

I smiled at her sincerity.

"Maybe you get on my nerves with your negative view on the whole world," I said.

"I don't think so. You never seem irritated by anything."

"You're right. I accept you just the way you are, the way God made you."

We had coffee together, but I had to decline a piece of cherry pie, for I had nowhere to put another bite of food after that sumptuous dinner.

We said good night to each other and I went to bed.

By the next late afternoon, the gate and the whole fence already had the first coat of paint that was slowly drying in the humid wind. The Romanian was in the living room, watching TV. He turned to me when I walked into the house and got up to help me carry the bags full of groceries. He was such a nice guy. I noticed that the whole place had been dusted, the floors cleaned and all the newspapers, magazines, and tons of my sheet music tidily arranged. He didn't have to do all that, but he did it.

"Tonight I'll make you a dish from the South of Serbia, where I come from."

"Kosovo?" he asked.

"No, that's more to the south. My hometown is about hundred fifty kilometers from here."

"I help?"

"Yes, if you want," I said.

He was a really good young man. He was nineteen and the youngest in the family. There were no jobs in Romania and laboring in Serbia was the only way he and his elder brother, who worked in the village next to this one, could support their parents and siblings.

"Tomorrow, the fence finished," he said.

"Great, you know your job."

We went to the kitchen and I explained to him what to do. He was chopping peppers and peeling tomatoes while I was sautéing onions with finely cubed meat. It was a super team work accompanied by the music from the radio. That night, they played Sinatra's evergreens.

After dinner, which was so delicious, we were relaxing in the living room over white wine and banana mousse chocolates. I lit a cigarette and he joined me.

There was nothing interesting on TV. I was switching channels, but other than politics – nothing!

"Tell me how I do it in Romania," he motioned to the pot with hardly anything left in it.

"To cook it for your family?"

"Yes."

"Here it is – "

Authentic Niš prženija or
Ratatouille à la sud de la Serbie
You need:
3 onions
1 clove of garlic
Half a kilo of lean pork
8 cubanelle peppers
2 hot green peppers, the hotter the better
4 tomatoes
Oil
Parsley
Salt and pepper

Chop the onions and garlic and fry them on low heat. About five minutes later add the meat cut in cubes and sauté for approximately ten minutes. Add the peppers, cut in squares and thinly sliced hot peppers. Peel the tomatoes and chop them finely. When the peppers are soft, add the tomatoes and stir. Cook for about ten more minutes, add parsley, salt and pepper. (If you like mushrooms now would be the time to add 250 grams of sliced champignons).

Turn off the heat and let the dish cook by itself.
Serve with fresh white bread.
Note: a whisked egg can be added at the very end if you like it, I personally don't.

As I was telling him the recipe, he was writing in Romanian. I was glad he was going to make our dish one day in his country.

We watched a video and then went to our respective rooms to sleep.

Somewhere in the middle of the dream I got scared and opened my eyes. He was in my bed, deep asleep, on my left side. When I tried to move him, he just hugged me tight, leant closer to me and went on sleeping soundly. I didn't know what to do. My thoughts were swarming. Maybe he was having a nightmare, but then, he wasn't a child. Why did he come to my bed?

I went back to sleep and immediately felt something heavy on my chest. It was his hand. I turned to my right side. He hugged me even more tightly and snuggled. It was a strange, yet a pleasant sensation. I could feel every single tremble of his sleeping body. He started moving his body in a rhythm unknown to me and exploring mine with his hands.

I jumped out of the bed as if scalded, pretending to be the three wise monkeys who see, hear and speak no evil, ran to the kitchen and made some coffee.

Soon I heard him coming down the stairs.

"Coffee smell nice," he said.

I ignored him, pushed a mug across the kitchen table in his direction, and went to take a shower and get ready for work. As I rushed out of the house, he was already outside, giving the fence the second coat of paint. I felt ashamed. I was so sorry for having given him the first morning coffee in such a rude way and disappearing in the bathroom without saying a word. I was punishing him for what hadn't been a bad intention at all. I came closer to him. He looked at me warmly and said:

"Thank you for all you give me."

"No, thank you," I said. "Please don't be angry with me for my outburst this morning. There's breakfast for you in the fridge, go eat first."

"No, paint first."

"No, breakfast first, please."

He put his brushes aside and stood up. At that very moment a ray of sunshine illuminated his face.

"Some boss give only little bread a day," he said. "And you, like brother, care, give best to eat and …everything."

That almost broke my heart.

I decided to invent as much work around the house as possible for him to do, to keep him a bit longer here and spare him of laboring in the fields and sleeping in stables with cows and sheep, which many of his companions had to endure.

My financial situation was tight, there was no salary, not even a mention of it, but I felt compassion for him and besides, where there's food for one, there's for two as well. I could still afford to pay him the peanuts he charged per day, but didn't want him to feel humiliated by just getting food and money, he had to earn it.

There were some cans with black paint in the basement, I saw them the other day while looking for light bulbs. That gave me an idea:

"If you can, I'd like you to stay a few more days to paint the metal work on the balconies and the railings inside, on the staircase."

The bright sun broke through October clouds.

He gave me a strong hug.

I saw how much it meant to him.

A few days later, while I was finding more things to be painted, cleaned, fixed, repaired or assembled, I knew that he knew I was making it all up, just to keep him safe and protected from the hard work in the fields and miserable living conditions.

Adrian, as was his name, was wonderful. He was painting the metal work on the balconies and the railings conscientiously and meticulously, without a single black drop on the floors. He was always happy to see my car driving into the yard. Just-brewed coffee would wait for me, for he knew I liked to have a steaming cup when returning home.

We made dinners together. He would wash the dishes and clean up the kitchen, and only then come upstairs to the room where I was working on my papers, sit down in an armchair.

We had a mutual secret.

At first, there was one: the secret of the first night when he came to my bed. Then it continued on the second, third and every night. Adrian would come to my bedroom when I was just about to fall asleep. I didn't know how to react. My body was telling me one thing, my brain something completely different. There were no winners in that battle. I was afraid of my own shadow in those days. Still, every time I saw Adrian's smiley face in the mornings, I felt gratified. We never mentioned those night escapades. They were a part of a dream.

Anita also got to like him a lot and often brought over the mouth-watering cakes and pies. He was teaching me Romanian words and I was teaching him Serbian. We called his family in Romania several times. They didn't have a phone, but there was one family in the village that did, so we would dial their number and ask them to fetch Adrian's mother. He would talk to her for a few minutes in a soft, gentle voice. I couldn't understand all the words, but I sensed the meaning full of warmth and love.

Then one day he came to me with sorrow in his eyes. I saw that something wasn't right.

"What's happened, Adrian?"

"I go to Romania tomorrow or after tomorrow," he said.

"So soon?"

"Have to."

I was looking at him. He explained:

"My brother dig and plough fields and can't do no more, got sick, say we go together. Can't stand boss and yelling. Have to go very soon."

I understood. Romanian hired hands were exhausted by laboring and the torture of the employers. I hoped they had made enough money to bring home and provide their families with decent life for at least a few months.

That day I finished my classes earlier and got home about three in the afternoon. I parked in front of the house and waved at Adrian. He was on the second floor balcony, putting finishing touches with a fine brush.

He ran out, happy to see me.

"Get into the car," I said.

He wiped his hands on a cloth and got in without asking anything.

"Nice fence," he remarked as we passed by the beautifully painted fence, the result of his work.

"It is, you did a super job," I agreed.

I drove to Požarevac, a town bigger than Petrovac, and we went to a department store. I didn't have cash or any money for that matter, but I had checks that could be post-dated and considering the speed the inflation was spreading its tentacles like an octopus, I figured out that whatever I bought and no matter how much I paid for it, would be eaten up by the inflation by the next month.

So I bought him a winter jacket and boots, warm, lined with fur. Also some shirts and sweaters and underwear. The underwear he had was terrible. I bought nice perfumes and scarves for his mother and sisters, and a watch for his father. Then I picked for him a gold chain and a pendant, A for Adrian, as a souvenir from me.

"Please, can be N?"

"Why N?" I was surprised.

"N like Nikola."

On our way back, he said he would tell everybody in his family how good I was and like a brother to him. I told him better to say that he had worked hard and earned a lot of money and that the gifts were from him, not from me. The less people knew, the better.

Anita, who had been feeling left out lately, came to dinner with us and brought best in the world home-made donuts with fluffy filling. I prepared oven baked sandwiches with chicken stripes, chopped tomatoes, goat cheese, and oregano.

We enjoyed the dinner, especially Anita's donuts.

She kept asking Adrian all sorts of questions:

"Where are you from?"

"How old are you?"

"Do you have a family?"

"Why did you come to Serbia?"

"Did you come here illegally?"

"Is it really hard in Romania?"

Adrian stoically endured Anita's "investigation" and answered properly all her questions one by one:

"Village near Timisoara."

"Nineteen."

"Mother, father, sisters, and brothers work here like me."

"Work, no job in Romania."

"Yes, across the mountain."

"Nothing there, no electricity, nothing."

Anita stayed till late that night, leaving the rest of the donuts to us.

Then we went to the living room, chatted a bit over a couple of glasses of chilled white wine, and were ready to go to bed. Just like every night, I went to my room, he to his. The second I turned off the light and got under the duvet, I heard knocking on the door.

"Come in, Adrian."

He came in and lay down next to me.

"You very beautiful, very good," he said.

Somewhere in the distance an owl howled.

Adrian left the next morning. He had a big traveling bag full of gifts. I also packed some sandwiches, donuts, coke cans, and water bottles for the journey. I gave him a lift to the place where he was to meet with his brother. His brother looked much older than him and weather beaten. I said good bye to Adrian. He started crying.

He hugged me tight and whispered, so his brother couldn't hear:

"I love you much, write letters, write in Romania."

"I will," I said.

"Promise?"

"I promise."

His brother thanked me for the food, saying I shouldn't have bothered but it was really nice of me. He shook my hand as a friend.

Then they left.

I went to work.

That day the children played extremely well. They may have sensed I was sad, for they played with all their souls.

Adrian crossed the border without any problems. He called me the next day. He said just a few words and the rest was explained by silence. Silence is sometimes so loud and powerful.

We kept correspondence. In his last letter, there was a picture from his wedding. He married a girl from the bordering region, who spoke both Romanian and Serbian. I could see by the previous letters how his Serbian was getting increasingly good. I was glad that he had found happiness, looking at the familiar face on the photograph. Adrian was wearing a blue shirt, one of those I had bought him just before he left. It was unbuttoned at the top and there was the chain with the pendant N around his neck. His wife looked beautiful, glowing in a simple white dress.

In that last letter he wrote:

Dear Nikola,

This is a picture from my wedding. My wife Milica is pregnant. If I get a son, I'll call him Nikola; if it's a girl, she'll be Nicole. I love you forever.

Adrian

I read and re-read it, who knows how many times.

Then I took the picture once again in my hands and saw there was something written on the other side:

Nu Te Voi uita nicodatā

(I will never forget you)

Later, when my tears dried, I showed the letter to Anita.

"I knew it, I knew it right away!" she said.

"Yeah, sure." I laughed.

"I'm telling you, the way he was looking at you and especially that evening when I brought the donuts, he could hardly wait to see my back so he could be all over you."

"Now you've gone too far! It's just your wild imagination."

"OK, I might be kidding," she said through laughter, "but I really knew it!"

"You know everything in the world!"

"Not exactly everything, but some things I do. Like so pretty and sexy-me, shake my hips, take the laundry outside to dry, pick flowers or pretend to do something in the garden, and he never even notices me. What kind of a man is that?" She said victoriously.

The evening after Adrian had left, I climbed the staircase of the quiet house and went to my room. I lay down and covered myself with the duvet. Sleep wasn't coming to me. The scent of Adrian's warm body was still lingering on the pillows and on the bedsheets. I could almost hear him breathing, his breath in my hair, at the back of my neck and on my face. As if again, like that first night, I could feel his hands and lips, torn between guilt and passion, between lots of 'no's' and only one 'yes'.

A tear rolled down my cheek.

I turned on the radio.

Through the dark and silence, Debussy's Prélude à l'après-midi d'un faune flowed in.

Then I went to sleep.

In the following few months, I didn't hire Romanians, never even passed by that part of the market. With the coming of spring though, I had to, for the overgrown branches of the trees behind the house had to be pruned. Like always there were lots of them leaning against the wall at the far end of the market. I approached a fair haired young man with sparkling eyes and asked him if he knew how to prune.

"Yes, I do," he said.

He had been working in Serbia for eight months and was speaking the language quite well.

At first I was thinking of not letting him sleep in the house, but to drive him back to the market at the end of day and give him a lift to the house in the morning, but as the night was descending I felt sorry for him. I knew he must have been sleeping in some burrow or a shed while I had the whole house to myself. He was very grateful for the dinner and the proper clean bed.

I tried to find Adrian in him, but that was impossible.

There were so many of them.

They were young, handsome, with gorgeous bodies and bright lively eyes.

Anita stopped counting them.

So did I.

Sometimes she would remark:

"This one isn't going to last."

Or:

"I'd love to hire this one to keep my feet warm."

I didn't find Adrian in the Romanian who cleared the vegetable garden of weeds, neither in the one who mowed the grass in the yard.

The last Romanian came to help me pack, at the end of my stay in Eastern Serbia. He had a wide smile and well-maintained soft hands, that were so at odds with a hired hand doing labor jobs. His Serbian was fluent. It turned out that he was a student at the Faculty of Music in Bucharest, specializing in piano. He couldn't afford the books and sheet music and that's why he used to come to Serbia illegally, every once in a while, to earn the money to buy them.

I wanted to make him happy. I wanted it with all my heart. The memory of Adrian was still strong, but I felt it was time I did a new good deed and the occasion just presented itself.

So I took him to my afternoon classes at the Music School, told him to sit in the back of the classroom and wait. My little students were coming one after another, playing various pieces while I was correcting and praising them, making sure they enjoyed the practice and the atmosphere. When the last student left, I turned to him.

"Alexander, would you like to play something for me?"

He couldn't believe his ears.

Instead of digging, ploughing, wood chopping, or stable cleaning, he was now being paid for playing the piano!

He started slowly, timidly at first, with Mozart sonatas. Then he suddenly went into the deep melancholy of Beethoven's Sonate pathetique. With the last accords still resonating in the room and my heart rejoicing, he got up, came to me and said:

"Thank you, thank you, thank you from the soul."

"No, Alexander, thank you. I'm so glad I could do something for you."

Over the next few days, Alexander was diligently packing the boxes while I worked, but at 4 p.m. was all too ready to jump into my car to get to the Music School and play for a couple of hours. At first I was always there with him, but then, trusting him to be an honest guy who wouldn't make any problems, I would leave him to play alone in the empty school while I ran errands or gave private lessons.

He stayed with me for a week.

Alexander was a genuine musician, giving all of his being to music. Since I was a professor, I wished to transfer him some of my piano expertise, so I gave him the score of Mendelssohn's Rondo capriccioso to practice. That piece had always been very special to me, but my personal temperament and technique had never made it possible to feel it as truly belonging to me. If you ever decide to listen to it, try to see the difference in character between the two leading melodies, one fast, almost fiery, and the other vivacious but with melancholic, diluted accords that follow one another like far-away constellations. Just as I thought it would, it came naturally to Alexander's fingers.

He never ventured into my bedroom, secretly, the way Adrian had a way to, but on the third evening while we were watching a video in the living room, he got up from the armchair and sat down close to me on the sofa. I shifted to make some room for him, when he suddenly took my hands, brought them to his lips and kissed them.

"You are the best, you give music to me... I... Thank you!"

He looked at me with tears in his eyes. At that moment I imagined myself not having the piano and somebody letting me practice and even paying me for that.

"It's my pleasure," I said.

I tried to turn towards the TV, to see what was happening in the drama we were watching with the wonderful, now late Lee Remick, when he pressed me tight to him and the next thing I felt were his lips on mine.

No.

I didn't want that.

Not at all.

I extricated from his embrace and went to the kitchen. Instantly, he was behind me, hugging me around the waist and kissing me in the neck.

Something clicked in me then. I couldn't tell what exactly, but something did, and it was strong.

I woke up before him.

He was lying on his back, completely uncovered.

I got up and went downstairs.

I made coffee.

That afternoon he played Chopin's Ballade in g minor, the most beautiful ever composed. It breathed out melancholy and suffering, but also passion, love and beauty.

It was like life – complex and uncatchable.

In the evening, while helping me wash the dishes after dinner, leaning close to me against the sink, he tried to kiss me.

I didn't want that.

Not at all.

He didn't try again.

That night I slept alone.

It felt good.

So much better.

He left happy. Kissed me on the cheek and pinched it lightly.

"You are so good, Nikola," he said.

The fence was navy blue the day I left the village, at the end of spring. It went through phases of being scratched and rusted, with no paint at all, through pastel green, white, beige, pink, and finally dark-blue. The trees were nicely pruned, the vegetable garden and the yard picture perfect, weed free and with the carpet of new grass. The wood that I hadn't got to use was neatly stacked in the shed. The balconies glittered. All the metal work and the railings were painted black. Looking at the balconies, I thought I saw Adrian bending and painting meticulously. It was just a shadow of the cherry tree branch, though.

Nothing else.

Nora's Impressions

I wish I could learn the art of giving from Nikola. Like, I generously give out my energy, knowledge, and advice to everybody around, but it has never occurred to me that people might need some bare essentials, such as food, clothing, and a place to sleep.

Call it 'God's will', 'destiny', 'karma' or whatever, the fact is that the distribution of wealth and poverty is so totally unequal on this earth!

Like, some people get to be born in palaces, some in stables (Jesus included). Personally, I'd prefer to sleep on hay rather than in a soft bed, so much healthier for the spine.

Just why would people who are not hungry enjoy lavish dinners while some starving people have to work their butts off for a slice of bread? I've been to so many formal dinners with elaborate candleholders, crystal, silver, china, silk, lace and all, which are only about showing off! I opt for Mom Vera's or Anita's or Nikola's cuisine in a nice warm kitchen, so much tastier!

Slave markets existed in ancient and early medieval times, according to my history books. I had no idea that such an institution has still remained, with some modifications though, to this day, in some parts of the world.

Right, nobody can know or do everything. People can be at their best playing music, dancing, writing, painting, teaching, accounting, engineering, selling, managing, marketing, field working, wood chopping, cooking... and what not. When you need someone to perform a job for you that you're not up to, do it in a civilized way, like Nikola; definitely not like that old asshole with alcohol-veined nose checking the muscles of his potential 'slaves'. Nikola should have punched him real hard into his red nose and what the heck!

Most of us do various jobs that require different skills, during our lifetime/s.

A pianist can come to your doorstep disguised as a laborer if in dire need of some food and somewhere to sleep.

We are all human beings and deserve to be treated as such by fellow human beings!

I go to Petrovac to see Nikola. Shopping for fruits and vegetables I see them for the first time, Romanians leaning against the wall at the very end of the market, clustered, waiting for someone to hire them for a couple of days. That day in that town there are Romanians, but I can sense that anywhere in the world, at the far ends of the most colorful markets, a group of people of some other nationality or race is also waiting for a local to offer them work, food, and shelter.

When I envision the procession of Romanians (who may epitomize any nation, from whichever country) happily eating delicious simple food after a hard day's work, taking a bath, and relaxing in front of the TV before going to sleep in a nice clean bed, so grateful for the most basic things in life, tears come to my eyes.

My eyes are watering heavily when I meet the Romanian who is diligently painting the huge gate and the fence of the yard of the house Nikola is spending his time in Eastern Serbia in. He takes the soap and towels for his bath in the large bathroom on the second floor as if they were jewels and so totally enjoys the inspirational meal I concoct, to the best of my cooking abilities, for our dinner.

The next day I leave for Belgrade. While the bus is slowly entering the curve on the village road, I see the Romanian on the balcony, looking for me among the passengers' heads. I wave at him and he waves back cheerfully. He's telling me something and without understanding the words, I know that they are:

"Bon voyage!"

My gratitude goes to Nikola for making it possible for Romanians at the time, especially for this special one, to experience life as it should be, at least for a few days.

"An accident of birth," a wise man once said to me.

We are all spread out all over the planet, in places we may not like to be and venture further.

It's the venturing further, in all spheres of our existence, that gives life its full meaning.

Show Me Yours, I'll Show You Mine

My salary was still nonexistent, a daily nightmare. In spite of my persistent complaints, phone calls, and explanations that we all work for money which is sort of necessary for living, all the responses were in the style, "The wind blows away a dog's bark" (Serbian saying, meaning: "It's all water under the bridge"). My only earnings were from private students but there weren't too many of them. Even though I wasn't paying the rent as agreed with my landlady in Paris and lived by myself, everything still cost. I was raking my brain as to how, in which way to earn a bit more.

Somewhere around that time, I started getting together with Dragan more frequently. He was a nice honest guy who wanted to show me everything in Petrovac and its surroundings, and to introduce me to some hidden corners of the area.

One Saturday, we drove in his beautiful new silver car to a nearby village that was spread out on the steep precipices of the Homolje Mountains. He said jokingly:

"You know, in this village, sheep graze under handbrake and beans are planted by a sling."

And it was almost like that.

The village was situated on a very high inclination. Some houses had three floors on one side of a hill and the ground floor on the other, because of the strange leaning of the earth.

That day Dragan took me to his friends' place, apparently a very well off couple.

"They are Vlach," he said.

The term 'Vlach' wasn't quite clear to me yet, but it started crystallizing, very slowly though.

Vlach people have been mentioned in lots of books, since the far-away times. Throughout history, they have been called different names and the very essence of their existence has remained a mystery. The Vlach population in Yugoslavia is mostly in Eastern Serbia, but also in the valleys of the Drina (Western Serbia) and the Drava (Northern Croatia) rivers and on the slopes of mountains. They speak Vlach language which is very melodious, sounds like a softer version of Romanian. Their folk tradition is wonderful, songs extraordinary, and the national costumes very colorful. Men wear white shirts tucked into wide red pants and high, conic-shaped fur caps. Women wear embroidered white tops with flowing skirts and tuck flowers in their hair. They have assimilated a bit with Serbs. There were some mixed marriages in all the regions around Petrovac.

The couple I was introduced to was unique. When the door opened, it was quite a sight. They were both dressed up as if just about to start performing in the Live Show in Las Vegas. He was wearing tight white leather pants, a matching short jacket with sequins, Elvis Presley style but more accentuated, a transparent red lace shirt and white patent leather pointed shoes. His wife was in one of the latest Valentino dresses ($5000 at least) and one of those incredibly expensive afternoon cocktail hats, typical for the ritual of the 5 o'clock tea in Great Britain. Such a hat would look perfect on a lady in the Ritz Carlton Hotel, dressed in a high quality tweed suit and a blouse in a soft, pastel color. It was definitely clashing with the atmosphere of the Homolje mountains.

They invited us in and offered us coffee and drinks. The living room was a reflection of their fashion style. The size of a department store or a railway station, it sported five extra-large sofas, all in white leather, with tons of multicolored cushions. In front of each sofa, there was a glass coffee table with a lamp underneath. In the middle of the room was a blood-red carpet, the reddest carpet I had ever seen. My glance fell on the walls with huge paintings, ultra-modern and probably very valuable, but hung up so haphazardly that instead of embellishing the space, they jumped out aggressively into the eyes of the observer.

The living room had one more unexpected feature. The ceiling, kind of a centerpiece, was three floors high. There was an opening of about twenty meters, going upwards. One of the reasons for that, they told us, was the chandelier they had bought in Vienna, Austria, a replica of the one from the Opera House.

I said it was magnificent. There it was, in all its beauty totally overseen, in spite of all the perfectly shaped millions of little glass pieces, round, oval, rhomboid or square, in the masterly polished Austrian crystal. The chandelier could be barely noticed from the clutter of wallpaper in striking colors and a multitude of Tiffany style lamps, mirrors in gilded frames, statues and vases with plastic leaves and flowers.

"We paid thirty thousand bucks for it."

"Pity to cut the rod, it has to hang."

"Lot of money, can't go to waste."

"Nice like this, real nice!"

They were admiring their chandelier.

They were admiring themselves.

They told us they always left it on all night so every time a car passed by, people could see its glitter.

Another reason for the high ceiling, regardless of the chandelier, was this: the comical couple liked to entertain, then would leave the guests sitting in the living room, while they climbed to the inside balcony on one of the floors, overhearing the gossips and who said what about the house.

"We listen and they don't know we're above their heads," they laughed.

"People love to gossip us."

Their parents as well as their parents' parents were all to one in Austria, working there. Money was coming in humongous quantities. The two of them didn't work, just kept buying more clothes and more things for the house. They were planning to have another house built.

I asked if it would be on a mountain slope or by the river, like a chalet.

"No," the wife said. "We already have a chalet in Switzerland, the new house'll be just here, next to this, so when we get into a fight, he and I, one sleeps here, the other one there."

"But we put in everything the same, all the details."

"All the same."

I caught Dragan's glance saying clearly, "They're nuts", and hid my giggles by lighting a cigarette.

It was fun talking to them, although they were real cuckoos.

They were telling us they were swingers and that once a month, couples from everywhere came to their place to fuck each and one another, and all together.

"Last week we had a famous porno actor from Germany," he said.

"Actually," she added, "he's from here, from Požarevac, but fucks there for money. He was so good!" she giggled.

Her husband roared with laughter and said she didn't get off the actor all night and wouldn't let any other woman ride him.

She got a bit serious at that and explained:

"What else could I have done? Believe me, like a horse's, a real rod, three hands can hold it and the glans still sticks out!"

"We have a video, if you want to see."

Dragan and I excused ourselves saying we'd love to stay longer, but had to go.

Later, in the car, we talked about them.

"Aren't they crazy, they wanted us to sit there and watch them fuck?" said Dragan.

"I agree," I said. "They don't exactly look like models for porno movies."

The couple was funny, but far from what I would like to see on the video. He was at least a head and a half shorter than her and fat, and she was like a giraffe without breasts and with long legs full of veins.

"They are so fortunate, with all that money," I sighed.

"Nikola, money isn't everything," Dragan said. "See what kind of life they have – fight all the time, sometimes don't talk to each other for ten days. They don't read, don't travel, aren't interested in things to explore and enrich their lives. They don't even go out to restaurants here, but pay a woman to cook for them. All day they're in front of the mirrors and admire themselves."

He was actually right. I needed more money for a better standard of living, but on the other hand, I was also fine the way it was, for my life was filled with music, research, and adventures.

That evening Dragan treated me to a nice dinner in a popular restaurant. We resumed our conversation about the wealthy couple and about being rich in general.

"I'd like to have money," I said to him, "but not to see it."

"What do you mean?"

"I don't want to save money, but would love to have enough of it so I could buy my mother everything she wishes, my friends everything they wish, and take Nora on vacation to Nordkapp in Norway."

"Why there?"

"Nora is very attached to that country, by some unexplainable ties we'll probably never figure out, the same way I'm attached to Poland."

"Poland?"

"Yes."

"Why?" he asked. "I didn't like it at all when I went there a couple of years ago. The people are rude, have no manners, it's like a waste land, the cities are all gray and everything's communist. There's nothing in it."

I was listening to him, thinking of how my Poland was so much more different from the one he was talking about. Mine was beautiful!

"Let's not talk about it, we have two diverging pictures in our minds," I said. "Back to money, I'd love to be able to treat all my friends to some special things."

"You think Nora would enjoy that trip?"

"Of course! She would absolutely adore it! A plane to Bergen, then by train or ship up north, or, just imagine, a horse-drawn carriage with a coachman and the two of us, Nora and I, wrapped up in thick warm polar bear fur and reindeer hide, heading to the furthermost northern point of Europe!"

I visualized Nora's long hair blown by the strong winds coming from the depths of the Arctic Ocean. Dragan's voice woke me up from my reverie.

"Trust me, the real wealth is only in the heart."

"Yes, I know, but it would be nice to be rich, if only for a short time."

He smiled.

Over the soft music and good wine, the conversation was flowing.

Dragan gave me a lift back home.

"Thank you for a great evening," I said.

"You're most welcome, just say when and I'm all yours."

There was something so warm about him.

The next morning, while I was buying burek, somebody tapped me lightly on the shoulder. I turned.

"You don't remember me?" a young man said.

"No."

I took a closer look at him, still having no idea who he was. A guy in his twenties, tall, with curly dark hair.

"So you forgot, I'm Djurica, a postman who delivered mail to the YPA Home when you were a soldier."

Right, that was him, just that he looked different now in sweatshirt and jeans, without his uniform. He used to be in a contagiously good mood and full of jokes and always had something nice to say about people, the weather or the nature.

"Now I remember!" I said.

We sat down at a small table with slices of burek and cups with yogurt in our hands. I had half an hour to spare before the classes.

"Are you still a postman?" I asked.

"No, I became redundant; there were too many of us for such a small place. People don't send letters these days, they barely have money to buy bread."

"I'm sorry you lost your job."

"Oh, it's OK, I work in the Leather Factory now."

The Leather Factory of Petrovac was kind of a brand name; shoewear produced there was sold in stores throughout Yugoslavia, I knew that long before the army.

"You're a professor in the Music School?" he asked.

"Yes."

"I've always loved music, but didn't get a chance to learn. Always wanted to have a piano and play."

"Would you like to come to the school and see the piano? I'll play something for you."

His face lit up. I noticed he had dimples when he smiled.

"I'll show you my job," I said as we were crossing the street.

His dimples expanded.

"Hey, this sounds good."

"What does?"

"I'll show you mine if you show me yours," he laughed.

In Serbian, the expression refers to winkies.

"You must be kidding!" I said.

"A deal?'

"A deal."

We went into the school building and climbed to the top floor.

He was looking at the piano, mesmerized. I opened it and started playing one of Chopin's mazurkas. When I finished, he asked for more. I played Beethoven's Moonlight sonata, the first movement. He was enchanted. Happy as a kid at a party full of balloons and candies.

The first student of the day knocked at the door. That was a signal for Djurica to leave.

"I have to work now," I said.

"No problem, Professor, but are we still on?"

"On?"

"You remember the deal, you show me yours, I'll show you mine."

"Oh, that," I remembered the joke. "Yes, alright."

"Come to the factory after eleven tonight, I'm a security there, will show you everything."

"So see you tonight."

It rained all day. My little students weren't in the best of moods, so I tried to relax and cheer them up in any way I could think of. It's interesting how rain steals the smile from some people. Rain, that I love so much for it gives me inner peace and vibrancy, makes some others sad and melancholic.

After work I went grocery shopping with Anita. I needed some meat, eggs, this and that. I wanted us to sit down at a bistro for a drink afterwards, but she said we'd better go home right away.

"People here are mean," she explained. "Tomorrow morning they'll gossip about us being lovers or something."

We made dinner together. Anita baked cheese and spinach pie while I was sautéing sausages and leeks. She asked if I'd like to watch a new TV series with her, but I declined, for I was meeting Djurica in the Leather Factory. On the way to the town the rain was thinning, until it became just a humid haze.

The Leather Factory looked frightening from the outside, in total darkness, with only a faint reflection of light from the lamp posts on the street. I discerned Djurica's figure in the security booth. There was a ramp in front of it. He opened it automatically and went out to greet me.

We chatted a bit while smoking in his tiny office. I could hardly wait to see the shoes, how they were made, styled, colored, varnished and everything.

I imagined a Santa Claus workshop.

I visualized the latest shoe fashion, already working out a plan in my head to ask him about his employee discount on the goods that would make mine, Mom's, and Nora's feet look amazing.

"The factory is closed by night, because of the economic crises. We work in two shifts only," he said as we walked to a huge metal door.

With a ghostly creak the door opened under Djurica's hands. Terrible stench filled my lungs. I didn't say anything as not to appear stupid, guessing it must be the chemicals used for coloring and varnishing shoes. It didn't smell anything like that, though, but of something rotting. Unbearable!

"Here, I'll show you all from the beginning," he said in pitch darkness. "Just stay where you are, I'll turn on the light."

If somebody had asked me in that moment, for a million dollar prize, what I would see when the light was turned on, I would have said: lots of beautiful but unfinished shoes, boots, sandals, slippers, all the imaginable shoewear, waiting for the finishing touches of laces, heels, buckles and other details. While imagining Santa's elves working at full speed to make lovely toys for all the children in the world, a strong light blinded me for a second. As I was adjusting to it, Djurica took me inside.

"This is how the process of making shoes and everything from leather starts."

I would have been less frightened if Dracula himself materialized in front of me with his sneering teeth.

I would have been less frightened if all the witches from all the cartoons I had ever seen came on broomsticks and goggled their eyes at me.

This was true horror!

I was standing with Djurica in front of enormous dark-blue containers. They were full of dead animals, just skinned that day. Terrified, I was unable to close my eyes or utter a word. I just stood there, looking at cows' eyes falling out of their skull and at rivers of blood. On the other heap there were sheep, with or without heads. Eyes, there were eyes everywhere.

I felt sick.

I was about to throw up.

I ran outside and stopped. The November wind from the mountains smelled of snow.

Djurica ran after me.

"What's wrong, Professor?" he asked worriedly.

"Nothing, just that I'm not used to..."

"Ah," he waved his hand. "Let's go to the hall number two, it's better there."

I followed him.

The next hall was a bit more decent, the hides were arranged by quality, thickness, and color. There were no heads, eyes, hooves, or tails. Then he showed me where hide was processed into leather, how it was dried and painted and the special machines that added the details.

The last hall was filled with boxes from floor to ceiling.

"Where are the shoes?" I asked.

"We don't do them here, just send the leather somewhere else and they make them."

We went back to his booth.

"Professor, you showed me yours today, now I showed you mine."

Of course it referred to our respective jobs, but the statement was ambiguous.

He was in a great mood.

"Mine is much bigger than yours," he said. "Look how huge these halls are!"

"But mine is a lot more beautiful than yours," I smiled. "These are just halls, and mine is protected by law in a national heritage building!"

We laughed like kids.

That night I had nightmares. Eyes of dead animals were chasing me in my sleep.

The rain drizzled all night and then, just before dawn, gave way to the shining sun.

I was telling Anita in the morning about my Leather Factory experience and the horror I went through.

"Stop it, you're giving me goosebumps!" she cried.

We were sitting at her kitchen table by the window, sipping coffee. The sunrays lit the yard, the freshly painted fence, and a part of the vegetable garden. Anita interrupted my musings about the beauty of the morning:

"Look, there's that whore, she sleeps with everybody!"

An ordinary woman was passing by the house. I had never noticed her before.

"You know everything," I said. "Like a real village gossip monger."

"Well, people talk."

"People talk and you prick your ears, like innocently."

"You men don't understand anything."

I went out into the rain kissed yard and inhaled the fresh air. It felt good.

"See you in the evening?" Anita asked.

"Yes, shall we make a crèpe cake?"

"Super!"

That evening after work I helped Anita make about thirty crèpes. NB: they are softer and thinner if you use water instead of milk.

Tarte au crèpes à la Nikola & Nora
Make a batter of flour, water, one egg and a pinch of salt.
Oil the frying pan and pour one ladle at a time, turning the contents upside down, preferably in the air. Repeat 20-30 times.
On the side, prepare ground walnuts, shredded chocolate, rosehip jam, and Nutella.
Layer the crèpes alternating chocolate, walnuts, jam, and Nutella until the last crèpe is on the top. Slice it like a cake and cover each slice with some melted chocolate.

Giselle in Krepoljin

The day was gray and gloomy, and I was playing Chopin's preludes in the empty classroom, for one of my students got sick and couldn't make it to the class. Suddenly the door opened and a man in his forties, with a jovial face, walked in.

"My apologies for disturbing you," he said. "Are you Professor Nikola?"

"Yes indeed," I got up from the piano.

"My name is Dane, I teach music in Krepoljin, a small place in the heart of the Homolje Mountains. We already have the snow, and it's still summer here, as I can see."

I smiled, for the temperature that day was -12 °C.

"Far from the summer," I said.

I had half an hour to spare till the next student, so I invited him to the school cafeteria for coffee. He looked honored. We sat down at a table in the large room void of other teachers at the moment. Dane had something on his mind and I waited for him to voice it.

"Well, Nikola, here's the thing…"

"What is it about?"

"You know, I live in a small place, it's not a village, more like a nice little town in the mountains. I've been working in the only school there for over twenty years. I have my orchestra and choir. What I miss is a music school. I have always dreamed of a music school in my Krepoljin."

"How can I help?" I asked. "You know, Dane, I haven't even got my first salary from September and what you saw upstairs is my own piano."

He had a solution.

"Nikola, if you decide to come to Krepoljin once a week and teach music classes all day, I'll make sure the parents pay you cash on the spot. Also, you'll have private students, children from our established and wealthiest families."

"How far is it from here?"

"About an hour and twenty minutes by car."

"It's up in the mountains and the winter is coming. My rickety Fiat won't be up to that."

"We'll fix it there," he promised. "Just come."

We continued talking about the weather and ordinary things. I got up when I saw my next scheduled student coming up the stairs. I could feel how much this man wanted me to come to that little town and work with him. He was an enthusiast, a creature of music and arts, working not for a salary but for the beauty of the work itself. Since I was made of the same fabric, I internally already accepted his offer.

"So, Nikola, are you coming?"

"When?"

"Next Saturday. If you don't like it, no big deal."

"OK, I'll be there on Saturday around eight in the morning."

All in smiles, he left bouncing and whistling Habanera aria from Carmen.

Running up the stairs, I heard a tiny voice behind me:

"Professor, am I too early?"

It was Maja, the elder daughter of my ex Captain Miha. She was always very polite and quiet.

"You are right on time, little doll, let's go to the classroom," I petted her on the hair.

Her fingers were small, so I chose for her only the pieces that wouldn't give her too much trouble and make all her hard work pointless. Today she beamed with pride because I praised her on how beautifully she played the whole program.

"Well done! That's my girl!" I said and gave her a candy.

She smiled and thanked me.

After my last student had left I leant against the window sill, looking at people, cars and carts passing by. It was only then that I realized I had started a new life, in a new town, with some new people, habits, and customs.

"Where are you going next Saturday? To Kre... what?" Nora asked that evening when I called her.

"To Krepoljin."

"What is it?"

"A little town in the mountains, probably very picturesque, just a bit colder than this place."

"Isn't it cold enough where you are?"

"It is, but you know how winter is romantic to me. I believe everything will be super."

"Right, just like the village school we used to work at was 'romantic', all with waiting for the bus for hours, dirty kids and stinky corridors, boring teachers and crazy locals. The frozen path to the school was also very 'romantic', you remember how many of our colleagues broke their arms and legs, even you fell down once and got all bruised," Nora was being realistic.

"But it was romantic to me, smiling children's faces, nice coworkers, rooftops with chimneys…"

"Oh, Nikola, will you ever grow up?"

I had no answer to that. Why would I grow up when it was so nice the way it was?

Nora went on:

"I'm worried about you, your car's not in the best of conditions and you'll be driving up the narrow roads."

"I'll be careful."

"Still, it's the mountain in the winter, icy and slippery, please take care!"

"Take it easy, Nora, I'll just go there once to see and if I don't like it I won't go back again."

"Promise?"

"Cross my heart."

I finished the conversation with Nora and was on my way to the kitchen to make a sandwich, when the phone rang. It was Mira. I told her about my new job offer.

"I may be working once a week in Krepoljin."

"You'll go work in what, Krepanja…?"

"Oh, God Almighty," I sighed. "Hasn't anybody ever heard of Krepoljin, a lovely little town in the Homolje Mountains."

"And why do they need you there? Aren't you already in a small town in Homolje?"

"They want to have a music school and pay cash after each class."

"Good luck," she said. "Have you got your first salary?"

"Not yet."

"That's all bullshit," Mira was increasing the volume of her voice. "You should come back! Get rid of those stupid villages, come back to where you belong!"

"Don't you worry."

"It's easy for you to say, but I don't sleep at nights, thinking about my daughters, making sure they get everything they need, and now I have to worry about you, too, in that God forsaken place!"

"It's not a God forsaken but a nice little place and I'm fine here."

"For Christ's sake, Nikola, why are you so stubborn?"

Mira was angry and we didn't talk for some time afterwards. She wanted me to come back to Belgrade, but I knew it wasn't the right time yet. My heart was telling me that.

I made some mint tea and sat down at the kitchen table to write a letter to Lieutenant Željko. His letter had been sitting at my bedside as a reminder to reply, but I had been putting it off for weeks. I took a deep breath and an old-fashioned ink pen. I always liked writing with ink pens, ever since I was a schoolboy.

Dear Lieutenant Željko,

I was very happy to receive your letter that brought warmth to these cold December days in the town you know well. I've been here for four months and it wouldn't be too bad if they at least paid me for my work. Unfortunately, there's no money for education.

I hope that you are doing fine, that you keep warm in the harsh climate of Monte Negro and stay away from married women, for men there can be dangerous when jealous.

Regarding the trip to Danilovgrad, I don't know what to say. I would like to see you, but on the other hand I'm a bit apprehensive, for I know you only as my lieutenant and it would feel strange to meet you in civilian circumstances. I don't want to refuse you, but please give me some more time to think it over.

Wishing you all the best, Happy New Year and (if you believe in God) Merry Christmas!
Yours truly,
Nikola

Krepoljin was a nice tiny place. I liked it a lot when I eventually got there. That Saturday I left home early, but it took me more than two hours through the mountains and I barely made it. The road to Krepoljin was a long story, winding, covered with snow, and frozen at many spots, constantly going upwards, lined with huge snow drifts at the sides. My little Fiat was struggling with each curve. Other than being old and suffering from lots of diseases, it had summer tires on top of everything. There was no way to get winter tires, so I was driving with these, thin and worn out, ready to slip at any moment. Still, destiny wanted me to get there safe and sound.

Dane was waiting for me at the school.

"How about some coffee?" He asked.

"Oh yes, please, a triple coffee would be great!"

He looked at me with concern.

"Bad road?"

"You bet! I was evaporating with three hundred sweats!"

We talked a bit. He said that thirteen students had registered for the classes that day. The parents were apparently delighted when they heard about the music school with a real professor.

Then we went to the second floor. The classroom was spacious and artfully decorated, with pictures of Mozart, Brahms, Beethoven, and Schubert. It smelled of music. There was a piano, an accordion and several violins, neatly arranged. Selected scores were in elaborate wooden frames and lots of photographs of Dane's small choir and orchestra from various competitions were displayed, together with the prizes they won.

"You are so successful," I said.

"But what's the point of it, Nikola, when the talent is wasted here? We are so isolated. And because of the mountain we can receive only one TV channel with just news and politics, there's no music, culture, or science programs for children to watch."

"Oh, that's a pity."

The children were lovely, sincere, and well-behaved. They were coming one after another into the classroom, introducing themselves and telling me their wishes: to learn how to play the piano, accordion, violin or to sing. The morning went by fast. At lunch break Dane and I crossed the street to an authentic restaurant.

"You have to try sausages with soft white cheese, they make the best ones here," he said.

He was right, those were the most delicious sausages I had ever tasted, served with freshly baked dark bread, sprinkled with linseed. The lunch was sumptuous and cost very little.

We went back to the school and I resumed work with the children. Dane was sitting quietly at the far end of the classroom, listening.

At the end of day I got paid in cash and slowly started the journey back. Dane promised to find a mechanic to fix my car the following Saturday.

Driving was now even more difficult because of the freezing rain that had fallen in the meantime. All the curves were covered with a thick layer of ice. It was windy and still snowing, so at times I couldn't see anything in front of me. The curves were sharp, I was navigating them slowly, waiting to see the monastery in the valley where I could stop and rest a bit, have coffee at a nearby café and refresh.

Finally, I saw the sign for turning and landed on the plateau in front of the monastery. I relaxed, savoring my coffee and cigarette. There was about half an hour drive left to Petrovac, but on a friendlier road.

When the flickering lights of Petrovac shone before me, I breathed the sigh of relief. I've made it, I said silently, contentedly.

Anita ran out of her house as soon as she heard the buzzing of my car entering the yard.

"How was it?"

"Not bad, just that everything's frozen."

She shook her head.

"I was worrying about you," she said. "Come in, I've just made donuts, sprinkled with sugar a minute ago. They're still hot."

Donuts are my Achilles tendon. I like them hot with a bit of sugar.

My dear aunt from the South of Serbia, now in the Heavens with Angels, used to make the best donuts in the world, filled with home-made plum jam.

I enjoyed the freshly fried dough and its aroma while Anita was giving me the latest update on neighborhood gossips, the situation in Croatia and Slovenia and the fuss about political parties. She knew everything. That woman was amazing: small, in flour up to her elbows, always humming while preparing food or tending the garden with an 'I don't care about anything' expression on her face, yet picking up everything that was going on in the village, the surrounding areas, and far beyond.

She poured us each a glass of wine.

"I'm getting more scared every day, Nikola," she said. "This war is spreading like cholera."

"I know, Anita, I'm scared, too."

She sighed heavily.

I understood her.

We had some more wine and then I went home. She gave me a few donuts on the plate covered with a napkin.

"This is if you wake up during the night and fancy something sweet," she smiled.

I told her about my habit ever since the childhood. If for whatever reason I got up in the middle of the night, I couldn't go back to sleep without a candy, chocolate, or something sweet.

The following Saturday, at the last curve, just before entering Krepoljin, at the spot from where a beautiful vista of the tiny town cuddled by the mountains opened, my little car decided to get seriously sick and to stop. It coughed a bit, then something inside it cracked and it came to a halt. Luck was on my side, though, for I was at the side of the road, not in the middle, and anyway, it was a country road, not a highway.

I covered the short distance to the school on foot. Dane's astonished face looked at me through the window. He hurried out.

"Where's your car?"

"At the entrance, by the bridge."

"I'll go get the mechanic, just give me the keys."

I gave him the keys and set to work. I asked the cleaning lady to make me a strong coffee and went to the classroom. Around four in the afternoon Dane came to tell me that the car was fixed.

"There's a lot to be worked on it, but for now it's OK."

I paid for the mechanic, the charge was reasonable.

The classes were unrolling one after another and at the very end of the day a small boy, sweet and polite, said his mom and dad were there and would like to talk to me.

A lively young couple was waiting for me in the corridor. They asked if I could give private lessons to their little Mike. He was very talented and a thirty minute class wasn't enough. They offered me a generous sum.

From the bottom of my artistic soul I would teach for free, but realistically had to comply with life's rules and take money for my work. Music is an inseparable part of me, of my heart; I am happy when I have the opportunity to transmit it to people, to open new horizons of beauty for them, and play a supporting role in fulfilling their music dreams.

From then on, every Saturday after the classes I would go to their house on a hill, impeccably clean and tastefully furnished, to teach little Mike piano, singing and ballet. I used to be a ballet dancer in my early youth and still remembered the positions and movements. Since little Mike was insatiable for all things beautiful, I decided to share my knowledge and skills with him and so he started making his first ballet steps.

The room in which we were spending our hour and a half of arts was full of light, with a spectacular view of the high peaks of the Homolje Mountains. Against one wall was the piano and along the other Mike's parents installed a big mirror and one of those bars that can be seen in all ballet schools, so he could practice.

Mike was eight years old, had an angelic voice, and long fingers made for Mozart's sonatas. That hour and a half was a pure pleasure for me and if I had more money I would pay them, instead of the other way round. The boy was progressing incredibly. He had enormous willingness to learn and perseverance, something that doesn't often happen at such a young age. His mom said he was practicing the piano at least two hours a day, then singing with the tape I compiled for him, and then ballet movements.

Just before Christmas I organized a mini concert at the school, so that my little students could show their performing skills. Dane artfully set up the stage and nicely decorated the hall. All parents and relatives came to attend. The children had stage fright, but I was calming them down and encouraging them.

They played wonderfully.

Little Mike was the first one to play. His brilliant interpretation of Mozart's minuet got a huge applause. Then, around the middle of the concert, there he was again. This time I was at the piano while he sang the aria from Traviatta:

Ah, fors'è lui che l'anima
Solinga ne' tumulti
Godea sovente piangere
De' suoi colori occulti!

At the very end, after the last composition was performed, Mike stepped on the stage in a navy leotard that his mom had made for him and danced a solo from Giselle. Everybody was impressed and his parents were glowing with happiness.

I tried to explain to them that I wouldn't be there forever, but that the child absolutely had to pursue the path of music and get further education. I suggested they moved to a bigger place, not necessarily Belgrade, but at least Požarevac, because their son had an extraordinary talent.

They said they would think about it.

A couple of years later, far from the Homolje Mountains, from that school and that tiny town, in the silence of my study in Belgrade, around the time I was getting ready to leave Yugoslavia for good, I thought about little Mike one evening. I called

Dane, my dear colleague, and asked him about one of my most talented ex-students.

Dane was delighted to hear from me, although sad about my leaving the country.

"You won't believe it when I tell you!"

"What happened?"

"Well, they went abroad, moved to Austria. Mike plays the piano and regularly attends the school of classical ballet, his mother says he's the best in the class. He already gave several piano recitals and is getting engagements with the Vienna Opera House and Ballet, every time they need a youngster for a role. The parents don't have your phone number and want to call you, to thank you for everything you have done for their Mike!"

When I put down the receiver, Nora came to me and asked with concern in her voice:

"Why are you crying, what's wrong?"

She sat down next to me.

I was crying of happiness.

"Remember my little super talented student from Krepoljin?"

"Yes."

"He has continued his piano and ballet studies in Vienna and is doing great!"

"Isn't that wonderful!"

It was holiday season. Anita's husband came back from the front in one piece, still his usual cheerful self. A thick layer of snow covered all the fields, the road and my yard. I was getting ready to leave for Belgrade for two weeks. Over coffee and coconut cookies in Anita's warm kitchen, I chatted with the lovely couple. Then I picked up my stuff and started the journey to Belgrade.

I was driving slowly, for it was still snowing and the visibility was minimal. They were saying on the radio that the highway was in a bad state and roundabouts were recommended, so I decided to take a longer, but safer road.

Nora was waiting for me, all in smiles when I finally arrived.

The Christmas tree was beautifully trimmed. There were lots of gifts under it.

That night we watched Charlie Brown's Christmas, ate prunes, figs and walnuts, and drank icy cold champagne.

It started snowing in Belgrade, too.

I was looking at the snowflakes fluttering between buildings with lit windows.

I visualized the snow in the yard of my house in the village, probably over half a meter deep by now, somewhere far-away, in the East, in a little town that was my prison, my paradise and my hell.

All together.

Winter

With its freezing breath, winter enchained the microcosm of the Homolje Mountains. I didn't remember it being so strong when I was in the army, but then, my mind at the time was who knows where, unable to register the cold of the winter or the warmth of the sun.

The winter was more severe here than anywhere else in Serbia, because freezing to the bone winds were blowing from the mountain peaks into the valley, where the small town was situated. Trees at the back of the house, the gate, the fence, everything was encased in a thick layer of ice. Under the light of the full moon, the yard looked ghostly but at the same time so magical, like framed in a moment of perfect stillness.

Mom was telling me on the phone that it was cold even in the South, but not nearly as much as in these parts.

I love winter.

I am a penguin.

I am a Siberian wolf or Arctic plankton.

My favorite movie scene is the one from Dr. Zhivago in the frozen village. I promised to myself that one day I would get on Moscow – Irkutsk train in the depth of a winter and spend all six days of the journey glued to the window, admiring the ice enveloped Siberian steppes and lakes, the dark tree branches hanging heavy with icicles. There's something about it that energizes and excites me. I love ice. I love the contrast of black and white with millions of shades in between.

My problems were of a different nature and started with the first <$0°C$ temperatures. My trouble was called 'the car' and I couldn't find a solution to it. There was no gas to be bought at gas stations and it was only thanks to Dragan, who had some connections, that I could get my tank full. It cost double the normal price but I had no choice. My trips to Krepoljin had been on hold for two weeks, because the snow was now so deep there was no way to get there, not even halfway.

Every morning, my car did its habitual thing – it wouldn't start. Every morning, I swore and cursed, but nothing came out of it. Irritated, I would start walking to work and it took over an hour because of the impossible winds in the open space between the village and the small town, space without a single tree. There were just fields on which the winds were free to dance the full scope of the vertiginous traditional dances, typical for that region.

I took my little Fiat for a check up to various mechanics. Each of them had a different diagnosis and none of them could repair it.

"I don't know what's wrong with it, maybe the electricity," a mechanic would say.

"Can you fix it?" I asked desperately.

"Just leave it here in the garage. I can, but later."

It made no sense being without a car where I lived. There was no public transport and it took forever to get to the town on foot in such weather. The sharp humid winds from the mountains were turning everything into ice in a matter of seconds. The Mlava River, fast and whimsical, was totally frozen.

At the edge of despair, I was spilling my suffering out to Anita one evening, over her melting in the mouth waffles with dried figs and dates, dipped in hot chocolate. I swallowed three of them and was full to the bursting, but my hungry eyes wanted more, so I put the fourth one on my plate.

"Anita, this is even better than sex!"

"Sex, what is it?"

We laughed.

Her husband was away from home for weeks, so she almost forgot the meaning of the word and all the pleasures the act can give you.

I finished my fourth waffle, complaining:

"If you go on making such delicious food, I'll turn into a barrel."

"Ah, shut up and eat, you're like a skeleton, just bones and some skin sticking to them!"

She was right, I was really skinny. Shopping for jeans or T shirts always implied a hard battle with sales people. They couldn't believe my size was easier to find in children's department than in men's.

While unlocking the front door of my house, I heard the phone ringing.

Bobby, an old friend from Pančevo (Vojvodina, North Serbia), called out of the blue.

"I got the job in the bank!"

"Super, that's what you've always wanted, right?'

"Yes, I've been on the waiting list for like two years."

"Congrats!"

"Mind if I come over to your place?"

"Not at all, you know you're always welcome."

Bobby and I had known each other for a long time and got together occasionally. Irresistibly handsome and charming, he could conquer women's hearts and all the other parts of their bodies in a fraction of a second. Every female wanted him.

So it was no surprise when Anita's eyes bulged at the sight of him as he got out of his blue sports car one Saturday morning and walked in the direction of my house. The pale winter sun delicately illuminated his features, making him even more attractive, if that was possible at all.

He barely had time to step inside and remove his coat when Anita showed up at the doorstep, bringing a platter of freshly baked cookies.

"Here's meringues with jam and honey, for a tired traveler," she cooed entering the hall.

I noticed she was wearing a new apron, was perfumed, and had make up on her eyelids. I winked at her when Bobby wasn't looking. She smiled.

The three of us agreed to go out to a nice restaurant in the evening, treat ourselves, and celebrate Bobby's new job.

Anita left with head in the clouds.

During the next two hours, she phoned me at least twenty times, asking for advice which top to wear with a matching skirt or maybe a dress, but what about handbags and other accessories? I listened to her crying and cursing her fat thighs and the butt "bigger than the Bulgarian Parliament". Many years later I went to Sofia, the capital of Bulgaria, saw that Parliament and was disappointed. I expected it to be much larger, for it was a synonym for all plump people in Serbia.

"I can't fit into any dress!" Anita was weeping, trying one after another.

"No worries, you're pretty in whatever you wear," I was consoling her.

As we all know, there's a big difference between sexes. I eventually got tired of her wailings, so I stopped answering the phone. I imagined her going crazy looking for some alluring attire.

Women.

Bobby was gorgeous.

Bobby had strong muscles that delineated so clearly under his shirt as if they wanted to break the constraints of the sleeves and the fabric and become free. Bobby always wore elegant suits and tight pants. He enjoyed being admired. He loved to see women blushing, muttering, and prostrating before him.

He loved men's envious glances directed to his pants that revealed, rather than hid, his genitals. He was a sex bomb.

But deep down, he was gay. Secretly.

And there was the problem.

Nobody in his social circle would have understood that. He could talk openly only with me and two of his childhood girlfriends; we knew the secret.

He slept with almost every woman in his town and the surrounding villages, seducing them while dreaming about something else. He was split and well aware he would spend all his life like that. Always encircled by tons of people, exchanging sexy stories, every once in a while he would get together with me or his two girl friends to share his other self.

That evening Anita looked lovely in a red dress. Her hair was styled and she had a lot of make up on her face.

"You look great!" I said.

"Wow," Bobby said. "A real beauty!"

She was just smiling and blinking with artificial eyelashes specially applied for this occasion over her own that were naturally long and thick.

We spent an enjoyable evening full of good music, food, and wine.

Anita, as a born top class cook, was finding fault with every single dish, even though they were all delicious. That was stronger than her. She would savor each bite and then blurt out:

"Hmm, they must have baked this meat with their left hands, imagine, no rosemary!"

Or:

"Smells good and looks good, but it's not sautéed enough!"

Bobby enjoyed the flavor of local dishes.

After dinner, we attempted a walk in the town center but the icy wind soon forced us to get into the car.

Anita went home.

Bobby and I were sitting in my living room, drinking cocoa with amaretto, smoking, and talking.

He was telling me all the stories he had been saving for me for months, stories nobody could know nor was allowed to hear.

He was telling me about a couple from New Belgrade who liked to play sex games. The wife indulged in having two men at the same time, while the husband was getting increasingly attracted to Bobby and wanted him only for himself.

"He started calling me at work, like every day," Bobby said. "So I had to meet with him for a serious talk."

"What did you tell him? It must have been a very delicate situation."

"Right, but on the other hand I have my job and parents to think about and I'm getting married soon. I didn't want him to ruin my life."

"I see."

"I told him not to call me anymore. He started crying. We were in that park in Zemun. He was getting on my nerves, sobbing there like a cunt. I wanted to hit him, to hurt him... fuck him!"

Bobby was visibly shaken.

"Calm down," I said. "It's all over now. When was it, this past summer?"

"This past fall," he sighed heavily.

"So how did it end?"

"Shit. It ended with me breaking his nose. He went on and on how he was dying to be with me alone, without his wife. Begged me and then cried even more and threatened he'd come to my workplace and say how much he loved me in front of everybody. I couldn't stand it anymore, so I hit him in the nose. He was angry, of course, but luckily I haven't seen him since. I changed my phone number, even though that doesn't mean much."

"A strange man," I said.

"A very strange man," Bobby echoed.

The next day I showed him around the small town, we walked up and down the main street. I took him to my favorite bakery for burek. We rented some movies from the town's only video store to watch in the afternoon. We were drinking vodka with lemon. Anita called a couple of times, but Bobby said he wasn't in the mood to entertain anybody.

"Except you," he smiled.

I smiled back.

"Right, you're entertaining me big time. I've been your tour guide in Petrovac, then your gourmet guide of its patisseries and am now acting as your waiter, making cocktails for you, all for free. Where's my part of fun in all this?" I said jokingly.

He laughed.

"What goes around comes around. What are friends for but to share? I'd do anything and everything for you, you know that."

"Yes, Bobby, I do, we've known each other for a long time."

He got up from the sofa and hugged me tight. For a moment I couldn't breathe.

"Right now I'll break you in half and eat you all up," he said.

"Cool down your hormones, boy, you always say that to me only because I'm skinny."

"No, on the contrary, you're slim, slender, fragile, gentle, and subtle like a birch tree, like a young poplar swaying in the wind, but not skinny, that's the difference."

Now it was my turn to laugh, for nobody had ever said I was fragile nor compared me to a birch or a poplar. I could hear Nora, Mira and all my friends doubling over with laughter when I told them about this. I was already imagining Marko giving me nicknames such as 'Birchie' or 'Poplary'.

"Like a delicate glass figurine of invaluable worth," Bobby continued.

'OK, now you're really exaggerating." I went to the kitchen for more booze to fill up our glasses and to get us some potato chips and pretzels. That strong vodka was making me light headed.

As I was slicing the lemon, Bobby came to me from behind and held me around the waist.

"Don't break the figurine," I laughed, using his metaphor.

"I won't, for it's invaluable!"

I brought the glasses and snacks to the living room, disentangling from his embrace.

The evening was unrolling pleasantly, filled with movies and our respective stories.

We drank a lot that night. The snow storm subsided and they said on the News that Eastern Serbia would remain very cold but without precipitations, which was good for Bobby's return home. We were so intoxicated and wobbly that we couldn't climb the stairs to the bedrooms on the second floor, so we unfolded the large sofa bed in the living room and slept there. At the crack of dawn I woke up with an irresistible urge to go pee, for all that alcohol had to find its way out. Just that I couldn't move.

Bobby was sleeping in my crotch, his arms wrapped around my waist.

I had to get up. My bladder was at the point of bursting.

So I got up slowly.

Bobby was mumbling in deep sleep. He was muttering words unknown to any dictionary while I was moving his head, arms, hands, and fingers and turning him sideways.

When I got back to bed, a couple of minutes later, he was soundly asleep on his back, snoring softly. The duvet fell off his body.

I smiled thinking of what girls would give to have a photograph of that moment.

When I woke up, Bobby's head was in my crotch and his arms around my waist, in exactly the same position as earlier.

A bit later we were having coffee.

Anita's voice refreshed our minds instantly. She phoned to ask when to come over. I said in half an hour.

Bobby put out the cigarette and ran his fingers through his hair.

"I'll go make myself presentable," he said.

He took a shower, shaved, put on an elegant suit, and ran downstairs.

Anita was already in the hall, with sandwiches she had prepared for his trip.

"Thank you so much, you shouldn't have bothered. Thank you, beautiful Anita!"

She blushed from her heels to the every single hair on her head.

"No bother at all and you're most welcome," she cooed.

He gently took her hand, brought it to his lips, and kissed it lightly.

I was afraid Anita would faint from a massive orgasm.

Getting ready to leave, Bobby hugged me.

"See you soon, just get out of this village, you don't belong here, run away from it!"

"I will, but did you notice how Anita blushed? You have a way with women, you really do."

He smiled, hugged me again, more tightly this time, and whispered:

"I'm even better with men."

I waved until his car disappeared in the white winter idyll.

It was nice spending a couple of days of enjoyment, but the reality was out there.

I didn't have a car.

Actually I did, but not it wasn't fixed.

Anita came to my rescue allowing me to use her husband's car, for he was at the front and the car was just sitting there in the yard. It was bigger than my Fiat and differently laid out and I was afraid of damaging it on the icy roads.

However, I took her generous offer and drove to a garage where my car was supposed to be repaired.

The mechanic was shaking his head.

"I couldn't do nothing, very complicated thing. Can't fix it."

"Do you at least know what the problem is?"

He kept shaking his head.

"No, maybe you leave it here some more."

"No, thank you," I said.

He coughed and came closer to me.

"Paying?"

"What about paying? You did nothing and fixed nothing."

"No, but I spend my time and that cost."

I was enraged. Still, I didn't want to make a scene and be a gossip topic in that provincial town for not having paid the mechanic.

"How much?"

"300 dinars."

I gave him the money.

I took my car to another mechanic. The story was always the same, with slightly different wording. Four garages later my Fiat was in no better state. I couldn't afford a new car. Good for nothing as it was, this one had to last till May or June, and then I'd throw it into the garbage when I get back to Belgrade. That was my plan.

"I'll go nuts!" I said to Dragan one evening at his place.

He had invited me over for dinner. I gladly accepted the invitation, for I hadn't seen him for a couple of weeks. I brought him a bottle of a nice men's fragrance as a gift. The interior of the house was really impressive. You could tell that the furniture cost a fortune, but everything was tastefully arranged. It was in all shades of white and red. We were sitting on a comfortable burgundy leather sofa in front of the fireplace and drinking martinis.

"I'll go totally nuts because of that car," I went on.

"So what's wrong with it?"

"No idea. One mechanic says electricity, another flange, the fourth one says crookity crank."

"That doesn't exist," he laughed.

"I know, I heard it somewhere and liked the sound of it."

"Where did you take it for repair?"

"Wherever I didn't! To the garage by the gas station, then to that stupid bold mechanic close to the market, then to the one next to the hardware store… They're all the same, just shake their heads, say they're very busy and to leave the car for a couple of days. Then they do nothing and ask for money. I'm sick and tired of the whole thing!"

"Don't you worry, it'll get fixed."

We had delicious stuffed quails and steamed root vegetables for dinner, as if prepared by the best chefs. Dragan made the dish by himself. We drank a lot. After martinis, Dragan switched to beer and I to vodka and with dinner we had exquisite vintage dry white wine.

"You'll stay here tonight," he said.

I had no other choice, being in no shape to drive and the taxi back home would have cost me an arm and a leg.

I fell asleep on the sofa in front of the fireplace, lulled by the music of Italian soloists from Dragan's stereo system. I woke up in a big fluffy bed by the window immersed in sunlight. The room was white, spacious, full of mirrors. A huge Japanese lantern was hanging from the ceiling. I guessed it was Dragan's bedroom. I got up immediately and felt a pressure in my head. Hangover! I took a cold shower.

"Good morning," he said cheerfully when I came to the kitchen.

"Morning."

"Fancy a coffee?"

"Oh, yes, a big one, and an aspirin, please!"

We were sipping coffee, chatting, and smoking.

It was almost noon, but it was a Sunday, so I wasn't in a hurry. I had one private lesson in the late afternoon, there was still plenty of time.

I looked outside. It had snowed heavily during the night. Then I realized that my car I had parked to the left of the house – disappeared.

"Dragan, my car's gone!"

"I know, I took it to a garage."

"When?"

"This morning, while you were sleeping."

That was so considerate on his part. Such a thoughtful friendly gesture. The next day the car was fixed. The mechanic explained it was old and had lots of problems.

"It'll last this winter and till the spring, but not longer," he said.

Whatever. At least for now I could drive it.

I called Dragan to thank him for the dinner and help with the car. I was happy to know him.

The winter became unbearable.

They started mobilizing again. The situation on the fronts of our once beautiful country was getting worse day by day. Battles were raging on the borders of Serbia and Croatia, Croatia and Bosnia. Brother against brother and father against son.

Each war is horrible.

There are no nice wars.

There are no winners or losers, just more blood and despair.

Our war was rotten.

Bloody.

I have never been able to comprehend, to this day, why so much hatred accumulated in the peoples of our Yugoslavia. It was stronger than the one in World Wars I and II, when the enemy came from the outside and was unfamiliar, first Austro-Hungary and then Germany with Hitler. This time people were fighting their friends, neighbors, and relatives. Mothers were expelled from houses where they had spent decades, for suddenly they were not good mothers anymore, because of their religion. I read about cases where father and son threw a wife and mother into the street and almost beat her to death, because she was catholic and they orthodox, or the same scenario, just another religion. There were too many of such stories. The unity of Muslims, Orthodox, and Catholics that was encompassing us all in former

Yugoslavia, living happily, was broken for some insane reason. I have never learnt to hate somebody because they believe in their God. And I never ever want to learn it!

The 8 o'clock evening news was more terrifying, and the winds more severe.

My house became icy cold and I got sick. The wood burning stove was working nicely, but it could heat only the living room. If I opened the door, the gelid air from the hall and the large staircase turned the room into an iceberg in a matter of seconds. There was no heating in the kitchen, so I kept alternating between warm and cold.

I stopped sleeping in the bedroom on the second floor, the cold was impossible to bear. I coughed a lot, because I often stepped out of the cozy room, into the freezing kitchen to make coffee or some food, back and forth.

Anita dropped by and looked at me disapprovingly:

"You've got fever."

"It'll go away."

It didn't, neither that evening nor the next day. It was hard to get out of bed. I was feeling weak, shivering and sweating at the same time. My body temperature was 42 °C.

"I knew you'd get sick," Anita said. "I knew it."

My blurred vision registered that she was holding something in her hand.

"You've got a letter."

I recognized Lieutenant Željko's handwriting.

"You have to drink a lot of tea and juices," Anita's voice trailed in my ear membranes.

I nodded, for it was hard to talk.

"I'll bring you some hot soup, just have to call my parents first; they're waiting to hear from me. Will be right back."

She left the room and closed the door.

I opened the letter.

Dear Nikola,
You say that my letter brought you warmth. It's nothing compared to your letter that heated my apartment on the second floor. I don't want to bother you with my laments and pleadings.

I just want you to know that you're always welcome to my place and my life, any time. I'm not after married women, thanks for the advice. As a matter of fact, I haven't fucked anything for months, somehow I'm not in the mood for that, pardon my French, but I'm not getting a hard-on on every skirt on the street. I hope they won't send me to the front and that I'll be lucky enough to see you again and spend some time with you.

Maybe I can't express myself well in writing, but I know what I know and that is I wish you to come to my place.

Happy New Year to you and everything you celebrate and believe in.

I believe in you.
Sincerely yours
Željko

Anita was back in less than ten minutes and thrust a bowl with steaming broth into my hands. I had just finished reading the letter. She had something on her mind. She was going out, coming in, carrying some cables. I was sitting on the edge of the bed bundled up in a thick duvet, watching her. Once she got everything under control, she said:

"Nikola, this is going to be our secret."

"What're you talking about, Anita?"

"Listen to me carefully. I don't pay for the electricity because my husband is on the front. I heat only the kitchen and the small room where I sleep. You'll get even sicker if you keep running from warm to cold and cold to warm."

I didn't understand her.

Did she want me to move over to her house?

No way!

Not for a million bucks!

Luckily, that wasn't a part of her plan.

"I've installed this extension cable, it's thick and strong, won't melt no matter how high you put the heating on your electric heaters."

It started dawning on me.

"Anita, I don't like stealing and that's what this is."

"And I don't like you coughing, and this is just the beginning of a more serious illness, I'm telling you!"

I had never stolen anything.

But this was an exceptional situation in exceptional times. I turned on the electric heater in the bedroom upstairs and another one in the kitchen. An hour later heath permeated my home. Even the hall and the staircase were warm.

In the morning, I felt much better and went over to Anita's place for coffee.

I looked through her kitchen window.

A thick long black cable connected the two houses. Everybody could clearly see I was stealing her electricity. I panicked. What if somebody reported me to the authorities and I got into a huge mess? I already visualized the front page of the local newspaper with the headline *Professor Abusing Benefits of an Officer's Wife*.

"Anita, this is so obvious, we'll be discovered any moment now!"

She took a look and waved her hand.

"Don't you worry, by the time you come back from work I'll camouflage it expertly."

"OK, if you say so."

I couldn't see any change in the afternoon when I drove back from the school into the yard. The big black cable was still there. It plainly stated that I was stealing electricity, so evident was its purpose.

I was about to give Anita a hand to carry out what she had planned, for she apparently hadn't done anything, when I spotted something white swishing in the wind. It was a dishcloth, half frozen, attached to the cable with two pegs. I picked it up and knocked at her kitchen door.

"Anita, what's this doing outside?"

"Why did you remove it? Give it to me!" She snatched the dishcloth from my hand, ran out, and put it back on the cable.

She marched in, rubbing her hands.

"Brr… Such a cold winter we're having this year."

Then she explained.

"That's the camouflage."

"Camouflage?"

"Yes, everybody will think the cable is actually a clothesline."

The only sound in the kitchen was the pork stew simmering on the stove. The silence lasted for less than two seconds.

Then we burst out laughing.

Tears were rolling down our cheeks while every now and then we pushed the curtains away to check how perfectly her camouflage was functioning.

I laughed in bed that night, before sleep. Only Anita could have thought of such a thing. The cable was thick, very unlike the clothesline and besides, who dried laundry outside in the snow on -20 °C? The very thought of the white swishing dishcloth made my eyes water with laughter.

It kept swishing till the beginning of March when the winter loosened its grip. I was using wood for heating again and gave Anita back her cable. The white cloth remained at the same spot to camouflage our secret mission.

Our theft.

Granny Jana's Song

Spring finally spread its white flowery veil over all the trees in my yard and over the whole town. Linden blossoms were generously giving out their scent to the main street and the promenade by the river. People were milling around, smiling to each other. No matter how bad the situation in the country was, getting worse by a minute, spring had that magic power to illuminate each face.

I was deep into ethnomusicology research for my Master's, traveling to remote villages and recording various types of singing. Every night I meticulously analyzed the material I had collected that day, listened to the tape recordings, and made music notations. At the school, it was business as usual. My colleague Julia and I started preparing students for the exams in June. Like every music school, ours also organized exams at the end of the school year. Students were required to perform a repertoire consisting of several pieces, write a music dictation, and sing melodies with only notes written on the blackboard. I was immensely happy that during all those months not a single student stopped attending the Music School. The children loved music and the two of us, their teachers, and we loved them all.

Saturdays were reserved for the elementary school in Krepoljin, where I taught classes to very talented students who were at the same time a part of my research project related to children's improvisations and imagination in creating a melody.

One Saturday, I was sitting with my colleague, Dane, in the teachers' room, telling him over coffee about my scientific work. He listened attentively and said:

"The only thing you are missing is the analysis of a mute song."

"A mute song?" I looked at him inquiringly. "What is it?"

"A song, but without words."

"Like Mendelssohn's Songs without Words for the piano?"

"No, this is authentic folk music. The song has words, but the singer doesn't say them, because they are love secrets and don't want to be revealed."

Intrigued and excited, I showered him with questions to which he simply answered:

"I don't know much about that, but tomorrow I'll take you to the right place, to the right person. Bring a kilo of sugar, some coffee and make a sign of the cross before leaving home. No sex tonight, just sleep peacefully. When I take you to her, you have to be pure in mind and body."

"To her?"

"Yes. She is an old woman, the most esteemed singer in this region. She also has a gift to see through lots of unexplainable things."

I wanted to hear so much more, but the school bell rang, announcing the start of the class and interrupting our conversation.

Driving back home, I wondered who that woman was and how she sang. What was it she could see? Why was Dane sort of mysterious?

I told Anita everything, over dinner that I prepared, for a change. I made a phyllo pie with potatoes and fried onions, sprinkled with oregano and chili peppers. She enjoyed it, to my delight. Through mouthfuls she said:

"Just so that you know, this region, especially the remote villages in the Homolje Mountains, are notorious for sorcery and white and black magic."

I looked at her incredulously. Yes, I'd heard a few times that someone was 'bewitched' by love charms and that some people had hard times because a neighbor hated them and put a kind of a 'voodoo' in front of their house, but I never paid any attention to that, for it was all superstition.

I was apparently living in an illusion, in an illusions infused place.

"It's dangerous," Anita went on. "It can change a person completely, I've heard about all sorts of things going on here."

"So strange, totally unreal."

"Advice for tomorrow – don't touch anything anywhere, definitely not the ribbons on the trees or on the ground and never look at anybody straight into the eyes."

"Now you're scaring me," I laughed.

"I don't want to scare you, just be warned," she said seriously. "This is a weird region."

Then we changed the subject and had some nice linden tea. Its scent permeates the whole house when you brew it. There are also fragrances that have linden blossom as a top note.

The early morning dew was sticking to my car tires as I slowly drove out of the yard. There were flowers everywhere. My geraniums were smiling to the warm sun. I've always loved white and red geraniums. I planted them in the fall, actually Adrian, my Romanian did, in the window boxes and in front of the house. When Nora came for a visit and saw them in full bloom, she exclaimed:

"Your house looks like a Polish Embassy, it's all in red and white!"

It hadn't occurred to me when I was planning my spring.

Lily of the valley was thriving in the shade behind the house. I picked a bunch and put it in a vase in the living room, to welcome me with its clean scent when I get back home. One of my favorite flowers, together with snowdrops and white roses.

There was nobody on the main road. Sunday was lazily waking up. The mountain greeted me with its winding roads lined by leafy trees. Driving smoothly through the green tunnel, I remembered how hard it was to conquer each curve in wintertime. I stopped at the Monastery of Gornjak, intoxicated by the beauty of the landscape. The monastery rose from a deep valley, surrounded by mountain peaks and hugged by blossoming trees. Like in picture books of castles, a small river was flowing by, gently caressing its solid walls. I stayed there a bit, inhaling the moment of serenity and deep peace before continuing my trip.

Everything was tranquil around me, my head echoing with Cherubic Hymn by Stevan Mokranjac, great Serbian composer from the 19th century. It so perfectly matched this idyll, the monastery and the colors and murmurs of the woods.

I was driving in silence, listening to the music in my heart. Soon I arrived to Krepoljin.

Dane got in my car and showed me the way. The road was narrow, curving to the left and to the right, every now and then opening vistas to lush meadows and fields. There were horses in the pastures, gorgeous and proud. The air smelled of freshness. The road was continuously leading up. After more than an hour drive, Dane said to stop.

"We'll walk from here."

A steep winding path was disappearing in the deep shadows of the woods. We walked through a thick forest with tall trees, followed by the bird song all the time.

All of a sudden, a village appeared before us. About two dozen houses, settled on the west side of the mountain. All the houses were white, with dark-red roofs. Here and there threads of smoke could be seen coming out of the chimneys. There wasn't a living soul on the little lanes spreading through the village like arteries and veins. Greenery was everywhere, lots of it. It looked as if the woods were in the village and not the village in the woods. Raspberry bushes were growing in neatly shaped circles, like some kind of a monument or a piece of art at an exhibition. There were several such bushes, taller than me, all perfectly round. I wondered at that.

Dane took us to the lane with water running down it.

"It's the stream that springs under her house," he explained. "People say it's magic and can cure all pains and aches, even lovesickness."

Amazed and curious, I climbed the narrowest path in the world, wading through the water. On both sides of it weeping willows were intertwining their branches over the stream, as if they wanted to wash in it. We arrived to the last house in the village, on the mountain plateau. Hens were strolling in the yard. There was also a cute cat and a cuddly yellow dog. The house was tiny but had a large veranda full of copper trays, clay bowls, flowers, and grasses hung upside down to dry in the spring breeze.

"Jana, hey! Jana!" Dane called her.

The heavy door cracked and a small old woman with sparkling eyes and a wide smile stepped out. A single look at her was worth thousands of words. She greeted us with spread out arms, scarf in vibrant colors on her head, rose buds sticking out of it. Over the white embroidered shirt, she was wearing lots of necklaces and miniature mirrors that reflected the sunlight as she swiftly walked towards us in her multicolored skirts. She affectionately hugged and kissed Dane. He introduced me.

"Jana, this is a professor of music from Belgrade, he is working in Petrovac and in my school in Krepoljin. I was telling him about your songs and he wanted to meet you."

"Good, good, welcome, Son," she said squeezing my hand. "C'mon inside, my dears, c'mon!"

She was inviting us in, but she herself didn't move. She was intently looking down the path we had come by as if expecting someone. After a few minutes of silence Dane said:

"Who are you waiting for, Jana? Is somebody else coming?"

She turned to me.

"Where's your brother? He should be here, too."

I was flabbergasted.

"I don't have a brother," I muttered.

She put her hands on her hips and looked at me suspiciously.

"Ah, it's not nice to lie to an old woman. Haven't you brought him with you?"

Dane was puzzled.

"It's only the two of us," he said.

She came closer to me and looked me deep into the eyes.

"Where is your twin brother?"

Blood froze in my veins. Nobody, absolutely nobody, knew that I had a twin brother who died at childbirth that Mom barely survived. This was scary.

"Granny Jana, he died, a long time ago," I managed to say.

"Why don't you say so, Son? 'Cause I see him next to you. I can see this world and the other," she waved her hand. "C'mon in, all three of you!"

I could hardly walk from the shock. We entered a room in the left part of the house. It was full of light and spotlessly clean, with a bed, a big icon of Virgin Mary, a cross above the door and jars full of wild flowers on the table by the window. A small wood burning stove was crackling in the corner. Granny Jana made Turkish coffee in a copper pot and distributed it into four cups. She saw a question mark on my face.

"That's for the one who somewhere in the world wants to drink coffee but has nobody to give it to him."

It was all so weird.

She was chatting with Dane about the past winter, about their common acquaintances, who died, who got babies... At one point she turned to me:

"I've loved music ever since I was a child. I love to sing, to be happy."

As if she knew what I wanted to ask her, she went on:

"I started singing as a little girl, went to villages, wherever they asked me to come, for joy or sorrow. I sang wedding songs and mourning songs, for going away from this world. People pay well at weddings and baptisms, but even better at funerals, 'cause it's sometimes hard to cry and what are the relatives and neighbors going to say if there's no one crying. I cried sincerely, for I could see the soul of the deceased leave and look at me."

"Dane says you can sing songs without words. What kind of songs are they?" I asked her.

She went to the window, looking somewhere in the distance.

"They're songs of love, secret love, forbidden love," she said. "Songs written from a sad heart."

"Why are they without words?"

She glanced at me for a second just to check in my eyes that I wasn't pretending not to know.

"They have words, Son, but you don't sing them, so that the birds can't hear."

"Birds?"

"Yes. If the birds hear you sing about a girl and you say everything in the song, how beautiful she is, her hair, eyes and all, they will carry the message and the whole village will know. What if the girl is taken? You don't want to make problems," she clarified.

"Can all the girls and guys in the village sing them?" I asked.

Dane and Granny Jana burst out laughing.

"No, Son. Only we women who have a gift from God to see in the dark, only we can sing them."

"There are only three of them in the whole of Homolje," Dane added. "But Jana is the best and the most respected, a star from the sky!"

She laughed with her lovely tinkling voice.

"When somebody falls in love and the heart is breaking 'cause the other one is married or who knows why they can't be together, they come to me and tell me their sorrow. When they leave, I take my peacock plume and put it on my head to give me strength and clear mind to save the words in my heart and to weave a song from my soul."

I was absorbing every word, every movement of this wonderful woman.

She went to another room.

"Isn't she amazing?" Dane asked me.

"Thank you so much for this," I said. "This is so unique, out of this world!"

Granny Jana came back, holding a big plume made of dried flowers and peacock's feathers. She put it on her head and covered a big mirror in the room with dark cloth.

"A mirror can read from the soul, and this is a secret song, that's why it has to be covered now," she explained and stood in front of the window.

Then she started singing.

The beauty of her song, its depth and primordial power cannot be described in one sentence, nor in volumes. From this tiny woman the song was gushing out with a mighty force of an unstoppable torrent. It was endless, poignant, extraordinary. At certain moments she paused, inhaled deeply, only to resume singing even more vigorously, from the depths of her very being. The song was sung like this:

Na na naaaaaa,
Ehmm na na naaaaaaa,

The nasal tones *mmm* and *nnn* rendered it a touch of mystery and her plume laced it with magic. Granny Jana was singing not only with her voice, but with her whole body and heart. The song lasted about ten minutes. The melody remained basically the same, but her sighs and specific vocal alternations were changing, dynamic from *piano* to *forte* and vice versa, accompanied by the expressions on her face. In the silence that followed, the reverberations were echoing in the corners of the room, on the ceiling, behind the icon, under the bed.

My eyes were full of tears. I was overwhelmed by the experience. Granny Jana simply saw me saddened by the song.

"Don't worry," she said. "The two of them got together. She's carrying a baby boy in her belly, it's been ten days. I saw her yesterday when I took the cow to the pasture."

I was intrigued.

"You saw that the girl was ten days pregnant?"

"Son, I can see when she's ten hours pregnant."

I was flabbergasted, for the second time that day.

Granny Jana looked tired, the singing must have used much of her energy. She sat down on the bed and took off her plume. I thought we'd better leave. I made eye contact with Dane and we got up from the table by the window.

Saying goodbyes at her gate took quite some time. I could see she was getting fond of me, as I was of her. She gave me apples and fresh eggs to bring back home.

"When are you coming again?" She asked.

"Next Sunday, if you don't mind."

"Not at all, you are a good guy. Just come."

She hugged me.

Dane and I went down the path with spring water to the center of the village from where we walked to the car.

"What do you say?" He asked me.

"What can I possibly say? An extraordinary woman, one-of-a-kind!"

I dropped Dane off at the entrance to Krepoljin and continued driving to Petrovac.

I couldn't wait to call Nora and tell her all about my adventure. She listened to me attentively and said to take care, like extra sensory perception could be dangerous, depending on how you use it. She was scared of those things and for me.

Anita made a sign of the cross when I told her that Granny Jana saw I had a twin brother.

"That's magic."

"Yes," I said. "But white. She's been given the gift by God, as she says herself, to do good."

Anita nodded briefly and changed the subject.

That night I went over to Dragan's place for beer and told him about my experience.

He listened, interested.

"I try to stay away of those things," he said. "I know they exist, but they frighten me."

"Me too, but this is different, she's good, she's such an incredibly soulful woman."

"I hope so," Dragan said.

The following Sunday I was sitting in Granny Jana's room. I brought her chocolates, cookies, sugar, coffee, and a new scarf. She thanked me profusely. I also brought my tape recorder to record her singing. She put the plume on her head, stood by the window and sang a song, very different from the one of the previous Sunday.

"What kind of song is this, Granny Jana," I asked her when she finished.

"Also without words, but from the other side of the mountain, it's a sad song of a girl who loves a guy, but he's married with a woman he doesn't love. The girl sends it to the field behind her house, a prayer to the field to take her and swallow her, so she could disappear from this world."

It was poignant, sung in another manner, with tones and melody so dissimilar from what I heard a week ago. It all went like this:

Nnnnnnn nnnnnnnn nnnnnnnnn

When I asked her why *nnnnn* and not *la la la* or *na na na*, she simply said:

"'Cause it can't be sung with any other letter!"

We were sitting on her veranda and talking. She brought some pears from the last fall, perfectly preserved. We ate while looking at the high mountain tops. She was telling me about that little village, just about eighty people lived there. The young ones were leaving far away, to big cities or abroad and never came back. The fields were overgrown with weeds and empty houses were slowly falling apart.

Granny Jana was in her nineties, but fast moving, youthful looking, and always cheerful.

I was slowly getting ready to leave when she said:

"Come into the house, I want to see something."

I entered the room.

"Sit down."

I sat down on a wooden chair. She put a white cloth on the table by the window, gave me a glass of water and an ear of corn. Then she sat down next to me.

"Take a sip of water and crumble the corn with your right hand, only once, the grains will fall where they want."

I followed her instructions. A few grains fell on the cloth, some on the floor, one in my and one in her lap. She was silent, watching. Then she got up, kindled the fire in the stove, fed it some new tree branches, and turned to me.

"Somebody's working against you. Somebody wants you to leave this place. It's not good for you to stay here, your destiny is written somewhere far-away."

I got almost panicky. Anything could happen to me, especially now that I knew about weird things, sorcery, charms, and curses.

Granny Jana saw fear in my eyes

"Don't worry, I'll keep you safe," she said. "I'll tell you when to leave, don't you worry, I'll keep you safe."

I wasn't exactly totally convinced or calmed down, but left it at that. I couldn't jump out of my skin or divert the course of destiny, anyway. Granny Jana and I said our goodbyes and hugged each other at her gate. She gave me a loaf of freshly baked bread and a big chunk of white cheese.

"For your dinner, Son."

I carefully navigated the curves on the road driving back home. Who could be working against me and why? I didn't have enemies, as far as I knew. I had never ever hated or hurt anybody. I remembered Anita saying at one point that local people didn't like newcomers.

Cold sweat ran down my spine.

Granny Jana and I became friends. We used to go for long walks in the fields. At certain spots she would suddenly stop and start singing. I was listening, carried away by the beauty of her songs. She would explain what kind of a song each of them was and why it should be sung in a specific way. They were about love, unfulfilled wishes, deep sighs, and longing. Some were very old, from her childhood, she had learnt them from her grandmother. Those songs were mostly prayers to the Almighty for rain or the sun, for good crops and full stables, lots of poultry and health in the house. They were different, faster and in a simpler rhythm. The songs that touched me most, to the very heart, were those without words. Some of them were inspired by a nightingale, some by a cuckoo. In some of them nature talked to men, in some men to nature. It was interesting that a cuckoo was always present and often taught a young soul what to do and how so that love could be requited. Love, oh love, so desired and so much sung about! Granny Jana's songs were precious pearls in the music necklace of eternity. They warmed many a heart in that village.

I was continually working with children and on my Master's, but always found some time, at least once a week, to visit Granny Jana.

Nora came one Saturday. I decided to take her to meet Granny Jana, who took a liking to her right away. Nora was scared to death by the strange things happening in the area and the unexplainable phenomena. She walked gingerly, not daring to touch a bush or a tree branch, fearing it might have been bewitched, with unlucky charms lurking everywhere. A couple of days later, exhausted, she said that was all crazy and it was really time for me to come back to the normality of the city.

"This is all freaking me out! It's so unreal, a weird region without a beginning or end, with soothsayers, sorceresses, and magic. It's terrifying!" She proclaimed.

I felt myself it was time to leave that part of the world. An internal voice was warning me, aware that the sand in the hourglass was ticking out my Petrovac days. Insisting on being paid all the salaries I had never got from the Music School was an excruciating task, impossible to accomplish. Not to mention all the surreality around.

For my birthday in May, I went to Belgrade and celebrated it with my friends. Every single one of them asked me when I was finally coming back. I said that was the plan for the nearest future, but I hadn't set up a date yet. Among lots of books, records, and tapes I got as gifts, there was an elegant snake leather wallet with a silver buckle.

It was so relaxing to forget for a moment about the house in the village, the yard, and the Homolje Mountains and enjoy the birthday party, music, dance, and laughter with friends. Belgrade, uglier than ever, was waiting for my return. Ridden by poverty, inflation, and full of some strange new people who now inhabited it, bringing with them some disgusting fashion. Still, to me it was the most beautiful city in the world.

On the way back to 'my little village', I stopped at a roadside café, ordered coffee and fuzzy water, and wrote a letter to Lieutenant Željko. It wasn't fair not to reply to his letter that had been sitting in my bag for quite some time.

Dear Lieutenant,

I hope with all my heart they don't send you to the front. Although a soldier, you are a wonderful person and there is a lot of room in your soul for things much better than the war. Pity we don't live in some other times. I'd so much like to take you to the National Theater in Belgrade and spend a lovely evening in your company. In this part of the country, it's the same old, the inflation is killing us slowly and steadily. If we don't die of it, then we certainly will from the TV news.

I passed by the barracks the other day and thought of you. I don't know if you remember, but even though you went by the nickname 'Horrible' among the soldiers, whenever alone with me you revealed, at least for a moment, your beautiful warm soul.

Be healthy, happy, and, at the risk of repeating myself, stay away from married women, find the single, good, and nice ones.

Can you send me a picture of you, preferably in the uniform?
All the best,
Nikola

I finished my coffee and went to a nearby post office to mail the letter. At that time there were no stamps because their price increased several times a day, so the only way to send a letter was to take it directly to a post office and pay on the spot.

A week later I was sitting on Granny Jana's veranda. We were drinking home-made elderberry juice and chatting. All of a sudden her expression changed. She closed her eyes.

"A snake! I see a snake! You have something made of snake?"

"Yes, a wallet, but I think it's fake leather."

She was silent.

Absorbed in looking at something only she could see.

I was afraid of what she might say.

"Fire. The snake is burning now. Somebody took it and burnt it. When you're back home, go behind the house, to the north, there's an old kennel, you'll find a trace there."

We continued talking about this and that, but my mind kept returning to what she had said. I couldn't wait to go home.

As soon as I entered the yard I went behind the house where the old kennel was. A dog used to live there, but had died before I moved in. I looked around and saw the buckle from my wallet. So somebody had stolen and burnt it, but why did they bring the buckle here? I never found out who it was. That morning I gave some money to Anita to pay the phone bills to the postman who was coming that day. I was in a hurry and probably left the wallet on the roof of the car and when I started it, it fell down, without me noticing anything. Anita said she built open fire in the yard shortly after I had left, to burn all the unnecessary stuff that had accumulated in her house during the winter, since there were no garbage bins in the village. Then her husband called and she was on the phone for half an hour. When she went back to the yard, something smelled strange. She didn't know that was my wallet. She also said the gate was wide open.

So they started 'bewitching' me.

Fine!

Now I was really scared. Somebody wanted to get rid of me.

I'm leaving in a month!

The decision has been made.

Nora's Impressions

"You have a psychic line on your palms. It's not fully developed, but you've got some great potential there!" a palm reader friend of mine says.

Well, I don't have the slightest intention of becoming a professional fortune teller, but have always been intrigued by what lies beyond the five senses. Like, my intuition is quite active and I can sometimes see people's auras, just like that.

I have a deep respect for clairvoyants, people who can see clearly, as the term literally means 'chiaroveggente' in Italian, derived from the Latin clarus – clear and the present participle of vedo, vedere – see, adopted in English through the French version. Some of them have that precious, God-given gift to see into the past and future and the present moment in between. Some others use tarot cards, crystal bowls, melted wax, or any other medium as a means of focusing. They basically tune into the universal energy and transmit the message to the person they are doing the reading for.

The most formidable reading I've ever had was when a psychic told me to hold my house keys in my right hand, covered it with her left, simultaneously talking and writing down messages directly from the Spirit Guides.

Left and right and the world is alright. Just why is 'right' a synonym for good, what about left-handed people, like Leonardo da Vinci; what about ambidextrous ones, like me?

I'm not into predictions, since whatever is supposed to happen, will happen one way or another and why bother. I just like parapsychology.

The psychics I've been in contact with interpret what they sense about you more or less accurately, for they are only humans. By the same token, you, being a human, can't know what the 'absolute accurate' is. So you take their advice if something unfavorable might be in store for you, like to be forearmed. It's all about energy flow.

They don't attempt to 'fix' anything like pouring 'magic potions' into the mouths and minds of people you want to change in order to serve your purposes. That's sorcery!

That's why I'm freaked out and shit-scared by the psychic scene of Homolje. To begin with, the division of the local fortune tellers into 'white' and 'black' is beyond my comprehension. Like, people go to psychics if they have a problem and need some sort of guidance, not bring harm to others, for it always backfires. Some strange ethic principles in this part of the world. Are the 'black' ones Morgan le Fay type, can they turn you into a frog or a beast or whatever like in the Sword in the Stone cartoon?

Granny Jana is 'white', all right or all left. She's a memorable and lively character with divine voice and a gift of prophesy, or so it seems. Her tiny figure is clad in the colorful national costume, all with flowers in her hair. She spreads her arms and smiles all the time. She's into birds' songs, dried herbs, fields, woods, streams, and the elements.

So far, I'm with her.

I delight in Granny Jana's archaic house, so perfect in its simplicity, smelling of the fresh mountain air.

I am still with her.

Having heard a lot about her psychic reputation, I'm puzzled when she serves me coffee with three spoonfuls of sugar. Can't she 'see' that I've always had my coffee black? Then she tries to stuff me with a delicious-smelling, but over-sweet pumpkin pie, still not getting it; I'm so not into sweets!

In spite of Granny Jana's whiteness, there's something slightly scary about what she does. Can't pinpoint exactly what it is, for her readings in corn grains are purely from the soul. My gut feeling tells me she has a tendency to fix destinies, rather than just read the corn. Sort of like she's playing God and you don't do it, no matter how sincere your intentions!

Anyway, Nikola and I walk in Granny Jana's meadows and fields and witness the performance of her little rituals at some special spots. This 90-year-old woman gracefully, like a little girl, extends her arms to the Sun, bends down to the Earth and makes some other movements in her own version of Sun Salutations, accompanied by her out-of-this-world singing.

I am totally with her here!

On our way back to civilization, i.e. Petrovac, Nikola and I stop at the Monastery of Gornjak. It's all white and zen-like, with a river running by its walls and the greenery all around; just that each blade of grass, all the branches of bushes and trees are 'adorned' with ribbons, strings, threads and some strange objects, like charms and spells.

I don't dare sit on the grass and wriggle my toes in the river, for fear of who knows what kind of 'magic' may befall upon me.

Get out of there Nora, get out of there Nikola!

Each in Their Own Way

The beauty of living in every country and city in the world would be complete if their cohabitants understood and respected each other. What could be more stimulating than getting to know different cultures, ways of life and local customs?

My country was slowly melting under the fires of hell and pressure from abroad. It used to be an inspiring, multicultural place where, before the war, people lived in harmony and learnt from one another. Unfortunately, the harmony now burst like a soap bubble, for everybody was currently busy hating each other and fighting as to who was a bigger nationalist and who that part of the wood or the river belonged to. A sad ending of a once-lovely fairy tale.

In Petrovac region, there were two major ethnic groups – Serbs and Vlachs.

Vlachs appear in early history as people living in the mountains of nowadays Macedonia, who later started to migrate to the north and east of the Balkans. There are lots of theories, but none of them is certain as to the etymology of the name Vlach. Much more interesting than the past is the present. Most Vlachs are orthodox, but also carry in their hearts beliefs from ancient pagan times. Some deeply believe in the secrets of quackery, sorcery, spells, and other 'magic' things.

When you walk in the town, at first glance there is no difference between Serbs and Vlachs; the distinction is more on the internal level. Vlachs love to dance, sing, and joke, just like Serbs, but their national costumes and melodies are unlike. Vlach songs are usually about nature and love for it, with lyrics of deep gratitude to the sun, water, wood, and life. Every single day of my stay in that enchanted part of the world, I was noticing various degrees of dissimilarities between the two peoples who lived happily side by side.

Vlachs tell jokes about Serbs, Serbs about Vlachs. Rumor has it that Vlach husbands are not jealous and that it's a sign of hospitality and respect for the guest to offer the wife, after good dinner and a glass or two of home-made wine, as a dessert I guess.

I liked the Vlach language a lot, so many unusual sounds, lined by vowels. What amazed me was the fact that it didn't have an alphabet. If a Vlach wanted to write a letter to another Vlach, it had to be in Serbian.

Vlach villages are full of joy and dancing. I enjoyed watching them dance and eventually learned some complicated Vlach kolos with intricate legwork. I was thrilled by the rhythm – irregular, interrupted, erotically-charged, and full of fire.

For the Saturday market in Petrovac, Vlachs from far-away villages would dress up in vibrant colorful clothes. Women wore bright ornaments, flowers in their hair, and glittering jewelry. Their children had somewhat unusual names, like Spaceship or Tractorette.

I was a guest in Vlach homes innumerable times, always enriched by a new experience. What I noticed most was their constant readiness to interpret all the possible symbols and sub symbols.

"Oh, look, look! The dog's wagging her tail, going out of the yard by the back gate, that means one of the women in this house has cheated on her husband in the last couple of days."

"Ah, look, look! The hen's pecking only at the left side of the fence; a misfortune is upon us, today or tomorrow. Quick, boil some rosemary and pour the water in front of the house!"

"The cock was cock-a-doodling this morning, stopped for a minute or two, then went on. A great news will come to this house, today or tomorrow."

Huge power, immense belief, myths, dream analysis, signs, trepidations on the face, the position of the Sun and the phases of the Moon; it was all very interesting to me at first, so I listened really carefully to everybody who had something to say about it.

The stories had incredible beginnings and unbelievable endings. Although fornication was freely enjoyed by both sexes regardless of their 'official' partners, since possessiveness didn't play a particular role in the lives of Vlachs, the desire for bewitching the wished-for person was very strong. Not a day passed by without me hearing something like:

"Poor him, that girl from the other end of the village put a spell on him, the one with long braids. She'll have it her way now and keep him to serve her as long as she wants."

Another story was similar, just that a guy went to a fortune teller hoping to conquer the love of a married woman. The fortune teller brewed a potion made of various common, less common, and totally insane ingredients. Then he had to perform some sort of a ritual, to say certain words at a specific time in a special way, under a designated tree, in full or new Moon.

The more I listened, the less I liked it.

In the course of a day I would hear countless of times:

"My nose is itchy, I'll be angry tonight."

"My left ear is ringing, bad news."

"My son's had toothache for two days, somebody cursed him. I'm taking him to a fortune teller to burn coal and put it out in water."

"Ouch, my right heel's hurting, somebody's getting married. I'm going to a wedding soon."

One after another, superstitions were multiplying, invading my reality. There were no such beliefs or 'magic' where I came from, so all that was very strange to me. If I accidentally coughed, somebody would immediately offer advice:

"Take one onion, let it stay overnight in cold water on the east side of the house. In the morning, make the sign of the cross, stand on the threshold, and drink that water while looking to the west."

When I mentioned to the cleaning lady at the Music School that I'd had headache for a few days, she had a ready solution:

"Drive in the direction of the Monastery of Gornjak right away, on the second curve go down by the river and look for one fir tree among thousands of pine trees. There's an old stump under it, with a small well of spring water. Cross yourself three times, wash your face with your right hand three times and take three sips of that water and you'll never have headache again!"

That afternoon, looking forward to a new adventure, I went there with Anita. Just as the cleaning lady said, among myriads of pine trees there was a single fir tree and by its roots an old stump full of water. I did what she had told me to, without much faith in the favorable outcome. 'Magic' or not, the fact is that it's been over twenty years since then and I haven't had a headache ever again. Knocks wood!

Threshold was very important for all Vlachs. When you came to their house, the host would greet you stepping over the threshold and on the way out, you would step over it while he stayed inside. Nothing that might have been unclean could cross the threshold. You didn't shake hands or wave to anybody over it. If somebody from the outside was talking to somebody inside, with the door open, no swear word was to be uttered, lest it got into the house and brought misfortune.

Millions of signs and sub signs were competing for the attention of, in their own way, unusual population in this region.

"Don't walk on the crossroads when you see the morning star, for then you'll be at the mercy of other less favorable stars."

"Don't pick up anything thrown on the fork in the road."

"If you come across two old women and they both wear black head scarfs, don't look at the one on the left, she'll bewitch you."

"When you see a mother breastfeeding, wish her good milk, goodness will come back to you."

The list of spells, potions, and antidotes was endless.

On one hand, it was all interesting to listen to, but on the other it made me increasingly alarmed. I abhorred the idea that somebody, a complete stranger, could gain power over me and change my life, health, and future by some inexplicable force. It would be awful to spend your days like a plant, a mushroom, charmed by an abominable person who happened to be head over heels in love with you!

I was born as a good soul, I am honest and open, and hold my heart on the palms of my hands. As such, I was an easy target for all kinds of 'magicking', according to Anita.

"Nikola, watch out, there can be a danger at every step. You're an only son, young and single, any woman may cast a spell on you and then you'll be done with," she worried.

During my piano classes the beautiful music made me forget all about it and I would dedicate myself to harmonic analysis.

Vlachs and Serbs lived in harmony which was exemplary. There weren't many mixed marriages, though. One of our rulers from the medieval times of the Kingdom of Serbia gave orders that Serbs were not to marry Vlachs. Nowadays they did, but not too often.

Vlachs had their beliefs, that cloak of uncommon rituals, and preferred to stick to each other. I decided not to pay attention to numerous words of warning, signs, and stories, simply to reduce my fear.

It worked to some extent, but didn't last long.

During late night phone conversations with Nora, I could feel apprehension in her voice; I could feel how much she was concerned about me. We were both firmly grounded and in spite of our open-mindedness, it was hard to rationalize paranormal things bordering the unreal that were yet so real.

I asked Granny Jana about it, but since she herself was a fortune teller, only white, she couldn't give me a straightforward answer.

"It's dangerous, Son, be careful," she said.

I knew that much myself. Uninvited, fear nestled in my heart.

The more I prolonged my stay there the harder it was to listen to stories and rumors about extraordinary phenomena and mind-blowing situations, about charms and spells.

The clock was ticking faster and faster.

The Month of Limburg

I noticed that time was measured somehow differently here than anywhere else in the world and started reading more about the history of these parts. Lots of researchers mentioned currents of subterranean waters, some talked about the underground sea, some delved into the influence of those waters on the soil of the Homolje Mountains. Everybody agreed on one thing: it was a scientifically unexplainable region. In my experience, regardless of all the beauty that nature generously gave to this area, there was something very strange about it, in the air.

When fear starts creeping into you, you become afraid of your own shadow. I tried with all my might not to let it happen, not to get overwhelmed by some stupid invention of my mind. I perceived, however, a significant change in my days and nights compared to a few months before. I didn't sleep well and invariably woke up sweating all over, out of breath.

Anita was in a bad mood because of the war that was destroying us all and gnawing us from the inside, for it was rotten and dirty. The media kept fighting as to who was more guilty and who more innocent. The offenders and victims changed with each TV channel. This war was torturing everybody with its pointlessness. Six republics constituting one once-proud country, had their own armies now, their own police, government, and flags. All of a sudden, all the past was forgotten, spat on, and left at the mercy of the present that was dreadful.

Death was everywhere, in each town and village. Endless lines of refugees were entering the cities. The pain was unbearable. They were coming with the bare essentials they managed to save in the chaos of running away from insane killing. A new term became increasingly present in the media – ethnic cleansing. Why would a nation try to exterminate another one? We had all been living side by side for decades, nicely and peacefully. There was no answer. The hatred was in the minds of the leaders blinded by their respective goals and urge for power, they were indifferent to human suffering. I sympathized sincerely with those poor people thrown away from their homes, fields, and woods where their ancestors used to live. And I cried bitterly after the midnight News full of bloody scenes in which, as always, the innocent had to pay the price.

The exams at the Music School were due in a week. I worked intensively on my students' performance for I wanted them to be at their best. I would leave home much earlier and come back a lot later than usual. One morning I bumped into the postman at my gate, bringing me a letter from Lieutenant Željko, I recognized the handwriting. I thanked the postman and got into the car. I had lots of classes to teach that day, but couldn't let the letter sit unread. I parked by the empty gas station at the entrance into the town and opened it. A photograph fell in my lap. I looked at the mildly smiling face of the lieutenant. It was a Mona Lisa kind of smile, secretive and only for me, like some kind of a secret code.

He was handsome.

He was really so very handsome.

He had something savage in himself, something uncatchable, something I loved.

Dear Nikola,

Sorry for not having written for some time – I was at the front. I don't want to remember a single moment from that period. I fucked around big time there and got an infection. I wasn't seriously wounded in the battles but got some injuries in my left leg and foot and am now hobbling, but it will pass. I would love to hear your voice. My phone number is at the bottom of the page and whenever you can, please call me.

Once you leave that small place and settle down back in Belgrade, I hope you could spare a couple of days to come visit me. I'll take you to a meadow that's out of this world and get some good old wine for us. I'll try to cook something nice. Oh fuck, I'm not a good liar, I'll pay a sweet lady from the neighborhood to bake something delicious for us. She's a Serbian married to a Muslim and lived in Bosnia for a long time and is an expert on pies and burek.

I still remember that New Year's Eve and your advice that saved my relationship with my now ex-girlfriend. I want to thank you for that. You are a very special young man.

I don't think I was that horrible in the barracks, but yes, I did give you a part of myself every time we were alone. When you got transferred to the YPA Home I felt a void, don't ask me about it, for some things I can't explain to myself.

Greetings and take care.
Yours,
Željko

I was sitting in silence.

Then I took a tape and soon Bach's *Ich ruf zu dir, Herr Jesu Christ* was cuddling my soul.

I started the car.

My colleague Julia asked me to come to her place after the classes to help her with a project she was doing for the College of Music in Skoplje, Macedonia. I accepted wholeheartedly.

Julia was a wonderful person, quiet, and intelligent. It had been a pleasure working with her at the Music School for almost a year. She was so sweet and dedicated to music. Occasionally she got on my nerves though, when in awe of my music education and experience. I kept telling her it was just a matter of practice. That afternoon we had pleasurable time absorbed in music analyses.

Driving out of her street, at the corner, I saw a group of children in heated argument about something. They were playing in tar, spilled out from a can. I jumped out of the car and told them to get out of there because tar wasn't a toy and was dangerous. They left involuntarily, looking back. Whatever was going on was wrong. I made for the place where they had been playing. What I saw was – a little whimpering puppy, all covered in tar. I ran back to the car and grabbed a blanket I always kept at the back seat in case my car stopped somewhere in the middle of the road and I had to spend the night in it. The puppy was shivering from fear. It was two months old at the most and had such a cute little muzzle and soft eyes. I quickly drove back home.

It took more than two hours of soaking the puppy in warm bath to remove the tar, but I finally managed, using brush and scissors. I had to cut its fur at some spots, from some others the tar went off fairly easily. Later, in the living room, I was lying on the sofa watching TV while the puppy was still shivering. I covered it with a blanket and it came to me and put its tiny paw on my leg. Then it licked my hand. It was such a gentle gesture of gratitude.

I decided to dial Lieutenant Željko's number. I had no idea what to talk to him about, but I sensed from the letter that he was lonely and needed a friendly voice. What if I were lonely and nobody to call me?

We talked for over half an hour. After the conversation I was pensive for some time, looking somewhere in the distance, as if I could see what was happening in Danilovgrad, more than 900 kilometers away. I took the puppy in my arms and carried it to the bedroom upstairs. The little one fell asleep in less than a minute and snored quietly. My thoughts were with the lieutenant. He was all alone and sounded different, a bit sad. We talked about this and that and laughed. I discovered only then how witty he was, describing things in a funny way. At the same time his voice emanated endless tranquility.

He asked me about Nora, my mom, my students, he was interested in everything related to me. I asked him if his left leg and foot had healed, if there was a chance for the war to be over. Our conversation flowed smoothly and I could sense I was talking to a friend. We finished with his sincere wish to see me as soon as possible.

"I'll send you the plane ticket, come over for a couple of days. Please, promise me you will, once this is all over and you are back home, in the capital."

I promised.

The next morning, my sweet little puppy looked at me with wide-open eyes as I patted it and gave it breakfast. Before digging in, it stepped close to me and licked me affectionately.

We became friends.

I called it Archibald – the name just came to me. He woke me up every morning pushing his muzzle into my armpit. He appreciated everything I gave him to eat. He loved the whole world. He would sit in Anita's lap like a little kid and give Dragan his paw to 'shake hands', the way I taught him. He brought joy to my last month there. There was one TV commercial that frightened him, because of the sound or the picture, I couldn't tell, but the moment it started he would jump into my lap and stay cuddled until the commercial finished.

The exams at the Music School were over and were successful. Both students and parents were glad and satisfied with results. They inquired about the next school year. I didn't want to commit myself to anything.

"We'll see how it's going to be with this war."

I knew I wouldn't be back.

Not in a million years!

Archibald was such a lovely, happy puppy. The first week he was just lying on the sofa all day, waiting for me to come back from work. At the sight of me he would wag his tail and lift his tiny paws to greet me. I grew very fond of him. Anita couldn't believe it when I told her how I had found him.

"It's outrageous!" She was angry. "Those kids should have been spanked!" She was holding Archibald in her arms, softly stroking his fur. He was basking in delight but every once in a while glanced in my direction to make sure it was OK with me that she was petting him.

My scientific project was progressing at full speed. The children I worked with and whose music improvisations I analyzed were so sweet and so talented. I wanted to 'steal' them all and send them to the best schools in Europe, if I only could. My research regarding children's imagination in composing a piece of music was engrossing and I was often amazed at children's reaction to my music questions and prompts. The idea was to find a way, using rhythm or melody, to motivate them to create, to invent their own melodies.

It was interesting to discover differences among children. Those from the town, especially if living close to the center and in rich families, with radio, TV, record, cassette, and video players, were less creative. Their melodies revolved around basic tones and were short and simple, just like the sounds they were exposed to. Their musical expression was affected by the newly composed folk music, media, and all the possible commercials.

Music language of the children from small remote villages with about a dozen houses was incredibly inventive and unique. They composed with their hearts, finding inspiration in the nature and in their own souls. So many times I witnessed the birth of a piece of art growing before my eyes.

One of my favorite students was little Faucette. She was eight years old and lived in a secluded village with only her grandmother, since her parents worked in Switzerland. She was named Faucette because her family was the first one in the village that had running water and faucets installed in the house. Every time the grandmother, always outside in the garden, saw me climbing the hill to their house, she would announce loudly:

"Faucetteeee, here's the professor coming!"

The little girl would run down from the top floor and give me a hug. We used to work in a quiet room on the far end of the house, overlooking vast meadows and high mountain peaks.

"What are we going to do today, Professor?" She always asked eagerly.

"Today, I would like you to tell me how you feel this music."

I played the recording of a melody that she herself composed about a month ago, but since it was one of the many, she forgot it was hers.

She listened attentively and closed her eyes.

"It's nice," she said.

"If you were a composer what would you do – leave it as it is or change something?"

"I'd change the beginning."

"Why?"

"It doesn't match the end."

"Can you sing it for me how you would like it to sound?"

"Of course."

She was singing, I was listening barely able to believe my ears. Little Faucette was criticizing her own work and embellishing it, not knowing it was hers. The first part of her originally composed melody was unusually divided rhythmically and the piece did sound asymmetrical. Now, with this modification, she created a precise music period. Both the first and the second part became equally clear rhythmically, and flawless melodically.

That's a real talent!

I never met her parents. During the ten months I worked with her, there was only grandma and nobody else. Faucette lived in a big house full of furniture, but without mother and father, without parental love and care. Her grandma was sweet, but very old and forgetful. I often asked little Faucette if she had eaten. I was afraid the grandma would forget about her and always brought her a bag of candies or a chocolate bar. When I went to that house for the last time and had to tell her we wouldn't see each other again, because I was leaving for Belgrade, she wept inconsolably, covering her face with her hands. I tried to comfort her, but I was crying myself. That child's talent cannot be wasted! She gave me her photograph and made me promise to write to her.

"Whenever you can, please write to me, Professor."

"I will, sweetie, I will."

I kept my promise. I sent her letters and postcards. She replied regularly. Then, about a year after my leaving Eastern Serbia, she wrote she was going to Switzerland, to her parents, because the grandma died and she couldn't stay alone in the house. I visualized her happy, with rosy cheeks, running down the mountain slope, and starting a new life in a new country. I was certain she would learn fast the new language and be the best student at school. That night, before falling asleep, I sent my prayers to Heaven for her bon voyage.

The school year was over in June and the classrooms in the High School, including the ones rented to the Music School, had to be painted. The building would be closed till mid-August. My piano was still there. I had to react quickly. I called Dragan.

"I need a vehicle that can transport the piano to the village, the High School is closing for the summer," I said to him. "Please ask around if somebody has a van or a truck, for if they lock up everything my piano will be stuck there!"

Efficient as usual, Dragan arranged everything in a couple of hours. That evening, with the help of two strong guys, his friends, we brought the piano from the third floor of the school to the ground level and put it in a small truck. A bit later, it was in my house. Archibald was excited to see the guests, running happily around their feet. He hadn't barked even once ever since I found him. He was such a quiet, sweet doggy. After his friends had left, Dragan stayed with me. I poured cold beer into the glasses and took them to the balcony at the back of the house. We were sitting there, surrounded by thick fronds, hidden from the world.

"I'm glad you're leaving," he said. "Not for me but for you."

"I'm kind of sorry I am," I said. "This is the final farewell to these parts, for leaving the Army wasn't a true parting, just the beginning." With all its good and bad sides, this part of the world had somehow crept under my skin.

Dragan was looking at me.

"This isn't a place for you," he lit a cigarette. "This isn't a place for me, either."

"I know."

"I'm going to the army in two months and when I get released I'm leaving for good, to Italy."

I nodded. I knew all that.

"I have to ask you something," he said.

"Of course, go on."

"You know," he laughed, "I wanted to ask you, if you can, when I'm in the army, to come to the barracks and take me out of there sometimes, we can get together for a dinner or a drink, just not to forget about each other."

I looked at him and smiled.

"Do you really think I can forget about you just like that, after everything you've done for me?"

"No, I didn't mean exactly like that."

"Good. Listen to me, when you're in the Army the only thing you have to do is call me and give me the address of the barracks. I'll be yours every Sunday."

"You're serious? No kidding?"

"Dragan, why would I be kidding? You are my friend and I want to continue our friendship."

We drank a lot that night and then, after midnight, we went to the living room to watch a good movie. Dragan fell asleep on the sofa halfway through it. I put a pillow under his head and covered him with a blanket. When the movie finished I took Archibald in my arms and went to the bedroom on the second floor.

It started raining as I was climbing the stairs. It rained heavily, incessantly. The raindrops were running down the huge window, two floors high, outside of the staircase. They were flowing and blending with the glass like tears on a face, following and joining one another and then disappearing. Archibald looked at me curiously, not understanding why I stopped.

"Don't you worry Archibald," I said to him. "Let's go to bed."

He glanced downstairs, towards the living room, where Dragan was soundly asleep. As if he reproached me for going to bed and leaving the guest alone on the sofa.

"Archibald, we can't wake him up now," I whispered. "That wouldn't be nice, he's already asleep."

Satisfied with the clarification, Archibald started skipping on the stairs, ran into the bedroom and waited for me in front of the bed. Only when I walked in and invited him to get to bed, he hopped on. The silence of the night was disrupted by the outpour outside.

Regardless of everything, I was sorry I was leaving.

Each parting hurts, even the smallest one. My mom says that farewells at railway stations are the most painful. The sound of the engine, the slow leaving, the screeching and squealing of the machine in movement, it's all so sad. For some others the hardest are goodbyes at airports, especially if you are on the observation terrace and watch the plane taking off faster and faster, farther and higher.

I was saying my farewell to Eastern Serbia slowly, as if I wanted to enjoy the suffering. Almost masochistically, I would wake up very early, at the crack of dawn, go to the market and watch it fill up with honest, hard-working people from the villages, bringing fruits and vegetables just picked up from the trees and the soil, eggs still warm from the hen house, young white cheese and freshly baked bread, watch them yawn, still sleepy. I was saying my farewell to Romanians leant against the wall at the far end of the market, from the window of my favorite bakery, savoring the delicious burek one of the last times. All of a sudden, the little town appeared nice, clean, and truly romantic to my eyes. I noticed that the church façade had a new coat of paint and was now more beautiful than ever. Even the drab post office got renovated and the concrete flower pots in front of it that looked presentable only in the winter, when the snow covered the garbage in them, were now blooming with flowers.

"Happy return to Belgrade and may luck always be with you," said Miha's wife, holding the smaller of the girls in one arm and the slightly bigger one by hand at her side.

Her husband, my Captain Miha, was at a front who-knew-where, while the three stars of his life, two young daughters and wife, were shining with loneliness waiting for him to come back. There wasn't a night when I didn't pray to God to keep him safe. He was one of the best humans I had ever met, an angel in the shape of a man. His wife, such a sweet and warm woman, was very saddened by my leaving. We used to enjoy conversations about music, arts, nature, weather, current happenings or anything really, while her elder daughter practiced the piano.

"All the best to you and come sometime to see us," said the florist from whom I used to buy lovely seasonal bouquets to decorate my classroom and my house.

"I'll miss you a lot," said the lady doctor with a sad expression on her face.

Friendship with her was quite an experience for me. We had never been too close, but respected each other and would occasionally get together for coffee and cakes to exchange our 'Petrovac stories', since we were both 'foreigners' there.

"Travel safely and good luck!" said the owner of the bakery. "Who's going to praise my burek now?" she added.

The saddest of all was the farewell to the YPA Home Manager. Even though a year had passed since the Army, my memories were still alive and saying goodbye to him now, in another set of circumstances, was at the same time a final goodbye to the army, to all those days spent in the YPA Home, days of sweet freedom, so different from the barracks, full of music but also drenched with salty tears in sleepless nights, mobilizations and fear of the next moment. We had a drink. We promised to stay in touch and then, in front of his house, under a big apricot tree, we gave each other a bear hug and parted.

My house was about a hundred meters away from his. It started raining again. I was walking slowly, the raindrops falling like little needles into my hair, behind my neck, on my arms. I went into the house and saw my reflection in the mirror in the hall. It was hard to tell what were tears and what was rain. Archibald whined, I knelt down and petted him. He looked at me with sad eyes, as if wanting to say he understood me.

"Right, Archie, I won't cry, let's go sleep."

Hearing those words, Archibald happily ran upstairs, stopping at every second or third stair to make sure I was following him. When I threw the blanket over me, he jumped on the bed and cuddled with one paw and his head on my leg and immediately fell asleep.

I couldn't sleep. I was remembering the YPA Home, how I planted geraniums in green flower pots, sewed the curtains, was on duty for nights on end, and filled the dead silence of after midnight hours with the sound of rickety typewriter on which I wrote letters to Nora.

If destiny has intended a long life for me, I'll ask Nora one day if she still keeps them and if the answer is positive, I'd love to read them and learn more about myself. Those letters were just impressions, fleeting thoughts and feelings. Maybe I'll publish them one day, who knows?

We are all in front of the Almighty and His decisions.

The piano arrived in Belgrade two days before I did. I paid the outstanding phone bills for the house in the village. I washed the curtains, yellowed from the cigarette smoke, dusted and polished all the furniture, including the large display cabinets, and brought the stuff I had originally put into the basement back to the rooms. Anita helped me wash the windows. The house was in a much better state now than when I moved in. The shed at the end of the vegetable garden contained neatly stacked chunks of wood for at least two months of heating. The gate and the fence were nicely painted, as well as all the metal work on the balconies and on the staircase. The grass in the yard was trimmed and flowers were blooming. I felt sure that the owners, who were coming back that summer, would be glad to see everything I had done.

The M Morning arrived. In the whole world, it was the month of June, but in Petrovac, it was as always Limburg, thirteenth month of the year, when everything is unreal or at best, hypothetical. I had my coffee alone, on the balcony. In the fronds, branches, and leaves of the tall trees I could hear the history of that balcony, hidden. I was hearing Dragan's stories, Anita's laughter, Oliver's gossips and Adrian's voice. I put out the cigarette, and washed the coffee cup. One more time, I did the rounds of all the rooms to make sure everything was fine. My little Archibald was following me, cheerfully wagging his tail. He sensed something big happening, but didn't know what. I went out into the yard. It smelled of a beautiful day.

Anita was standing at her kitchen door, wiping her tears.

"Don't cry now," I came to her. "Please don't, I don't want to leave like this."

"I can't help it, I've got so used to you."

"So have I to you, but this is the reality. I have to look for a job in Belgrade, if I don't get it now, there'll be nothing left in the fall."

She understood. She took Archibald in her arms, petting him gently.

"I'll miss you, too, my little sweetie," she whispered into his ear.

About twenty minutes later the last suitcase was in the car trunk, fragile things and the TV set on the back seat and Archibald on the front. I opened the gate for one last time in that yard. A few yellow ribbons fell on the ground.

"Don't touch them!" Anita screamed. "These must be spells, somebody's put them here purposely to bewitch you!"

"No, Anita, that's just superstition," I took them in my hands. "If there's one thing that's been driving me crazy in this region, it's that belief in sorcery and spells."

I came closer and hugged her. She could barely hold her tears.

"This is for you," she proffered something in a plastic bag.

"We said no gifts, Anita," I reminded her.

"It's just plum noodles, made especially for you."

That was so thoughtful!

I opened the window on Archibald's side and started driving in reverse. Anita was waving and Archibald was waving back, with his tail. Then I took off. At the crossroads, I stopped. To the left – the town center, road to the past, to the right – road to Belgrade, to future.

The umbilical cord between me and this town was too strong to be cut with one turn of the wheel. I turned left, driving slowly, passing by the old church, the post office, the clinic, the high school, the market, the bridge, and stopped just in front of the YPA Home. I didn't want to get out of the car, only to say a proper farewell to that building. We were looking at each other for a few minutes. It had grown older in a year, but was still beautiful and still mine. The curtains were drawn, which meant that soldiers hadn't kept the geraniums on the window sills. The bistro was no longer there. Instead of it, an empty space was gaping through the window. The YPA Home and I were looking at each other, knowing we would never see each other again. Archibald was panting from the heat, his tongue stuck out. He looked at me and wondered why I was lingering. I patted him.

"Archibald, this place was my Heaven in Hell."

Then I took off for real. Slowly, as if I were afraid. The YPA Home was still there, but now from the back. I turned my head for a moment to better remember its roof barely visible through the trees. Then I drove straight and turned right into the main street. More than twenty years later, at a business meeting in New York, in a high-rise building on Broadway, one of my colleagues said that car windows were like life: the back ones smaller, so that the past couldn't block us, and the front, the windshield, bigger, to open up our path to the future.

I was driving towards the future. I left the town and passed by the house I had lived in for almost a year. I slowed down, but didn't stop. The windows glittered under the high morning sun. Somewhere among the fronds of the tall trees a hidden balcony could be discerned. I looked at it one last time and pressed the gas pedal.

"Let's go, Archibald, let's go to Belgrade."

Archibald wagged his tail cheerfully.

In the early afternoon, we parked in front of Nora's grandparents' house. I rang the bell by the gate. A minute later, Nora was running to greet us. Archibald was beyond himself of happiness. He loved Nora, even though he met her only once when she came to the village a few weeks ago.

"Welcome, both of you," Nora said and hugged me. The embrace could have lasted much longer if Archibald hadn't tucked his muzzle into her neck, asking for his portion of tenderness.

"You jealous little one," I said to him jokingly.

Nora took him in her arms, petting him as we entered the house.

A thunderstorm was about to start, unusual for that time of the year.

It was the month of June 1992 in the whole world, except in my ex little town in Eastern Serbia.

There, it was still the month of Limburg.

Act VIII
God Has More than One Name

- **Music on the Cobblestoned Street**
- **Nora's Impressions**
- **Between the Two Fires**
- **Good People**
- **Nora's Impressions**
- **Before You, I Stoop Humbly**
- **Nora's Impressions**
- **Fog**
- **Nora's Impressions**

Music on the Cobblestoned Street

The waiting room at the unemployment office wasn't exactly a five star hotel, but it served its purpose. It was early in the morning, and I the only person there. There were about fifteen more minutes before the counters opened. I took my book, to pass the time. In that period, I enjoyed Hungarian novelist Lajos Zilachy. A middle-aged gentleman walked in, courteously said "Good morning" to me, sat down on a chair across from mine and started reading a newspaper.

I was ill at ease. After everything I had done for the school where I used to work before the Army, they didn't want to rehire me and now I had to wait at the unemployment office and look for a job. Me, who made that school famous with my performances and engraved its name in the history of Belgrade choral music! A week ago, when I returned from Eastern Serbia, I gave myself a day to settle down and rest and then went to see the principal. I was sternly admitted to her office. The conversation lasted less than two minutes. She made it clear that my position had been filled and that the school had nothing to do with me anymore.

"Can I teach only choir singing, part-time? A few classes a week at least?" I asked.

"How can you, an educated man, not understand the meaning of my words," she said icily. "No means – no."

So I left. The heavy wooden door slammed after me. I remembered how I used to guard blackboards and chalk for nights on end there, and how I prepared the children's choir to win at competitions. That was now the past.

"You'll find a job," Nora kept saying. "Everybody in music circles knows and respects you."

It sounded optimistic, but the reality was different. All the elementary, high, and music schools were cutting down on staff, due to the economic crisis, and the Faculty of Music didn't have an opening for me at the moment. The unemployment office was my only chance.

"Are you a professor?" The gentleman sitting across from me in the waiting room asked.

"Yes."

"May I ask you something?"

"Of course," I said.

"You probably have lots of colleagues. Do you by any chance know somebody who is a professor of music? I am a principal of a well-known school in downtown, but haven't had much luck with musicians for two years now. I can't seem to be able to find the right person to work with the choir and teach music."

I looked at him closely, to make sure he wasn't an angel, accidentally fallen from the Heavens into this waiting room. I smiled:

"Sir, I am the one you are looking for."

He couldn't believe his ears. He clapped his hands, like a little kid. At that moment the office door opened and a young woman with nice make up appeared.

"How can I help you, Gentlemen? Who is the first one?"

We both stood up. The principal said:

"Luckily, Miss, we have found each other – the young gentleman is looking for a job and I for a professor."

"Excellent, congratulations!"

The principal and I left the gray building and made for the nearby park. The birds were chirping and the sun was tickling my face through the singing treetops. Life was beautiful. I could have flown high into the sky if I had only spread out my arms! At the end of the park I thanked the principal once again and went to the tram stop.

How wonderful it felt being employed again!

There were no trams so I slowly walked home.

Nora was ecstatic.

"I knew it! And it's not just any school! That's the most romantic school in Belgrade. I love that part of the city, the cobblestone, the tranquility of the old streets lined with trees... I'm sure the children there are polite and lovely."

I was overjoyed.

Nora was making tomato sauce à la Nora, stirring in the herbs. I was helping her by finely chopping basil leaves. Archibald was stretching in the shade of the kitchen table, listening to us. The day couldn't have been more perfect.

As it often happens in life, happiness doesn't last long. The steps of Nora's father could be heard on the staircase. He marched into the kitchen and immediately, without a greeting, fired away at me:

"My daughter has two University Degrees and look what you're making her do, stand by the stove, she's not your servant!" He seethed.

"You have no reason to yell at me. I also have a University Degree and am about to get my Master's, but here I am chopping basil. Also, I've never made her do anything, she has her own will."

"Don't you lecture me, I know everything!" he snapped angrily.

Then he turned to Nora:

"Sweetheart, stop it right now, start looking for a job that will pay well for your knowledge and competence."

Nora ignored him. That was her most frequently used defense mechanism which sometimes worked, but often didn't. Her father was annoying like a bug, like a mosquito in a tent. It was next to impossible to get rid of him.

One year and one month after her mother's death, just before my comeback, Nora decided to move from the apartment into her childhood home, to the old house that grandpa had bequeathed to her. She thought it right that her father should live in the apartment that was his anyway. The switch could have been so simple and easy if her father wasn't what he was – a stubborn irrational man. He couldn't give up his 'treasures' kept in big black garbage bags in the attic and the basement. They contained corks, old newspapers, rags, eggshells, rusted nails, or broken bottles.

He would come to the house every day and spend hours and hours 'cleaning up' the basement and the attic. After a few weeks, we discovered that not a single eggshell or cork had been discarded, just shifted from one bag to another. He maliciously wanted to stick around, to harass us as much as he possibly could, day after day.

As the summer was getting hotter, he was becoming more unbearable. We couldn't enjoy our morning coffee on the terrace, watching our geraniums grow, and looking over the rooftops of Belgrade, because somewhere from behind the bushes in the garden his nasal voice would trail on:

"It's bad to have coffee on an empty stomach," followed by detailed descriptions of ulcers in the intestines and of the complete digestive system.

If he found us out drinking Coca Cola with dinner:

"This is poison, you should drink quince juice!" Again followed by long boring explanations, so we couldn't even eat anymore. There was no quince juice in the supermarkets, anyway.

If we happened to have chewing gum in our mouths:

"Chewing plantain leaves is good for the gasses, not that shit." There were no plantains in the garden and we just wanted to refresh our breath.

Whenever we went to the market early in the morning, he would comment acidly:

"Rational people go to the market at noon when farmers sell everything half price, because they want to go home." We only needed to get some fresh food.

Whenever Nora and I watered the flowers on the terrace in the evenings, the nagging would continue:

"Tap water is not good for plants, it has to be stale or rain water." We did use room temperature and rain water, but he didn't want to notice that.

My bicycle was his eyesore. Wherever I parked it, it bothered him. He constantly grumbled and actually cursed it.

Then, one day, the glass of bitterness was full over the brim. I gave him a piece of my mind. There were no impolite words in my monologue, for respect of elderly people, but there was everything else, every single thing he had done to embitter our lives.

Nora was listening, standing aside. When I finished, she stepped forward and gave him a piece of her mind as well, mentally punching him right into the face. It was high time he disappeared, got lost out of that house, and let us live peacefully. He owned a three-bedroom apartment but wanted to stay with us, to intentionally make our mornings and evenings sour and our days impossible to go through.

His leave lasted for days. He was taking with him old rags, dirty, and torn to the thread, wash basins full of holes, cement, sand, and rotting wooden boards. All the time he was grumbling and cursing. Whenever I heard his mumblings, I would sing from the top of my lungs, just to irritate him a bit. That man had sent me to the army, to the worst branch of it, and had taken away mother from his own daughter with his malice.

Archibald was thriving in his new home, quite different from the one in Eastern Serbia. He enjoyed running and exploring the garden but most of all sitting like a sphinx on the stone by the gate where he would spend the bigger part of his day watching passers-by. In just a couple of weeks he managed to get tons of fans. One group was passing by that part of the street in the morning, on their way to work, bringing him fresh burek, pastries or juicy bones left from supper and another one in the afternoon, with some more delicacies.

Nora and I started living together. I had never lived close to somebody till then. I hoped, just as Nora did, for the best. Both Nora and I were the only children, coming from different family backgrounds and used to being by ourselves. Our roads had always been parallel and now we crossed them. Our friends were happy for my final return from Petrovac, my new job in Belgrade and our togetherness in the house.

The summer was fierce and the war even fiercer. Almost the whole country was in flames now. The worst part was that everybody was guilty and everybody blood thirsty. They started fighting with each other in battles, within the same nation. Each new commander wanted his piece of the war cake and became more powerful and more dangerous than the previous one. We were listening to the News automatically, taking for granted what they wanted us to hear. On rare occasions we had a chance to see a short BBC or CNN report. Other than being fratricidal, it was also a media war. Croatian media were trying with all their might to convince television and press of the Western countries that Serbs were to be blamed for everything that was going on, while Serbian media were doing the same thing, accusing Croatians. Ordinary people like Nora, I, and everybody around us were suffering, for the atmosphere was saturated with intolerance and hatred, preventing the air of normality and humanity to flow through. Political parties turned the National Assembly into an arena, yelling and jumping at one another, competing for the most spectacular image on the media. At the same time, innocent people were dying in a war that should never have happened.

The sky was against farmers, the sun was scorching the poor crops. There hadn't been a drop of rain for almost two months. Nora and I had beans and carrots, thanks to her aunts from the country who supplied us. Markets were a waste land, with just a few stalls. There were no peppers that summer, all were burnt while still young by the merciless heat. Tomatoes were stunted but could be bought, together with some previous year's onions and potatoes. It was a hungry July.

I was to start my new job at the end of August. Nora didn't work. My overdue salaries from the Music School in Petrovac never came. We were penniless. We knew it would all be better with the beginning of the new school year, but the long weeks before that were really hard. With our last coins we paid for the ads in newspapers for private English, Italian, and piano lessons. Luck was on our side. We started getting small, but so valuable money. I was teaching piano and sight singing to aspiring music students and Nora English to a bunch of little kids. She also prepared Italian Literature students for their exams.

Our special food at the time was bean burgers. We would soak the beans overnight, then cook and mash them the next day, add some chopped onions, spices, rosemary, and minced tomatoes and make spoon size burgers that we fried in a bit of oil. They were quite tasty with pureed carrot soup. Another speciality was pickled peppers that my mom had conserved, stuffed with the same beans mix and baked in the oven.

My mom came to see us and brought several jars of apricot, plum, and rosehip jam, all freshly made, by her and my aunt Kankica.

"Crèpes!" Nora and I exclaimed in unison.

We invited our closest friends for a treat of crèpes with homemade jams.

There were ten of us sitting on the terrace, wrapped up in a balmy late summer evening. The crèpes were piled on a large platter, bowls full of jams, and ground walnuts (from the big walnut tree in the garden) arranged around it. We were all happy to get together. Mira brought her two little daughters who had grown up so much in a year that I barely recognized them. Marko, and Lela with her four-year-old son and husband, completed the tableau.

The main topic of conversation was, uninvitingly, politics. We, who used to talk for hours about music, poetry, and all the beautiful things, were now sticking to politics, like clutching at the straws. Goes without saying, the more people are gathered together, the more different political opinions transpire, leading to high pitched tones and unpleasant moments of silence. We had all caught the virus and were venting.

Lela's husband had a strict political stance that opposed my vision of democracy. Lela's and Mira's views were discordant, as were Nora's humanitarian and Marko's utilitarian ones. All of a sudden everything became so entangled and awkward. A potentially lovely evening was spoiled, we all sensed it, wondering how we got to that point. We could have simply enjoyed the crèpes, jams, and walnuts.

Nora, my mom and I were left with a bitter taste in our mouths after everybody had left. Mom's silhouette was outlined against the pale night sky, smoking and looking at a distance. I came closer to her.

"A penny for your thoughts."

"I am thinking how everything beautiful we had had to be destroyed and annihilated," she sighed pensively. "And how now young people are wasting their time discussing politicians."

"You are so right!" Nora said, smoking next to mom.

We stayed on the terrace till the late hours, without a need to go to bed. Each of us deeply absorbed in contemplation.

The new school was fantastic! I liked all the colleagues at first glance, well, most of them. It was situated in the Old Downtown core and the windows of the music classroom had a view to a quiet street lined with tall trees. The children were absolutely fabulous! We clicked right away. From the very beginning I had that good feeling that can't be described in words. I simply knew that we would totally enjoy each other's company and make a public success out of it.

A bit out of 'sweet revenge', but a lot more because of the genuine quality of children's voices, I decided to perform at the media as much as possible. I applied to all the choir competitions, one after another, winning most of them. I felt sort of satisfaction when the school I used to work in, with that stern principal, ranked the last. You reap what you sow.

The young students I was working with composed an incredible choir of about twenty powerful voices. Each child was in their own way a music genius in the making!

How we loved one another!

To those sweet children I represented escape from the gray reality, shortages, stories about the war, TV that always and only broadcasted news about horrible things happening in once a beautiful country. I was their friend, professor, and father. I understood them perfectly.

The children were my reality, but at the same time my own escape from the TV and war images, from poverty and misery. We found ourselves caught up in the vacuum of the beauty of music. Every day after the classes, the twenty or so of them would stay for about two hours of choir rehearsals. We started preparing for concerts, we practiced songs that no other children's choir had ever performed. My super musical children were getting hungry for more difficult pieces, and I, fascinated by their divine singing. We sang Liza Minnelli from Cabaret and The Age of Aquarius from Hair. We sang melodies I arranged for the choir, those from Eastern Serbia, complicated and archaic. My singers were one-of-a-kind. They loved blues and soul, but could immediately switch to cheerful children's songs. At the very end of the rehearsal, I always liked to ask them:

"What shall we sing now?"

"How about that song from Mary Poppins?"

"Chim chiminey?"

"Yes!"

"Right on!" I was already playing the introductory accords. We would sing it in English and Serbian, alternately.

The energy of music was filling my heart and eliminating the political poison around me. I was coming home all smiling and leaving for work happy, anticipating a new joyful day. Not even the shortages of basic things affected me much. We performed on TV at least once a week. We were winning the competitions. We had such a wonderful time together.

The children.

And I.

Then, one sun-illuminated September evening, we decided to give our contribution to the oldest cobblestoned street in the city, with its authentic 19th century houses in the shade of ancient oak trees. We walked its length up and down all day, singing popular songs and old time ballads. Passers-by stopped to enjoy our music and we got lots of invitations to give concerts at their schools, companies, or factories. We sang all the imaginable kinds of melodies. Tuning in with people who were passing by that truly romantic street at a particular moment, we would sing arias from Nabucco or a rock song In the Blues.

Belgrade public opinion applauded to this event. Radio and TV reporters came to get interviews and take shots of us. It was all in the newspapers the next day. A week later we did the same thing, at the same place. Our singing on the cobblestoned street became sort of a landmark, a tradition. We were frequent guests at the morning programs of TV1 and other channels.

I was bursting with happiness and pride in my choir.

Mira lived just a few blocks away and used to drop by for coffee, during my breaks. From my classroom on the third floor I could see her in front of the school, always nicely made up, youthful looking and incredibly fit.

"You guys can be heard three streets from here, singing so nicely," she would say.

True, the windows were always open and the early autumn mild wind sent our songs traveling over the neighboring streets of the Old Town.

Sometimes she waited for me after the classes and we would go for a walk, get some ice cream or lemonade, and talk for hours. Everything was fine in her small family, but she was lonely. There was one man on the horizon, but she didn't know how to approach him. I gave her advice:

"Shake your butt a bit. You're a woman, right?"

"Oh, shut up, why should I shake it?" she laughed. "If he wants to be with me, fine. If he doesn't, fine again!"

"Oh, Mira, long hair short brain, it's not like that. You have to let him know you like him. Smile seductively, touch him gently, you've got to do something, for God's sake!"

"I will, you'll see."

Eventually she did. By whichever spells or charms I couldn't tell, for although assertive in all other areas of life, she was very shy in that respect. He entered her life discreetly, so as not to disturb her children. In the meantime, I went to live abroad with Nora. They remained friends after love, which was even more beautiful.

October rains brought a different rhythm into the music hearts. My choir and I didn't let the rain sadden us, so we chose to sing more cheerful and faster songs. There was no end to our music!

Then the cold winds from the rivers chilled bones through every jacket and sweater.

"This is going to be a bad winter," people on the tram said.

"Just what we need, when the country doesn't have money for heating," they added.

Archibald was warm in his own wooden house we made for him. He had grown up, gained weight and got thick winter fur, but in his face and mind, remained a playful puppy.

I was coming back home from the school one cold November evening. The accords of the songs the children had been singing were still echoing in my ears. I opened the gate quietly. Archibald ran out, beyond himself of happiness, like every time he saw me. I hugged him and petted him behind the ears. All of a sudden, I stopped.

"Listen, Archie, can you hear how the whole city is quiet now?"

Archibald was cheerfully wagging his tail.

Soft snowflakes were caressing my face and hair. Silence brought them, the way it always does in its mysterious way.

Snow was covering rooftops, withered tree branches and the cobblestoned street in the Old Town. The street on which the refrains of just sung songs were still hovering over the forged iron lamp posts.

One night I was awaken by an inspiration. Nora lifted her head from the pillow and looked at me curiously.

"Shhh, go back to sleep," I whispered. "I want to compose, I have a melody in my head!"

I made some strong coffee, lit a cigarette and the candles on the piano.

D minor.

The song was creating itself that night by candlelight. In the morning, I presented it to my choir, to my sweet children. They were delighted.

"Every word is true," Isidora said.

"The refrain is so beautiful," Matija said.

"Who is going to sing each part?" they asked.

I thought for a couple of seconds and then decided – the refrain would be sung by the choir and each stanza divided between a boy and a girl. The title of the song was I Vote for Peace. My children experienced it very emotionally.

> *I vote for peace, love, joy, and cheer,*
> *A song from the heart and all things dear.*
> *I vote for play, cartoons, and smiles,*
> *Let all the people join us in lines.*

It became a hit. Lots of my colleagues called me after one of our TV performances and asked for the score. Over the next few months, I listened to its various interpretations at numerous choir music festivals. We were voting for peace in the middle of the war. We were voting without ballots.

The children needed cartoons, and we, toilet paper and food. I was getting sick of the beans, bread, and sometimes jam, when days were good. I longed for salami, dreamt about ham, cheese, scrambled eggs…

There was nothing to buy. Empty shelves were gaping through the dirty store windows.

Nora and I would wait for hours to get a minimal quantity, prescribed by the government, of oil, coffee, sugar or laundry detergent, in long lines of people in front of supermarkets. We were all the same in poverty. The sky was black over Belgrade.

One day, on my way home from the school, I came across Dragana, my ex colleague from the Faculty of Music. We were talking about this and that when an ear piercing thunder split our words in two.

"Thunder in the middle of the winter isn't a good sign," Dragana shuddered.

And it wasn't.

No sign those days was good.

In the spring, as a gesture of gratitude for her extraordinary songs and their contribution to my scientific work, I invited Granny Jana to Belgrade. I wanted to introduce her to the TV audience as a guest of honor in my show and had already organized her concert in the National Museum. My plan was to pick her up by car from her village, drive her to the capital and then back to her lovely house in the mountains.

That involved a lot of gas. There was no gas at the stations and it was possible to get it only through connections. Apartment buildings in those days were life threatening. Frantically trying to improve a bit their living conditions with some solid cash, people were hiding smuggled cans of gas in the basements and sold it for foreign currency. The very thought of an accidentally thrown cigarette and the explosion that would follow made me freeze. Innocent lives would pay for the survival of the others.

Somehow I managed to get enough gas for the round trip and made for the East. This time my heart didn't hurt while I passed by the familiar area. The wounds had healed. I was driving slowly through the town that now looked even smaller than before. Then there were the curves of the Homolje Mountains, the monastery, the bridge, Krepoljin and the steep road to Granny Jana's village. She was ready for the journey, smiling as always, but also apprehensive. She had never been in a big city and was afraid of everything in advance. I reassured her saying I would take care of her every single moment, and that she would be away from home for only a couple of days.

Nora was very glad to see her. Our friends could hardly wait to meet her, eager to hear about their destinies read in corn grains. Granny Jana was an expert in that. You had to put 21 or 22 corn grains wrapped in a piece of red paper under the pillow and sleep on it, so she could read properly. I didn't believe in it, but I liked the idea of our friends getting a glimpse of an impressive personality and finding out something more about their lives.

That evening Granny Jana was a special guest in my music TV show. She looked spectacular in the national costume, colorful scarf with fresh flowers sticking out of it and the peacock plume that crowned her head. She sang incredibly beautifully in her specific, archaic way. After the show the phones in the studio were ringing for a long time, people were asking for more of Granny Jana's songs, but she had already left with me to Nora's house for dinner.

The next day I showed her around the city, but she didn't like it because there were too many people, and she got tired of saying 'Good morning' to everybody, as was customary in villages and small places. To my attempts to explain to her there was no need for that in a big city, she responded by helplessly shrugging her shoulders.

She was to perform a solo concert in the evening at the National Museum. The cultural circles of Belgrade, musicologists, ethnomusicologists, artists, writers and poets, and all our friends attended, to finally hear live that voice they had heard about from me countless of times. The hall was full of people, some of them standing for there were no seats left.

Granny Jana didn't have stage fright. She stepped on the podium and untucked a wild rose from her scarf.

"I picked it up while I was tending to sheep in the mountains," she said.

Then she started singing. Enchantingly, from the top of her lungs, as if she were alone, somewhere in the fields. She chose a song in Vlach language, about a fairy who came to see a newborn infant, to give it advice for life, to tell it if it would be happy and how long it would live. The song was cheerful in character, but in a slow rhythm and very long.

The applause was tremendous. Granny Jana won every single heart in the hall.

Then she sang my favorite one, without words, the one that only birds knew. Through the silence of the National Museum her voice was expanding, reaching out to all the corners and seats, behind the shadows of old paintings. Then the whole museum was reverberating, permeated by the vibrations of her powerful voice.

Later that night, on the way to Nora's house, Granny Jana asked me to take her back to her village the first thing in the morning, for she couldn't endure the stink of the city, the pollution, and the noise of so many people any more. I understood her and did as she asked.

The phone was ringing for days with invitations to Granny Jana to perform at other cultural institutions and at the Faculty of Music, but it was too late. She was already in her lovely little white house on the top of the hill, surrounded by flowers and birds' chirping. That was the last time I saw her.

She stayed in my memory exactly the way she was dressed up for the concert, with her plume, smiling, filling up the hearts of the audience with her unique singing. That year I dedicated one of my research papers to her. I was invited to present it before university professors and ethnomusicologists from all over Serbia at the annual music event Mokranjac Days in Negotin. Stevan Mokranjac was a 19th-century composer and music educator, considered the most important figure of Serbian romanticism music. My work was highly praised. During the presentation, illustrating my words, Granny Jana's voice was heard from the tape recorder. Her songs really had a magic power and deep beauty, so primordial in their essence.

When she got out of the car, Granny Jana deeply inhaled the fresh mountain air and looked like reborn.

"I'm already feeling better," she said. "Go, Son, go home, it's getting dark."

And so I left, hesitantly. I could see her tiny figure ascending the narrow winding path to the highest point of the village, to her house, to her peace, her herbs, and songs that echoed much more vibrantly in the fields, under the vast skies of Eastern Serbia than in the concert halls of the capital.

I didn't know then that I would never see her again. I was standing and waving at her. She was climbing slowly, turning every now and then to give me a sign to leave, but I didn't want to. Only when the whiteness of her blouse couldn't be discerned in the distance any more, I got in the car and started it.

Nora wasn't at home when I came back that evening. On the dining room table there was a letter from Lieutenant Željko, I spotted it right away.

I sat down in Nora's grandfather's antique armchair and opened it.

Dear Nikola,

I'm very happy that you got a job, congratulations! I was sent to the front again. I'm writing to you from the hospital I hope to be released from soon. It's nothing serious, a few deep scratches on the legs and one on the neck, but I was bleeding too much, so they took me to this abominable place.

Can you come next weekend? It's my 35th birthday and I would like you to come as the most beautiful gift. I have no friends or family here and other than your letter there will be no birthday cards for me. I have a feeling that this shit of the war won't end the way I wanted it to, shortly, so I'm asking you to visit me and make my reality tolerable. If you can't come, I'll understand and you don't have to apologize.

From the heart,
Željko

"Why are you sitting in the dark?" Nora walked into the room and turned on the light.

As if awoken from a dream, I lifted my head. She looked gorgeous, her hair and clothes soaked through from the sudden downpour, so typical of Belgrade.

"Nora, I'm going on a short trip. A dear friend of mine is having hard times," I said.

She understood everything.

Later that night, Nora was soundly asleep on my left hand side in the old mahogany bed, and I was somewhere in my thoughts. Nora had the uncanny ability of reading feelings. If she could have somehow produced it in tablets she would have been a millionaire. So many friendships, loves, marriages, relationships of all kinds break up because of misunderstanding and redundant words. Nora would feel first and then say. She would listen with her soul and talk from her heart. That evening she understood that a friend needed me. She didn't ask who, why or where. She was Nora. She was like the theme from Rachmaninoff's Symphony No.2 Op.27 III. Adagio, theme that everybody likes to listen to, but very few can entirely comprehend, because its beauty is hidden in the most various nuances of violoncellos, violins and violas, intertwined with steady love born out of trombones.

The next weekend I flew to Titograd now Podgorica, Monte Negro. Željko was waiting for me at the airport. He was thin, actually quite skinny, like a shadow of the robust lieutenant I used to know. Regardless of everything, he somehow looked more handsome than ever. I got into his car and saw a bouquet of white roses on the front seat. I looked at him questioningly.

"For you." His sensual lips spread into a brilliant wide smile that could open all the gates in the world.

"Thank you!" The roses were beautiful, all in buds, angelically white.

It was the beginning of a long night.

Candles were glowing on the table that evening when I entered his cozy apartment. Music was playing from the old record player. The soft voice of Hose Feliciano was hovering above the bright candlelight. We had dinner, talked and drank. He showed me his badge collection he was so proud of. It was really impressive. Hundreds of badges, neatly arranged by size, color, and theme.

We toasted.

"To you, Nikola! To your good health!"

"To your good health, Lieutenant!"

To each of my "Lieutenant" he would make a funny grimace that made me laugh.

"I can't call you otherwise, even if you kill me on the spot," I said.

"Please."

"I can't, why don't you believe me?"

He was holding my hands. He said he had noticed I had nice hands, at our very first meeting in his office at the barracks of Petrovac. I was perplexed, for the memory of that day still gives me goose bumps.

"You were very strict, maybe too much," I said.

He gave me a stern glance that for a fraction of a second froze the blood in my veins, but then he smiled and melted all the glaciers.

"Nikola, that's the Army, no thinking or feeling, only short orders and subordination."

"I think I understand the whole concept."

Then we changed the subject. We talked about Danilovgrad, its people, and their way of life and about life in general.

We were drinking white wine, a lot of white wine, rivers of white wine. It was delicious, it smelled of the sun and the grapes.

"From the Island of Hvar," he said pointing at the bottle.

I liked it even better then, for each sip brought back memories of the resplendent beauty of the town of Hvar on the Island of Hvar, the white cathedral, pebble beaches with crystal clear blue sea, and marble paved town squares glistening under the summer sun.

We drank more and more.

We toasted to each other.

To the days past.

And to the future ones.

We reminisced each day we spent far from each other.

Then we went to another room and opened a bottle of cognac.

We were drinking it slowly.

At one moment the candles burnt out.

For the life of me, I couldn't figure out where Željko and I made a mistake.

The sun was rising on the right wing of JAT Boeing 737, painted in platinum gray. On the plane it still said Yugoslav Airlines, even though the poor Yugoslavia was internationally belittled, internally butchered and mutilated. I was sitting on the window seat, witnessing the birth of a day.

Days are born invariably, whether we are sad or happy. They were born before our birth and will be born again and again, when there's none of us there anymore.

I was immensely sad.

I was sadder than Chopin's Prelude No.20 in c minor, if that's possible.

Still, I didn't cry.

I spent two extraordinary days in Danilovgrad. Željko and I stayed in his apartment all that time. He was reading to me the poems of Rakić and Dučić, Serbian romantic poets, and explaining the underlying ideas of Krleža's short stories. Miroslav Krleža is the Croatian equivalent of Chekhov.

In the morning we didn't feel like going out, so we baked bread our way. It didn't look nice, was even less tasty, but we ate it anyway. It accompanied chilled wine, olives, and tomatoes.

Then the second night came.

The drinking opened the door to even more drinking and then to sobriety.

The image he had in his mind didn't match the image I had in mine.

He wanted a lot more than I could give him.

I wasn't ready for that.

It pained me to unintentionally inflict pain to him.

Behind us, there were loads of unwashed dishes and overflowing ashtrays left.

"I'm sorry, I'm so sorry," I was saying.

The noise of the plane engine deafened my whisperings.

I landed at Belgrade Airport.

It was the end of May, but spring couldn't be felt in the air. The trees were too sorrowful to blossom. The day after my return, by the international decision, sanctions were imposed upon our country and the airport was closed. The metal birds were grounded.

I got on the bus to the city, old and rickety, and sat down by the window.

"I'm sorry, I'm so sorry," I kept saying inside myself, louder and louder.

The noise of the bus was overwhelming and my words and thoughts disappeared in the void.

Just like our friendship.

Lost forever.

Nora's Impressions

Nikola is back to Belgrade! Archibald is here, too! I am so happy, hugging them both, one at a time or both together, this is so wonderful, like being reunited with the family!

The summer storm, all with thunder and lighting, starts in the evening. The sky opens, pouring cats and dogs, no pun intended. I run out to check on Archibald, pushing hard on the terrace door, for the furious winds slap it back into my face. I frantically call out his name in the flooded garden, among rose and hydrangea bushes. No answer. I've got to find him, make sure he's alive and well! Running like for dear life, my legs intuitively bring me to the shed, with the door ajar. And there he is, safe and sound, wagging his tail, jumping and licking me. Our friendship is sealed in that moment.

He is teaching me that instincts are always to be trusted.

If my annoying father hadn't been fooling around with some crap from the shed all day, the door would have been locked and Archibald – no, I don't even dare think of what might have happened to him!

Nikola and I rearrange the centuries old furniture in the house, adding some personal contemporary touches. The place looks spectacular now!

All the garbage accumulated over the years is out, with the exception of my father, who's still hanging around, but not for long.

Paradox – the civil war is raging, the country or what is left of it is in deep economic crises, Nikola and I have hit our financial bottom, but parties are thrown in the house like every second day, just like in the times of my njanja and mom. Not exactly extravagant ones, but still. The candles are lit, the baby grand piano ready to be played on. When times are bad, people tend to stick to each other more than in normal circumstances. When food is scarce, you get creative with what you have and want to share it with others.

"Archie, take it easy sweetie. Hey, I've just washed this dress!"

I have to change several times a day on account of Archibald's hugs. He's grown a lot in the last couple of months and his way of showing affection is to stretch on his hind legs and wrap his front ones around my shoulders and neck, jumping and laughing. Which is lovely, since I thoroughly enjoy playing with him and appreciate his expressions of love, just that he runs in the garden all day, rolls in mud and dust and leaves imprints of his paws on my clothes. Then he licks me all over the face. Why do I bother with make up at all these days?

He is teaching me that true feelings are so much more important than the appearances.

Archibald is basically a mongrel, but a gorgeous one! Has the body shape of a German shepherd and a face like Lassie, with long hair and noble looks. His coloring covers the whole spectrum of browns, beiges, and whites, interspersed with yellows.

He is the most cheerful and charming creature on the planet and becomes the star in the neighborhood in no time, in addition to being Nikola's and my dearest friend ever, among humans or animals.

I start my private English Play-school in the house. The kids and I have such fun together, with nursery rhymes, singing, drawing, playing... And along the way they learn quite a bit of English. Kids never cease to amaze me. They are so open, smart, and inventive! They pick up everything I teach them like sea sponges. We do performances for parents on New Years' Eves (no electricity in the city, but what are candles for?) and at the end of each semester. We also get fifteen minutes every week in Nikola's TV show. I am so proud of my children! None of them has butterflies in their bellies, they demonstrate what they have learnt like little professionals!

Kids are the only species Archibald is not crazy about. At his best, he simply ignores them, at his worst he quietly growls at them, which is totally out of character. That's why he has to be tied to a wire between the cherry and the apricot tree every time I teach classes. The wire extends all the length of the garden, so he can still move around, and the classes are only twice a week, two hours in the afternoon. He bravely survives the 'imprisonment', intent on seeing the last kid leave, so he can run into Nikola's, mine or our friends' arms, as we chat on the terrace.

He is teaching me freedom.

His puppy trauma caused by some nasty little humans who covered him with tar has left an imprint and he's dealing with it by being extra cautious of small beings and breaking free, releasing.

There is so much that people can learn from dogs in general and from Archibald in particular.

Nikola has been restless lately. I am not asking anything, just letting him be.

One lazy late summer afternoon, I emerged in books and Archie asleep in his kennel, he rushes out for some fresh air.

Comes back a few hours later telling me about a new friend.

A cute guy with a hamster-like face appears in our house the next day. His name is Pega. Brings me a fragrant bouquet of wild flowers. He is into arts, dry pastel is his medium, always on Carson paper. Talks easily about everything and has dimples when he smiles; and he smiles a lot.

Archie is all into jumps and licks when he sees him. We soon establish a weekly ritual of walking him for miles along the neighborhood streets lined by big leafy trees providing shade and protection to the old mansions.

Pega, Nikola and I spend many a pleasurable evening together, simply talking, and being ourselves: smoking cheap cigarettes, sometimes sharing one between the three of us, drinking even cheaper wine, and eating whatever I can concoct out of flour and water, with some toppings, like: tomato sauce or cream cheese if we're lucky to get it.

At one point, Pega produces a business card of a certain Klaus from Switzerland, currently working in Warsaw. He met him at the Prague Airport some time ago.

Little do we know that this little piece of paper is to become Nikola's and my ticket to freedom.

Between the Two Fires

I dream a lot.

I dream in novels, volumes of them.

I dream in vivid colors and in three languages.

There were two persons within me. One was sleeping, the other one was dreaming. My two personalities were always together and tormented me. One was enjoying each new day, the beautiful house, quiet life and a great job. The other one was craving something else, something potentially dangerous, obscure.

A few times, I went to the porno movie theater by the Railway Station, dilapidated, stinky, and with half the seats missing. The ticket booth was in a brightly-lit part, and right next to it there were pool tables where lots of young men were playing. One hundred steps separated me from entering the darkness of the cinema. Those were hard steps. I was petrified that some of my friends or acquaintances might see me. My legs were shaking every time I ventured there. On the way out, I always made a promise to myself that was the last time.

"Hallo?" I answered the phone.

"Greetings," said a voice on the other end of the line. "It's Dragan, I hope you remember me."

I was happy to hear him.

"Who can forget you?" I said. "A millionaire from Petrovac, soon to become Italian."

He laughed, delighted that we got in touch again.

"When shall I take you out of the barracks?" I asked.

"This Sunday, if it's OK with you."

"Of course it is."

"So, see you on Sunday then."

"Right, just tell me which barracks it is."

We talked some more and confirmed the place and time. I put down the receiver, looking forward to seeing him. I found Nora at her dressing table doing her makeup and said Dragan had just called. She met him a couple of times during her visits to Eastern Serbia.

"Shall I make some coffee?" I asked her.

She looked at me sadly.

"We ran out of coffee," she said. "We've got some Divka, though." That was a substitute for coffee, a weird mix of ground grains. Dissolved in water it became brownish and smelled of poverty.

"At least something," I made two cups of it and sat down at the piano. I was in the playing mood.

Dragan went out of the barracks in the military uniform. It suited him nicely. He seemed to me even more handsome than he was a few months ago. Probably because of the uniform. I love uniforms.

"Aren't you going to change?" I suggested. At those uncertain times soldiers were allowed to change into civilian clothes when going out, for their own safety.

"Sure, just wait for me a bit."

He came back shortly, in jeans and a t-shirt. Now he looked shorter, probably because in the full uniform he was wearing a cap. We went to sort of a pub downtown and started gulping pints of beer, one after another.

I think I'm a natural, alcohol-wise. Other than the unsuccessful attempt to drink the whole bottle of rum when I was in grade seven, followed by terrible vomiting and almost ending up in hospital, I've never had any dramatic consequences. I didn't like getting drunk, but enjoyed the taste of a drink. That night was a beer night. We were drinking, but also eating salads, ćevapčići (barbecued minced meat rolls) and freshly-baked proja (corn bread), so we could go on drinking. Around 11 p.m. we took off, since he had to report at the barracks by midnight. We agreed to book a hotel room for the following Sunday and drink to our hearts' content.

"Nicer, more comfortable and less expensive," Dragan said.

We caught the tram. Two stops away from the barracks, Dragan grabbed my hand.

"Let's get off now!"

Outside, the crisp wind lifted my heavy eyelids.

"I want to walk a bit, to refresh and sober up," he explained.

We were walking slowly through a park. On our left, through the bare tree branches the night lights twinkled on the street, on our right there was pitch blackness. We were talking about one thing or another when I felt his embrace. The image of his room in Petrovac came back to me, my car, all those little thoughtful things he had done for me. I had the impression that he was experiencing all that at the same moment. We turned right, unwillingly, towards the barracks. Towards total darkness.

"So, next Sunday at the same time?" he asked.

With the swollen tongue I barely managed to say:

"Yes," and stumbled to the bus stop hoping to catch the after midnight transportation. I found a vacant seat onboard and sat down. An elderly woman was looking at me suspiciously. Since I didn't appear dangerous or belligerent, she decided to address me:

"Son, your fly is open."

That night I dreamt I was working in a garage, fixing cars, together with some young muscular guys, mechanics, smeared with oil. I woke up with fire in my stomach.

Dragan was waiting for me patiently. I wasn't punctual, which was out of character. I'm always on time, in all kinds of circumstances. I was late because there was no public transport. After a long and futile wait I decided to walk all the way to the barracks.

"Sorry," I said out of breath. "The tram never came."

"I know, no tram or bus passed by in over an hour."

We made for downtown.

"I booked a room in the Park Hotel," he said.

"Super!"

We got to the hotel on foot and checked in. Then we went to a corner store, bought some cold beer and snacks. A movie was just about to start on TV when we opened the first bottle.

"Come, lie down next to me," Dragan said.

"In a second, just to light up."

We were lying next to each other, watching the movie. It was excellent. The empty beer bottles were piling up on my and his side of the bed. I didn't remember what time it was when I fell asleep. What stayed in my memory was a dream. An erotic one.

I have always dreamed a lot.

Ever since my earliest childhood.

Dragan and I didn't just drink ad infinitum, we went to concerts and theater performances whenever they coincided with his days off. I introduced him to Jasmina, my ex private student. I wanted both of them to be happy, to unite the opposites. Dragan was handsome, polite and rational, while Jasmina was gorgeous looking but unpredictable and on the edgy side. They weren't impressed by each other. It turned out I wasn't a good match maker, even though absolutely certain that once they got together, there would be great sex. As a matter of fact, I think there was, but nothing else between the two of them was compatible.

I gave up attempts to find a girl for him while he was in the Army. Whoever I recommended was declined. Eventually I let things flow their own course. Dragan was a sweetheart and always had a little surprise for me: a bracelet he made himself over the week in the barracks or a hidden chestnut chocolate bar in his pocket. I was glad he was in Belgrade.

The news from the fronts were horrible, worse day by day. The vacuum in which we existed was increasingly less tolerable for living. Other than the everyday shortages of the most basic things, we were all sinking deeper and deeper mentally. We were surrounded by the war and the confrontations of all kinds we never wanted or asked for. The innocent always suffer. We worked for the money the value of which was getting more absurd by the hour. Like weeds, dealers germinated on street corners and you could hear:

"Foreign currency, to sell or buy."

At first we didn't notice them, for they were sprinkled here and there. Then they occupied the whole streets and squares. Simultaneously with the dealers, stalls with Western European goods started to spring up. They were makeshift, just cardboard boxes with German or Austrian chocolate bars, two liter Coca

Cola bottles, and some trinkets from abroad placed on them. The prices were, of course, in German marks, for the Yugoslav currency dinar was slowly disappearing from the face of the earth. Actually, it was already buried alive to the throat.

Dragan went on his two-week leave to Petrovac, for his whole family was coming from Austria, and also the family from Italy, of the girl he was going to marry the following year.

"Travel safely and good luck!" I wished him.

He was waving at me from the bus, until he disappeared from the view. It was a late afternoon. I was at the bus station, bordering the railway station. I was a stone's throw away from the cinema I had promised to myself never to put my foot in ever again.

I didn't go in.

I wanted to.

Instead, I sat down on a bench in the small park across from it and lit a cigarette. I needed to settle down my thoughts a bit.

"Do you have a lighter?" A young man with curly hair and smiley face asked me.

"Yes, here you are," I said.

In the next half an hour, I got to know an incredibly sweet teacher from a town close to Belgrade who wanted so very much to go to the cinema, but was ashamed and afraid of all the eyes that might recognize him.

"I sweat all over every time I buy the ticket," he said.

"Me too."

"I have a feeling everybody's looking only at me."

"Critically."

"Yes, and giving me grades."

We burst out laughing, for we both had the same symptoms of the same disease. We got up from the bench and went for a drink to a nearby Balkan Restaurant.

"See this?" He pointed to the lipstick traces on the half washed glass. "I know it's the crisis, but if we all try in these hard times to give out even more of ourselves, to bring out the internal beauty. Everything would be so much better."

"I agree totally," I said. "I'm a musician and trying, as much as possible, to inspire my students and give them beautiful moments, far from the everyday reality and vulgarity."

"I'm doing the same thing with my students."

It felt so good talking to him.

I invited him to come over and meet Nora that weekend. Nora clicked with him instantly, at first glance. He was easy-going and imaginative, and it was enjoyable listening to him. He became a part of our lives and dropped by at least once a week. We had great conversations and good laughs over some dinner or drinks.

One evening, out of the blue, we started talking about Poland. As a matter of fact, we were talking about places we would like to live in forever. Nora, of course, said Oslo, Norway, for she had always had some sort of attachment to that country, its culture and people. Pega said he was drawn to the floating islands of the Lake Titicaca, in South America. I said Warsaw.

"Why Warsaw?" he asked. "I've been there and didn't like it at all."

"We've been there twice together," Nora said, "and had a great time. It's a gorgeous city if you know how to look at it. Poland as a whole is such a wonderful country."

I didn't know where to start from or where to finish, so I decided to give a short explanation.

"Warsaw is the place where my heart dances, as if I had been there before, in a past life, if there had ever been one."

"I believe in reincarnation," Pega said.

"I'm not so sure about it."

"I deeply believe in it," Nora said. "Nikola must have been Polish at one point in time, he loves that country so much, it's simply incredible."

Pega was shaking his head. I could see he was searching his brain for some memories of Poland that were cheerful, unusual, unique. He could find none.

"Nikola, to me everything seemed so dark and gray there, poor and sad."

I looked at him with astonishment.

"I'm at home there, like in a paradise!"

Nora brought the freshly brewed coffee, the substitute for it actually, for there was no real coffee to be bought. We lit up. The bluish cloud was hovering above the big dining room table. All of a sudden, as if remembering something, Pega said:

"I have a friend who is Swiss, now living in Warsaw. I believe he would be glad if you called him and gave him my regards," he pulled out a business card from his wallet and gave it to me.

I took it, not knowing then that the small business card would change two lives – Nora's and mine.

The time was not right for that yet.

Everything in its own time.

Good People

The phone ringing was echoing through the inside of the house as I was trying to unlock the heavy gate that was resisting to my keys that day. Finally, I ran in and picked up the receiver in the kitchen. It was my dear professor Zora, with marvelous news.

"We have an opening, twenty hours a week, full time, made for you."

"Do I have a chance?"

"Of course you do," she said cheerfully.

Soon afterwards, like in a beautiful dream, I got accepted as a lecturer at the Faculty of Music. Of course, I didn't resign from the elementary school, because I knew I could fit in everything. I was scheduled at the Faculty for Saturdays and Monday, Tuesday and Thursday afternoons. I talked with the school principal about rearranging a bit my classes there.

"Everything for you," he said. "Just go on winning at competitions and getting the best results!"

He was so proud of all the first places we had been winning at competitions. The principal was a good man. With some peculiar political opinions, though, opposite from mine, but was an excellent principal nevertheless. He devised a schedule that enabled me to teach at the Faculty and still work full time in his school. If Serbia had been in normal circumstances, I would have been earning a lot. Unfortunately, the situation was far from normal. Each salary, other than being irregular, was extremely difficult to get.

There were no paychecks or direct deposit at the time, only cash. The second the money was in our hands, we would run to the first intersection, to the first dealer, to exchange it for a few German marks. My monthly salary as an assistant at the Faculty of Music was about twelve German marks, which would now be the equivalent of six euros or nine US dollars. The elementary school paid less, about eight German marks per month. It was a pittance, but on the other hand, that was the reality. I was sadly watching the denominations of the poor dinar getting more worthless by a minute. The government was 'fighting' for it by printing banknotes with more and more zeroes and then denominated them, hoping to suppress the galloping inflation which, like an epidemic disease, sneaked into our wallets and lives. Overnight, people lost any idea about values and prices. At the markets, the farmers, honest simple folk, didn't know how to charge for their goods anymore.

"How much are the eggs, Ma'am?" Nora asked a woman at the market stall one morning.

"One egg – five hundred billion dinars."

Her first neighbor who was selling onions, corrected her:

"It's not billions, it's trillion."

"Then, five hundred trillion dinars."

Nora produced the banknotes we had. A pile of them. The woman was looking at them closely.

"This one I know. This one I don't; this one's no good."

"Why isn't it good?" Nora asked.

"They said on TV last night it's not current or something."

We hadn't heard about that. With wallets bulging with money, we could barely buy some potatoes, onions and four eggs. Toilet paper was sold only for German marks. The supermarkets had been out of it for almost six months, but it overloaded the stalls of the improvised mini markets on Slavija and other squares in our city. Wherever you looked, you could see toilet paper. I was embarrassed at the thought that an accidental visitor from abroad might think we had overactive digestion and shat a lot, for how else to explain the invasion of the city by the stalls overflowing with tons of toilet paper?

The school principal used to call me at midnight, the salary had just arrived and was being distributed. There was something clandestine about the whole thing. I would get to the school by some night buses, pick up the money, throw it in a big plastic bag, and immediately run to the first dealer to exchange it for a few German marks. It was impossible to pay your electricity bill with the whole salary. Or any other bill. We paid as much as we could, just the minimum of the required sums that kept increasing together with the inflation.

My TV show was progressing at full speed. Wednesday nights were reserved for preparations and on Friday evenings it went live. I structured it like this:

- The guest – somebody whose profession is music, a composer, conductor, singer, or performer.
- Visit to a music institution – philharmonic hall, ballet school, or opera house.
- Choir or group of singers' presentation.
- Ethno moment – singing an old, authentic folk song.
- Instrument – a child who plays an instrument says something about it and plays a piece.

From the very beginning, this thirty minute show became a hit among the children and adult audience. Everybody enjoyed it and I was getting innumerable letters of support and wishes as to what children would like to see in the forthcoming episodes. I had great, wonderful guests. I was fortunate and honored to host the most brilliant music minds from all over Serbia. I wished I could have gathered together the most brilliant artistic souls from all over Yugoslavia, but that was technically impossible.

My life in general became so much better, because it was more fulfilling. I didn't have time for anything other than work, and the work I thrived on. I taught full time at the elementary school, full time at the Faculty of Music and hosted TV shows. Sundays I had for myself. And on Sundays I gave private lessons. I worked all day, every day, and that became a part of me.

Teaching at the Faculty of Music was truly inspiring. I was surrounded by young aspiring and ambitious musicians. During the afternoon sessions, we were thoroughly absorbed in harmony analysis, and on Saturday mornings, dozens of bright-eyed students, eager for learning and knowledge, would gather around me and the baby grand piano in the main hall.

One day, accidentally, hidden behind the scores, a business card of a Swiss living in Warsaw popped up before my eyes, the card Pega gave me that night when we were talking about Poland. I decided to write to an unknown person. I said I would like to come to Warsaw and spend a couple of days there, but had no means to pay for the hotel. If he didn't mind my staying at his place, I would be delighted, for that would be an excellent opportunity to shoot a mini-series about music life in Warsaw and about Chopin, for my TV show. I added that Pega, our mutual friend, was sending his best regards. I mailed the letter the next day, not setting my hopes too high.

Soon, much to Nora's and my surprise, a letter came with the invitation and guarantee statement that I brought to the Polish Embassy and got a visa for five days. The TV station paid for my air fare. I was sorry there wasn't a possibility for Nora to go with me this time.

"I'll bring you something nice," I promised her at the airport.

She knew I would. I always brought her nice things from all my trips.

I was on board of a small ATR-72, flying by LOT, Polish Airlines, from Budapest. The sky was pristine blue, without a cloud, and the sharp high tops of the Tatra Mountains under the snow looked miraculously beautiful.

Klaus was in his forties, well-built and groomed, with a short mustache and lively eyes. He waited for me at the airport with a young Polish couple, his friends. Since I had visited Poland quite a few times before, my ears were already familiar with the sounds of the language and its melody that I picked up from Polish songs. I was able to follow an easy conversation, but we all communicated in English, for Klaus spoke no Polish at all.

"This is the hardest language on the planet," he said. "There's no way to learn even a word of it. What kind of a language is this? Only consonants, impossible to pronounce!" He was fluent in German, French, and English, so Polish came to him as a shock.

Klaus was an exceptionally good host. He rented a luxurious apartment on the third floor of a building in Wola, a quiet, upscale part of Warsaw. He showed me to the room that was set up for me and said to feel at home. He had been living there for two years and would stay for another three, for the contract with his

Swiss company was for five years. Over a copious dinner of pasta primavera, steaks, salad, baguette, and wine, he was telling me how Warsaw was a tricky city to find your way around by yourself. That's why he had his friend Soroczko who acted as his interpreter, tour guide and a body guard. Soroczko and his fiancé Margoszata were a wonderful couple, they loved Klaus and did him lots of favors. They simply had a magnet that attracted me when I first saw them at the airport and I sensed they could feel my vibrations. I had a feeling that a genuine friendship was being born between us.

Is it possible that anything happens by chance in this world? Was it by chance that establishing the friendship with this couple would secure a visitor visa to Poland for myself and Nora, some months later, when we had to flee from our country? Who could have known, during those delicious dinners in Klaus' apartment, filled with joking and laughter, that one day Klaus would give us shelter from the whirlwind of the war in Yugoslavia and that Soroczko would welcome us like family and make sure we stayed safely in Poland for some time.

Is anything happening by chance?

My Warsaw time was flying too fast. I shot a documentary featuring the church organ in St. Clements, where I met a wonderful young priest, brother Krzysztof, who was also a choir conductor. We became friends instantly. He wanted to know everything about the situation in ex-Yugoslavia, which he had visited and liked a lot. I told him as much as I knew. Polish news were transmitting a different picture about the situation in the Balkans, which was understandable, because, as I mentioned earlier, each confronted party presented their 'truth' to the media. Then we switched the conversation to a much more enjoyable subject of music, spiritual in particular, and about concerts he was organizing in his church.

I attended the choir rehearsal that afternoon. Brother Krzysztof was a very handsome man. The canonicals emphasized even more the beauty of his face. Deep in my head I could hear a little devil telling me that such a gorgeous man must be having tons of sex, hidden by his church vestments. I didn't want to listen to that voice. After the rehearsal, the choir, composed of young girls and guys who all looked with adoration at brother Krzysztof and I, went to the church hall for some hot tea, the most favorite drink of Poles (after vodka), and szarlotka (apple pie). Upon my leaving some time later, at the church door, wrapped up into the crisp night air, brother Krzysztof and I hugged and parted like old friends.

The following day the four of us, Klaus, Soroczko, Margoszata, and I went to Żelazowa Wola, not far from Warsaw, the birth place of Frederick Chopin, where I shot a documentary about his childhood and youth. It was snowing and I was melting of happiness. My new friends were so wonderful, absorbing my words about Chopin's music as we walked on the small winding paths around his house. We went inside, admired the furniture, paintings, and objects that belonged to him. The curator was a very nice girl. Soroczko exchanged a few words with her.

"She said you can play a bit on the piano."

"On Chopin's piano?" I asked, amazed.

"Yes."

I sat down, my hands hovering over the keyboard. Nocturne in D-flat major came to my fingers and I started. The tones were ascending high to the ceiling and then fluttered around, spreading all over, into the starlit afternoon, over the show outside and the warmth inside. The other tourists stopped by to listen, mesmerized. It was a moment worth of eternity.

I called Nora once. Klaus kindly allowed me to use his phone. I had to tell her I wanted to stay there, forever; I wanted Warsaw to become my home, my reality, and everyday life. But I knew I couldn't and that it was only a dream.

"Nora, they have everything. The stores are full of meat, cheese, all kinds of things. This is a totally transformed Warsaw from what we saw last time, everybody's glowing!"

Nora couldn't believe her ears.

"I can't wait for you to come back and tell me all!"

On my last day in Warsaw I was walking alone. I wanted to pass by the streets I had walked on so many times before, to experience them from a new perspective. Warsaw was slowly putting on some pretty dresses. Architecturally, with the exception of the Old Town, it was still a gray city built in communist manner, with unappealing façades and huge government buildings, but it started beautifying. Here and there, neon lights were illuminating it. The stores resembled those in Western countries and were full of goods. What a joy filled my heart when I saw dozens of most various chocolates, nicely arranged on the shelves – like in a fairy tale! At home, there was nothing on the shelves, maybe only a few stray cans past expiry date. Our stores sported angry sales people by the cash register, chain smoking, in the boredom of an aimless day. Here, they were all smiley, in white coats, with lively eyes and quick tongues.

I wanted to get-together with Alfred, my old friend. I dialed his number, but it was out of service. I called Pani Maria and found out that my dear Alfred passed away a week ago, from a heart attack, without pain, after a party he had thrown for about twenty people. Tears were running down my cheeks. I asked Pani Maria to take me to the cemetery and laid white roses on his tomb. I was immensely sad. Alfred was such a good man, full of love and understanding for the whole world. I sat on the bench by his grave, mourning my friend with whom I had spent so many beautiful moments.

As I was leaving the cemetery, twilight descended on the city. I walked the familiar boulevards, got on trams and buses. I was looking around and listening. I was getting increasingly fond of the language, of this city and the country. It had been quietly conquering my soul, ever since September 1985, when I first went there, through lots of visits to my friend Alfred, visits with tour groups, to music festivals or just because. Each time I was falling more and more in love with Warsaw and Poland.

That night Klaus took us for dinner to his favorite restaurant, Pod Gryfami. I felt like in a family. Klaus was an extraordinary man, with high moral values and an artistic soul. Soroczko and Margoszata were cheerful like always. The dishes were prepared according to the recipes of the old Polish cuisine and their taste was divine.

Later that night, while I was packing, Klaus came into the room and asked if I would fancy a drink. I always fancy a drink. We were sitting on the sofa in the living room. Klaus' face was serious. He said he had heard on the News that the situation in ex-Yugoslavia was getting even worse. He didn't understand anything about that war, who was against whom and why. There was no point explaining it to him, for I myself was confused by everything that was going on. Klaus was visibly worried. We were drinking and talking as if we had known each other all our lives. Before I went to bed he said I could always count on his help and that, if it got very bad, a room in his apartment would always be there for me.

The next day, over the morning coffee, he said:

"Last night, when I said I had a room for you, I meant for you and Nora."

My new friends came to see me off, on the verge of tears. We were standing in front of Okęcie Airport, saying our goodbyes. Soroczko then said something in Polish that will forever stay engraved in my memory. Forever! Translated, these were his words:

"It's very bad and getting worse in your once beautiful country. Gosia (diminutive for Margoszata) and I have grown very fond of you. If you have big problems, if you don't have money for food or if your life is in danger, I want you to call me and immediately to come here, to safety!"

Klaus was guessing what Soroczko was saying, so he added:

"Any time! If you decide to come, you and Nora, you can stay at my place, for the beginning. You are welcome any time! Remember our conversation from last night?"

I quickly said my final goodbye and went into the airport building. I could hardly wait for the plane engines to warm up and for the propellers to start turning. One tear rolled down my cheek, swiftly, imperceptibly, a tear of joy.

Such wonderful people they were!

They could barely get to know me during those five days, yet they were offering me a place to stay and live; to me, and Nora, who they knew only from my stories about her.

Nora couldn't wait to hear everything about the trip. She absorbed every word of mine and was deeply touched by what Soroczko and Klaus had said. She replied by the Latin saying:

"*Similis simili gaudet.* (Birds of a feather fly together) There are good people in this world and they need good people to unite against the bad."

I left with a small traveling bag and returned with two suitcases. Klaus gave me two jackets he never wore, new and elegant. He loaded me with cheese, ham, and salami, to send some to my mom, too. Soroczko bought me some nice shirts and a warm sweater for cold Belgrade days, as he said. Gosia sent a beautiful blouse for Nora. I also had a few chocolate bars, a couple of cartons of juice and, for a joke, some kind or irony, I brought a roll of toilet paper, yellow, with a flower pattern and the scent of violets.

Since Nora and I somehow lived in our own world and our friends were also mostly people of arts or beauty in its various kinds, we were not aware to which extent the relations between Serbs and Croats had deteriorated, actually between the orthodox and the catholic.

The following Wednesday I spent almost an entire night at the TV studio montaging the documentary about Chopin and another one – about the church organ.

The show dedicated to Chopin was amazing and highly praised, with all the positive feedback from the audience. It was rerun several times. On the other hand, the show featuring the organ from the church of Saint Clement in Warsaw divided the opinions. Some people liked it, but most didn't. The sad thing was the fact that nobody minded the organ as such, but the religion, the Catholic Church. Everything passed without major consequences, though. Nora then realized it was some sort of gunpowder waiting to be ignited.

"It could have been worse," she said.

It wasn't in the remotest corners of our minds that somebody might disapprove of my show about the organ, like a music instrument, just because it was shot in a catholic church. Intolerance is dangerous and has no limits.

The everyday life brought few changes. I was working, had three jobs and private students. Nora decided to do something with her talent and was seriously thinking about opening a private English play-school, for small groups of preschool children who would learn the language through games, singing, and drawing. I was ecstatic with the idea.

That evening Nora and I sat down at the big dining room table and started creating first Serbian flyers. We were typing till late in the night, on the old typewriter:

Dear parents,
Private English Play-school
Opening soon in your neighborhood!
If interested, please call...

On each flyer, we put pictures of Donald Duck, Daisy, Mickey or Goofy, cut out from the comics. Over the next two days, we walked for kilometers and distributed them to every single mailbox in the area.

And the phone started ringing and parents enrolling their children. Those were times of poverty, but people still found means to provide for their children's education. They somehow managed to save on the bare necessities for the little ones. Kids needed to play and learn, to grow physically, emotionally, and mentally into healthy people, which was so important especially in the war time.

On the other side of life, some other young people, from the territories of ex-Yugoslav republics, carried away by another kind of embers and flame, were enrolling to paramilitary organizations and went to fronts to kill one another. The cemeteries were full of crosses with pictures of young men, 18 or 19 years old, died in pointless battles against their recent countrymen, neighbors, and friends and often against their relatives and family.

All the craters of the raging lava opened up and spilled out the fiery mass over us. We were all scorched, some more, some less, but all burning and smoldering under the tyranny of the devil. People were sinking lower and lower, to the lowest possible level. People became embittered and irate, nobody cared about anything anymore. The most beautiful city squares were turned into makeshift markets with goods smuggled from abroad, cigarettes, fruit juices, foodstuff. Going home from work in the evenings, I would look with sorrow at hundreds of cardboard boxes thrown around a square, waiting for the morning to become stalls again, behind which someone also miserable would stand and sell Coca Cola for half a German mark.

Like in every chaos, hopelessness, times when people get lost in lawlessness, confrontations, and deep political gap, there come people who present themselves as saviors. So overnight in our poor city some new characters appeared, came from who knew where, loaded with money and greedy for more. They addressed to people who barely had means for the basic survival and promised them big money if they invested everything they had in their newly opened bank.

One morning, looking through the dirty bus window, I was totally astonished by the scene: thousands of people were standing or sitting on folding stools, in a kilometers-long line winding around several streets, everybody eager to invest the little they had and then get rich. I had no savings and neither did Nora, so we didn't bother about it. To make the things more exciting, another bank in the same genre opened shortly afterwards. Now people were divided even by this – some were for him, owner of one bank, and some for her, owner of the other.

In that frantic struggle for a better tomorrow, for money, people were ready to wait for two days and two nights in endless lines. Family members were relieving one another. A few blocks away a new line was forming for some new banks.

While some were waiting in lines for the banks, the others were gathering in front of various government buildings and argued there, shouted, demanded this or that, but were most often against somebody who said something about someone. A hodgepodge of nonsense.

The kiosks displayed a variety of political newspapers, magazines and tabloids, all drenched in poison. They were exposing the faults of this or that party and the parties were spitting back.

One evening I was slowly making my way back home, for the tram didn't come after an hour of waiting. I decided to enjoy the charming streets of the city center. I had better not. What met my eyes were broken lamps on the old-fashioned wrought iron posts – aftermath of countless street demonstrations. The lawns and big pots once containing flowers were now overflowing with cigarette butts and garbage. Belgrade wasn't a white city any more.

I walked briskly to the tram stop one early Saturday morning. I planned to teach my students an original approach to singing that I invented the previous night and couldn't wait to share it with them. There were tons of people at the stop, so I continued walking down the street, hoping that the tram would show up eventually. I heard the squeaking of brakes. A car stopped in front of me.

"Sorry," said the driver I couldn't see.

I bent and gave him a closer look. To my surprise, it was Sava, the supermarket manager I met a few years ago.

"I knew it was you," he said. "Get in!"

I got into his car. I was very glad to see him after a long time. Before I left for the army, I had moved all my things from the garage apartment to Nora's place and somehow misplaced his phone number.

"What have you been up to? What's new?" I asked.

Sava's gaze was fixed on me. He took my head in his hands and shook it gently.

"You look good," he said. "I'd say you've put on about a kilo, thank God."

"Well, I lived in a village in Eastern Serbia for a year and shared the yard with a Hungarian woman who was a super cook and made for me any dish I fancied."

"Any sex?" He winked.

"That was instead of a cake," I laughed. "No, nothing along those lines, we were friends."

Sava was driving, but had his eyes more on me than on the streets.

"Let's go somewhere for coffee," he said.

"I can't Sava, I've got students to teach. The class starts in ten minutes."

"And after that?"

"After that will be fine," I said.

He parked in front of the Yugoslav Drama Theater. I got out of the car and made for the Faculty of Music, right next to it. Sava honked twice and left.

My students sang like angels. I was teaching polyphonic harmony examples, each more complex but also more beautiful than the other. Time went by fast and in a blink it was already noon and the end of the class.

Sava was waiting for me in front of the Faculty. He was wearing a blue jacket, white turtle neck and jeans. He had put on a few kilos, but they suited him. He hugged me, lifted me up and swirled me around a few times.

"Hey, man, calm down your hormones," I said laughingly.

Out of breath, he said:

"Don't disappear from my life like that anymore. I was looking for you at all the schools," he took some air. "All the music and elementary schools in Belgrade. Then I was afraid you might have been sent to the front, so I was looking for you on the lists of killed in battles, praying to God I didn't find you there."

"I was in the Army, Sava."

"A few years?"

"No," I felt irony in his voice. "Just that everything happened in such a rush, I lost your phone number and you don't work in that supermarket any more, I went there several times."

"Right, I'm working in Zemun now."

"See?"

We were both overjoyed to have met again.

"Shall we go to the restaurant across the street for some baked fish and wine?" He asked.

"Sounds good," I agreed.

During the time we had been out of touch he got another daughter, a better job and a raise, but the inflation and the shortage of foodstuffs were destroying his chain of supermarkets, as they did everything and everyone. We spent that afternoon together. He gave me a lift home. Before saying goodbye, in his car, he gave me a piece of paper.

"Don't misplace it his time," he said. "This is my new phone number at work."

I gave him a piece of paper with my home phone number.

Sava remained my dear friend that and the next month. We gathered together after my classes or his work. We would sit on the bank of the Danube at dusk, sipping beer, or coffee as the first morning guests at the café on the riverfront.

One morning while I was shaving, Nora came into the bathroom and said I had an important phone call. She didn't know who was on the line.

"Hallo?"

"Hi Nikola, it's me, Sava."

It was him, but his voice was somehow confused and strange.

"You sound different," I said. "What's going on?"

"I'm calling you from a phone booth in Novi Sad. I'm leaving the country with my family. We're going to Austria, to my brother in law. They keep trying to mobilize me, I can't even go home any more. We decided to flee from here. We have four suitcases and the four of us. I wanted to thank you for everything."

"Thank you, Sava, I wish you all the best."

"I'll come back one day when everything gets back to normal," he said.

"I know you will. Bon voyage!"

"Thank you. Well, bye, Nikola."

"Good luck!"

"You know?"

"I know."

Nora's Impressions

Creative as I am, I'm running out of ideas how to make a decent and nice looking dish out of water, flour, a few drops of oil, an occasional tomato, and some herbs still growing in the garden. Our beans supply is running low but we still have one jar left of the rosehip jam from Granny Jana.

Nikola revisits his and our Warsaw. I can't sleep at all those five days, like, what if he gets sent to the front, and dragged out of the bus before reaching Budapest airport? Or what if the borders get closed?

He comes back safely, his mouth bursting with stories about his new friends, and his suitcase loaded with nice clothes for him, me and his mom, and good food!

I can finally make a proper breakfast with bread, cheese, salami and orange juice and real coffee!

Warsaw is calling us back, I can sense it. Klaus will make it possible. Such a sweetheart of a man, Archie would lick him all over! Soroczko and Gosia will be our staples there.

What are we waiting for?

If it hadn't been for one lazy late summer afternoon, Nikola wouldn't have met Pega. Without Pega, there would be no Klaus. Without Klaus, there would be no Soroczko and Gosia. Without them, there would be no exit for us.

If I hadn't been immersed in books and Archie asleep in his kennel on that late summer afternoon, and if Nikola hadn't rushed out for some fresh air, none of this would have happened.

But it did.

Fortunately.

Before You, I Stoop Humbly

> *Wie soll ich dich empfangen,*
> *Und wie begegn' ich dir,*
> *O aller Welt Verlangen*
> *O meiner Seele Zier?*
> *O Jesu, Jesu, setze*
> *Mir selbst die Fackel bei,*
> *Damit, was dich ergötze*
> *Mir kund und wissend sei.*
>
> (Chorale J.S. Bach)

God exists in various ways.

What He is called, what He looks like, the ways in which people of all nationalities and races show reverence to Him, makes no difference. True faith comes from the pure heart, but is unfortunately often misunderstood. Religion as an institution can sometimes be spoiled by money or some other unholy things. To me, all places of worship are beautiful. I enjoyed visiting catholic churches in Belgrade with the same joy as the orthodox ones.

One day I met a wonderful young man in the garden of a lovely catholic church in the very downtown, hidden in the deep shade of ash and poplar trees. His name was Vita. He was a poet, talked in a sophisticated language and was a great cook. The friendship with him was like a jewel. Nora and I took to him right away and so did he to us. We started getting together more often and became more acquainted with each other every time. Once, while we were sitting at the big dining room table in Nora's house, he said:

"Nikola, there is a church that needs a music director. The choir has a great potential, the church is marvelous, and the vicar is made of pure gold, trust me."

"I really don't have time for anything more in my busy schedule," I said honestly. "Believe me, I can't fit it in, even though I'd love to do it."

He didn't press, just said:

"Can we go to a choir rehearsal sometime? I would like you to see the church and meet the vicar."

"Yes, that I can promise."

The way it happens in life, a week later I was walking in the well maintained garden of an impressive catholic church. It was really marvelous, outside and inside. The first thing that caught my eye was the floral arrangement at the altar, a masterpiece. A combination of flowers, budding branches, grasses, and lush greenery intertwined with tulle and lace, so ethereal and divine.

"Who created this?" I asked quietly.

"A choir singer, very devoted woman. She is exceptionally talented, isn't she?" Vita said.

"Yes," I was looking in amazement at lots of floral decorations throughout the church.

I heard steps coming closer and a jovial looking middle-aged gentleman with cheerful eyes materialized in front of us.

"A very good evening to you, young man," he said. "You are a professor of music, soon to be kapellmeister of our small but exquisite choir, if I am not mistaken."

"Good evening, sir," I said. "It is such a pleasure for me to be here, but as I explained to our mutual friend, I am doing two full time jobs and have a weekly TV show. I don't think I could find some spare time for what you are offering me, even though I would love to work at this magnificent place."

The vicar was looking at me. The smile never left his face. He gave me a light hug and took Vita and me to the staircase leading to a lower level. Soothing music was playing. The choir was there, waiting to be introduced to me. There were about twenty people, men and women: believers, more or less musically educated, but with a strong desire to sing to God and to beautify the church by music. I introduced myself and asked them to sing a song they knew well. That was my starting point to see at which musical level they were and how much time I would need to rehearse them to perfection. I told them not to worry about anything and to let go of stage fright, for I wasn't there to criticize them, on the contrary, to admire them.

They started singing one of their favorite hymns, a polyphonic piece. It wasn't bad, but their voices were unsynchronized, each one standing out, one too loud, one shrilly, one too open, far from a professional choir sound. Still, deep, deeper under all of that, a wonderful potential was there and immense love for sacred music.

It was a hard decision. I really didn't have time, the Faculty of Music, the school, TV, private students, and on top of everything I recently started writing a column for a magazine about everyday life. But there I was, in front of them, such dear people, and I simply couldn't say no.

"Yes, I accept your offer," I said to the vicar.

"I knew you would," he beamed. "I can see you are a good man at heart. I will pay you for your efforts as much as I can."

"Money isn't what is motivating me to work with this choir," I said with tranquility and inspiration. "It is the love of these people for music and our faith in God, regardless of how we pray to Him!"

He tapped me on the shoulder and invited me for coffee in his office. It was an artistically arranged room full of books and beautiful paintings. The vicar was a cultured, intelligent, and soulful man. He was managing the church and his parish with strong skillful hands, taking care of the poor and the sick and of everybody who was in need of help. Friendship with him enriched my and Nora's treasuries of life.

I rehearsed the choir three times a week. I worked mostly on my singers' careful listening to other voices so they could all blend their personal ways of singing into an overall great performance.

My heart wanted to jump out of my chest from joy when two weeks later the smiley vicar came to congratulate me, after the Sunday Mass.

"Well done, Professor! You have transformed my choir! How did you do that? They were singing so sweetly and pleasingly, the whole congregation noticed!"

I was elated, my singers even more. They were glowing with happiness, proud of their achievement.

The winter was unusually cold and bitter. It was getting increasingly hard to wait in lines for hours to get some bread, coffee, sugar, or anything, whatever could be got. Nora and I were lucky, though, for ever since I started working with the church choir, the wonderful vicar was helping us, bringing us flour, oil, cheese, canned ham, pasta, rice, and chocolates. Life could have been tolerable were it not for the terrible threat hanging in the air – the likelihood of forming fronts in Serbia itself.

Nora and I went to the South of Serbia for a few days to see my parents and relatives. Misery and poverty was what we found there. The public transport was paralyzed because of the shortage of gas. Most schools were closed down for there was no heating. The stores were empty. The whole town was enveloped in a shroud of destitution. Nora and I brought from Belgrade what we could and distributed the essentials equally to my relatives. My mom looked sad, with sunken cheeks and hair that hadn't been dyed for quite some time. I had never seen her like that. In some nice times, only a couple of years ago, my mom regularly went to hairdressers' and beauty salons for facials, manicure, and pedicure. It was a pleasure for me to afford her all that. Now I worked more than ever, but the economic situation was extremely bad and the government invested all the money in the war, useless, horrible war, while everything else was rotting from negligence, pennilessness, and grayness of the everyday life.

Nora packed lots of the goodies the vicar had been giving us and gave them to my mom. How lovely was the dinner on that cold January evening! Mom baked bread and made stuffed dried peppers, with rice only, for meat was impossible to get. Nora enjoyed the taste of hot pickled peppers, cucumbers, and cauliflower while I was indulging in ajvar. Mom managed to make only a few jars of it, for the lack of oil or money to buy it. In spite of the circumstances, there was plenty of food for all of us. The dinner was also special because my father joined us at the table in good mood. It was probably the poverty and the unstable situation in the country that loosened his rigidity, at least a bit. I had always tried to avoid eating with him, because he would invariably make up a reason to raise his voice, to criticize mom or me, to find fault with this or that, just to spoil any meal. Even today, after so many years, whenever people start a discussion at the table laid with food, I get up and leave.

That evening my father was in good mood. He was chatting with Nora about everything. Mom was relaxed, for that was one of the rare moments without friction and problems. The four of us were eating happily and gratefully, feeling the taste of food on our palates. For dessert, that we didn't even dare to expect, Mom brought from the oven her famous apple pie, to crown the night.

The next morning we went to see my dear aunt Kankica who welcomed us with wide-open arms and piping hot piroshki filled with cheese in her cozy kitchen. She had always been a master for all kinds of pastries, focaccia, bread plaits, scones, donuts, you name it. My aunt is no longer among the living. I believe that God took her to be close to Him because of her immense goodness, warmth, and open heart that encompassed all beings.

A few days later, we returned to Belgrade. We arrived in the late afternoon and I said to Nora I'd go to the barracks to see how Dragan was doing, it had been quite some time since my last visit. I was waiting for the bus for an eternity. When my ears totally froze and turned into icy red head holders, it finally came, packed with people. I managed to get on somehow, excusing myself for pressing against a soldier, who was obviously heading to the barracks, a bit drunk.

I was sure he would bring spring with his smile. Dragan's face was so radiant.

"You've forgotten about me," he said, half-jokingly and half critically.

"No, Dragan, honestly I haven't, but so many things happened in the meantime. I didn't have time to come, and I phoned hundreds of times, but nobody ever answered."

"How come?"

"No idea."

He went to the booth by the entrance and came back five minutes later.

"They changed the phone number and didn't tell me," he was angry.

"It's alright, I'm here now, go change."

He went out in civilian clothes. His hair was long for military standards, but it charmingly framed his face.

"Where are we going?" I asked.

"I'm taking you to something special," he beamed.

"Why?"

"Tomorrow is my birthday, I want to treat you."

"Ha, right on," I said. "You thought I wouldn't remember it, but I did. Happy 23rd birthday, Dragan!" I took a nicely wrapped flat box from my bag and handed it to him. He was touched by the attention, I saw his eyes watering. He opened it and pulled out an etching of Warsaw I bought for him when I was in Poland.

"It's beautiful! I'll take it with me to Italy!"

"I got it for you purposely, because I want you to know it will be the city I'll go to with Nora. That will be my future," I said with deep faith.

"So you guys decided to leave?"

"Yes, Dragan. This here is hell."

He looked at me.

"Nikola, you know it can get even worse."

"I know, but on the other hand, let it be. Let there be war in Serbia, so I'll know it's the war and have 50/50 chances to survive or be killed, but not live like this. Each day is a struggle to buy bread, a battlefield to get on the bus, fight to get your salary. People yell at each other on the streets, they are desperate and angry. People here started really hating each other. I can't go on like this."

"We don't need to talk about it," Dragan said. "Didn't I say this was a special evening?'

"Indeed you did."

"So, let's go to a tavern."

"Let's go!"

We spent a phenomenal evening. The music was superb. We were singing and forgetting about everything around us. The tavern was full of people who, like us, were celebrating their own or someone else's birthdays, or were there simply to ignore the reality. Interestingly, outside the tavern walls, there was nothing except poverty and empty shelves in stores. Inside, there was everything: food and drinks, flowing liberally, and quite affordably priced. Two worlds, the dream world and the real one mixed together.

I woke up with a heavy head, in what looked like a hotel room. It took a great effort to get up. I went to the bathroom and splashed my face with cold water. Dragan was still sleeping, quietly and motionlessly, like always. Contrary to him, I'm a restless sleeper. I talk in sleep, toss and turn, change positions, jiggle my arms and legs in all directions, and I am constantly either too cold or too hot. I envied him the way he slept. Not a tiniest sound could be heard. I took a shower, got dressed, then went down to the restaurant on the ground floor, and ordered two coffees. It was the Kasina Hotel, I found out. How I had got there, I didn't have the slightest idea.

"Good morning," I said, bringing steaming cups into the room.

Dragan woke up and went on his elbows.

"Morning," he yawned.

I lit up and took a sip of the coffee. It felt so good. Dragan came out of the bathroom, lighting his first morning cigarette.

"Why are you smiling like this?" I asked. He had a strange expression on his face.

"Nothing."

"C'mon, tell me, or I'll start tickling you!" He hated that.

"Oh, how dangerous you're today," he laughed.

"Tell me!"

"Alright, OK. You drank a lot last night and were in such high spirits. You were singing with the musicians at the tavern, then we went to a bar across from the theater, remember?"

"No."

"There, you sat down at the piano and played some great music, got tons of applause and drinks on the house."

I had no idea what he was talking about. I usually remember almost everything.

"There was no chance to talk you into going to a hotel. You wanted more fun, so we went to another bar, in the same area. You didn't like it, because it was too loud, with too many half naked singers."

"And?"

"Then you finally agreed to go to a hotel. The rest, I'll keep for myself, because it's so sweet that I don't want to spoil the loveliness of it by telling you a single word."

I gave him my 'tell me or I'll kill you' look, but he didn't budge. He was obviously enjoying keeping me in the dark.

"Right," I said. "You can say whatever you want, because I don't remember. You can make up everything."

"Made up or true, it's mine," he clicked his tongue.

"You're getting on my nerves now," I smiled at him. "I've got to go, Dragan. I have a rehearsal in church."

"What church and what rehearsal?"

"I conduct a church choir – gorgeous place, good-hearted people…"

"Such a role model of a religious person you are," he burst out laughing. "Yesterday, you were so boozed up you could barely walk – to say nothing about what you did last night – and now you're going to church! Ha, ha, ha!"

"You're always right, yes, we know that, the same old story."

"Of course I am," he winked.

"I'm taking off."

"Fine, call me when you can."

"I will," I said and left hastily.

If my singers noticed how sleepy and tired I looked, they didn't show it. We were practicing Bach's chorale O How Shall I Receive Thee (Before You, I Stoop Humbly in Croatian translation). Its harmonies were so wonderful, it was a pure pleasure for me to conduct it. That day after the Mass, in the vicar's office, over coffee and conversation, I felt energized.

"May I ask you to do me a big favor?" the vicar looked at me like a hopeful child.

"Certainly," I said. "I'll do whatever I can."

"I would love it if you could work on a Mass in Latin with the singers, my favorite Easter Mass."

"For you, by all means! You have my word!" Practicing a Mass in Latin would require lots of rehearsals with a non-professional choir, but I was confident in my singers' capacities. I was looking forward to it.

The vicar thanked me warmly and offered to give me a lift home. I gratefully accepted, for I still had residues of hangover from the previous intoxicated night.

Nora's English Play-school was a real hit. The children attended it regularly and we got some new admissions, so now we had four groups. Nora enjoyed her work and was thrilled to be a guest in my music T.V show with her little students. The show was amazing and brought us even more kids. People were watching it and called us for days afterwards. Whenever my time allowed, I loved being with 'Nora's kids', playing on the piano the songs they had just learned, and participating in their games. The parents were wonderful, intellectuals, people like Nora and I, open-minded, caught up in the whirlwind of general discontent and abnormal everyday life. The children were great, each with their own distinct character and all of them so sweet and adorable and totally in love with Nora. Our 'pet' was little Daki who couldn't wait to come to our house for English classes. He liked doing tricks and his favorite one was to misplace things. Often, after the classes, we would find his sock in my shoe, the potpourri bowl from the dining room table in the washing machine, or his cap on the rosebush in the garden.

"Sorry, Nikola," the editor in chief of the magazine I was a columnist for said. "We don't have money to pay you, but I can give you a chunk of mozzarella, two pairs of jeans, and a big sack of flour in lieu of the wages."

I admired her. She was a dragon woman and born leader, straightforward, full of energy and passion. In some other times, that woman could have easily become the president of the country. Everything about her was perfect: the voice, looks, clothes, and gestures. I didn't mind not being paid, for even if I were handed that money, I could buy nothing, since there was nothing to buy. This way, at least I got flour, two thirds of which I could send through a connection in the railways to my mom and aunts, and keep one third for Nora and I.

"No problem, Milena," I said, gazing at her. "You look stunning in this navy blue suit, it fits you like a glove!"

"You are always full of compliments, Nikola," she gave me a quick smile, rushed out of the office to see if there were other journalists waiting for her, checked with her secretary, made sure everything was running smoothly, then came back and turned to me.

"Your latest article was phenomenal! The phone was ringing off the hook, my mail box was full; people were totally into it. Congratulations! Keep it up!"

Nora was delighted by flour and jeans, but most of all, by mozzarella.

"Pizza!" she clapped her hands.

"Pizza it will be," I agreed.

"Do we still have some of that tomato sauce left?" she asked.

"I'm pretty much sure I saw a bottle of the hot one in the pantry," I said.

We invited Mira, Marko, Lela, Pega, the vicar, Vita, and Dragan for dinner. My professor Zora wasn't feeling well, otherwise she would have joined us. Nora and I made several pizzas with most various combinations. Our tomato sauce was a mixture of ketchup and home-made tomato juice that Nora's aunt had brought from the village. One pizza included onion rings topped with an egg, one with finely-chopped smoked meat (from Mira) and one with thin slices of pickled peppers (a gift from a wonderful woman, mother of one of my private students). It was a pleasant, relaxing evening. Everybody chatted friendly with people they hadn't met before and nobody disturbed the idyll with discussions about politics. Archibald was beyond himself of happiness, seeing so many people around him and was wagging his tail as fast as possible. A couple of months earlier, we discovered that Archibald was actually a she. After having made an acquaintance with a local dog, which I found out by chance, and which happened due to a hole in the fence that was hidden by a hydrangea bush, it made it possible for the 'lover' to get to

Archibald; he got pregnant. It was funny to everybody that Archibald was a mother, even funnier to himself.

He was a bad mother. He refused to breastfeed his sweet little puppies who were whining. Nora and I had to feed them with various milk mixtures from a baby bottle, often in the middle of the night, because Archibald totally ignored his offspring. He kept courteously greeting the whole neighborhood as they were going to or coming back from work, and basked in the affection that every human showed to him. The puppies were just a burden and a hassle for him. As soon as they grew up a bit, we gave them for adoption, having found some nice people to take care of them. Archibald was overjoyed when the puppies were not in the garden any more. His face exuded relief, like there was enough bother with the little ones; the time came again for a royal life of the only pet in the house, without any competition.

The spring sneaked in, without glamour and the usual pomp. White blossoms gleamed on the trees, only to be washed off by the rain. The sun would appear at dawn, just to cast its rays for a moment on the rooftops and the windows, then disappear behind the clouds.

Spring existed only on the calendar and in our agendas, but in the souls and hearts of us, winter still reigned. The war was an unbearable burden, day and night. The war started taking some extremely deformed shapes. There was a rumor about concentration camps in Bosnia, like in World War 2. Why? What for? Haven't we grown stronger and wiser during the last fifty years? Haven't we learnt enough from the concentration camps of the past? Haven't we evolved for at least one degree of higher intelligence? Why are we going back to Jasenovac and Auschwitz? Americans were sending rockets to space, in Denmark the power of the sea was utilized and windmills placed deep into it, so that by the energy of the wind they could get cheaper electricity. The whole world was putting their minds into creating something better, newer, more modern – something that would bring a brighter future to everyone, especially to young generations. What are our descendants going to say, one day, if that day ever comes? Will they talk about waiting in long lines, misery, and destitution?

What about the fact that only those doing something illegally could prosper, while decent people were doomed?

Nora was trying to calm me down – actually to placate my anger, but wasn't successful. Maybe it was my nature, maybe my zodiac sign, Taurus, or the distribution of planets at the moment when I was born. At any rate, I went into a phase of resentment and wrath which held a firm grip on me. I was embittered that people who used to be brothers, friends, and close to each other were now killing each other for the sake of the politicians. *'Why all of that?'* I asked myself. Then we heard about rapes and massacres of the innocent. The innocent always suffer. The News reported, again, about villages being burned down to their very foundations. The same events were broadcasted from three sides: Serbian, Croatian, and Muslim, with completely different wording, and participants with three dissimilar versions of the truth, different attackers and different victims. It became sickening to turn on the radio or TV became sickening to be alive.

On the foggy political terrain, disgusting dirty matches were played. The parties were fighting to come into power, spitting on one another, the more the better, and poor people were somnolently turning to one or another, seeking salvation in the times without entertainment, beauty, and culture, in the times that should have never happened. My rage was smoldering deep into my heart, spreading over the veins in my body, tormenting my brain. The more clearly I saw injustice at every single step, the less I could stand it. My beautiful Belgrade stank of the rot of ex-communists, now favorites of the leading Socialist Party of Serbia, who were getting rich at vertiginous speed, buying land for a bargain and building huge buildings, investing in some unforeseeable future, visible only to them.

Mira was trying desperately to provide for her family: her two daughters, to feed them and buy them everything they needed for school, by working extra hard, teaching tons of aerobics, and stretching classes on top of her full-time job as a Physical Education teacher. I admired her and helped her as much as I could, by simply being her friend and talking to her, since I had little money and few food-stuff to offer her. Marko was doing fine. He worked in a private funeral home; the business was going well and he was paid in German marks. Lela belonged to the Belgrade élite now, not the intellectual, but the financial one – but I didn't think she was thriving. At that time, overwhelmed by my jobs, the choir and everything around me, I wasn't keeping regular touch with her, for even though I promised to myself and swore not to, I would still have to fight with her husband about politics, because I had eyes and ears and could see and hear what was happening, unlike him, who looked upon it all from an opposite view point, protected by big money and cardboard fortresses.

An unidentified pain in the stomach was added to my aches. Even after numerous examinations, the doctors couldn't find the cause of it. It would occur suddenly, at night or in the morning, and was unbearably piercing, like a stab of a knife.

The tape I recorded with my children's choir, a fruit of my deep love for the authentic folk music, was selling like hot cakes. But after all the paperwork regarding copyrights and other bureaucratic issues was completed, I was left with a sum total of about $100, which quickly melted in the hot pot of inflation. By the time the money was paid on my account, it was a ridiculous sum, so ridiculous that it couldn't be converted into any currency because it came to less than one dollar. I wasn't particularly surprised or disappointed. I was happy that the first (and only) edition of the tape was sold out, that thousands of children would listen to it, and that those beautiful, old authentic songs wouldn't be forgotten and disappear in the whirlwind of the newly composed folk music.

Easter was approaching. My church choir was getting better and better as we practiced the Latin Mass in the F-minor, which the venerable vicar loved so much. It was so uplifting, harmonically and melodically complex, and in spite of all the energy my singers were putting into it, there were some complicated parts in the score, too; demanding for an amateur choir. I asked six of my best students from the Faculty of Music, if they didn't mind, to join my choir in singing the Mass. I said it would be in a Catholic church, and that they shouldn't feel obliged to help me out just because I was their professor. Deep in my heart, I knew they would accept, for those were girls made of beauty, good-hearted and full of understanding. It didn't matter to them which church it was; what mattered was music.

All six of them agreed, my dear, dearest students. I was so honored to have met them, they brought so much joy into my lecturer's days at the Faculty. In the years to come, far from my country, my prayers to the Almighty for health and happiness have always included them. They were intelligent, honest girls and excellent students, passing exams with honors. One of them, Biljana, a flute player, was my right hand at many concerts. The state of war and incredible fear took me away from the country too fast, so I lost contact with her. Whether after completing the studies she went back to her hometown of Negotin (where a great 19th-century composer, Mokranjac, was born) or stayed in Belgrade, I didn't know and I'd give everything to be able to hear her voice once again.

The Easter Sunday came.

The church glowed magnificently under the bright April sun. The churchyard was full of believers. Inside, it was gorgeously adorned with a multitude of spring branches with tiny yellow flowers, gently enveloped in pristine white tulle. Bouquets of daffodils and delicate apricot blossoms sprang out from each pew. It all looked beyond this world. The vicar was visibly excited.

My singers sang like never before. Aided by the angelic voices of the girls from the faculty and the skillful hands of the organist, also a university professor, the Mass elated the audience and opened hearts even more towards God. Nora was all in tears.

"It was fantastic!" she said.

"Bravo maestro!" the vicar gave me a big hug. "Excellently done!"

Later, that night, when we were sitting on our terrace, surrounded by darkness, because the electricity restrictions hit our part of the city, Nora said quietly and frighteningly:

"You know, I was so very afraid today."

"Of what?"

"Nikola," she said into the night, "Today was Catholic Easter, but we all gathered together in church, in the name of God –of resurrected Jesus. It was a divine white oasis in this ocean of blackness. An insane mind from the outside could have used today's day as an easy target for doing something evil, for provoking chaos and for… "

She couldn't go on.

I understood.

The truth was that: hatred ruled people, most of them. The reason was in deep sleep. Evil was awake, keeping company to stupidity.

That night, on the terrace, in pitch black darkness disturbed only by the glow of our lit cigarettes, Nora and I definitely decided to leave our country for good and go to Poland, while there was still a chance to leave. We didn't say anything, yet we said everything. The smoke whirling from our cigarettes was speaking of sadness, melancholy, and the graveness of the moment. Archibald, half asleep by our feet, suddenly lifted up his head.

"He is sensing it," Nora sighed deeply.

There was no sign of electricity that was supposed to be back on at midnight. Nora and I lit candles and went to the bedroom. There was no need for words, silence was talking.

Through the clouds, for a moment, the full moon appeared, just to say "Good night" to Belgrade, drowned in gloom.

Only for a moment.

Then it hid again behind the clouds.

The night became gloomier, and darkness darker.

Through silence, Bach's chorale was floating in my ears.

> *Before You I stoop humbly*
> *O Savior my sweet.*
> *Looking at Your face, Holy,*
> *With wounds heavy and deep.*
> *Looking at the crown of thorn*
> *On Your Sacred head low,*
> *I step closer to the throne*
> *And cry with all my soul.*

Nora's Impressions

In the summer of 1989, while touring Northern Italy, Nikola and I happen to be in Basilica di Sant'Antonio in Padua at one point. We don't know much about the Saint at the time, but put our hands on his coffin, for the tradition says that Saint Anthony is a miraculous healer and protector, and can make all your wishes come true.

Nikola's wish is not to go to the Army. Well, he eventually does, but is protected all the time.

Mine is to marry Nikola.

On June 13th 1993, we get married. The date is picked purely on the basis of when the registry office can fit us in.

A year later, Nikola conducts a church choir and a big celebration is on June 13th which is, as we find out, St. Anthony's day!

Life spins its yarn in most miraculous and subtle ways.

Some months later, our first apartment in Warsaw, Poland, overlooks the National Theater, the Opera House and, the Church of St. Anthony – just across the street!

Some more months later, I get the original prayer to St. Anthony, in Italian, from Cyprus. I always keep it in my wallet which is often empty of money but full of grace.

A couple of years later, I buy the icon of St. Anthony in St. Michaels' Cathedral in Toronto. It is above my bed here in Montreal, watching over my dreams and greeting my mornings.

I have always been attracted to churches, synagogues, mosques, temples, and all places of worship.

To the beautiful architecture and artwork.

To spirituality and tranquility.

I just walk in, light a candle or an incense stick, say a silent prayer, and simply be.

Feel the peace.

Feel the eternity.

Catch a glimpse of the Universal Love.

I prefer these moments to attending the regular service.

In these moments, there is like a direct link between God and me, between God and the few people who are here – praying, whispering, spilling out their souls.

God listens and radiates His/Her smile upon us.

The Church of St. Anthony in Belgrade shows me that such magical moments can be experienced during official Masses.

The magnificent flower arrangements are made by a truly inspired woman.

The choir sounds divine.

The vicar likes doing Masses in Latin and totally wins me here!

St. Anthony is venerated within the Franciscan order of monks and priests who are traditionally poor, clad in simple brown habits with a cord around the waist, just like San Francesco D'Assisi when he walked the late 12th and early 13th century Italy barefoot, talking about humility and brotherly love. Italian literature starts with his poem, Cantico delle creature (Canticle of Living Beings) celebrating pantheism.

Our vicar, Fra Leopold, is a Franciscan of the 20th century and makes sure everybody leaves his church nourished in soul and body.

After the Mass, there are always pastries (made by the masterful hand of Vita) and wine.

He also provides food for Nikola, and me and Nikola's mom and family in the South of Serbia.

When Fra Leopold comes to our house, I cut the most fragrant roses from the garden, so the inspired lady can make a new arrangement for the altar.

I become a regular church-goer.

Tuesday evenings, soft and relaxed.

Sunday mornings, energized.

My step is lighter and my heart bigger, every time I leave the church, as if infused by the Omniscient's Love.

On Nikola's and my last day in the country of our birth, heading into the unknown, it is the choir of the Church of St. Anthony that wishes us well into the uncertain future.

It is Ruža, a lovely soprano, who takes pictures of all of us, sending Nikola and me with God's blessings.

St. Anthony, Fra Leopold and Ruža are watching over us.

Nothing can go wrong, so let's go!

Fog

Fog is here, fog is all around,
From a distance faintly echoing a sound.

The mesmerizing voice of Josipa Lisac was permeating a small café hidden deeply inside a building, with only four tiny tables, three of which were empty. The waitress went outside to smoke, so Dragan and I were the only people there. He was done with his military service and came to say goodbye. In a few days, he would go to Italy, get married, and start a new life. His eyes, always so cheerful, had a melancholic shade that day.

"Don't be sad," I said to him. "This is a happy moment for both of us."

"I know, but I am sad. This country is falling apart, like everything I have believed in."

I looked at him. His face expressed anguish, the same one I was seeing on my face in the mirror, and on the faces of people on the streets of my city, of my country.

"It would be great if we could get drunk by vodka now," he laughed.

"I agree, but we won't. We made a deal, right?"

"Right."

We drank our espressos and walked down Balkanska Street to the bus station. I loved that street, cobbled, winding, and full of charming little shops from a bygone era. It had always been buzzing with life and vitality. All my friends from the province who came to Belgrade for a visit had to experience Balkanska Street with me. In some happy times, we would treat ourselves to broken chocolate that I used to buy in the grocery store next to the grand Moscow Hotel. There was nothing wrong with the chocolate, but since it was not foiled and was in pieces, it cost very little. So many times, I enjoyed boza, a drink made of fermented wheat in the Turkish cake shop at the end of the street. Buying guitar strings with Marko was like an adventure. Needles for Mom's brand of knitting machine could be found only there, in an antiquated shop owned by a smiley old man, nowhere else in the city. That day, Balkanska Street looked joyless and gray, and was lonely, because there was nobody to visit it. The shops that were one-of-a-kind were disappearing under the galloping inflation and giving way to modern cafés. Dozens of cafés, one next to the other. If there had been foreign tourists in Belgrade in those days, they would have probably looked in wonder how everything was being pulled down and turned into a sea of cafés. They were usually empty and nobody knew why they were opened by some new young people, the only ones who had money. Lots of people from the war zones were coming to the capital. Some with just bundles of old clothes and bare necessities they could salvage, some with hundreds of thousands of marks, dollars, or francs. They were all refugees, some suffered and some reigned.

That day, Dragan and I were walking side by side in silence. When we got to the bottom of Balkanska Street and the yellow building of the Train and Bus Station, old and dilapidated yet somehow unique, could be discerned in the distance, I stopped.

"I am not going any farther," I said.

Dragan looked at me questioningly, but didn't say anything.

"I'm sorry," I tried to explain. "Something's silly with my head. Too many seeing offs, leavings, wavings and sadness. I simply can't, as if something is going to happen to me there; I can't, I can't, I can't."

"You don't have to apologize," Dragan said. "I understand."

I had to spill it out, for that was the truth. During all those long years of my youth, there had been so many goodbyes and partings, more sorrowful than sorrow itself, and I didn't want Dragan's leaving to drown in that sea, which was already too salty from so many tears.

The rain fell suddenly and heavily, followed by lightning and thunder. We ran to a nearby apartment building entrance for protection. The paint of an undefined mushroomy-mustardy color was peeling off its mildewy walls and it smelled of urine and poverty. If I had been in the mood, I would have made a joke about the setting looking like one from Alan Ford comic strip, but there was no place for joking in that moment.

"You won't see such buildings in Italy," I said.

"Neither you, in Poland."

We hugged tightly. I held my breath so I could hear the rhythm of his heart and memorize it. The rain stopped all of a sudden, the same way it came.

"May luck be always with you," I said.

"And with you!" he replied. "May you have success in music and life!"

"Write to me."

"Of course. You too."

Real friends never part forever, for that's why they are friends. They keep in their hearts the torches always lit. I believe that destiny is rewarding me for some nice things I have done in my life, because I have always been surrounded by such wonderful people. That day I was sad, but only in my eyes. My heart was happy, for my friend would be safe, far away from this shit in the country and the pestilent stench of the war. I took a deep breath.

"Thank you for everything," I said.

My words fluttered with some pieces of paper, leaves, and plastic bags, blown by the strong wind.

"No, Nikola, thank you for everything." Dragan was on the brink of crying, his eyes were full of tears.

"Good luck," I said.

"Good luck," he said.

Then we went our ways unsteadily, one towards the West, one towards the East. He – to the safety of Italy and marriage, me – to a possible, uncertain future in Poland, if fortune granted Nora and me to get there and stay.

I was feeling his glance on the nape of my neck, but didn't turn. The friendship with him encompassed the depth of my Petrovac time. I realized how sweet and dear he was to me in those far-away days in Eastern Serbia, days that were now fading, suppressed by the fear of everyday life. The farewell scene from

Cabaret movie came to my mind: when Sally parts with Brian at the railway station and leaves. Then, without turning her head, she lifts her right hand, waves for a second and disappears. A phenomenally encapsulated moment!

I didn't wave. I was slowly walking up the steep Nemanjina Street, to Slavija Square. If I had had a crystal bowl, I could have seen most of that street destroyed by bombings five years later. At the time, when I was climbing it, though, I was thinking about Dragan and his future life in Italy, mentally sending him my best wishes.

The following month, I got two letters from him from Italy. He was thriving there, I saw it in his smile on the photograph he sent me in a padded envelope, together with the tape containing one of my dearest songs in the whole world, Caruso. Lucio Dalla composed it in 1986 and performed it at an Italian festival in 1988, while Nora and I were watching TV, snuggled on the comfortable sofa in her beautiful apartment outside of the city center; in the period of developing and strengthening our endless friendship, stronger than any kind of love, even the one between man and nature. Later, through the time tunnel, the divine voices of Luciano Pavarotti, Ginette Reno, Lara Fabian and Anna Oxa sang that wonderful refrain, bringing me back to the cozy evening with Nora.

> *Te voglio bene assai*
> *ma tanto tanto bene sai*

I knew it was going to be my last summer in Belgrade. I believed that with God's help, I would manage to get out with Nora far away from that swamp of hatred my country had turned into. Still, the parting hurt.

I was thirty years old and had thirty million partings behind me.

I had the best friends in the world.

I had immense love for music and jobs I truly enjoyed.

I had neither serenity nor peace. Each day could bring total mobilization and even wider spreading of the horrible war.

I was thirty years old and had thirty million partings engraved deeply somewhere in my heart and soul.

Painful partings have been following me all my life. A dear Canadian friend of mine from nowadays, a woman who has in her veins the blood of Indians from North American forests, and is a psychotherapist by profession, said to me on one occasion that they were somehow intentional; they were a part of my being, created by me by looking for jobs that included relocations and understated separations, like a pattern. In my childhood, I constantly fought with loneliness and tried to always be surrounded by tons of kids. To be with Mom was lovely, to be with Dad meant being alone. My friend, Mo, also said that the very fact I was born a twin signified that all my life I would be looking for that other person and parting from a multitude of others, subconsciously searching for my twin brother who died at birth. He was born five minutes before me, stronger, perfectly healthy and almost double my weight. I believe that in the still unborn state I wanted to get out of loneliness as soon as possible and be with him again. I believe I was disappointed by the cold hands of doctors in that hospital in the South of Serbia. I believe I cried, with or without tears, asking to be brought to my brother who I had been sharing everything with during all of my existence up to that point, all those nine months.

My genes and life have always been directing my actions and reactions towards separations. My youthful loves were invariably in some other towns. Trains, buses, planes, partings for shorter or longer periods of time. Leaving for the university in the big city, the truck, the piano, my family and relatives gathered together. That day, the last Saturday of August 1983, was impressed indelibly by unshed tears into a deep wound in the heart. My aunts with red eyes, my mom realizing that the umbilical cord was irretrievably severed, my father rushing me and shouting not even to think about crying, because I was a man and men didn't cry in that part of the world.

I didn't cry.

Mom's comings to Belgrade, over the course of the following years, every two or three months, just like my goings to the South, were always accompanied by sadness of an unavoidable parting. Between them, there was a sea of some other partings, seats by the window, the right side on a bus, the left side on a train, by the wing on a plane, tears shed or unshed. Sandwiches prepared for Mom, so she didn't go hungry while traveling, or hers made for me, for my trips.

I am now breaking the promise I gave to my mother years ago not to mention an incident that brought me more emotional pain than anything I have ever experienced. Forgive me, Mom!

It was during my first year at the university when hunger was my constant companion, together with mildewed walls of the small icy cold room where I lived, on the outskirts of the city. Mom was coming to see me at regular intervals, bringing me everything she possibly could, since she herself lived on a shoe string. She knitted a lot, so some money came to her hands and then to mine. We were all alone in the world, we cared so much about each other to the point of arguing, however strange it might sound. Whenever Mom was on her way back to the South, I would give her some of the money she had brought me. Then she would start crying, pleading that if I loved her, I should keep all the money for myself.

After one of our most heated discussions, Mom took the first bus available. It stopped somewhere in the middle of Belgrade-Niš highway for a half an hour break. On that hot day, all the passengers got off the bus and went to a nearby motel for some refreshments. All of them, except her. My mom didn't have a single cent and in the haste of leaving, she forgot to take from the table a bottle of water and two slices of bread with apricot jam I prepared for her three-hour long trip. She made that jam especially for me a few days before coming to Belgrade. Now she was sitting there all alone, on the scorching bus, dying for a cold drink. My mom, the woman I would give my life for, was thirsty and hungry, looking pensively at the sunlit fields of Serbia. If somebody had taken a closer look at her, they could have seen a radiant smile on her tired face.

It was only a year later that she decided to tell me about that episode in her life.

"Let the others eat and drink as much as they want," she was reminiscing that day. "My son is an excellent student and a good honest man, and that makes me the happiest person in the world!"

The pride of her heart overcame hunger and thirst. I didn't let Mom worry ever again. I studied extra hard, knowing that each exam I passed with a high mark would erase a line from her beautiful face.

Still, even now, as I am writing these lines on a 12-kilometers altitude, carried by Boeing 777 to one of my business trips, I am crying, hiding my tears from the passenger on the seat next to mine. That episode is one of my life wounds that won't heal. I still cannot forgive myself for not having persuaded mom to take some money from me and buy herself a cold drink that day. Mom gets all flustered when I mention how much that incident hurts me and regrets ever having told me about it. Ever since that day, regardless of how white or black my reality was, one thing was for certain – Mom would always have the existential minimum and I would take care of that. Later, I could afford Mom the most beautiful spas, trips in the business class, and dinners in exclusive restaurants.

My countless trips became emblematic, a deep beating artery of my being. The days of my youth were filling up with maturation, learning, and better understanding the world around me, but also with separations; and every single time, each one of my love affairs or genuine friendships had to be somewhere far-away, which naturally involved comings and goings and partings. On the railroad of my life, locomotives were whistling like in the unforgettable scene in the movie Ana Karenina, with the most beautiful actress in the world, Greta Garbo; the scene where she throws herself on the rails and dies under the hissing steam liberated by a sharp painful shriek of the running train. I saw that movie for the first time with one of my closest high school friends, who later became a renowned opera singer and who is no longer among us. We cried our eyes out while going back to our respective homes, choosing roundabouts and lonely streets, so we couldn't be seen crying, for we were both men and in the South of Serbia men must not cry.

In the years to come, my partings acquired all the melancholy but also the strength and depth of the impossibly emotional and orgasmically charged Scriabin's Etude Op.8 No.12, the only piece of music able to express the way I felt every time I had to part from a dear one.

My Belgrade days were coming to an end, dissolving my sweet secrets, hopes, and aspirations.

I was saying farewell to my beloved buildings and streets, where my heart left its imprints in the tar of the sidewalks.

I was saying farewell to every single tree in Karadjordje Park, to the benches telling me about some clandestine loves.

I was saying farewell to my friends, acquaintances, and colleagues, suffering in advance the indeterminate separation.

At the time, I didn't know that the war would really come to Serbia, that the bombs would really fall from the sky to my beautiful Belgrade and destroy so many dear people, memories, and happy moments.

At the time, I didn't know that it was my and Nora's literally last chance to leave the country, and that a few months later, everything would take the turn for even worse, that people would become even angrier and more scared.

I didn't know that a few years later, hundreds of fires caused by the bombings of foreign countries would burn all over Serbia, most fiercely in my hometown in the South, once upon a time the center of a Roman province, once upon a time a town on the west border of the Ottoman Empire. The bombs in 1999 were ferociously falling on the town of my childhood, ruining streets, bridges, buildings, and parks that were a part of my life. They were aimed at military targets, orchestrated by high decisions of big foreign powers in order to help my people get rid of the tyranny of their leader, who was hated by the whole world. What they unfortunately missed to calculate were possible mistakes, so the bombs also fell on schools and hospitals, taking away completely innocent lives in those joyless spring days of April and May.

When it started happening with such intensity, when the streets of my hometown became the breaking news on CNN, BBC and all the media, I was already in Canada, glued to the TV screen, all in tears, watching the destruction of what was left from the former Yugoslav dream. When the famous centuries old bridge in Mostar, Bosnia and Herzegovina, exploded with a blast, a part of my heart flew out in pieces with it, for that bridge had been a part of me, of the books I had read and history I had been taught.

My mom firmly refused to go to a shelter during air raids, having experienced it once as a stifling and depressing place, packed with people who made the reality even more fearful and fear even deeper. She preferred to sit in her kitchen, because it had a small window that she covered with a blanket to protect herself from broken glass in case a bomb fell close to our house. In spite of all mom's prayers, a bomb did fall, about one hundred meters away, damaging the house and eradicating the chestnut trees in full bloom. Fortunately, my mom remained uninjured on that day in May that happened to be my birthday. On that very day, my thirty-fifth birthday, I was going to my work places as usual. Ever since I arrived in Canada, I had two – sometimes three – jobs, to pay the bills and support my mom and aunts somewhere far, far away in the Balkans. I was walking to the subway station, not knowing that at the same time sirens in Serbia were announcing another air raid. People around me were sitting quietly, reading the newspapers, while my mother was praying to God to save her life, on my birthday, to spare her from the storm of bombs and grenades that were pouring from the sky like ominous black rain, destroying her reality and my memories.

Belgrade looked more appealing to my eyes, day by day, in that July of 1994, since I knew I was leaving it. The schools were closed for the summer, the Faculty of Music as well. I said my farewells to all my private students, to the TV station and to the magazine I was writing for. Finally, I parted with my dear professor Zora. She wasn't glad to hear I was going away and leaving the position at the Faculty she had fought so much for me to obtain. She wished me all the best but with sadness and disappointment in her voice. I didn't know then that we would never see each other again. I purposely didn't take the elevator, slowly descending five flights of stairs instead, carried by a secret wish that the door of her bohemian apartment would open, that the professor would come out and say she wasn't sad or disappointed. The door stayed closed.

Sometimes, I open her Book of Melodies and play some of them – most often, my favorite one in C sharp minor:

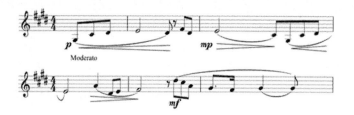

I seldom finish it though, for my eyes quickly fill up with tears and my hands start shaking. My professor was a brave woman, a brilliant musician and fighter on music battlefields. Her wise words must have stayed deeply rooted in the minds of the students who were honored to attend her classes and learn from her. I was the most honored of all, being so close to her. May she rest in peace.

That day, after the sad parting with my professor, I found myself on the street full of people. The sun broke through the clouds, bringing smiles to people's faces. Children were running and laughing. Even the fountain in the downtown's biggest square started working after a long time, cheerfully spraying jets of water. The tram I got on was half empty, there were vacant seats. Suddenly, I wished for Nora and me not to leave the country, not to go anywhere, just to stay where we were. The internal pain of separation was tearing me apart, so I started deceiving myself that the situation wasn't that bad, that things would look up, even though deep down I knew it wasn't true. To prove to myself that I was right, I indulged in making more new friends who, like me, believed or wanted to believe that there would be a happy ending, that everything would take a turn for the better and that Yugoslavia, as it was still called, would survive all the troubles and become a part of European Community one day. Those fairy tales inevitably ended in a trinity: intoxication, fornication, and hangover.

Nora and I were in the process of packing the boxes and storing them in the attic, for one day, we would come back. If we only knew we never would, we could have spent those last few weeks in leisurely walks with Archibald and play in the neighborhood park, instead of sadly parting with vases, sweaters, books, and other inanimate and insensitive things. People somehow get over-attached to them and along the line, the balance is lost between what just serves its purpose and what truly fulfills a part of your being by its existence.

Archibald looked pensive in those days, which was completely out of character. If he could talk and write, I think this would be his story:

Archibald's Saga

The world went totally crazy, one hundred percent, I'm telling you. Where are those nice housewives who used to bring me juicy bones and some tasty leftovers from the previous night's dinners on their way to the market in the morning, and then a croissant or a piece of burek on their way back?

Where is that sweet neighbor from the end of the street, used to come every day and whisper in my ear:

"Who fancies a bit of bacon?"

I always made it very clear to her, by wagging my tail, giving her my paw for a handshake and my charming smile that it was me, and she would give me a good slice of deliciously smoked bacon.

Where is that cheerful young man who used to pet me gently behind the ears and leave bread with foie gras spread on my throne by the gate? I saw him in a camouflage uniform the other day, probably going to a carnival or a costume ball. Very ugly costume, if you ask me. He hasn't passed by ever since.

Where are those two sisters, one brunette, one with hair the color of fire? What is going on with them, I wonder. They called me Archika and treated me to a pig knuckle every week.

There was also that wonderful neighbor in the wheelchair who adopted my son, one of the litter, anyway. What a great man, I'm telling you! How nicely he used to play with me and what interesting stories he told me!

Where are all those people?

People, where are you?

Maybe I offended them somehow. But how? I never barked at night so as not to wake them up, I'd always get up early to see them off to work or to the market, and often stayed awake till late to greet them on their way back home from work or whatever.

There are none of them anymore.

That student of Russian literature, the girl with big blue eyes, where did she vanish? I miss her kind words.

"Sabaka," that's what she called me (means 'dog' in Russian), "keep your fingers crossed. If I pass the exam somebody will get something nice."

I would impatiently pace in the garden, thinking what to do since I didn't have fingers, so I clutched my paws and wished her all the best with the exam in my mind. I would recognize her from a distance, all smiling:

"Sabaka, I got the highest mark! Here, this is for you for bringing me luck." She would delicately place slices of heavenly tasting sausage on the stone by the fence that serves as my chaise longue.

I have an impression that people are avoiding me. But then, everything's turned upside down now. Even the street doesn't smell like before at sunset. Is anybody cooking these days? What happened to those soups with meaty bones? Other than the smells, the sounds I loved also disappeared. Nikola used to play the piano, the first neighbor to listen to the radio, the granny down the street to folk music, Damnjan, the little boy from the house number 8 was always watching cartoons. Now everybody's watching and listening to only one channel on TV that I can't quite understand. It isn't funny and makes people sigh like they're afraid of something.

People are very strange. Why are they watching that channel if it doesn't suit them, if it just makes them frightened? "Switch the channel, people!" I'm barking, but I am a dog and people don't listen to my sort.

Nikola has been coming home very late and smelling weird recently. He would normally pat me a lot and tell me everything that's happened that day, but now he just says to me sadly:

"Good night, my beautiful Archie."

Nora and he have been talking about something I don't understand. They've started packing boxes and taking them to the attic. Whenever I come to lick them and cuddle a bit, they sigh deeply and say:
"Poor Archie, poor Archie."
Why are they saying that to me?
Something's going on here and I can't figure out what.
Days are becoming long for a dog like me.
"Where are you, neighbors, friends, where are you?" I call.
The street is quiet and deserted.
Where are you peeeeople?
Where are youuuuu?
Why are my masters climbing to the attic and taking suitcases? What do they need them for?
A car is speeding on the street.
No, false alarm.
It's my heart beating very fast, like it wants to jump out of my chest.

This life of ours is full of roads and crossroads. Lots of them are hard and thorny, sometimes impassable. I deeply believe that regardless of everything, our destinies have been written somewhere, by some magic plume. When I look at Nora's and my leaving the country, now, after so many summers and winters, I can clearly see that some kind of a higher power intervened, and in its miraculous way, directed us to decisions, simultaneously opening new paths and closing dead ends. The events playing in front of our eyes, people we were meeting, conversations we were sharing, all of that was gradually intertwining into a braid of leaving for a better tomorrow. That tomorrow was uncertain, unclear, foggy, but had at least one sure thing about it – the beginning.

In less than a month, thanks to the set of circumstances provided by the touch of destiny, Nora and I held in our hands the fourteen-day visitor visas to Poland. The vicar of the church, where I conducted the choir, helped us obtain them.

"They couldn't give you more than two weeks, because of the war state here," he said. "Go in peace."

We understood. Our destiny wanted to tempt us and see how much we were capable of finding a way ourselves to extend the stay in that country, safe and with supermarkets full of food, the country we both loved but whose language, unwritten rules of conduct, and actual living there, we still had to explore. The last hook in the chain of faces, smiles, old friends and those who appeared only once, on a particular day or for just a moment, brought by a sparkle in the Universe to enlighten our way and push us forward, that last hook was an honest and worried face of the lady at the Polish Embassy in Belgrade, and her kind words of encouragement:

"Serdecznie mam nadżieje że państwo znajdżiecie sobie pracy i zostaniecie tam w Polsce, bo tutaj, to nie dobrzre," she said. *"Myślę że my też musimy przeprowadżić się wkrótce."* ("I sincerely hope that you will both find jobs and stay in Poland, because things aren't looking good here. I think we will also have to leave soon.")

And then, August 8th came.

I was lying awake, waiting for the subtle transition of night into day.

Two suitcases: one gray, like the uncertainty of the whole journey, one black, like the reality.

We had arranged for Archibald to be in care of a nice elderly couple who had a house with a garden. None of our friends had enough living space to take him. We hoped he would be fine.

He was whining at the sight of our suitcases in the trunk of the cab.

I wanted to hug him and take him with us. Still, since Nora and I were sure we would come back as soon as the situation in the country calmed down. I managed to overcome the pain of separation and got in the cab waiting for us. If I had known that our journey would turn into an exile and immigration, if I had known then that some years later, one of the bombs would fall from the sky into the garden next to the one where Archibald lived, scare him and make him run away somewhere into the unknown, if I had only known that, I would have found a way to take him with us.

To my prayers on another continent, I have always added the wish that a nice person gave home to my dear friend. I am sure that Archibald, our sweet, dear Archibald, found a friend for himself. Who could possibly resist his smile, his tail wagging and proffering of paws, first left and then right!

The cab driver was silent, as were the two of us. Nora, absorbed in her thoughts, was looking straight ahead, while I was leaning to the window.

Coincidentally, the bus to Budapest Airport (Belgrade Airport being closed under the sanctions of Western countries) was parked by Nora's Faculty of Philology, right in front of the room where classes in Polish language were held.

At first, softly and then gradually intensifying its rhythm, the rain fell, heavy – tired – as if my beautiful Belgrade was saying a farewell to me. Nora always wanted to leave it with all her heart. I wasn't sure about anything anymore. My thoughts were unclear, influenced by the dread of the war. The rain was drumming on Nora and me as we got on the bus to take us to the airport in Budapest. The bus was packed and smelt of fear. The doors closed and the driver turned on the radio. A familiar voice gently trailed through the silence:

Fog is here, fog is all around,
From a distance faintly echoing a sound.
Fog is here, fog is all around,
It's too late, all in vain, our fate is bound.

A few days later, Yugoslav's borders were closed.

Nora's Impressions

Bye, bye, Serbia, Yugoslavia!

As the bus is pulling out just across from the Faculty of Philology where I have spent many happy years, I feel only lightness in my heart.

New cities, countries, and horizons to explore – unbounded. New languages to learn.

Vive la liberté!

I sense how emotionally charged this moment is for Nikola. He is saying a silent farewell to all the dear people, places, and memories left behind. There are so many of them.

He is bravely gazing through the window, without a single tear in his eyes, in spite of the turmoil whirl-winding in his soul.

I tend to burn the bridges behind me in pursuit of a new adventure, come what may.

I know that no harm will come to the people dearest to us, no matter how dreary the economic and political situation might be. Mountains and people meet, over and over again, if meant to, and when the time is right.

I miss only Archibald! Like, how do we get him shipped to wherever we are? But then again, he is the smartest and the sweetest of all dogs and will survive in all kinds of circumstances.

The first stop my Budapest!

The next one our Warsaw!

The next, next one who knows and who cares!

The fog is behind us, a new day rises right in front of us.

Nikola and I cross the Serbian – Hungarian border on foot, on account of long line-ups of buses and cars; our legs are asking to be stretched. So, we walk, along the wheat and sunflower fields, spreading out like a sea, gently swaying in the soft summer breeze in the wee hours of the morning. The night is not over yet, but dawn is slowly making its way through the first sunrays.

We simply walk on and on. At one point, I say to Nikola:

"The air smells different now. Hey, we're already in Hungary!"

Sure enough, the customs officer smiles and lets us in, without even checking our passports. I guess it's my Hungarian charm, inherited from my njanja that does the trick.

We cross the border, with only our handbags containing: passports, toiletries, and some German cash stacked safely under the insoles of my ballerina shoes.

We catch up to the bus that contains all of our earthly possessions packed in two suitcases – just stuff.

We spend a wonderful day in Budapest, the promenade along the Danube River, Zacher, torte in the oldest patisserie in the city, street musicians, cobbled steep shady streets of Buda, and lovely boutiques of the flat Pest.

We fly to Warsaw later in the afternoon.

We are FREE!

Cadenza

Through various periods of classical music, in lots of compositions, there could be found an added piece, usually at the end of each or only after the last movement, called cadenza.

Cadenza is a moment where the composer gives a chance to the performer to express his or her virtuosity. It is customarily written without signs for dynamics, without details for tempo or character, simply Ad Libitum, allowing for the freedom of performance.

Our Cadenza is a story about people, times, and events.

The tapestry of these stories has been woven out of loving yarn for the world and people, intertwined by threads of sorrow, caused by the destruction of the Yugoslav dream. Our wish has been to share a journey through the tough years of the downfall of a country, a time that was also sprinkled with unexpected joy, memorable moments of beauty, and genuine human compassion.

The idea about this book started forming in our voluntary exile in Poland, over tea and biscuits with our dear friends who were urging us to write a book that would explain the hardships of Yugoslav's transformation, and everything that was happening prior to, during, and after that. Emil, who turned out to be our staple in Warsaw, was adamant:

"Po prostu ty i Nora na prawde musicie to napysać! To będzię wspaniała książka dla każdego: dla Jugosławianów, dla Polaków, dla wszystkich!"

("You and Nora simply have to write it, really! That will be a great book for everyone, for Yugoslavs, Poles, for everybody!")

We learnt in Poland, along with 'the most difficult language in the world' according to our friend Klaus, how hard it was to extend our temporary visas every three months, apprehensive of the outcome. We also experienced that wonderful feeling of exploring the new, found ourselves in a multitude of tragicomic situations, and lived through lots of sweet and sour moments.

The next stop on our journey was immigration to Canada, where we have been living for twenty-one years. My Canadian days have been filled with various jobs, but one thing has been common to all of them. People I have worked with kept saying:

"Write a book about your life."

Destiny wanted each piece of the puzzle to set in its own time.

In 1997, I was working as a fragrance consultant and would go outside of the store on my breaks to light up, accompanied by my colleague, Mo, whose friendly love has been warming me ever since. During our chatting, an airplane would fly over our heads. I could instantly tell her which type of the aircraft it was, the passenger capacity, and all the technical details, then sigh deeply. She would gently hug me and say:

"Don't be sad. You'll become a flight attendant one day, I know that."

She was always telling me that my life was like a fairy tale and should be transposed into a book.

The most persistent ones, in terms of transposition of my life into a book, were my dear colleagues from Air Transat, where my dream to become a flight attendant finally came true three years later. It often happened, during the long night flights, in the aft galley of Loocheed 500, or Airbus 330, that they came to me and asked:

"Come on now, tell us again that story…"

The leader was my 'sweet sister' Jelica, who was even more persistent than the others in urging me to write this book. She read the first few stories and encouraged Nora and me to continue creating this work. Jelica is a wonderful friend, and a great co-worker on overseas flights above sleepy oceans and cities all over the world.

One evening in January 2011 deserves a special mention. It was my Patron Saint's Day: St. John. My close friends gathered together in my downtown Toronto apartment on the 27th floor, with a panoramic view over Ontario Lake. I just got back from a flight and didn't have time to prepare food, so I ordered barbecue and salads. My friends brought tons of home-made delicacies: red peppers stuffed with white cheese, spinach pie, crèpes with ham and sour cream, cookies and cakes. That night gave birth to the official idea of the book; fully supported by Nenad, Edita, Gordana, Mila, and Jelica.

Nenad was bugging me every day, in order to remind me to write something. From the very beginning of our friendship in 1996, he'd been telling me that my life was like a book: so full of interesting stories, and that it would be a shame not to share them with the world.

My dear friend, Mila, put all her heart into wishing this piece to be composed.

Still, that drop of water that either fills up or overflows the glass, and in our case the spark to light up the passion for writing, was Anna Maria, wife of my old friend Dean (stories Army and House of the Rising Sun). Dean came to Montreal on a business trip in May 2011, with his sophisticated wife and their lovely daughter. We met again, after so many years, and went for dinner to a restaurant famous for authentic French cuisine. The line was too long and we too hungry to wait, so I took them to a Polish restaurant nearby. Poland seemed to have sent a message. And so casually, over pierogi, pork chops, and potato fritters, we talked about days old and new. At one moment, Anna Maria, herself a published author, said:

"You have, you simply have to write a book! Everybody will love it!"

After dinner, I hurried to catch the train to Toronto. Nora was waiting for me at Gare Centrale, fresh from her swimming, which was the reason why she couldn't join us for dinner. Given the choice between food and physical activity, she would always opt for the latter. The moment I saw her, I said out of breath:

"Nora, I'm starting to write a book, right now!"

I told her everything I had in my head, I wanted it to be our book, mine and hers. She was ecstatic and immediately gave me the story line. I hugged her as she was on the brink of tears from excitement and ran to the gate.

On May 17 2011, this book was born. The date happens to be Norwegian National Day, so dear to Nora's heart.

Her stories were told from the second floor of a Montreal apartment building, facing a church and a huge park, in the intermissions of her gym classes. Mine were almost all written on planes, during my breaks or heading to business trips. I was writing incessantly, most often sitting on the right side of the plane, by the window. Every once in a while, I would take a look at a beautiful landscape, a mountain peak covered with snow or an archipelago spread out in the blueness of the sea, then conscientiously continue writing.

It was on the trains, though, that the book was started and finished. It completed its full circle from Montreal to Toronto and from Toronto to Montreal, from May 2011 to October 2011.

Nora and I enjoyed exchanging our reflections as we experienced a certain time in a certain country, filtered through our individual narrative goggles.

Our heartfelt thanks go to our friends and colleagues, especially to Alexia, Jennifer, Elizabeth, and James who proofread the manuscript, gave us a precious feedback and thumbs up.

Also to our cats, Poppers and Archie, who supervised the editing by purring from the top shelves of our computer desks.

A very special appreciation to my partner Georges who normally reads only French books. He decided, however, to bring the manuscript of Yugoopera to one of our vacations in Cuba. Just looking at him completely absorbed in the book and listening to his enthusiastic comments made it all worth it.

Nora's and Nikola's adventures continue in Poland and in Canada. They will form the second and third book of The Way of Life Trilogy.